Tread Softly

Tread Softly

Wendy Perriam

Peter Owen
London and Chester Springs

PETER OWEN LTD
73 Kenway Road, London SW5 0RE

Peter Owen books are distributed in the USA by Dufour Editions Inc.,
Chester Springs, PA 19425-0007

First published in Great Britain 2002
by Peter Owen Publishers

A catalogue record for this book is available from
the British Library

ISBN 0 7206 1176 8

Printed and bound in Great Britain by
MPG Books Ltd, Bodmin, Cornwall

This was the world when you stepped into it. The thick charge of blame and assault and love and murder and unbelievable acts of kindness and the bitterest sunken levels of disappointment that you could imagine and then, quick as a flash, from nowhere, jokes!

Susie Boyt, *The Last Hope of Girls*

For my Mother.
In loving memory

I

1

BUNIONS

were inherently absurd. The very word made people smirk – perhaps because it rhymed with onions. But the reality was far from funny. Distortion, swelling, constant pain. Agony in bed at night.

Lorna surveyed her feet: granny-shoes, at thirty-nine; ugly low-heeled lace-ups, bulging at the toe-joints. The Creator, if He existed, had done a lousy job. This waiting-room was proof enough, full of the walking wounded – plaster casts from thigh to ankle, arms in slings, bandaged knees – and a bald, squint-eyed baby wailing fretfully. Even the posters crowding the walls reinforced the theme of mortality: 'Meningitis can kill.' 'Tobacco seriously damages health.' 'TB – still a major threat.'

She turned back to her magazine. 'Tempt him with our haddock savoury.' Unlikely. She and Ralph ate separate meals at different times in different rooms. Anyway, he hated fish. Haddock – another comic word. Gudgeon, flounder, turbot, winkle: all a shade ridiculous. There were fish in the tank opposite, dazzling, iridescent creatures, the only healthy occupants of the room. She closed her eyes, letting her swollen feet melt into graceful fins and propel her through warm, turquoise-coloured water. Pursued by a shoal of lusty males, she zigzagged sinuously between fronds of weed, flirtatious bubbles streaming in her wake.

'Mrs Pearson?'

Startled, she surfaced, abandoning her bevy of sleek suitors with their kissing mouths and gossamer tails.

'How d'you do? I'm Mr Hughes.'

Pin-stripes, silver hair, a pale, solemn face with joltingly dark eyes. Her father, resurrected, stepping out of his photo frame into three-dimensional reality. In a daze, she shook his hand, gripping the cool, reassuring fingers for rather longer than was suitable.

'This way, please.'

Stay alive, she murmured, as she followed him into his room. Don't leave me again. Don't slip back to your sepia flatness.

*

'Six weeks? I can't spare you that long, Lorna. We're up to our eyes as it is.'

'I'll be able to *work*, Ralph. I just can't walk, that's all. Well, I can hop around on crutches a bit, but he said not to overdo it. I'm meant to keep the foot up as much as possible. But I can still type and answer the phone.'

Ralph poured himself a glass of something. Whisky, from the smell of it. He had his back to her, as usual. 'I've heard it's a very painful operation. How on earth will you manage?'

'With pain-killers. They have fantastic ones these days. Anyway, I've got to have it done. He said it'll only get worse if I leave it. It was extraordinary, you know. He looked just like my father.'

'Your father?'

'Well, the photograph. I was so struck by the resemblance I forgot half the things I was meant to ask.'

Ralph said nothing. Was he listening, she wondered, or still worrying about her being off work? The latter, she decided. Over the years she had learned to read his back: anxious, tense, annoyed, withdrawn. Today it was all four. Since he'd given up smoking a week ago his stress level had soared.

'He says he'll have to operate on all the toes, not just the bunion itself. Break and reset five bones, cut a couple of tendons . . . ' She kept her tone light-hearted. As a child she had been taught stoicism. When she broke her ankle falling off a pony, she was told she was lucky to have legs at all, just as she was lucky to have food on her plate when millions of children were starving. She had imagined the world as full of amputees with empty bellies. 'At least he's not doing both feet at once,' she added, valiantly ignoring six weeks' immobility, six months of still painful walking and a year before the swelling went down. 'He says he'll leave the right one till next year. Otherwise I'd be completely out of action.'

'Couldn't the left one wait till Christmas, when things are slacker?'

'I'm not sure if surgeons work over Christmas.'

'Well, the week before, then.'

She pictured herself hobbling out of hospital on Christmas Eve, cooking the turkey from a wheelchair. Except there might not be a turkey. Last year, having a deadline to contend with, they'd had time for only a quick cheese-and-chutney sandwich in front of the computer.

'It really would help, darling. The next three months are going to be absolute bedlam.'

'OK,' she said, 'I'll ask Mr Hughes.' The prospect was appealing. On the way home she had relived the sensation of him handling her bare feet, resting them on his pin-striped knee, palpating each toe in turn. He had endowed distorted growths with a peculiar sort of dignity, worthy of his art.

'You know, I hadn't realized till today what complex things feet are. That', she said, pointing to her left foot, 'contains twenty-eight bones, thirty-five joints and a hundred-odd ligaments. Which is why the operation's so difficult. There's a lot more to go wrong than in, say, a hip replacement. People imagine you just hack off the lump and hey presto! But – '

'I'm sorry, Lorna, I must get off. I'm late already.'

'Get off? Where? We're going out this evening.'

'We can't be. I've arranged to meet John Allan.'

'Ralph' – she tried not to let her irritation show – 'we're having dinner with the Kirkwoods. It's been in the diary for weeks.'

'Well, I didn't see it.'

Didn't *want* to see it. Ralph liked his meals on a tray, alone. 'Look, I'll phone John Allan and tell him you're not well.' As he turned to face her, she noticed the tiny muscle in his cheek was twitching again. She felt sorry for that overworked muscle.

'No. The last thing we need is clients thinking I'm going downhill. What time are we meant to be there?'

'Half past seven.'

'That's OK then. Cobham's only fifteen minutes' drive, so I can see John Allan first.'

'Don't be silly, Ralph. We've less than an hour. You'll just have to put him off. Say something unexpected's cropped up.'

After Ralph had left the room she remained sitting on the sofa, gazing at the oppressive grey-green walls. For ages she had wanted to redecorate, but somehow they never managed to get round to it. Besides, she doubted if redecoration would change the basic character of the house – a character not unlike Ralph's: dour and rather isolated.

He was the one who had chosen it, long before her time, and, despite now being in their joint names, it still seemed his, not theirs.

'You're lucky to have a roof over your head,' she heard Aunt Agnes cluck, 'when hundreds of people are sleeping rough.'

Lorna saw them huddled drunkenly in doorways on their cardboard pallets or sprawled supine on the pavements. She ought to visit Agnes, soon – before the operation certainly. It was a long way to go on crutches.

Picking her way through the rows of inert bodies, she went upstairs to change.

'John Allan didn't mind,' said Ralph, putting his head round the door. 'As a matter of fact, *he*'s not very well.'

'Good. I mean rotten for him but good for you. Are you going to drive, by the way, or shall I?'

Ralph ignored the question, correctly interpreting it as: Do you intend to drink? He yanked off his tie and picked irritably at the label. 'When d'you think we'll be able to leave?'

'Ralph, for heaven's sake! We're not even there yet.'

'It's just that I've got an early start tomorrow.'

'Tomorrow's Saturday.'

'I know. But I'm going to Devon. I've only just arranged it.'

Lorna forced her feet with difficulty into the nearest she possessed to normal shoes. Another weekend alone. Which meant the Terrors were bound to strike. Most normal people found terror inexplicable unless it had a cause – a bomb scare, for example, or rapists at one's bedroom door. Anything less was neurosis. But Ralph understood, thank God. He could hardly be much help, though, two hundred miles away.

'You're fortunate to *have* a husband.' Aunt Agnes again, lifelong spinster.

Yes, Aunt, she replied feelingly. I am.

'Come in, come in! How lovely to see you!'

Lorna felt herself pressed against a generous, fleshy bosom and overpowered by floral scent. The sensation was not unpleasant – like being softly smothered by a honeysuckle pillow – and was a distraction from the pain in her feet, exacerbated tonight by shoes that made her bunions scream. Was it beyond the wit of shoemakers to construct special lump-accommodating shoes, on the lines of hamsters' pouches?

Olive Kirkwood released her at last. 'It's wonderful to meet you, Lorna, after all our little chats on the phone. And of course we've heard so much about you from Ralph.'

So much? Ralph rationed words and regarded compliments as unnecessary, if not hypocritical. But perhaps he was different when she wasn't there. How odd, she thought, that she'd never know how he behaved in her absence. With the Kirkwoods he might praise her to the skies: 'I adore my wife. I'd be completely lost without her. She means the world to me.'

'You must meet Hugh, my other half. He's seeing to things in the garden.'

Hugh. Hughes. Lorna's mind flipped back to the surgeon. Sitting on his knee. Not just her feet, the whole of her. He was stroking her hair, caressing her cheek. He smelt of coal tar and security.

Olive was now embracing Ralph, unaware that he regarded physical contact as an invasion and a threat (and anyway would rather be at home). 'Great to see you again, Ralph! Do come through, both of you.'

As Olive led them into the sitting-room, Lorna covered for Ralph's taciturnity with a tidal wave of compliments: what a lovely house it was, so light, so bright, so spacious . . . Weren't the pictures charming, and what an original colour scheme. She was, in fact, dizzied by the patterns – stripes on the curtains, squiggles on the carpet – and by the profusion of flowers: flamboyant lilies, shaggy-haired chrysanthemums, snooty scarlet roses preening in cut glass. Olive herself was a living bouquet in flounced peony-printed silk, and there were more flora on the chair-covers: an extravagant (if seasonally inaccurate) display of delphiniums entwined with pussy-willow. She had imagined the house quite differently from Ralph's terse descriptions.

'Yes, we love it,' Olive smiled. 'Especially the garden. We decided to have drinks alfresco this evening, to show off your handiwork. Hugh's made a nice fruit punch.'

Ralph's smile failed to reach his eyes. He actively avoided any drink with an alcohol content of less than 40 per cent.

'Or would you prefer something else?' She indicated a daunting array of bottles on the sideboard. 'We've got all the usual – gin, whisky, sherry, Martini – and a few exotics brought back from trips abroad. This is medronho,' she said, cradling a weird-shaped bottle in smoky-brown glass, 'which we picked up in the Algarve. Or there's ouzo from Cyprus, or – '

'Whisky, thanks.' Ralph was still standing by the door, as if poised for a speedy getaway.

'And I'll try the medronho, please.' Lorna wished she had something of interest to say about the Algarve, but her fears put paid to foreign holidays. She eyed the family photographs, which, even on the expanse of the dazzlingly white grand piano, seemed to be jostling for space. She and Ralph were not just singularly ill-travelled but short of living relatives: no parents on either side, and no children – only pregnancies.

'There we are!' beamed Olive, handing them their drinks. 'Now let's go outside and find the others.' She led the way through the French windows on to a patio that rivalled Kew Gardens in its abundance of plants, the only difference being that the Kirkwoods' were largely artificial.

A paunchy fellow in a loud tweed suit spotted them and came bounding over. 'Hello! Hello! I'm Hugh,' he said to Lorna, pumping her hand with painful vigour and then giving Ralph a friendly thump on the shoulder, all the while somehow managing not to spill his drink (a lurid mulberry-red concoction stuffed with an awesome amount of tropical fruit salad – the punch, presumably).

'Cheers!' he said, raising his glass. 'Here's to us.'

'Cheers!' Lorna echoed, wondering what he meant by 'us'. Surely they had nothing in common beyond an interest in fake grass.

'How's business?' Hugh asked, as if reading her mind.

'Fine,' Ralph lied. 'We've landed a big contract for Broom Hall's hockey pitches. It's a boys' public school in Devon. I'm off there tomorrow, to measure up. With all this rain we've been having recently, artificial grass is really coming into its own.'

'Yes, we're thrilled with ours,' Hugh said. 'It saves us a hell of a lot of work. No mowing or weeding or maintenance.'

'And no hay fever,' Olive put in. 'Last summer I was sneezing night and day.'

Ralph should put them on the payroll, Lorna thought – let them proselytize to all and sundry with their unprompted customer endorsement. Far cheaper than an advertising agency.

'Our guests are admiring it at this very moment. And they're all frightfully keen to meet you.'

Hugh steered them across the Astroturfed lawn to the Astroturfed tennis-court, where some six or seven people were peering down at the velvet-smooth green surface. Well, green in part. The garden was illuminated by a variety of coloured lights, which cast psychedelic swathes of pink, purple, gold and turquoise across the extensive vista.

As Olive made the introductions, Lorna grasped at names and hands. Was Alice the one in the red, or was that Caroline? And had Olive said Joan or Jean?

'So you're Mr and Mrs Astroturf!' Joan/Jean laughed.

'You could say that,' Ralph put in quickly, scenting further business. 'We're actually called Astro-Sport, and we use every sort of material and do every type of job – private gardens, of course, but also putting-greens, cricket-grounds, tennis-courts, you name it.'

'It's a brilliant notion,' the woman in red enthused. 'You could never tell it isn't real.'

'And it's much healthier for children.' Ever loyal, Lorna backed Ralph up, stressing the messiness, inconvenience and health hazards of *real* grass. And ditto of real plants and shrubs. Although the Kirkwoods had real water, she noticed, cascading in a miniature Niagara from the gaping mouth of a corpulent bronze frog into a landscaped pond surrounded by frog siblings. Further statuary (of a human kind) was dotted among ersatz rhododendron bushes in full purple bloom – a rare sight in mid-September.

'Can I tempt you to some nibbles?' Olive proffered bowls of roasted nuts.

'Mm, lovely.' Lorna took a handful, wondering when they were going to eat. Tantalizing smells were wafting from indoors: garlic, roasting meat. She still wasn't sure what the dinner was in aid of. Did the Kirkwoods simply like to socialize with business contacts, or was another order in the offing? But what was there left to Astroturf? The sitting-room? Hugh's bald patch?

'This weather's a bit iffy,' observed a man in a blue blazer and matching cravat. 'I wouldn't be surprised if we were in for a shower.'

17

Lorna looked at the sky expectantly. A nice sharp shower would mean they could go in and sit down. There *were* chairs and loungers in the garden, but no one was actually lounging, and she could hardly sprawl horizontally while the others remained vertical. Bunionless mortals couldn't imagine the torture of standing. For some time now excruciating spasms had been stabbing through both feet. She wished she could unscrew them and stand on her stumps. Or perhaps borrow one of the statues' plinths for support. Not that she would change places with the naked Venus in her rose-bower (synthetic roses, of course). It was cold enough *with* clothes. People's predilection for congregating in gardens regardless of the temperature never failed to amaze her. Regardless, too, of the insect population. Squadrons of midges and mosquitoes were mingling with the guests, and two inebriated wasps clung to a pineapple-raft in the punch.

'Yes, the long-term forecast isn't good,' Alice/Caroline remarked, gold bangles jangling as she sipped her punch. 'Not that we're too worried, are we, darling?' She smiled smugly at the man beside her. 'Bill and I are off on a Mediterranean cruise next week.'

'Oh, lovely,' Lorna said, recalling the nightmare of her honeymoon cruise with Ralph. The Terrors had assailed her the very first evening. The trouble with ships was that you couldn't get off, apart from brief trips ashore. Sightseeing in Alexandria, she had been severely tempted to make a bolt for it and return to the safety of home. 'Where are you going?'

'All over the place. Athens, Venice, Malta, Rhodes . . . '

'Lovely,' she said, third time. She stole a glance at Ralph, who was regaling a bespectacled man with more sales patter: the advantages of artificial grass for children's playgrounds. She was glad it wasn't around when *she* was a child. She remembered lying on her back in a nice, wet, muddy field at the age of six or seven, gazing up at the sky in the hope of a glimpse of her parents. Should heaven be so grey, she had wondered anxiously?

'Lorna . . . ' Olive bustled up again. 'Did Ralph tell you we had a new grandchild?'

'No, he didn't mention it.'

'Yes. A little girl, born on Monday. I've been boring all the others with the pictures. Would you like to see them?'

'Pictures so soon?'

'Oh yes. And Brian videoed the birth, right from the moment Daphne's waters broke.'

Lorna hoped she would be spared the gory details. She took the padded pink album, glad of an excuse to sit down. It was surely physically impossible to look at photos standing up with a drink in her hand. She studied each page politely, although with a growing sense of emptiness. No children meant no grandchildren; your world unpeopled, futureless. 'What a gorgeous baby,' she said, wishing she had something to show in return. Perhaps she should have videoed her miscarriages or come armed with a sheaf of photos of bloody little foetuses. 'And what's her name?'

'Brianna.'

'That's unusual.'

'Yes, isn't it? They were hoping for a boy, who was going to be Brian junior, so they chose it as the female equivalent.'

Lorna pondered the irony of childbirth: everyone beginning life inside someone else, yet, once they emerged from the womb, becoming isolated from other human beings; each adult person separate, cut off.

'My daughter likes exotic names as well,' Olive continued. 'She called her two boys Zachary and Sheldon. My son-in-law wanted James and John, but I'm afraid he was outvoted!'

'You can't beat James,' Blue Blazer declared. 'My name!'

Lorna smiled at him gratefully – at least she'd got one straight. And Clarence she remembered because the name didn't suit its owner – a weaselly individual with a straggly grey moustache. 'Our son's called James,' he was saying, as he dislodged a lemon-pip from his teeth.

'Yes, how *is* he?' asked Jean/Joan. 'We haven't seen him in ages.'

'Oh, he's doing famously. He got ten GCSEs this year and passed Grade 8 in violin.'

Lorna pictured the teenage prodigy: a budding Einstein-cum-Menuhin, mortar-board on head, violin case under arm, and not a trace of acne or adolescent angst.

Having expounded further on his son's accomplishments, Clarence broached the subject of television. 'Did anyone see *The South Bank Show* last week?'

Lorna groaned inwardly. Children and television were two conversational zones she could enter only in a state of total ignorance. Ralph monopolized the television each evening, while she sat in the study with a book.

As the discussion moved from Melvyn Bragg to *Newsnight*, she studied the women's shoes. Amazing that they could stand at all in such torturous creations: strappy sandals, slingbacks, towering stiletto heels. She had never owned such footwear in her life. From an early age both she and her feet had been 'difficult' (Aunt Agnes's word).

She dragged herself up from her chair. Being the only one sitting, and thus on an eyeline with people's stomachs rather than their faces, made her feel somewhat out of things. She just hoped dinner wouldn't be long. Dusk was deepening into dark, and a contingent of fluttery moths had boosted the ranks of winged gatecrashers. Brushing one from her face, she noticed the goose-flesh on her arms. A pity the coloured lights couldn't double as a source of heat. An idea for Ralph, perhaps, once the entire world was Astroturfed and he needed pastures new.

'Dinner is served!' Olive announced, conveniently saving her guests from pneumonia. 'Hugh, if you'd take everybody in I'll dish up the soup.'

Soup. Perfect! Something warming to start the meal. Lorna tried not to appear too eager as she followed Hugh back into the house, although just the prospect of a long-term chair seemed a blessed relief. Ralph, she knew, would have liked another drink and was lingering on the patio, possibly planning a hasty retreat through the artificial shrubbery. Again she sought to compensate as Hugh ushered them into the dining-room. 'Oh, what a lovely table! You've gone to so much trouble.' Indeed, raided the silver vault. Candelabra, napkin-rings, goblets, cruet, mustard-pot – all were gleaming silver. There were even silver name-holders at each place, the names written in curlicued script. She did a surreptitious check. It was Jean, not Joan, and there was also a Robert she didn't remember meeting.

'You're here, my dear,' said Hugh, pulling out a chair for her. 'And Robert opposite. Clarence, you're at this end. And, Ralph, if you'd like to sit next to Jean . . . '

Lorna watched her husband peer at his name, his eyebrows rising

20

slightly – in disbelief? Amusement? (If she invested in silver name-holders would he join her for meals at the table at home?) She could see him twice – facing her in the flesh and the back of his head reflected in the mirror on the wall behind him. He looked tired tonight, and worn. Sometimes people mistook them for father and daughter, which was both embarrassing and hurtful. Not that there was any physical resemblance. Her eyes were dark; his faded blue. Her thick, straight hair was tawny-brown; his, once blond, was now grey and thinning. And, while he was tall and effortlessly lean, she was barely five foot two and could put on weight just looking at a chocolate bar.

Olive brought in garlic-bread. Its pungent smell made Lorna want to grab a hunk and sink her teeth into the moist, butter-oozing flesh. But she sat demurely, storing up a word-hoard for the meal to come. Enough of 'lovely': it must be superb, delicious, exquisite from now on.

'Superb,' she rehearsed, only to see her mocking reflection in the mirror, exaggerating her faults: childishly red cheeks that made her look as if she'd overdone the rouge; the tiny but maddening gap between her front teeth. Hugh had prominent teeth, like tombstones. 'All the better to eat you with, my dear . . . ' Did he and Olive still make love? What was he like in bed? A wolf? A pussycat?

Olive entered with a tray of soup-bowls (flower-patterned, of course). 'It's vichyssoise,' she said, setting them out with a flourish.

Lorna rubbed her chilly arms. If there was one soup she loathed it was vichyssoise – a bland, insipid sludge that for some inexplicable reason was considered socially superior to a more robust kind like oxtail. Yet oxtail had a kick to it, was colourful and spicy and served vibrantly hot, not cold like congealing porridge.

'Delicious!' she said, holding the first spoonful in her mouth like a particularly vile medicine. Eventually she forced it down, turning the instinctive shudder into a little start of delight. 'You must let me have the recipe.'

'Oh, it's simplicity itself. Just potatoes and cream, basically.'

Lorna toyed with her spoon. If only she could tip the stuff into Ralph's bowl. He was eating in his usual morose fashion, but that was no reflection on the soup. If Olive had served him truffled *foie gras* his expression wouldn't have lightened.

Lorna stared at the gobbet of cream swirled into the surface of the soup – white on white. White like bandages and hospitals. No, she mustn't think about the operation. Anaesthetics were the ultimate in Terror: sinking down, down, down to some nameless hideous void. Maybe still awake but paralysed, screaming silently in pain. No one able to hear. She glanced around at the deaf, oblivious faces – Olive's glistening crimsoned lips opening and shutting as she prattled on.

'Yes, Brian's just been promoted. We're frightfully proud.'

White. White like bones. The surgeon hacking off great lumps of bone, slicing into tendons.

'We're taking them out to celebrate next week. Daphne's worried about a babysitter, but . . . '

White. White like shrouds. Her parents had died instantly, according to Aunt Agnes, and went straight to heaven, hand in hand. Now she knew there wasn't a heaven. Food for worms, that's all.

'Mind you, they could bring the baby with them if we went to that nice Italian place. Do you know it, Ralph? – Marco's, in Guildford?'

Through a fog she heard Ralph's voice, ponderous and slow. Nothing else was slow. Her heart was racing and there was an avalanche in her stomach, tilting and churning its contents. Her head throbbed and burned, droplets of perspiration trickled down her back, yet at the same time she was shivering. She was hot and cold, like the soup and the garlic-bread. She ought to be eating, but her throat felt constricted and her hands were trembling so much she couldn't hold the spoon. Why had no one noticed? Bill was laughing, for God's sake, and his wife filling the air with words words words words words.

'I'm having trouble deciding what to pack for the cruise. Bill says I always take too much, but it's easier for men. They don't need evening dresses. Or leotards and tights.'

Lorna dabbed at her face with a napkin. Distraction – that was the key. The Panic Manual suggested offering to wash up, but there weren't any dirty plates yet and, anyway, Olive didn't seem the type to let guests help in the kitchen.

She pressed her hand against her chest to stop her heart from racing out of control. Vigorous exercise was also recommended – running on a treadmill, jumping up and down on the spot. Not possible in Olive's fancy dining-room, with an audience of nine.

'The trouble with you lovely ladies is you're far too vain. It beats me why you need a dozen different outfits every day just to watch the waves.'

'Oh, Bill, you are a tease! I bet you're just the same, aren't you, Lorna?'

Lorna caught sight of herself in the mirror. How could she look so normal when her mind and body were disintegrating? Reflection blurring, walls closing in, voices no longer issuing from people's mouths but darting round the room, spiteful little arrows piercing her skin, skewering her eyes.

'Go on, Lorna, tell Bill you agree with me. I mean, if you're invited to sit on the captain's table you can't appear in any old thing, can you?'

With a despairing cry Lorna staggered to her feet and lurched towards the door. If she didn't escape she would die.

'How *could* you, Lorna? In front of the Kirkwoods, of all people.'

'I'm sorry,' she murmured, not daring to meet his eye. For once, he was facing her.

'Being sorry's no help. We've obviously lost them as clients. And the others are bound to talk. It'll be all round Surrey that my wife's a nutcase.'

Lorna picked at a loose thread on her skirt. It wasn't just a matter of losing business: she had humiliated him in public, and that for Ralph was unbearable. 'Olive . . . seemed to understand.'

'Oh, she was humouring you, that's all.' He struck a succession of matches in an attempt to light his pipe. 'What's wrong with these damn things?'

'Ralph, you promised you wouldn't smoke any more.'

'I *haven't* smoked. For eight days. And it's practically killed me, I'll have you know.'

'You've done brilliantly, darling. Don't spoil it now. It's so bad for your lungs.'

'After your performance tonight, my lungs are the last thing I'm concerned about.'

More guilt. 'But the doctor said – '

'Don't change the subject, Lorna. We're talking about the Kirkwoods.'

'Look, I . . . I'll write them a note in the morning, to explain.'

'Explain? What on earth can you say?' At last he got the pipe alight and exhaled a belch of smoke.

He was right. No mere words could explain the Terrors. Liable to erupt at any time, they could flare from a spark into a blazing conflagration, leave her prey to fear of fear itself: fear of madness, physical collapse. Usually Ralph was sympathetic, but tonight she had pushed him to the limit.

'You're not the only one with problems. Do you know how much we're in debt? I can't sleep at night, wondering how we'll manage.'

Each of them lying awake in their separate rooms. The moon with a contemptuous clock on its face, ticking out the hours. If only they could listen to its tick together, cuddle up, console each other. 'Perhaps we ought to sell the house. Find somewhere smaller.'

'That's no solution. Moving house takes time we haven't got, quite apart from the upheaval. Anyway, with the enormous mortgage on this place it wouldn't release much capital.'

'Let's give up BUPA then.'

'Before your operation? Don't be ridiculous. All these years we've been paying in, and this is the first claim we'll have made. Bugger!' he muttered, noticing that his pipe had gone out. He struck another match with such force that it snapped in two, then tossed both pipe and matchbox into the ashtray. 'Besides, you'd wait for ever on the NHS.'

'I don't mind.'

'Well, I do. It's out of the question.'

Was he ashamed of her bunions too? Wanted a wife with straight feet and a placid disposition? Not that much to ask, perhaps. Olive and the rest of them probably managed to combine the two.

'I'm going to bed. Goodnight.'

She listened to his angry footsteps slam up the stairs, followed by the slam of a door. Yet he was still there in the room, in the acrid, accusing smell of tobacco. Last week she had cleaned the whole house, removing the dull film from walls and paintwork; picked the sticky brown shreds out of every pocket of every jacket; cleared the tangle of bent pipe-cleaners, dead matches and broken pipe-stems from his desk and bedside drawers. Most men made do with three or four pipes. Ralph had twenty-seven.

But then Ralph wasn't most men. Which was why she'd married him. Her long-sought maverick.

She levered her feet from the crippling shoes. Even through her tights she could see how red the swellings were, and the pain was agonizing. If only she could wear her granny-shoes for parties, or, better still, the ones specially made by Surgical Appliances. But if she turned up in those great clumping things she would be written off as seriously disabled.

Which she supposed she *was* – on several counts. Just thinking of the débâcle this evening brought her out in a cold sweat again. Olive's friends were probably still discussing her: 'What a ghastly, hysterical woman. A total headcase. How does her husband put up with it?'

How indeed? Being married to her had imposed restrictions on Ralph, and he'd had to cope in the bad times with a shaking, sobbing wreck of a wife. And he *had* coped, pretty well. He had seen her at rock bottom, yet continued to stand by her.

Wretchedly she slunk upstairs, a shoe in either hand, and tiptoed past his bedroom. Hers was smaller, a child's room. It seemed right that he should keep the master bedroom, the one he had shared with Naomi. Yet she hated sleeping alone. It wasn't just the physical contact she missed – the solid reassurance of another body touching hers – but that there was no one to share a chat or a joke. Long ago, when she and Tom were an item, they would spend whole days in bed together – making love, of course, but also laughing, talking, hatching plans for the future. That future hadn't happened. Tom, like most men, soon tired of panic attacks. And even stoical Ralph had finally suggested they sleep apart, after years of being woken by her nightmares – horrific dreams that made her scream and thresh about. Who could blame him? A less patient husband might have simply walked out.

She placed her shoes side by side in the wardrobe, then took off her dress and put it on a hanger. Tidiness was important when chaos threatened your life. She tried to imagine the wrench of moving house, of exchanging Mr Hughes for a cack-handed youth barely out of medical school.

'Other people manage without four bedrooms and private health-insurance schemes.'

'Yes, I know, Aunt Agnes.'

'If you're in debt, then you'll have to economize.'

'Yes, Aunt.'

'And look at you now – mooning around feeling sorry for yourself when you're the one that's done the damage. If you can't sleep, then for goodness' sake get on with something useful.'

Obediently she retrieved the Panic Manual from under her pillow and reread the section headings:

YOU ARE NOT ALONE.
YOU WILL NOT DIE.
YOU CAN RECOVER.

I am not alone.

I will not die.

I can recover.

I am not alone I will not die I can recover.

In the manual, Panic was depicted as a fire-breathing monster with a long forked tail and horns – something between a devil and a dragon. She sat with the book on her knee, leafing through the well-thumbed pages now stained with sweat and tears.

'Take control of your monster,' ran the instructions. 'Even take it to bed with you. But be sure to show it who's boss.'

Her own Monster had a capital M and, although invisible to Ralph, was virtually a third person in the house.

Dutifully she turned back the covers. 'In,' she ordered. '*Down!*'

To her surprise it subsided, and she stretched out beside its scaly limbs. 'I can recover,' she whispered, wishing she could share her bed with a rampant Mr Hughes rather than a temporarily quiescent Monster.

2

'Lorna?'

'Mm . . . ?' She opened her eyes. Ralph was standing in the doorway, naked except for his underpants. Which meant he must be feeling randy. She only saw him naked when he decided (intermittently) that separate rooms had their limitations.

'Fancy a . . . ?' His voice tailed off. He never had the words for it. 'Sex' was too bald, 'cuddle' overly twee, 'shag' downright crude and 'sleeping with' factually inaccurate.

'What, now? Today?' It was the morning of the operation, so her fear level was infinitely higher than her libido. Yet it would be unwise to refuse. Of late, Ralph's erections couldn't be relied upon, but now she could see a creditable bulge pushing out his underpants. Even years ago, in his forties, he had tended to look sheepish with a hard-on, as if it didn't quite belong to him and might do something wayward.

With an awkward laugh he took a step towards her. 'You'll be out of action for a while, so I thought we might . . . '

'Yes, of course. Let me just have a wash.'

'No.'

She had learned to interpret even his monosyllables. 'No' meant 'Don't delay. I can't trust the thing not to lie down and die.' Ralph was a proud man and would rather embrace her unwashed body than risk the shame of failure. She shifted over towards the wall to make room for him in the narrow bed. *He* had washed, and smelt of soap – although not coal tar: that was Mr Hughes's soap, the one she imagined for him, as she imagined his underpants, his bedroom. Malcolm D. Hughes. Could it be D for David – one of her father's names? Or Daniel, perhaps. Or Derek . . . Would she ever know? A fortnight ago she had seen him at the hospital to go over the details of the three osteotomies and the procedure for her two subluxated toes. In an attempt to appear efficient, she had jotted down a few notes, then scrawled at the bottom, 'I love you, Daddy.'

'I love you,' she whispered to Ralph. He suddenly seemed precious, the one who would drive her to the hospital, be there when she woke up (*if* she woke up), take her home again a week later.

'Love you,' he muttered, embarrassed. He preferred sex to be silent and certainly free of clogging endearments. After more than a decade of marriage, words weren't necessary.

She lay back on the bed while he positioned himself above her, then she slid her feet up his chest and on to his shoulders – Mr Hughes's shoulders. She closed her eyes, saw his dark-as-treacle-toffee eyes gazing down at her. Weirdly, he was clad in pin-stripes at the same time as being naked. Pin-stripes were erotic, the uniform of fathers, two-dimensional fathers. Even Mr Hughes's penis had a seductive pin-striped foreskin. Enticingly rough yet soft inside her. The jargon he'd used at the consultation had become bewitching love-talk: ' . . . dislocation of the second MTPJ . . . titanium hemi-implant . . . '

'Yes!' she whispered back. 'Dorsal subluxation . . . flexion deformity of the first metatarsal . . . '

They were building up a rhythm, an electrifying rhythm – long, fierce, sliding strokes, interspersed with gasping cries.

'Wait,' Ralph panted. 'let's do it the other way.' Swiftly he withdrew, arranged her on her hands and knees and knelt above her on the bed. It was even better that way – tighter, more exciting. She cupped his pin-striped balls, felt him thrust more urgently in response.

'Oh yes!' she shouted, screwing up her face in concentration, tossing back her hair. 'Yes, oh Malcolm, *yes!*'

'Christ! What's that?' The engine had begun to stutter ominously and then suddenly cut out. Ralph punched the hazard-lights button and yelled to Lorna to stick her hand out of the window. He wrenched the car to the left, narrowly missing a van which swerved round them with a furious blast on the horn.

There was a further volley of hooting from the traffic roaring past. Lorna hardly dared to look as Ralph somehow managed to steer the car into the nearside lane before it slid to a halt. Cursing again, he opened his door and got out.

'Careful!' Lorna warned, as cars and lorries thundered by, within inches. There was little he could do, she feared, in the way of a major repair, dressed in his best suit and cashmere coat. To make matters worse, it was minus two outside and a malicious flurry of snow was already settling on his back and shoulders as he lifted the bonnet and peered inside.

Having tinkered vainly for some minutes, he made his precarious way back to the driver's seat. 'God knows what's wrong. It could be anything. I'll have to get the AA.'

'But they'll be ages.'

'Not if we're stuck in the middle of the A3. We're a hazard to other drivers.'

'I'll be late, Ralph, even so. My operation's scheduled first on the list.'

'You'd better take a cab then.'

'Go . . . alone, you mean?'

'Well, I can't abandon the car – not here.' He grabbed his mobile. 'Let me try the AA. They may be able to fix it.'

While he phoned, she checked the time. They were already running late, thanks to broken traffic lights at Tolworth Broadway.

'They'll be twenty minutes minimum,' he muttered. 'And they said we must get out of the car. It's not safe in this traffic.'

'Oh no!' In her sunshine-yellow jacket she was even less prepared for snow than Ralph. She had worn it specially, to counteract the inner and outer gloom, but the wretched thing was only waist-length and far from waterproof. 'Look, let me order a cab first.' Please, God, she prayed, as she dialled. Although if there was a God He would hardly have got them into this mess. 'Shit! The soonest they can do is eleven.' That was the time she was due at the hospital. 'They blame it on the weather.'

'Lorna, we *must* get out.' Ralph winced as a forty-ton lorry rumbled past, all but taking off their wing-mirror.

Reluctantly she opened her door and stepped into the snow. Surely someone would stop to help. But there was no let-up in the heedless stream of traffic.

'I suppose I could always walk to the hospital!' she shouted above the din, gamely attempting a joke and gesturing at her gaping slip-ons, chosen for bunion-ease rather than a twenty-mile hike in a snow-storm.

'Get off the road,' Ralph bellowed, taking her arm and helping her over the barrier. 'You won't *need* an operation if you land up in the mortuary.'

They stood disconsolately side by side, heads bowed against the snow. She glanced at her watch again in dismay. Much as she dreaded the operation, postponing it would be worse still. Since September, hardly a day had gone by without her thinking about the ordeal to come. Not that the last two weeks had left much *time* for thinking. She felt as if she'd been running a marathon, working all hours to leave everything in good order for Ralph, as well as battling with crowds (and panic) to do the Christmas shopping, and writing a hundred cards to clients past and present. A week in hospital would probably be a respite, anxiety or no. But now it seemed she'd have to start the hideous waiting process all over again. Even with private medicine, surgeons couldn't fit you in at the drop of a hat if you happened to miss your scheduled date. Besides, next week was Christmas, and after that Mr Hughes was going away for 'a spot of winter sun'.

Winter sun. If only . . . She was so cold her teeth were chattering and she had lost all feeling in her hands. She wished a genie would appear with a sheepskin coat and a pair of woolly gloves, although Ralph looked so morose that even a brace of genies was unlikely to console him. A grounded car, in his view, was much the same as a limp penis – a source of personal failure.

She squeezed his hand (which at least felt warmer than her own). 'Don't worry,' she mouthed. 'It's not your fault, darling.'

Any reply he might have made was lost in the wail of a siren as a police car glided to a stop behind them, its blue lights flashing dramatically.

'Thank God!' said Ralph. 'They may be able to help.'

One of the officers got out of the car – a short, squat man with sandy hair. 'Hello, sir and madam. What appears to be the trouble?'

Nothing, Lorna bit back – we're just fresh-air fiends enjoying the first fall of snow this year.

Fortunately Ralph did the explaining, then the policeman helped him push the car further off the road.

Ralph brushed snow from his eyes. His hair was dishevelled, and there was a streak of oil down one cheek. 'The thing is,' he said, 'my wife's due in hospital for an operation.'

'Kingston? No trouble, sir, we can drive her there.'

'No, it's the Princess Royal in north London.'

'In that case, sir, I'm afraid we won't be able to help. If it was local we'd take you with pleasure. But look, I'll check with the AA and see how long they're going to be.'

Lorna fought an urge to laugh. The situation was so awful it was funny. Even Aunt Agnes would have trouble coming up with some edifying remark. 'You're lucky to have a car at all' perhaps.

The policeman was soon back. 'Ten minutes, they reckon. And in the meantime you're welcome to sit in our vehicle rather than standing around in the cold.'

Lorna followed him somewhat unwillingly. She had already been inside a police car, thirty years ago, when she had run away from school. The local Somerset constabulary had returned her promptly to an incandescent headmistress.

'I'm Andy, by the way. And this is my colleague Pete.'

'Oh, how do you do . . . ' Lorna introduced herself and Ralph, although Ralph's curt nod signalled his disdain for such extraneous pleasantries on a busy road in blinding snow.

'You look drenched,' said Pete. 'But you'll soon warm up in here. And if you're feeling peckish I can offer you a bar of fruit and nut.'

In 1971 there had been no offer of chocolate, only a stern talking-to and then, back at school, detention every night for a week and exeats cancelled for the rest of term. (Not that she minded about the exeats. She only went out when other children's parents took pity on her, and she invariably felt superfluous.) 'That's kind of you. I'm sure my husband would love some.' She handed the chocolate to Ralph, watching enviously as he broke off a couple of squares. 'I'm not allowed to eat,' she explained. 'I'm having an operation. Well, that was the general idea. I suppose now it rather depends on the AA.'

Pete turned round with a sympathetic smile. 'I can imagine how you feel. Just yesterday we were called to another breakdown. The lady involved was nine months pregnant and we had to rush her to the labour ward – in the nick of time, as it transpired.'

'There you are, you see,' Aunt Agnes put in triumphantly. 'Didn't I tell you things might be ten times worse?'

As Ralph bit into the chocolate, Lorna could taste its creamy richness slowly dissolving on her tongue. She crunched an imaginary nut between her teeth, savouring the contrast in the textures. She would probably fast all day only to find the operation was cancelled in the end. Still, at least she wasn't panicking – a miracle given the circumstances. But then panic was of its essence unpredictable. It could erupt for no reason at all, yet fail to materialize in a bona-fide crisis.

With a sigh of resignation she sank back in her seat, listening to the crackle of the radio. The whole area, it seemed, was experiencing a spate of burglaries, muggings and horrific accidents.

'. . . *suspects breaking in now at 15 Burlington Road. Both men armed . . .*'

'. . . *pile-up in the Kingston one-way system. Believed serious injuries.*'

'. . . *burglary at 7 Fairfield North. Two masked men seen running away . . .*'

Not very tactful of Ralph to sit there scoffing chocolate while bodies were strewn pell-mell across the county: bleeding, coshed, unconscious, robbed, raped or dead.

'What operation are you having?' Pete asked. 'I hope it's nothing serious.'

She hesitated. Something serious would actually sound more impressive. A triple bypass, for example, would induce instant respect. Bunions, like mothers-in-law, were merely fodder for jokes. 'It's, er, on my foot.'

'Well, I wish you all the best. Certainly the Princess Royal is said to be first class. And very snazzy, so I'm told.'

Spoilt bitch, they probably thought, swanning around in luxury while the have-nots languished for decades on the waiting-list. Perhaps the car breaking down was her punishment for queue-jumping. Private schools, private doctors, and she had the gall to call herself a socialist!

'It's not a bunion, is it?' Andy continued remorselessly. 'A friend of the wife's had hers done and said it was worse than having twins.'

Luckily an item on the radio diverted their attention – more bloodshed or skulduggery, she assumed, although she couldn't decipher a word of it. She stared glumly at the back of Pete's bald head. The car was getting fuggy and, far from being a haven, felt cramped and claustrophobic. Its blue lights seemed as restless as her thoughts, circling on the same obsessive track. She could see snowflakes trapped in their beams, frenziedly trying to escape.

Pete switched on the heater to clear the misted windows, while Andy pursued the subject of his wife's friend's bunion op.

'Yes, Janet wishes she'd never had it done. After all that pain and aggro her feet are just as bad. In fact she has to walk with a stick.'

Lorna swallowed. 'Yes, well . . . '

'Aha!' said Pete. 'Rescue is at hand!'

Yellow flashing lights were now added to the blue as the AA van drew up in a flurry of slush. Ralph and Andy got out and stood talking to the patrolman, who then strode across to the stranded car and inspected the engine.

Please be able to fix it, Lorna pleaded silently. As soon as humanly possible.

Ralph returned glowering to the police car. 'It's an absolute bugger. There's nothing he can do here, he says. He'll have to tow us to a garage.'

'Oh God!' she wailed. 'I should have booked that cab when they offered it. I'd better see if it's still free.'

It wasn't of course. There was now a delay till two o'clock.

'Ralph, what on earth shall I *do*?'

'Ring the hospital. Tell them with any luck we'll be there in an hour.'

'But that's impossible. It's an hour's drive from here, and we haven't even got to the garage yet. And what if they can't mend it straight away?'

'Phone the hospital anyway.' He handed her the mobile. 'And get a move on. The AA man's waiting to tow us.'

'Engaged,' she groaned. 'I can't believe it.'

'Well, try again in a minute.' Ralph helped her out of the car.

'Good luck,' Andy called. 'I hope the operation goes well!'

'If I have it,' she muttered, slipping on a patch of slush and practically measuring her length.

Ralph caught her arm. 'Be careful or you'll break your leg.'

Mm, she thought – not a bad idea. A broken leg sounded a good deal more dramatic than bunions.

3

'Your blood pressure is still extremely high, Mrs Pearson.'

Lorna grimaced. 'I'm not surprised. The journey was a nightmare, as I told the other nurse. After hanging about in a totally useless garage, we had to walk miles to the station. And when we eventually caught a train it stopped for half an hour outside Clapham Junction – the wrong kind of snow no doubt. Then in the cab from Waterloo every single traffic light was red. I was beginning to think someone up there had it in for us!'

The nurse pursed her lips. 'It's no laughing matter. Mr Hughes won't operate unless we can bring it down in time.'

Better to laugh than cry, Lorna thought. Since their arrival, wet through and dispirited, it had been all systems go. First the paperwork – concerned less with the state of her health than with that of her bank balance. (If she died from the strain, they probably wouldn't care less, so long as she could pay.) Then a change of room when her original one was found to have a mysterious stain on the carpet (blood? urine? absinthe?). Next a briefing on the formidable array of call-buttons, lights and switches, requiring a degree in computer science. And last, and apparently least, her medical history was taken and her raised blood pressure discovered. And now here she was, lying in bed in a hospital gown, awaiting further developments.

Clearly a stiff upper lip was called for, and a quick tally of her blessings: she had a room to herself, a luxurious en-suite bathroom, a view through a decent-sized window (mainly of traffic and tower blocks but far better than a blank wall) and, best of all, Mr Hughes had rescheduled his list and fitted her in at five.

'He'll be tired by then,' sneered the Monster. 'His scalpel is bound to slip.'

'Go away!' she hissed.

'Well, I'll leave you to rest, Mrs Pearson. I'll be back in half an hour to check your blood pressure again. Please don't get out of bed.'

No chance of that. The trembling in her legs wouldn't let her move at all. She tried to console herself by looking at the tag on her wrist. 'Mrs Pearson/Mr Hughes' – she and her father bracketed together. She hadn't seen him yet. He'd be in theatre, knee-deep in blood.

'It'll be *your* blood soon,' the Monster warned. 'Gushing all over the floor. Then you'll need a transfusion, and you'll get Aids sure as dammit.'

'You can't frighten me.'

'Oh really? Just you wait. Your blood pressure will shoot up even higher. You could have a stroke any minute, finish up as a vegetable.'

'I *like* vegetables,' she said desperately, resorting to visualization (an anti-panic technique) and summoning up carrots, cabbages, aubergines and swedes – giant-sized to crowd the Monster out. She peeled them, chopped them, simmered them in an orgy of distraction.

At that moment Ralph walked back in. 'Well?' he said. 'Are they going to operate?'

'Yes, if my blood pressure comes down.'

He made a noise between a grunt and a cough, settling himself in the chair. For the last hour or more he had been up and down like a yo-yo. The hospital's strict no-smoking policy meant if he wanted to indulge he had to go outside and brave the snow. And he *did* want – his latest attempt to kick the nicotine habit had lasted a mere three days. What with the stress and the exertion, his blood pressure was probably higher than hers by now.

'He'll die and you'll be left a widow.'

'Go *away*,' she snapped.

'What?'

'Sorry, darling, I was talking to someone else.'

Ralph glanced uneasily around the empty room, then subsided into his habitual silence.

There was plenty of other noise, though. Footsteps of varying weight and urgency in the corridor outside, the sound of patients' buzzers, nurses calling to each other and, in the background, the constant drone of traffic, which even the double glazing couldn't entirely block out. Cars roared past, uncaring, as they had on the A3, and the snow continued to fall remorselessly. Well, did she expect the world to stop just because she was about to have some footling operation?

'*Major* surgery. And you know how dangerous anaesthetics can be.'

'You're lucky to *have* an anaesthetic.' Aunt Agnes had joined the Monster now. 'Not so long ago people had their limbs chopped off with only alcohol to dull the pain. And they usually died anyway, from shock.'

Ignoring them both, Lorna turned to Ralph. 'Did you manage to get something to eat?'

'I'm not hungry.'

'There you are, you see. He's sickening already.'

She bit back her retort. You were supposed to speak out to the Monster in a loud, defiant voice, but not at the risk of being classified insane. She wiped the sweat from her forehead. 'There's a coffee-bar downstairs.'

'I know.'

'You could have bought a sandwich.'

'Don't fuss. You're the one who's ill, not me.'

'I'm not ill, Ralph, just . . . '

'Who are you kidding? Look at the state you're in! I doubt you'll last the night.'

'You ought to be on your knees, child, thanking God for all this luxury! When I had my hysterectomy I was in a great big noisy ward with . . . '

Lorna sank back against the pillows. This four-way conversation was exhausting. 'I'm fine,' she repeated through gritted teeth, trying to rid herself of the Monster – preferably with Aunt Agnes slung across its shoulder. 'I'm as calm as a mill-pond, as cool as a cucumber.' She visualized a mill-pond on which ice-cold cucumbers floated serenely, with the odd tranquil swan gliding past. Deep breaths in, deep breaths out . . .

'And yes, Aunt, I *am* lucky,' she said *sotto voce*, squinting through her eyelids. Private hospitals had something in common with country-house hotels: wall-to-wall carpet (hers was tasteful grey); bland, non-threatening non-art (two watercolours of sun-kissed poppy-fields); bowls of flowers in reception; and tropically warm central heating. All that was very pleasant: it was the patients she found unnerving. Walking past their rooms she had caught sight of the occupants – attached to yards of tubing or ominous-looking machines, legs in traction, arms in plaster, drips in veins, bandages on feet. And she kept thinking of the horrors going on in other wards: colostomies, cardiac arrests, heart and liver transplants. Whatever happened, she must cling on tight to her vital organs, in case some passing surgeon needed a donor kidney in a hurry or decided to help himself to her womb or spleen in the interests of research.

Mill-pond, she reminded herself, boarding a cucumber-boat and drifting downstream as she tried to continue counting her blessings. 'My husband's still alive; he still has his own liver, heart and kidneys; he can eat and excrete without technological assistance. And he's not even watching television.' (Although he *was* casting furtive glances at the set.)

'Oh, Lord!' he said suddenly.

The cucumber-craft capsized as she sat up in alarm. 'What is it, Ralph? What's wrong?'

'Nothing's wrong. It's just that I bought you a present and I completely forgot about it.'

'A present? What for?'

'Not for anything, just . . . you know.' He handed her a Jiffy bag. (Ralph was notorious for never wrapping presents.) Inside was a small padded box.

She opened it. 'Oh, *Ralph* . . . '

'Put it on.' He leaned over and fastened the clasp for her. She gazed in awe at the delicate gold-and-diamond bracelet. How had he found the time to go shopping? Or the inclination? Ralph would rather be murdered in cold blood than face a crowded high street in the grip of pre-Christmas hysteria. And where had he got the money? 'Darling, it's absolutely beautiful! I feel . . . quite overcome.'

Ralph frowned in warning. Gratitude embarrassed him. 'I hoped you'd like it.'

'Like it? I love it! And it looks terribly expensive.'

The door opened and a nurse came in – a new one again. It was worse than a cocktail party, trying to remember names and faces.

'Hello, I'm Pat. I've come to take your blood pressure.'

Lorna kept her eyes on the bracelet, endowing it with magic powers. Ralph thought her worth all that trouble and expense, which was magic in itself.

'Good,' said Pat. 'It's gone down considerably. I'll get a message to

Mr Hughes and tell him we can go ahead. And I'll pop back in ten minutes or so to give you your pre-med.'

No! she wanted to shout. It's all a dreadful mistake. I'm leaving – now. I was just trying out the facilities. They're great. Congratulations.

'Are you comfortable, Mrs Pearson?'

'Yes . . . fine.' Any hint that she was prone to panic and they'd pop back with a strait-jacket.

Ralph stood up. 'I . . . think I'll get a breath of air.'

A lungful of pipe-smoke, he meant, and an excuse to escape before Pat returned with a needle. He hated injections – his own or other people's – although he would never say so in a thousand years. That was the trouble with fears. Nobody admitted to them.

There was a sudden commotion outside: shouting, running foot-steps. An emergency? A death? She concentrated resolutely on the two paintings on her wall: azure sky, white puffy clouds. Below the sky were the poppies, though – Flanders Fields; the Cenotaph.

She was startled by a tap on the door. Perhaps they needed her bed. A crazed gunman was on the loose, and his maimed and bleeding vic-tims were being stretchered in by the score . . .

'Hello, Mrs Pearson. It's good to see you at last. I understand you had a rather gruelling journey.'

She stared. Mr *Hughes*. Or was it? The pin-stripes were replaced by baggy theatre greens, the elegant calfskin shoes by ugly wooden-soled clogs, and the silver hair was bundled beneath an unflattering nylon cap.

'I'm glad to hear your blood pressure has stabilized.' The voice was the same – vintage brandy topped with double cream. But shouldn't he be in theatre, his clothes bespattered with blood?

'Could I take a look at your feet?'

Extricating her legs from the covers, she inadvertently revealed the voluminous paper bloomers they had given her to wear. Mortified, she pulled the gown down over her knees. But Mr Hughes was concerned only with her left foot: beyond that one deformed extremity her body didn't exist for him.

He whisked out a black marker pen and began drawing lines on her toes. 'I intend to make an incision *here*. And *there*. And . . . '

She tried to block her ears. It was as if the pen were a scalpel and he was already slicing into her flesh.

He continued explaining the procedure, expounding on various risks he had never previously mentioned: she might develop another bunion even after surgery; the second toe was extremely tricky and if it stiffened it might require a further operation; the balance of the foot might change; there could be problems with the arches . . .

'So, if you're happy with what I plan to do . . . '

Happy? She was delirious. Who would forgo the pleasure of having their foot ripped apart and then cobbled together again, only to be left with it worse than before?

'If you'd just sign here, Mrs Pearson . . . ' The black felt-tip had turned into a gold fountain-pen, which he was holding out to her along with the consent form.

'You're insane,' the Monster growled. 'Signing away your life.'

'Read it first,' Aunt Agnes tutted. 'It's high time you were more responsible.'

She studied the sea of print. The Os in the osteotomies were expanding into cavernous mouths howling in terror. She closed her eyes. Your father's here, she told herself. So everything's all right. He's the person you love best. He chose your name – a romantic name.

'Mrs Pearson?

Call me Lorna. Call me your pet, your sweetheart. Stroke my cheek; ruffle my baby hair.

'Is anything wrong?'

'N . . . no . . . ' Her hand was shaking so much she could barely write. If only she could put a cross instead. A goodnight kiss for Daddy. He was tucking her in, bending over the bed, the dark eyes devoted, loving . . .

'Thank you, Mrs Pearson. I'll see you later then.'

By the time Pat returned with a metal bowl and a syringe, the Monster was crunching her in its jaws, spitting out her pips and rind.

'Turn over on your side, Mrs Pearson. That's it. Now, just a little prick . . . '

A javelin stabbed into her buttock. If she had an unexpected haemorrhage, would someone . . . ?

'You should feel nice and floaty soon. If you need me, ring the bell.'

I *shan't* need you. I'll be too far gone.

*

'Lorna, are you all right?'

'Absolutely A1! I'm on top of the world.'

'There's no need to be sarcastic.'

'No, I mean it, Ralph. I want to dance. Fancy a quick tango?'

'Lie still, for Christ's sake!' Ralph instructed. 'It must be the morphine,' he muttered.

'Morphine?'

'In the pre-med.'

'Really? Well, buy me a load for Christmas then. I want to feel like this all the time.'

'What happened to your bracelet, by the way?'

'In its box. You have to take everything off – or out. Nail varnish, jewellery, false teeth . . . ' She began to laugh. And laugh. 'Oh, Ralph, I'm so glad we came. I *adore* it here, don't you?'

'Frankly, no.'

'You are a spoilsport! Why don't I ring for some tea?'

'You're not allowed tea, Lorna.'

'Yes I am. I'm allowed anything I like. I'll order buttered scones and crumpets and a big wodge of gooey cake. My word is their command. See, here they come, before I've even rung the bell!'

'Right, Mrs Pearson, we're ready for you now.'

'Great!'

'Lorna?'

'Yes?'

'G . . . good luck.'

She looked at him in surprise. It was clear that he was worried, concerned about her safety perhaps.

'It's OK, Ralph. There's nothing to it. I'll be back in no time.'

He didn't seem convinced. And as she was transferred to the trolley-bed he took her hand (in spite of his distaste for displays of emotion) and leaned down close, so that no one else could hear. 'I love you, Lorna,' he whispered. 'And don't forget: diamonds are for ever.'

4

A patch of glaring blue came into focus. Only to disappear. Everything beyond it was shadowy and blurred. The blue loomed again, slowly taking on a shape – the outline of a nurse. The nurse was saying something. Couldn't hear. Sounds were muffled, jumbled. Couldn't speak. Teeth chattering too much; body shaking uncontrollably.

Someone holding her hand. She clutched at the person – another blue blur. Two nurses, one each side.

'Why . . . am . . . I . . . shaking?' she tried to ask, but the words were lost in the shaking. There was nothing but the shaking. Arms, legs, head, hands, back, all jerking and twitching like a mechanical toy. She prayed for it to stop. That was all she wanted in the world. Any other wish was pointless.

'Mrs Pearson, can you hear me?'

She nodded, shook her head. It made no difference. Hearing didn't matter. Nothing mattered except to stop shaking. '*Stop*,' she told her body, but it didn't. Couldn't.

She was aware of another bed. And someone in it – close, yet miles away. The voice was deep. A man's voice. Could it be her father? Had he died again?

'Are we dead?' she asked. 'In heaven?'

'No, Mrs Pearson, you're in the Recovery Room. And you're perfectly safe.'

'So . . . why . . . am . . . I . . . ?' The shaking took over, completing the question for her.

'It's a reaction to the anaesthetic. It does sometimes give people the shakes.'

Anaesthetic. She vaguely remembered a needle in her arm. Then nothingness.

'And you got very cold in theatre, being immobile for so long.'

Yes, cold. Frog-cold. Her teeth were still chattering. But she mustn't make a fuss. She was lucky to have two nurses to look after her. One was taking her blood pressure again. The other tucked a blanket round

41

her. The blankets were shaking too. And the tube in her arm. Why did she need a tube? Had something gone wrong?

The man beside her was speaking. 'I feel sick,' he said. So did she. Waves of nausea were rolling through her body, nudging at her throat.

She shut her eyes, surrendered to the sickness. Surrendered to the shaking. Shaking, shaking, shaking. No relief. No change.

Time passed. Still shaking.

'We're going to take you back to your room now, Mrs Pearson. All right?'

No. Not all right. How could she go anywhere like this?

The trolley rattled over bumps. Unsafe. She might fall off. Glaring lights. A corridor. Clanging doors. A lift. Then the room with poppy-fields, blood red. And a familiar voice. Angry.

'What the hell's going on? They told me an hour and a half, and she's been gone four hours.'

'I'm sorry, Mr Pearson, there was a slight problem in – '

'A problem? What do you mean? She's not in danger, is she? Why is she shaking like that, for God's sake?'

The voices faded.

'R . . . Ralph?'

'He'll be back in a moment, pet. He's just outside, talking to the other nurse.'

Pet. Mr Hughes called her Pet. But Mr Hughes was dead.

Another voice. Male again, but cheery: 'Hold still, Mrs Pearson, we're going to put you back into bed.'

Hold still? How could she? The shaking wouldn't stop.

As they moved her from the trolley, she caught sight of her foot. Bandaged, with the toes sticking out. Wires in the toes, caked with blood. Her lower leg was bruised. Red and purple blotches. She couldn't feel the leg. Or the foot. Just a sort of numbness.

Someone took her hand. A bigger hand than the nurse's.

'I'm here, Lorna.'

Ralph's voice. She clung to it.

'Darling, are you all right?'

'Fine,' she mouthed. Mustn't cry. If she cried he'd leave. Like Tom.

*

42

'What time is it?'

'Ten past two.'

'In the afternoon?'

'No, two in the morning. I'm the night nurse, Eileen. I've come to top up your drip. How's the pain?'

'I can't feel anything.'

'Good. Do you need the commode?'

'Er, yes.' Her bladder seemed as numb as her leg, but it would be humiliating to have an accident.

The nurse removed the cradle from her leg and helped her to sit up – not easy with a tube in her arm. 'Careful! Don't put any weight on that foot.'

She manoeuvred herself on to the commode and somehow managed to pull her bloomers down. Though numb, her left leg felt huge and unwieldy, as if it no longer belonged to her. She sat like an obedient child, trying to perform. But peeing was impossible with an audience. Impossible full stop. 'I'm sorry, I . . . don't think I can.'

With an audible sigh, Eileen helped her back to bed. Resentful of time-wasters no doubt. All the staff seemed perpetually busy and hadn't time to chat. She wondered if Ralph was asleep. If only she could phone him . . . But he wouldn't know what to say, and anyway he needed his sleep. He had looked shattered when he left, and would have had the snow to contend with, and unreliable trains again, most likely. All very well for her, tucked up in the warm, away from demanding clients phoning at all hours. She admired his fortitude. He would never dream of giving way to panic, although from a psychological viewpoint he surely had reason enough. As a child, he had suffered more than she had: an indifferent mother, a pig of a stepfather, no Agnes to provide a home, no security whatever. Nor had his misery ended there. His first wife, Naomi, had developed multiple sclerosis early in the marriage and had become a mental and physical cripple over the next ten years. And even his present life wasn't exactly a bed of roses, what with the pressure of work, the debts, and a second disabled wife. But his method of coping was to bottle everything up, to use silence as a defence weapon. She had been aware of that from the start, accepted it almost gratefully. It meant they complemented each other: his control counterbalancing her emotional outbursts.

43

'There's nothing *else* you need, is there?' Eileen was already making for the door, and her tone of voice implied that any further request would be as greedy and unreasonable as asking for cream as well as custard on your apple tart. Forget apple tart – a cup of tea would be heaven; a slug of vodka better still.

'No, thank you,' Lorna said to the closing door. 'I'm . . . fine.' Fine was a crucial word in her armoury. The Monster hated fine.

She remained sitting up against the pillows. Outside, a few cars sped past, and she could see a plane in the dark night sky, its tiny red and blue lights flashing. Across the road there were lighted squares of windows in a tower block. Other people sleepless? Mourning? 'No man is an island . . . ' A lie, of course. Everyone was an island, and at 2 a.m. the bridges were closed and the ferries didn't run.

She wormed herself down the bed, propping her foot on two pillows. (It had to be kept higher than her heart, to help the swelling go down.) She preferred to sleep on her stomach, but that was more or less impossible with the bandage and the wires, and sleeping on her back felt awkward and unfamiliar.

'You're lucky to *have* a bed. In the war we slept in shelters.'

'Yes, I know, Aunt Agnes, but it happens to be peacetime now.'

Peace must be what the angels felt, a concept as foreign to her as growing up with parents – the Monster saw to that. Perhaps she could conjure up an angel: kindly and sweet-tempered, with soft, protective wings. Yes, there he was, with a steaming-hot apple tart in one hand (cream *and* custard) and a bottle of Smirnoff in the other.

'Come in,' she murmured sleepily. It must be Eileen again, with more pills.

'I'm sorry to disturb you at such an unsociable hour, but I'm due at the Royal Free at seven thirty, so I thought I'd look in first.'

Mr Hughes. Impeccable in a dark suit and dazzling white shirt. While *she* was lying in a jumbled bed, sweaty and dishevelled. If she'd had advance warning of his visits she could at least have combed her hair.

'How are you, Mrs Pearson?'

Embarrassed. She tugged the skimpy gown over the unprepossessing bloomers, before sitting up gingerly. 'The feeling's come back in my foot.'

'Good. Any pain at all?'

'No.'

'We've got you on an very high dose of pain-killers, so you shouldn't experience any discomfort. And I'm glad to say that basically the surgery went well.'

'Well? But why did it take so long? My husband thought I . . . I'd kicked the bucket!'

Mr Hughes gave an awkward laugh. 'I'm afraid there was a slight mix-up, Mrs Pearson. My . . . saw went missing.'

Saw? The image of a lumberjack came to mind, hacking through a massive tree-trunk. How could a modest bunion require an implement on that scale?

'They told me it was on loan to another hospital. As you can imagine, I was exceedingly annoyed.'

Was this some kind of joke? Didn't hospitals have their own saws, or was there only one to go round? And surely the theatre staff checked that all instruments were there before putting a patient under. She couldn't conceive of a carpenter or plumber embarking on a job without his tools, so why should a surgeon be any different?

'A motorcycle messenger was dispatched to retrieve it, and was gone for some considerable time . . . '

It *must* be a joke. Even the Monster couldn't have dreamed up such a scenario.

'Eventually he returned, saying the Gresham didn't have the saw. Which precipitated another search. And, would you believe, it was here all the time.'

No, she wouldn't believe.

'So I'm afraid you had a rather protracted sleep, Mrs Pearson.' He smiled apologetically.

Sleep? She'd been pumped full of dangerous anaesthetics for four solid hours, simply because of staggering inefficiency. And poor Ralph had been going demented. When he'd asked why it was taking so long, they'd just said vaguely she must still be in theatre. Yes, in theatre while Mr Hughes sat twiddling his expert (and extremely expensive) thumbs.

'And there was another complication . . . '

'Oh, heavens – what?' Perhaps one of his minions had sewn up a needle inside her foot, or the anaesthetist had ingested his own drugs and dozed off.

'Your skin is paper-thin, Mrs Pearson. Which is very unusual in a woman of your age. And of course it made things much more difficult. I had to use nylon sutures instead of the absorbable ones.'

The Monster burst back in. 'See, you're falling to pieces! When he takes the stitches out your skin will probably pull away in great lumps.'

'And your second toe was, frankly, a mess. There was a lot of debris in it and severe arthritic changes, which again is unusual in patients under forty.'

She swallowed. It was obviously time for her bus pass, or a merciful injection from the vet. Agnes was a martyr to arthritis, but it hadn't come on till her seventies. And what on earth did he mean by debris?

'There's very little movement in that toe. It's essential to keep it mobile. I want you to wiggle it up and down for a minute or so every half-hour. Up down, up down – like this.'

She flinched as he yanked the poor aged toe almost at a right angle to the others.

'Now you carry on doing this as often as you can. I must be off now, but I'll look in again this afternoon.'

'Told you so,' crowed the Monster after Mr Hughes had gone. 'What an incredible balls-up!'

'It went *well*. He said so himself.'

''Course he did. Saving face, that's all.'

'My foot's *straight*, isn't it?' Which was indeed a triumph, although with the trauma of the anaesthetic she had hardly taken in the fact. Whatever else had gone awry, all her toes now pointed in the same direction – on one foot anyway.

'Don't you be so sure. That bandage hides a multitude of sins.'

She turned her back on the Monster as the door opened again and a lanky, dark-skinned man appeared. 'You like breakfast?' he asked.

'Yes please!'

'What you like?'

Bacon, eggs, mushrooms, beans, fried bread. 'What is there?'

'You not see menu?'

'No.'

'I fetch.'

Half an hour went by. She tried to use the time profitably by exercising her second toe, ignoring the Monster's jibes that it wouldn't do the slightest good since that toe was already a write-off. Eventually she turned on the news to drown him out: a massacre in the Congo, a bomb scare in Calcutta, flooding in Bangladesh and more casualties in Afghanistan.

'All *right*, Aunt Agnes, I know I'm lucky not to live in a war zone. But I do happen to be extremely hungry. I haven't eaten for twenty-four hours, and then it was only a slice of toast.'

The lanky man returned with two impressive-looking menus. Unfortunately they were for lunch and dinner, not breakfast.

'This not breakfast,' she said, unconsciously lapsing into pidgin.

'You not want breakfast?'

'Yes, I *do* want. But this isn't it.'

His soulful eyes stared at her in bafflement.

'D'you think I could have a boiled egg?' Best to keep it simple. If she mentioned kippers or black pudding, God knows what would turn up. 'Boiled egg,' she repeated slowly, wondering whether to mime the action of tapping an egg with a spoon. Except it might confuse him into thinking she wanted a hammer (if the hammer hadn't gone the same way as the saw).

She reached across to her bedside drawer for a pen and a scrap of paper. 'Boiled egg, tea and toast,' she printed clearly. If he couldn't understand it, maybe someone in the kitchen would. She passed it to him with an encouraging smile, but he looked still more dismayed. Perhaps he imagined it was a *billet-doux* – a lonely female patient making unwanted advances to him.

'Give note to kitchen, please,' she instructed, wishing she'd brought a translator with her, or, even better, a private chef.

To pass the time she studied the two menus, which were illustrated with colour pictures of fruits and vegetables. The food sounded remarkably good, despite the spoilsport caveats: 'Unsuitable for Diabetics' or 'Not Recommended for Slimmers'. Ignoring the healthy dishes, she selected the highest-fat, highest-sugar options, restraining herself with difficulty from ticking two choices for every course. While she was deciding between banoffi pie and tiramisu, the phone rang – Ralph, asking how she was feeling.

'Ravenous!'

'Well, that's a good sign. Blast! The other phone's ringing. I'll call you back.'

Ten minutes passed without the promised call, so she turned on the television. Gruesome pictures of the massacre, close up. She switched to another channel: violence in Ireland now. The shrill of the phone coincided with an explosion in Belfast. 'Hello, darling,' she muttered, shuddering at the carnage.

'It's not darling, it's Anne.'

Lorna gritted her teeth. Anne Spencer-Armitage was an acquaintance rather than a friend. (What friend would phone at this hour?)

'I expect you're in agony, aren't you? They say it's one of the most painful operations you can have.'

'I wouldn't know. I'm drugged to the eyeballs with pain-killers.'

'You want to be careful, Lorna. Those drugs can cause bleeding of the stomach. In fact a girl at work developed a full-blown ulcer after just two weeks on ibuprofen.'

Who needed the Monster when Anne was about? Only half listening, Lorna tried to turn off the television, but succeeded merely in increasing the volume.

'What's that awful noise?'

'Gang warfare in Chicago. Oh dear, there's someone at the door.' Breakfast, with any luck. Which she had no intention of sharing with Anne. 'Can I ring you back?'

'Yes, do. I'm dying to hear the gory details.'

The lanky man slunk in again, with a piece of paper in his hand. Another menu? A reply to her note?

No, another consent form. Would she accept the risk of eating a boiled egg? Presumably it referred to salmonella but, having just survived major surgery, she would doubtless survive a few germs in an egg. As she signed her name, the phone rang once more: Ralph's return call at last. This time she asked him how *he* was, inventing the ideal reply: I miss you desperately. The house is bleak and empty without you. It's lost its heart. I'm bereft.

48

'What d'you mean, how am I? There's nothing wrong with *me*. Bugger! There's the other phone again. It's Patrick Gillespie, I bet. He's . . . '

With the TV blaring, she couldn't hear the rest of the sentence. She punched the buttons on the remote-control, with no more effect than before. It would probably switch off at the set, but she wasn't allowed out of bed until she had seen the physio and been issued with her crutches. Enforced immobility was frustrating. She longed to go to the bathroom to clean her teeth and have a proper wash, but could only lie and listen to atrocities – all the crises and accidents beloved of the Monster. Existence must have been easier in medieval times, when you didn't hear about events beyond the confines of your own small village. She tried to turn herself into a thirteenth-century goodwife, with nothing to worry about except a hen not laying or a faulty stitch in her tapestry.

'No anaesthetics,' the Monster sneered. 'No penicillin. No fridges. You'd be panicking before you could say Black Death.'

'Go away!' she ordered, then 'Come in' as she heard another knock at the door.

The egg at last, with any luck. By now her stomach was rumbling audibly and her mouth felt like the bottom of an ancient, boiled-dry kettle.

In walked a bouquet with a small, red-haired man on the end of it. 'Flowers for you, Mrs Pearson.'

She looked nervously at the pompous blooms shrouded in Cellophane – the sort of thing one might order for a funeral.

'I'll fetch a vase.'

'Thank you.' She prised the card from the bouquet: 'From Heather and Sebastian, with fondest love.'

There must be some mistake. She didn't know anyone called Heather and Sebastian. Perhaps she could eat the flowers for breakfast, though – scrambled lilies on toast – and drink the water in the vase.

Swiftly reappearing, the red-haired man proved a model of efficiency. He turned the television off (having first explained the controls), filled her water-jug, promised to sort out the mystery of the flowers, and finally gave her the number of the kitchen.

'Hello. It's Mrs Pearson in room twenty. I ordered a boiled egg . . . Oh, on its way? Wonderful!'

Within a couple of minutes there was a tap on the door. 'Yes!' she whooped. 'Come *in*. I'm so hungry I could . . . '

In walked Diane Morris, the wife of one of their wealthiest clients. 'Lorna, how *are* you? Do forgive me barging in like this, but I'm on my way to work and I literally pass the door. I just couldn't resist popping in to see you. Did everything go well?'

'Mm . . . fine.' She was rigid with embarrassment. Diane's appearance – elegant cream suit, immaculate hair, scarlet lips and nails – highlighted her own state of dishabille. Worse was the contrast in their feet: Diane's shod in dove-grey kidskin ankle-boots; hers ignominiously naked – the right twisted and deformed, the left bloody and bristling with wires. Quickly she pulled the sheet over them and forced her face into the semblance of a smile, although making stilted conversation with a comparative stranger was not a welcome prospect.

'Do sit down. How lovely to see you!' Whatever her feelings, she must make an effort for Ralph's sake. 'And what's the weather doing out there?'

'It's perishing, my dear! You're lucky to be here in the warm.'

Shades of Aunt Agnes. 'Yes, they do keep it nice and snug.'

'And how long will you be in?'

'Oh, barely a week. I'll be home well in time for Christmas.'

'Don't mention Christmas, Lorna! I've hardly begun my shopping . . . '

'Are you and Bob going away?'

'Just to our country place in Shropshire. Both the girls are coming, with their families, so it'll be the usual houseful. How about you?'

She wouldn't be going anywhere, that was for sure. Well, maybe hobbling on crutches from the bedroom to the kitchen. Christmas was lonely at the best of times, without being incapacitated. If only she could hire a ready-made family: parents, children, cousins, aunts . . . Her one living relative, Aunt Agnes, was otherwise engaged – spending Christmas in a hotel with an old friend from her teaching days.

'Lorna, if there's anything you need I'll be delighted to help. You only have to say.'

'No, honestly, I'm fine.' Fine was true, for once, because at that very moment the breakfast-tray arrived: grapefruit segments, two boiled eggs, buttered toast, and tea and milk in a flower-sprigged pot.

'Oh, my *dear*, you haven't had your breakfast! I'm so sorry. I'm disturbing you.'

'No, please. It doesn't matter. It's sweet of you to come.'

As the phone rang yet again, Lorna began to wish she was in a National Health ward. She wouldn't have a phone then; nor would visitors be allowed to swan in at breakfast time.

'It's me again.'

'Oh . . . hello, Ralph.'

'What's up? You sound peculiar.'

'Er, Diane Morris is here. She's very kindly come to see me.'

'I'll ring off then. I'm a bit pushed, actually. I've got to see that useless contractor in Staplehurst, so I shan't be able to ring again till tonight.'

Ring? Wasn't he coming in person? She couldn't ask with Diane there. How long was the wretched woman going to stay? It must be getting on for nine by now, but Diane worked in advertising, which was noted for its relaxed attitude to timekeeping. She and Ralph were at their desks by seven.

'Don't let your breakfast get cold, Lorna – not on my account.'

'Actually, I . . . I couldn't face eating at the moment.' What she couldn't face was conversing with her mouth full in front of the fastidious Diane. Or, worse, dripping egg yolk on the sheet. She eyed the untouched food – butter already congealing on the toast. Even the smell of the toast was lost in the blast of Diane's Chanel No. 5.

'But what's wrong, my dear? I thought you said you felt fine?'

'Oh, just a bit . . . sick, that's all. You know how it is after anaesthetics.'

'Well, I *don't*, to tell the truth. I've never been ill in my life, let alone in hospital. Bobby says I'm so healthy it's disgusting. Anyway, if you're feeling sick you won't want visitors, so I'd better make myself scarce.'

'Well, it's been a pleasure. Thank you . . . ' Any second now she would be able to sink her teeth into the toast, devour each egg in a couple of gulps, wash them down with pints of glorious tea.

But no, it seemed she wouldn't. Another intrusion, in the shape of Nurse Pat, accompanied by a porter with a wheelchair.

'I'm sorry to disturb you, Mrs Pearson, when you have a visitor, but Mr Hughes has requested an X-ray. Oh, you haven't had your breakfast yet. Aren't you hungry?'

Yes! she wanted to shout. I could eat a horse. Why stop at one? She could eat an entire stud farm. But she could hardly contradict what she had just said to Diane. 'I seem to have lost my appetite.'

'Don't worry, that often happens. I'll get someone to take your tray away.'

She cast a last lingering glance at the breakfast, tasting the refreshing tang of grapefruit on her tongue, the tea slipping down hot and sweet and strong. Well, at least she was saved from salmonella and – another blessing – the nurse was actually helping her on with her dressing-gown, concealing the offending hospital robe.

'Goodbye, Lorna,' Diane called, teetering to the door. 'Good luck!'

Yes, I'll need it, Lorna thought, as she was wheeled along the corridor, her leg up on a metal strut and sticking out at a right angle. It felt horribly vulnerable – she was terrified the orderly might bang it against the wall.

Mercifully, though, she arrived unscathed at the X-Ray department. He parked her just outside and, with a jaunty 'Cheerio!', strode off.

Stay, she begged him silently. I can't move without you.

Suddenly, above all else, she longed to stand up and walk away. She couldn't, of course: she was trapped. For endless weeks she would be reduced to limping and hobbling, and dependent on other people to help her do the most basic things. The prospect was appalling.

'You'd better get used to it. Judging by the mess that stupid surgeon made, you'll probably be permanently disabled. And there's still the other foot, remember. Once he's let loose on that you might as well make your will and be done with it.'

'*Scat!* They don't allow Monsters in X-Ray.'

'It's so crowded I doubt they'll notice.'

True. All the casualties in this morning's news seemed to have congregated there – broken arms, broken bodies, crocks like her in wheelchairs or supine on trolley-beds. Despite their common plight, the famous English reserve prevailed. Not a single person spoke; each sat in their own separate purgatory, unwilling (or unable) to communicate.

'No man is an island . . . ' Her island was drifting further and further from the mainland; Ralph and her friends were tiny dots in the distance waving her adieu.

No! she pleaded desperately. Come back.

5

'It's perfectly simple, Mrs Pearson,' Phil explained. 'When you go upstairs you lead with the good foot, and when you go down you lead with the bad.'

Lorna gazed at the flight of stairs looming before her as if into the stratosphere. Nothing was simple on crutches.

'Remember that little tag I told you: "The good go up to heaven and the bad go down to hell." Right, let's try again. Transfer the crutch to your other hand – hold it horizontally and try to balance its weight. That's it. Now put your good foot on the first stair and pull yourself up. No, no! You must support yourself on the banister-rail and the left crutch, not on your bad foot.'

Phil was female, not male, with a burly physique and a baritone voice to match the masculine name. Her manner of barking instructions made Lorna feel distinctly cowed – especially just now, when she could barely tell right from left. She had experienced the same confusion when learning ballroom dancing – slow, slow, quick, quick, slow. There was nothing quick about *this* process, though. Dragging herself up even a single step was a major undertaking.

'That nightie's most unsuitable,' Phil admonished. 'It's too long. It'll trip you up. Have you nothing shorter?'

Lorna shook her head. She had borrowed the exotic lacy creation from a friend, concerned less with its length (the friend was five foot ten) than with arousing Mr Hughes's passion.

'Well, hitch it up and tie it with your dressing-gown cord.'

The dressing-gown was borrowed too: Ralph's navy-blue-striped towelling one, which must have looked a shade incongruous with six inches of frilly pink satin trailing below it. But her own night-clothes were non-existent. Normally she slept in her skin or a T-shirt, and, working such long hours, had never found much use for dressing-gowns.

Phil held the crutches for her while she balanced on one foot and made the necessary adjustments.

'Right, let's continue,' Phil said testily, handing back the crutches. 'We haven't got all day. Bring the bad foot up with the crutch. No, leave your right foot where it is. You want both feet on the same stair.'

Lorna tried to concentrate. She was going home the day after tomorrow, and if she didn't learn to negotiate the stairs she would starve when Ralph was out.

'Now we'll try going down. The bad foot leads, remember – "The bad go down to hell."'

Agnes had been a great one for hell. Adulterers were banished there without mercy or exception – including adulterers in intent. When Mr Hughes had popped in yesterday Lorna had stripped him naked and seduced him. Strangely, today she had lost all vestige of desire. If he came slavering to her bed she would simply show him the door.

'Now we'll walk along the corridor back to your room. Both crutches forward first, please, then move the bad foot up to them, resting it on the heel. It's not hurting, is it?'

'Yes.'

'Well, it shouldn't be.'

'And so's my back. In fact my back's almost as bad as my foot.'

'That's because you're not mobile.'

'Actually, Janice said she thought it might have been damaged during the op.'

Janice was the other physiotherapist and as different from Phil as Mary Poppins from Attila the Hun. She was young, petite and giggly – a friendly chatterbox who had admitted in an unguarded moment that patients were sometimes manhandled in theatre. 'And, you see, if you're moved awkwardly when you're anaesthetized it can cause an injury.'

Especially if you're anaesthetized for four solid hours, Lorna had bitten back.

Sergeant-Major Phil, however, dismissed the idea out of hand and continued relentlessly with her drill. 'Take more weight on the arms! No, don't grip the crutches so tightly. Relax, relax! You're far too tense. And look up, not down. Bend your knees. You're holding them too stiff. Take smaller steps. There's no need to stride out like that – you're not competing in a marathon.'

Nor ever likely to. Any increase in pace was simply to propel herself back to her room so she could flop out on the bed. They were nearly there, thank heavens.

'Right, I'll see you tomorrow, Mrs Pearson. And don't forget: practice is essential.'

And so is a rest from my labours, Lorna thought, undoing the special shoe on her bad foot. Provided by the hospital, it was a monstrosity in air-force blue, a cross between a trainer and a sandal, but fastening with Velcro straps and made large enough to fit over the bandages. Not exactly this year's fashion sensation.

Her foot was throbbing and burning, and her back hurt so much it was impossible to get comfortable. In fact she felt worse today than she had all week – exhausted whether upright or flat out. And her lunch had gone cold, of course. It was an unwritten rule in the Princess Royal that, whenever a meal arrived, someone or something would turn up almost immediately and disrupt it. Thus Phil had appeared thirty seconds after the duck in port-wine sauce and chocolate soufflé. The soufflé had collapsed and the port-wine sauce was edged with an orange frill of solidifying fat. Not that it mattered – she wasn't hungry anyway.

Too lethargic to read, she lay slumped against the pillows, gazing at the implausibly blue sky above the sun-kissed poppy-fields. The real sky outside was leaden, and this morning's forecast had warned of floods in Wales. Clare was in Wales, which meant she couldn't visit. They might have had a good laugh together. Or more likely a good cry.

Lorna counted on her fingers – fourteen days till Clare was back, eight till Christmas Day. Much of her time was spent counting days: two until she left hospital, twenty-one until the stitches were out, forty until she could dispense with the crutches, a hundred and eighty until she could walk really well, three hundred and sixty before the second operation, which she didn't dare to contemplate. She thought of the charts she had made at school, ticking off the days to the end of term – although memories of school were best avoided. She had been a pariah then: an orphan, to be shunned, as if the condition were catching. Often she had lain awake in the dormitory terrorized by images of car crashes: her parents bleeding in a tangle of wreckage. Had they suffered dreadfully? Would she see them again when *she* died?

Ralph seldom mentioned his schooldays, yet from what she could gather he had been equally miserable. And it had forged between them a bond no less powerful for being unspoken. He was the only person she had met who understood the pain of a lost childhood, and who'd also been forced to come to terms with grief before he knew the meaning of the word.

'It's a pity you can't be more stoical, like he is. Now get up and practise your walking, as Phil told you.'

'But it *hurts*, Aunt Agnes.'

'I don't wonder, child, with all this lying around. God gave us our bodies to use.'

With a groan, Lorna reached for her special shoe again. (One thing she had learned was to keep everything close at hand, otherwise it meant hopping – strictly forbidden by both physios.) Doing up the ordinary shoe on her good foot, she stared dejectedly at the mismatch: the left foot a wodge of white bandage in an ugly, clumping blue thing; the right pink-socked in a black lace-up. As she leaned forward for the crutches they fell to the floor with a crash.

'*Damn!*' she muttered. When you were immobile, picking up things you had dropped was a struggle. Several of her possessions had already vanished under the bed: a book, a pen, a handkerchief, one of the pink socks. The cleaner – a manic-depressive Spaniard, Dolores – didn't appear to have noticed: too busy complaining about her husband. ('He bad news. He go with other women.')

Having retrieved the crutches, Lorna crawled on her hands and knees to recover the other items, then rested with her head on the floor. This was a baby's-eye-view of the world, nose to the carpet, aware of its smell and feel, and dwarfed by beetling crags of furniture. Babies had it easy – sleeping all day, with no little Hitlers bossing you about. Cooed at by strangers. Cuddled by your mama.

She had no real sense of her mother, despite the photographs – which, somewhat disconcertingly, portrayed a younger version of Agnes. Occasionally she invented a different mother, with no resemblance to Agnes in either looks or temperament. But on the whole she preferred to stick with her father – an only child, as she was. She liked to imagine him free of *all* ties, except the one to her: she his wife, his love, his enchanting little princess.

Safe in his arms, she stretched out full-length on the carpet and closed her eyes, barely registering the knock on the door.

'Mrs *Pearson*! Are you all right? What happened? Did you fall?'

'No, I'm . . . fine.' Scarlet-cheeked, Lorna heaved herself to her feet. Didn't it just have to be Nurse Ingrid, a humourless harridan who had already caught her talking to a potted plant earlier in the week?

'Let me help you back to bed. Good gracious! You're extremely hot. Has someone taken your temperature? No? I'll do it then. You stay there and rest. I'll be back in a second.'

She was, with a thermometer and an air of agitation.

'It is rather high, Mrs Pearson,' she said, shaking down the thermometer. 'We'd better let Mr Hughes know. Fortunately he's just along the corridor, seeing another patient.'

'Another emergency, no doubt,' the Monster gloated. 'I expect all his patients develop fever and delirium.'

Lorna kept her eyes on the get-well cards clustered on the windowsill. She had friends. They cared. Clare had even sent a bouquet of pink tulips (miraculously spring-like in midwinter), although the poor things were drooping in the heat.

'Watch out! – here he comes, the strutting little quack. I wouldn't trust him an inch. Remember those scandals about botched operations and mix-ups with the – '

'Good afternoon, Mrs Pearson. I hear you're not so well.'

'Er, no.'

'How's the foot feeling?'

'It's been hurting a lot more today.'

'Have you a cough?

'No.'

'Or any problem with your waterworks?'

'No.'

'We'd better take the dressing off. Nurse!'

Lorna could hardly bear to watch as Ingrid unwound the crêpe bandage, revealing a disgusting layer of other, blackened, bandages encrusted with dried blood, which had to be prised off with hot water. The gauze pad beneath was sticking to the wounds and proved even more painful to remove. But the sight of her foot was the real shock. It resembled some grotesque exhibit in a sensationalist avant-garde art show – hugely swollen, with the black stitches standing out against the deep puce of the flesh, and yellowish pus oozing from two red and puffy toes.

Clearly Mr Hughes was no happier than she was. 'I think this might have been brought to my attention a little sooner,' he remarked, his irritation evident despite the measured words. 'And Mrs Pearson's temperature chart doesn't appear to have been filled in for the last couple of days.' His raised eyebrows signalled further reproof, although he was graciousness itself as he turned to speak to her. 'I'm afraid it is a bit infected, Mrs Pearson.'

'A *bit*?' the Monster spluttered. 'The whole thing's a mass of gangrene!'

'So I think we'd better keep you here a few more days.'

Her first thought was for Ralph. Already he was pushed to meet the deadline on the Staplehurst job and had to fight his way across London to see her every evening on top of a hard day's work. Last night he had looked washed out and did admit he wasn't feeling well. Perhaps it was just the pressures: letters piling up unopened, invoices not sent out, and clients annoyed at getting the answering-machine instead of her personal attention. If she told him she had to stay in hospital when he needed her so desperately at home he might –

'Nurse, take a swab from those toes,' Mr Hughes instructed. 'And get the RMO to put a drip up. We'll give Mrs Pearson some intravenous flucloxacillin. Keep her on bed-rest, with the foot elevated, and I want a four-hourly check on her temperature and pulse. I'll look in again first thing tomorrow.'

'Why bother,' shrugged the Monster. 'She'll be dead by then.'

6

'Here we are then,' said Colin. 'Safe and sound.'

Lorna felt neither as she peered through the ambulance window. Oakfield House seemed singularly ill-named, with no sign of a field or an oak (or indeed of any tree): just an austere expanse of tarmacked drive darkened by the rain, and a grim grey-stone façade that reminded her unsettlingly of boarding-school.

'No, don't move, Mrs Pearson. We'll help you out.'

Colin set up the wheelchair while Jack got down from the driver's seat and opened the doors at the back of the ambulance. She found it acutely embarrassing to arrive with a uniformed escort: Colin holding her case and crutches, Jack wheeling her down the ramp and up to the front door. Not that there was anyone to notice. The entrance hall was empty, the reception desk unmanned.

'Are they expecting you?' Jack asked.

'Mm.' She was eight again, blinking back the tears as the hated school engulfed her. Big girls didn't cry.

'I'll give a shout.'

Jack's 'Hello there!' was answered by a long, low, desolate wail. Had they come to the wrong place – a torture chamber rather than a nursing-home?

'Ah, here's someone,' Colin said, as a scraggy woman in a badly ironed blue uniform walked into the hall. 'Can you help us?' he asked. 'We've brought Mrs Pearson from the Princess Royal. She's staying here over Christmas.'

'I don't know nothing about it.'

'Well, can you find someone who does?'

Another unearthly howl echoed from the floor above. Lorna fought an overwhelming urge to seize her case and bolt. Even now she hadn't quite accepted the fact that she was a prisoner of her chair. If she wanted to go anywhere beyond a scant fifty yards, someone had to wheel her.

Nervously she glanced around the hall. The grey lino and beige walls did nothing to raise her spirits. The only splash of colour was the Christmas decorations: paper-chains in red and green, and a lopsided Scots pine planted in a red plastic bucket and hung with garish baubles. The Princess Royal seemed a palace in comparison. However, despite the aftermath of her infection, she had been summarily discharged from there. Over Christmas and New Year they kept only emergency cases, being reduced to a skeleton staff. She pictured gaping skulls leering as they brought patients' medication, jangling bones lurching along the corridor.

'I see you're admiring our Christmas tree.'

Lorna turned to see another blue-uniformed woman – a definite improvement on the first: not only neatly dressed but actually smiling. And pretty, too, with short, dark, curly hair and grey-green eyes.

'Hello. I'm Sister Kathy. Mrs Pearson, isn't it?'

'Yes, that's right.'

'Welcome to Oakfield House. I'll take you to your room.'

Lorna felt strangely bereft as she said goodbye to Jack and Colin. They had become friends in a friendless world, Jack chatting to her all the way from London and even confiding that he, too, was dreading Christmas. She pressed a £10 note into his hands – an over-generous tip, maybe, but as well as thanks it represented a plea for them not to abandon her in this ghastly place but take her back with them to normality.

Alas, it was not to be. Sister Kathy picked up her case and wheeled her down a corridor that smelt depressingly of urine. Through open doors Lorna caught glimpses of white hair, white faces, white cardigans, dead eyes. As they paused a moment outside the lounge, she gazed in at a circle of chairs, each occupied by an inert ancient female. The only sign of animation was a bouncy girl on television prattling away to the impervious stares of her audience.

'You're on the top floor,' Kathy said, manoeuvring the chair past a trolleyful of incontinence pads, then standing back to let a tottery man on a Zimmer frame weave his slow way to the lounge. 'I'm afraid the rooms are rather on the small side up there, but we're chock-a-block over Christmas and it was the only one we had free.'

'That's OK.' At least it might be quieter away from the screams of the demented. Counting blessings should prove a doddle here. Compared with the inmates she had seen so far, she was not only in the prime of life but in the pink of health. Coming towards her was a poor wretch in a wheelchair, his face porridge-pale, his hands blotched with purple bruises, his whole body jerking and twitching. Lorna's tentative smile of greeting was met with a hostile glare. Perhaps people kept themselves to themselves, and friendly overtures were discouraged. If only she knew the protocol. Shades of school again – that frightening first day when all the other girls seemed years older than her and she had no idea what to say, how to be and whether she would ever find her way around without a permanent guide.

'Lousy weather, isn't it?' Kathy remarked as they waited for the lift.

'Yes, awful.' She had hardly noticed the weather – she had too much on her mind. Besides, in a hospital there wasn't any weather, only endless fug. Weather belonged to one's visitors, along with functioning feet, outdoor clothes and an interest in turkey and mince pies.

As the lift groaned and shuddered upward, she tried to curb her fear. Lifts, heights, the Underground, deep water – all could bring on palpitations. To avoid every source of panic she would have to enter a nunnery (and then suffer claustrophobia).

The lift doors clattered open and she was trundled down a passage-way past rows of numbered doors.

'This is it, Mrs Pearson.'

Kathy had stopped at number thirteen. No wonder the room was free – thirteen was a death warrant.

'The house is very old, so we don't have bathrooms en suite. There's a toilet just round the corner.'

'But I . . . I'm not meant to walk. Not for another fortnight, the surgeon said.'

'Oh, it isn't far. But we can bring you a bedpan, of course, if you prefer.'

'No, I'll manage, thank you.' She'd had enough of bedpans. While her foot was infected they hadn't allowed her out of bed at all, and since the antibiotics had upset her bowels and stomach the humiliation had been total.

Kathy wheeled her into the room, which was dark and low-ceilinged and looked out over the dustbins at the back. No thick-pile carpet or poppy-fields. The floor was covered with a scruffy sort of matting, and the only art on the walls was a tasteful gouge in the plaster, surrounded by a collage of dirty marks. Lorna did her best to ignore the smell of urine (stronger even than downstairs). She had a bed, a chair, a wardrobe, a small table and a television. What more could anyone want? Well, an escape-ladder might come in handy.

Kathy helped her into the chair, placed the crutches beside her, and showed her where the call-bell was. 'Just press this if you need anything. Sister Joyce is the nurse in charge of this floor and she'll be along to take your details. I wish I could do it myself, but I'm afraid I have to rush off. I've left a new care assistant bathing a patient, and I'd better make sure she's coping. We're terribly short-staffed.'

'Oh . . . right. Thank you.' Lorna was sorry to see her go. Left alone she might succumb to the Terrors (although, incredibly, the Monster hadn't yet pursued her here).

Should she undress? she wondered. It had been difficult enough putting her clothes on; taking them off again might be worse. One leg of her tights hadn't fitted over the bandage and so was wound around her middle. The bare leg was cold and the room itself distinctly on the chilly side. She levered herself up, using her crutches to hobble over to the radiator. Barely tepid. Ah well, too much heat was bad for the complexion.

While she was on her feet (foot), she decided to unpack, knowing she would feel less desolate with familiar things around her. Unpacking wasn't easy, though. You couldn't carry much on crutches, and there were no hangers in the wardrobe and only one tiny drawer, which jammed. She laid Ralph's gold-and-diamond bracelet in the drawer. She couldn't fasten the fiddly clasp single-handed, and the staff hadn't time to be helping her put on jewellery, with emergencies on all sides. The gift still meant a lot, though. Ralph seldom gave her presents and when he did they tended to be uninspiring things he wanted himself, such as a steering-lock or an automatic video rewinder. But the bracelet was truly special, as was her wedding-ring – Victorian rose-gold, engraved inside 'For Ever'. Ralph was a romantic at heart, but he hid his feelings for fear of seeming vulnerable.

There was certainly nothing romantic about the new nightdress he'd bought her for the nursing-home: a brushed-nylon affair (spinsterishly high-necked and long-sleeved) in a shade between mould

and mushy pea. She stuffed it into the bottom of the wardrobe and collapsed, exhausted, into the chair. Mr Hughes had told her to keep her
foot up on two pillows, but she hadn't the energy to get up again and
fetch them – if indeed there were any. The bed looked worryingly flat.
At least the TV remote-control was within reach, so she switched
from channel to channel in search of some distraction. It was shameful to admit, but even earth-shaking events failed to make much
impact at the moment. Pain turned you into a cretin, too fixated on
your malfunctioning body to take an interest in the wider world. Her
back still hurt as much as her foot. The X-rays had revealed degenerative changes in the vertebral bodies, with some loss of disc space –
whatever *that* was supposed to mean. All she had really gathered was
that she was degenerating. Fast.

There was a knock at the door. 'Mrs Paterson?'

'Mrs *Pearson*.'

'Hi! I'm Sharon.' A small blonde girl appeared, looking about thir-
teen-and-a-half and wearing a gingham overall with a name-badge
saying, 'Valerie'. There seemed to be some confusion regarding names.

'I've brought your tea. I hope you don't take sugar. We've run out.'

Running out of staples like sugar didn't augur well. Still, there were
worse tragedies in life than unsugared tea. She took the plastic beaker,
which had a slight greasy scum on top. No flower-sprigged cups and
saucers as in the hospital, although there was a biscuit to go with it: a
custard cream (minus its top layer).

'Anything else you want?'

'I'd love a cushion for my back. It's hurting.'

'Mine too. It's agony! And my feet are killing me. I've been on duty
twelve hours and there's no chance of going home yet, not with new
admissions.'

'Look, don't worry about the cushion if you're busy.'

'Sure?'

'Yes.'

'By the way, what d'you want for your tea?'

'Isn't *this* tea?'

'No, I mean the evening meal. It's served at five, so the kitchen
staff can get off.'

'Oh . . . What is there?'

'It's sausage rolls or sandwiches tonight.'

'Um, sandwiches.'

'Ham, cheese, Marmite or sardine.'

'Sardine, please.' At the Princess Royal the sardines had been fresh, grilled with basil and oregano. Not that she'd eaten more than a mouthful. A waste, she realized now, to lose her appetite when four-star food was on the menu. Here the only menu was Sharon's sing-song recitation.

'And afters is stewed prunes or tapioca.'

'I, er, think I'll pass on afters.'

'Pardon?'

'No pudding, thanks.'

'Please yourself. Will you be coming to the dining-room?'

'Do we have to? I'm not feeling all that brilliant.'

'Matron does prefer it. It's less work, you see. We haven't time to be lugging trays around, except for them that *can't* move.'

'Could you let me off just once, seeing as it's my first day?'

'OK, Mrs Paterson.'

'Pearson.'

'What?'

'Oh, nothing. Look, before you go could you wheel me to a phone? I've got to ring my husband.'

'We don't have phones – not public ones.'

'Well, is there any way I could order one for my room? I'll happily pay extra.'

'You'd need to arrange it yourself – you know, get on to BT or . . . '

'Without a phone I can't get on to anyone.'

Sharon laughed. 'Yeah. True.'

'Look, could you ask Sister if I can use the nursing-home phone? My husband's not well and – '

'Got this awful flu, has he? They're dropping like flies here. We had two deaths only yesterday.'

Lorna swallowed. Ralph might die, alone and unattended. It was a particularly virulent strain of flu that had more or less prostrated him and was in fact the reason she was here. With a high temperature and a streaming cold he could hardly look after an incapacitated wife. Although, when Nurse Ingrid had suggested a nursing-home, Lorna had imagined a cross between a health farm and a hospital, with patients of all ages, not a geriatric waiting-room for Death. Still, she was lucky to have found a place anywhere, especially one in Woking, only five minutes' drive from home. The first half-dozen establishments they'd phoned had no vacancies at all. Sickness and old age were clearly growth industries – and jolly profitable too, judging by the fees. Fortunately BUPA had agreed to pay, otherwise she and Ralph would have landed in the bankruptcy court.

'Sharon, you won't forget to ask Sister about the phone. Tell her it's urgent, will you?'

'If I see her, yes. Must fly, Mrs Paterson!'

This time Lorna didn't correct her. There was something to be said for being Mrs Paterson: then she wouldn't have to worry about Ralph. Unlike her, he had no one to wait on him, no one to stew him prunes or make him sardine sandwiches. At this very moment he might be suffering dehydration, too feverish even to fetch himself a drink.

'No, I *won't* go!' yelled a strident female voice. 'I'm not budging and that's that.'

'But, Mother, it's all arranged.' A male voice now, also unnaturally loud.

'Well, you can *un*arrange it.'

'I can't. Fay will be frightfully upset. She's – '

'Bugger Fay!'

A door opened and then slammed.

Lorna shifted uneasily in her chair. Her neighbour, by the sounds of it. She could hear the two voices through the wall, the mother deaf to the son's pleading – and literally deaf, judging by the way he had to shout.

'I'm *not* being pig-headed, Mother. You can't disrupt everything just because . . . '

Eavesdropping on a family row was not a pleasant pastime. But Lorna had no alternative – unless she perished from cold in the next few minutes, which did seem increasingly probable. She had forgotten to ask Sharon about the radiator, and the room must have been sub-zero. She dragged herself up once more, hopped over to the bed, heaved the blankets off it and hauled them back to her chair. Bundling them round her as best she could, she sat staring at the window. Dusk was falling and the dwindling light was the colour of bonfire ash. According to the calendar, yesterday had been the shortest day. Strange that today should feel the longest.

She winced as a string of expletives reached her through the wall. Was it just the television, now blaring out with a rival shouting-match, or was the woman next door about to murder her son?

Then all at once an uncanny silence descended. Lorna could almost see the corpse lying bleeding on the floor, the deaf and doddery murderess staring aghast at her lifeless offspring.

'I was *watching* that programme, John, I'll have you know. Will you kindly turn it on again.'

'No. It's tea-time, Mother. I'll take you down.'

'I don't want tea. It's muck they give us. Anyway, I'm not ready.'

'Yes you are. You only came up here to fetch your teeth.'

After further protracted argument the door finally opened and shut and the voices faded to a murmur along the passage.

Within minutes there was more disturbance: Sharon and some other girl bickering outside.

'It's not my turn – it's yours.'

'I did it yesterday. And the day before.'

'Poor diddums!'

'Oh, shut your face!'

Lorna's door crashed open and Sharon stormed in, red-eyed. 'I'm giving notice,' she announced, slapping a tray down on the table.

'Oh dear. What's wrong?'

'If I told you, you wouldn't believe the half of it.'

'It can't be that bad, surely.'

'*You* try working here. It's living hell. They never give you a break. I'm on all Christmas Day. And Boxing Day. And – '

'Look, sit down and – '

'No, they'll kill me if I stop. I'm way behind as it is. Good grief! What's happened to your bed? I only made that an hour ago.'

'It's OK. I'll put it straight. But could you please do something about the radiator. It seems to have . . . '

Too late. She'd gone, banging out in a whirlwind of further complaint. Lorna felt *she* ought to take the trays round and let Sharon have her bed, as the girl was so distraught. A waitress on crutches would be a novelty, at any rate – a much-needed diversion in this forbidding place.

For the first time she looked at her tray. They had given her the tapioca she'd said she didn't want, although perhaps it was just as well, since the sandwiches were minuscule. She balanced the plate on her knee and took a bite of one, gagging on something slimy. Pulling the bread apart, she discovered not sardines but a large piece of white ham-fat, smeared with margarine. Was this someone else's tea, or had they run out of sardines as well as sugar? No point summoning Sharon – she would have a nervous breakdown on the spot. Best to leave the fat for the birds, if any, and eat the bread on its own.

Which took precisely three minutes. The bread seemed flavoured with urine, but maybe she was muddling taste and smell. The smell was strongest in the chair – the previous occupant must have had an accident. But at least the chair wasn't wet: another blessing to be counted.

Next she tackled the pudding – or tried to. They had forgotten to give her a spoon, so she struggled to her feet again and rummaged through her sponge-bag to find a suitable alternative. But neither comb, nail-file, nor toothbrush handle proved particularly efficacious in transferring glutinous tapioca from the bowl to her mouth. Having spilled some on her lap (and on to the blankets she would be sleeping under tonight), she abandoned the whole exercise. She disliked tapioca anyway, especially lukewarm and unsugared. The tea was also sugarless, of course, but she drank it gratefully in the hope it might warm her up.

Supper over, she ventured out on her crutches to the toilet, surprised to see that most of the doors along the corridor were open. Was it to make the patients feel less isolated, or for the benefit of the staff? Curiosity overcame good manners and she couldn't help glancing into the rooms. They were much the same as hers: small and cramped, with little in the way of a view. Each bed held a body, lying comatose. Were they already dead, and Sharon too busy to remove the corpses? The televisions shrilled on regardless – tuned to the same programme in every room: *Wheel of Fortune*.

Turning the corner, she all but collided with a nurse.

'Hello, dear. You must be the new arrival. I'm Sister Joyce.'

'Oh, how d'you do?'

'I was just coming to take your details.'

'D'you mind if I find the loo first?'

'Go ahead. It's that door opposite. I'll be with you in five minutes.'

The bathroom was cavernous. A throne-like porcelain toilet sat beside a jarringly modern bath full of complicated equipment, including a plastic chair and a hoist. A battered wooden shelf-unit held packets of medicated wipes, disposable rubber gloves and yet more incontinence pads. Was she the only one with bowel and bladder control? A bumper blessing to add to the list – as was the chance of an early night. There weren't likely to be any late-night revels here.

Hobbling back to her room, she found someone sitting in the chair – not Joyce but an elderly lady in a sleeveless off-white nightgown, her limp grey hair straggling on to her shoulders.

'Hello, Ethel,' the intruder said in a voice surprisingly forceful for her scrawny frame. 'Nice to see you again.'

'I'm, er, Lorna actually. And I don't *think* we've met.'

'Yes, they told me. You've got to bring the yellow one.'

'I beg your pardon?'

'They don't want green, they said.'

'Oh, I see.' She didn't. Resting her crutches against the wall, she perched on the edge of the bed – there was nowhere else to sit.

'You can't take them with you. It's not allowed.'

'Really?'

'No, you have to leave them outside.'

'Well, thanks for letting me know.'

The ensuing silence grew uncomfortable, but Lorna felt unable to contribute more to the conversation. Besides, it might encourage the woman to stay, or even to lay claim to the bed (although in its present state it didn't look inviting: a crumpled counterpane atop a plastic sheet).

Lorna consulted her watch. Joyce should be along any minute, so best sit tight and say nothing. She noticed that her visitor was studying the tea-tray with great interest, eventually picking up the piece of ham-fat and putting it into her mouth.

'I wouldn't eat that if I were you,' Lorna cautioned.

'You will bring the yellow one,' was the only response, mumbled through a mouthful of fat.

'Yes . . . all right, I will. But, look, that stuff's not very good for you.'

'Green's no use, they said.' Still chewing enthusiastically.

Lorna pressed the bell. She was afraid the woman might be sick, or choke – or both. Worse, sitting in thin nightclothes in an unheated room in December, the poor soul was in danger of hypothermia. A red light came on above the bed and continued flashing. At least the bell was in working order, if her visitor was not.

'Ethel?'

'Yes?'

No further remarks were forthcoming, so Lorna lay back on the plastic sheet. Her foot was throbbing unbearably – a result of failing to keep it elevated. She reflected on her new persona: Ethel Paterson. Ethel, she decided, was not only completely fearless but a stunning beauty, with first-class honours from Cambridge, Harvard and the Sorbonne, a string of Byronic lovers and –

A sudden crash made her jump. It was followed by a screech, this time from the room directly below. The woman carried on placidly chewing as if nothing had happened. Perhaps deafness was the norm here, along with incontinence.

She pressed the bell again. Why did nobody come? If the woman had a heart attack a delay could prove fatal.

'You're lucky to *have* a bell. Think of that poor husband of yours, alone and seriously ill, with absolutely no one to . . . '

Yes, Agnes was right – poor Ralph. He was less than a couple of miles away and had two phones, a fax and e-mail, yet the pair of them might have been on different continents for all that they could communicate. She felt horribly cut off from him, from friends, from everyone.

'Stop it!' she told herself. 'You're Ethel Paterson, remember, so you *never* feel isolated. Nor do you feel the cold. You're super-resistant to bugs, germs, unkind remarks, hunger, pain, unpleasant smells, noise and extremes of temperature.

'Ethel,' the woman said again, having finally swallowed her mouthful. 'It *is* Ethel, isn't it?'

'Yes,' Lorna said with a determined smile. 'It most certainly is.'

7

Lorna opened her eyes, blinded by a light. A torch was shining directly into her face, the room beyond in darkness. A shadowy figure – broad-shouldered, burly, black – was looming over her bed. My God! she thought, a mugger . . . 'No!' she shouted. 'Go away!'

'It's all right, Mrs Pearson. My name's Oshoba. I work here nights. I'm a care assistant. I didn't mean to wake you, but we have to check on the patients.'

'Oh gosh, I'm sorry,' she murmured. He'd think she was a racist. 'I was having a bad dream and . . . '

'Yes, I heard you calling out in your sleep.'

Not a good sign. Was senile dementia catching? If so, she might forget her own name or find herself wetting the bed. 'I . . . think I'll spend a penny now I'm awake.'

Oshoba looked blank. His English, although impressive, obviously didn't encompass euphemisms.

'I need to go to the toilet.'

'I'll bring you a commode.'

He left her on her own to perform, and returned a few minutes later with extra pillows and blankets, a cradle for her foot and a jug of water – all the things she had craved last night. Better still, he remade the bed and even tucked the covers round her, tenderly as if for a small child.

'You're far too young to be here, Mrs Pearson. How old are you – twenty-three?'

She flushed. 'No, almost forty.'

'You can't be!'

Was he flirting with her? Well, a little flattery was harmless enough. And his voice was deliciously sexy: a rich, black-treacle bass that sounded as if it came from the depths of a well.

'Do you know what the average age is here?' he asked, lingering by her bed.

'No, tell me.'

'Eighty-seven. My poor mother died at fifty.'

'And mine at thirty-one.'

'Oh, that's terrible. I'm sorry.'

His words seemed genuine, and his eyes were kind – huge, dark, rather bulgy eyes, the dazzling whites a contrast to his skin.

'Tell me your name again. I didn't catch it.'

He grinned. 'Yes, everyone finds it a mouthful. It's Osh-*show*-bah.'

'And where do you live, Osh . . . oba?' Making small talk in the middle of the night was a trifle odd, but it was a relief to talk to someone both calm and *compos mentis*.

'I've got a place in Woking, but I come from Nigeria. I only left a year ago.'

He must be lonely too, uprooted, far from home. 'And are your family still there?'

'Yes. All except one brother. We share a flat. He works as a chef.'

'That sounds nice. Does he cook for you?'

'Oh no. I'm out so much I hardly ever see him. I'm doing Business Studies at Brooklands College.'

When did he sleep, she wondered, studying all day, skivvying all night? Sharon had told her how disgracefully low the care assistants' wages were.

'Well, I must let you get your beauty sleep. Although you're a beautiful lady already.'

He *was* flirting. No matter. Compliments were rare. Ralph never commented on her appearance. Indeed if she were to dye her hair and embark on plastic surgery, including total body reconstruction, she doubted if he would even notice.

'Goodnight,' Oshoba said, switching off the light. 'Have nice dreams, beautiful lady, not bad ones.'

Yes, she thought, I will: dreams of a torrid encounter with a broad-shouldered, kind-hearted and wildly passionate black man.

She woke with a start. An appalling noise was jangling on and on. The fire alarm! The building was alight. She would burn to death. No escape on crutches. She sat up, sweating, shaking, her heart pumping so hard it could have fuelled the national grid. Fear was worse than fire – would probably kill her first. Already she was paralysed. Couldn't move, couldn't stand. The noise crescendoed, a wail of terror stunning the whole house. Had someone called the fire brigade? No, jumping out of the window on a knotted sheet or going down a wobbly ladder would be as bad as burning to death.

'Help!' she screamed. 'Please help me!'

No one came. She could feel the flames licking at the door, smell the charred remains of burning timbers, burning flesh.

'Help!' she yelled again. Still no response. All the staff must have fled, leaving her to perish in the flames. She could no longer see or breathe. Smoke poured through the room. She was dying – now – her last gasps stifled by the contemptuous bray of the alarm.

Then silence, suddenly – almost as shocking as the noise. Disoriented, she opened her smarting eyes. There *was* no smoke; the only smell was urine and, amazingly, Sister Joyce had appeared.

'Are you all right, Mrs Pearson? I thought I heard you shouting.'

'Yes. No. I . . . '

'You did know about the fire-drill, didn't you? We test the alarm first thing every Thursday.'

'No, I wasn't told.'

'Oh dear, that *is* remiss. And no one's emptied your commode. I'd better do it now.'

When she'd gone, Lorna lay recovering. Every panic attack left her bitterly ashamed, and this one more than most. She hadn't spared a thought for her dozen octogenarian neighbours. Any decent person would have rushed to rescue them first, not given way to hysteria. Some brave souls risked their necks to save a *cat*, for heaven's sake. 'Total fear casteth out love,' a wit had once remarked. Shamefully true.

Joyce reappeared with a tumbler of water and four pain-killers in a plastic pot. 'You should have had these with your breakfast.'

'That's OK. I haven't had breakfast yet.'

'Not had breakfast? It's nearly half past nine!'

'Look, please don't worry. I don't want any.' A craven coward like her didn't deserve to eat.

'How about a cup of tea?'

'No, really. This water'll do me fine.'

'Well, it's the Christmas party this afternoon, so you'll be able to eat your fill. It's quite a feast, by the sounds of it.'

'Oh . . . good.' Somehow she couldn't imagine a party here. Was a party frock *de rigueur*? Which reminded her – she hadn't had a bath for over a week. If Christmas celebrations were planned, she didn't fancy being singled out as the new arrival with BO. 'I wonder if I could have a bath.'

Joyce looked dubious. 'We are exceptionally busy. How much assistance would you need?'

'Well, if someone could help me in and out I'm sure I could manage the rest. Though of course I mustn't get the bandage wet.'

'I'll see if Tommy's free.'

Tommy? A man? No, remembering Phil, perhaps not. While she waited she swilled her mouth with water. Even cleaning her teeth was a trial – she might hobble all the way to the bathroom only to find it occupied.

Joyce popped her head round the door again. 'Oh, by the way, there was a message from your husband. He phoned to send his love.'

'Is he better?'

'He didn't say.'

No, he wouldn't have done. Ever the stoic, Ralph. He must be getting weak, with only pipe-smoke to sustain him. And of course smoking could lead to complications: pneumonia, TB. Perhaps it was just as well they couldn't wish each other a happy Christmas tomorrow. Given their individual circumstances, happiness seemed a remote prospect.

There was a rat-tat-tat at the door. Sharon with an ultimatum? No – a man of about forty, with rimless spectacles and reddish hair, manoeuvring a wheelchair into the room.

'I'm Tommy,' he said curtly. 'I hear you want a *bath*.' He made it sound as self-indulgent as asking for a ton of Beluga caviar or a personal slave to cool her with an ostrich-feather fan. (During the night the radiator had gone from tepid to red hot.)

'Well, yes, I – '

'You'll have to make it sharp then. I'm meant to be taking the drinks round.'

Drinks? Did the Christmas party include a mid-morning gin? She'd need one if she was going to be bathed by a man. 'I, er, thought it would be a female – '

'It's me or nothing. Where's your sponge-bag?'

'In that drawer.'

The drawer jammed of course, and Tommy's muttered 'Fuck!' reminded her of the woman next door. (She seemed mercifully quiet today, but perhaps her son had dragged her home for an apocalyptic Christmas.)

Sponge-bag under his arm, Tommy helped her into the wheelchair, then whistled tunelessly as he jolted her down the passage. The passage was stiflingly hot, the bathroom corpse-cold. Evidently the heating at Oakfield House was as old and temperamental as its residents.

'Soap?' said Tommy.

'I haven't any.' Considering the mammoth fees, surely they could run to a bar of soap.

Tommy's sigh was hurricane-force as he stalked off on a soap quest. He returned with a bar of Pearl, which she recognized from a TV commercial featuring an ultra-glamorous model with a cascade of ash-blonde curls lolling sensuously in a bubble bath – an unfortunate contrast with herself. Her own hair hung lank and greasy after eight days without a wash, the antibiotics had brought her out in a nasty rash on her chest, and she felt acutely self-conscious about taking off Ralph's dressing-gown to reveal the mould-green number. Tommy, however, paid her no attention – too busy running the bath. She sat nervously in the wheelchair wondering what the procedure was. Should she strip, or would it look brazen or, worse, provocative?

Tommy turned to face her. 'Ready?'

'Yes.'

'Towels?'

'I wasn't given any.' Did they expect you to provide towels as well as soap (and cutlery)?

'Shit! Why didn't you say?' He disappeared again, this time for much longer. She could hear some sort of skirmish going on outside – several voices raised in altercation while a particularly vituperative character demanded access to the bath. Well, it was big enough for two.

'Bloody cheek!' Tommy grunted, reappearing with a large towel marked 'Property of Oakfield House'. (Since it was virtually threadbare, she couldn't imagine anyone wanting to steal it.)

'Are you able to stand, Mrs Pearce?'

'-son,' she added *sotto voce*, although it was an advance for him to address her by name. Up to now his manner had verged on insolence. 'Yes,' she said, 'on one foot.'

'OK, let's get moving.'

He hauled her up, pulled off the nightie (with no delicacy, in any sense) and plonked her into the plastic chair. As the machinery groaned into action, she was lifted over the side of the bath, then lowered slowly into it.

'Keep your leg up!' Tommy warned as her bottom made contact with the water.

She managed to lodge it on the side, and kept her hands crossed over her chest, trying to conceal her breasts and the rash. Being naked in front of a man, and a total stranger at that, was unnerving in the extreme. She was intensely conscious of her thighs (too fleshy), her pubic hair (wiry, with a copper tinge) and the fact that her nipples were erect (only from cold, although Tommy wasn't to know that). However, he clearly had no interest in her body other than as an object to be soaped, and set to with Herculean force. She hoped he wasn't so violent with the elderly residents, whose bones would be much frailer than hers. Flinching under the onslaught, she tried transposing herself to the television commercial: veiled modestly by bubbles and indulging in a languid reverie rather than being subjected to a drubbing by a misogynist. At least the water was pleasantly warm, and it was bliss just to be clean.

'Do you think you could wash my hair?' she asked him tentatively.

Without ceremony, Tommy dunked the back of her head in the water and, seizing the soap again, pummelled her scalp as fiercely as he had the rest of her. Shampoo must be an unknown refinement here, never mind conditioner.

'That's it, Mrs Pearce. All done.'

'But shouldn't you rinse the soap out?'

'I have – mostly. You're lucky I even washed it. Most people go to Betty.'

'Who?'

'Bulbous Betty in the hair boutique.'

'Oh, there's a proper hairdresser?'

'Well, I wouldn't call her proper, but . . . '

'Can I make an appointment?'

'Not today. She's fully booked. They're all getting dolled up for this damn-fool party – the ones that know what's going on. A lot don't, of course. One poor old bugger thinks he's still fighting the First World War. OK, let's have you out.'

More strong-arm tactics, this time with the towel, which left her looking as if she had a rash all over. Still, the stimulation warmed her up, as did the wheelchair-dash down the passage.

'Need any help dressing?' Tommy asked, already backing away through the door.

'No, I'll manage, thanks.'

The question was: What to wear? Her grey skirt and sweater would look distinctly drab if the others were being beautified by Betty. A pity Clare was still away, otherwise she could have borrowed something from her, plus a hairdryer and a decent (non-bald) towel.

She sat, locks dripping, on the end of the bed, wondering if the exotic satin nightdress would double as an evening gown. Except it was creased and sweaty by now, and the low neck would reveal her rash. Well, it would have to be the grey outfit and soap-streaked hair. Never mind – however well coiffed and togged the others might be, she did have youth on her side. Twenty-three, Oshoba had guessed, so she couldn't look that bad. If *he* had bathed her instead of Tommy it might have been a rather different experience.

She closed her eyes and imagined the creamy-white bar of soap in his broad, black, teasing hand. He was letting it smooch slowly across her stomach and along the insides of her thighs, tracing tantalizing circles as it inched towards her bush. Whorls of pearly lather frothed across the copper curls, making her exquisitely moist. Tiny tendrils of hair lassoed his long dark fingers, which then slipped deep inside her, to fondle, to explore.

What did it matter that she had nothing to wear for a dreary Christmas party, when she and Oshoba were enjoying a blissfully naked celebration?

8

'And this is Marjorie.' Sister Kathy indicated a big, shapeless woman who had slipped sideways in her wheelchair. Everything about her was slightly askew. Her skirt was rucked up, her cardigan misbuttoned, and her spectacles were sliding down her nose.

Lorna murmured a hello through a mouthful of potato crisps. (The Christmas party 'feast' hadn't yet materialized, and lunch had been cold macaroni cheese without the cheese.)

'And next to her is Dorothy.'

Puzzled, Lorna glanced at the imposing-looking lady with iron-grey hair and aquiline features. 'But I thought Dorothy was that other . . . '

'They're both Dorothys!' Kathy explained. 'We have eight Dorothys altogether.'

'Oh, how . . . unusual.' Given the confusion engendered by her own relatively simple surname, it occurred to her that perhaps the staff called all the women Dorothy, to make things easier. Would she, too, be Dorothy by nightfall? The men were less of a problem, since there were so few of them. So far she had met only Fred and Sydney. Statistically it was well known that women lived longer, but at Oakfield House they outnumbered the weaker sex by roughly ten to one. With Ralph so much older than her, was she doomed to decades of widowhood?

'And this is Marjorie's son, Trevor. He's come all the way from Poole today.'

The tubby middle-aged man was visibly perspiring in his tight blue suit. Lorna could see from his expression that he would rather be back in Dorset. And, offered the chance, she would have gone with him like a shot. The room was stuffy, smelly and crammed with wheelchairs – hers but one among dozens, locked almost wheel to wheel. Her foot was causing further obstruction, propped up on three pillows atop a padded stool. One elderly woman had been using it as an overflow plate, depositing half-chewed morsels of crisp and Twiglet into the folds of the bandage. No one seemed to have noticed, which was hardly surprising in the general chaos. She hadn't realized that relatives were invited to the party, including the under-fives. Babies' screams mingled with the wails of the demented; children fought and squabbled, while a cracked recording of Christmas carols quavered in the background. She could do with a stiff drink – or three – but the only liquid refreshment on offer was orange-squash or the ubiquitous tea. However, Sharon and another girl were just emerging from the servery, carrying trays of what looked like food. How they would negotiate the obstacle course of Zimmer frames, wheelchairs, walking-sticks and obstreperous toddlers wrestling on the carpet remained to be seen.

Lorna kept an eye on the progress of the food while trying to follow the conversation between Dorothys One and Two – an account of their respective operations, going back a good fifty years. The saga of Mr Hughes's lost saw paled into insignificance beside their grim experiences. Dorothy One had inadvertently lost a kidney during a routine appendectomy, and Dorothy Two had lost several pints of blood (and all remaining hope of a child) when at the age of thirty-five she was given a hysterectomy instead of a D and C. They continued in the same vein with graphic descriptions of vital organs damaged or mislaid, which Lorna feared would put her off her food. Luckily, though, the discussion moved on to a comparison of knee-replacement scars. Most of the women's knees were, in fact, on view. Despite the wintry weather, ankle socks were popular, or hold-up stockings (which failed to live up to their name and sat concertinaed around the patients' calves). And as for shoes, she was in good company. Normal footwear was restricted to the visitors; the residents wore carpet slippers or shapeless felt contraptions with Velcro fastenings. And, judging by the swellings and protrusions, Mr Hughes could have a field-day here, slicing off a plethora of bunions and straightening renegade toes. Legs too were in need of medical attention – many bruised or ulcerated, some swathed in crêpe bandages or elasticated supports. With every hour that passed her gratitude increased. A rash on the chest was nothing compared with suppurating sores, metal kneecaps or varicose veins the size of bell-ropes.

And now cause for yet more thanks: Sharon was standing before them with the tray of snacks. Gnarled and wrinkled hands stretched out to grab sandwiches, cheese tartlets or sausages on sticks. One lady took six sausages but, having sniffed them suspiciously, put them back again. Lorna helped herself to a sandwich, taking the precaution of first pulling it apart to see what it contained. In fact it contained nothing, but that was preferable to ham-fat, and at least the bread was fresh.

'Take plenty,' Sharon urged. 'Then I won't have to keep coming back.'

Lorna willingly piled her plate with food. Some of the other sandwiches looked more promising, with a pinkish-coloured filling. But whether it was fish, fowl or face-cream she couldn't tell, even when she'd swallowed it. Like the sausages, it had no taste whatever. One man was eating the sausage sticks instead and appeared not to notice the difference. She kept wanting to intervene: to wipe faces or noses, brush crumbs from laps or help those who lacked the coordination to feed themselves. But that was the job of the staff, who already had their hands full restraining the more murderous of the children and dealing with relatives' complaints. Trevor, for example, was demanding to know why his mother hadn't had a bath for two weeks. Instantly Lorna felt guilty. Had it been Marjorie this morning trying to storm into the bathroom? No, the poor woman looked incapable of speech, let alone creating such a fuss. Neither did she smell – which was more than could be said of some of them. Still, one learned to develop an imperviousness to smells, as the only way to cope with malodorous rooms and residents.

This room was actually quite attractive, with floral curtains, a squiggled carpet and a dozen round dining-tables, six people to each. Christmas decorations abounded, in the form of paper-chains, bunches of balloons, artificial holly-wreaths, and Christmas crackers piled on every table. The staff sported Santa caps or tinsel in their hair, while the residents' dress varied from 1930s cocktail frocks to baggy, food-stained sweat-pants. (One woman was trying to *un*dress, much to the consternation of her son.)

It would be better, Lorna thought, had the ratio of food to decorations been reversed. She would have been satisfyingly full by now, munching holly and balloons, whereas in fact she was still ravenous. Biting into a sausage roll, she found only a smear of grey gunge in the tough and greasy pastry. However, she was lucky to be able to bite. Teeth were by no means a standard commodity here.

A sudden bang startled her. Some of the children were pulling the crackers, which without exception contained plastic whistles or noise-makers. Soon a cacophony broke out, eclipsing the strains of 'Silent Night'. Sydney trembled in alarm, possibly confusing the din with a past campaign when he had been under enemy fire.

The care assistants began picking up the paper hats that had fallen out of the crackers and placing them on residents' heads. The contrast between festive hats and bleak expressions was marked, and deeply sad. But this was Christmas Eve, so everyone must enjoy themselves, even if the jollity was forced. Would they play party games later on: Pass the Parcel or Blind Man's Buff? – although more were deaf than blind at Oakfield House. (Perhaps just as well considering the volume of noise.) Another potential game might be throwing balls – or food – into the many permanently open mouths. Not only were teeth valuable, she realized: so was the ability to close your lips. Several residents dribbled constantly or made repeated chewing movements, even though their mouths were empty. Others simply sat with gaping Os.

Another tray of food had materialized – the second course, presumably: iced fancies, Penguin biscuits, slices of Swiss roll, and individual pots of shop-bought trifle. These last posed a problem since they still had their foil lids on, which few of the elderly could manage to remove. Even the relatives were having trouble: one woman broke her thumbnail, and Trevor finally resorted to jabbing Marjorie's lid with his penknife, spattering himself and his mother with cream. Lorna decided not to risk it – she had only a couple of outfits to wear and didn't want them messed up (especially if laundry facilities were as scarce here as were bathrooms).

Watching Trevor feed his mother with spoonfuls of the trifle, she was reminded of Ralph again. He was partial to trifle and she always made him one on Christmas Eve – a gloriously alcoholic concoction with brandy, sherry, raspberries and ratafias, toasted almonds and proper custard. She could just imagine his reaction to this wodge of orange-jellied sponge, topped with synthetic cream and a meagre sprinkling of hundreds and thousands.

But her attention was jolted back to the proceedings when the activities organizer, Val, fought her way to the centre of the room. A Titian-haired giantess, she bore an uncanny resemblance to a lampshade in her fringed pink tent-style dress. Clearing her throat commandingly she announced the cabaret.

Cabaret! Lorna waited with bated breath while Val somehow managed to coax the children to sit down and be quiet – a minor miracle – before ushering in a man in a black evening-suit. The music switched abruptly from 'We Three Kings' to 'Isn't It Romantic?' and he burst into song, crooning into his hand-held mike and wiggling his bony hips.

Many of the audience continued to gaze into space, as if they hadn't actually registered his arrival, while Lorna found it incongruous that he should sing so passionately of romance yet be so blatantly over the hill. His dyed hair and haggard face made his Elvis Presley-style gyrations acutely embarrassing for the relatives and induced sniggers in the children.

He bowed low in all directions, acknowledging the tepid applause and declaring grandly, 'My name is Rodrigo' (Brian or Keith, more likely, Lorna thought) '. . . and I'm absolutely delighted to be here. Are you all enjoying yourselves?'

'No!' a small boy yelled.

'Oh yes!' gushed Val. 'We *are*.'

'Now I'd like you to put your hands together for a charming young lady – Carmen. She comes from sunny Spain and she's going to sing all your favourite numbers.'

This time Val led the applause and the relatives dutifully joined in as a female of uncertain age in a sleeveless, backless, strapless creation teetered into the room on four-inch stiletto heels. With the extravagantly frilled black-and-scarlet dress she wore elbow-length red satin gloves and a red feather boa flung around her scrawny neck. Her hair was dyed exactly the same shade of black as Rodrigo's (perhaps they economized by sharing the same packet) and was adorned, as were her shoes, with artificial roses – red, of course.

With her long black lashes fluttering and the dangling flesh on her upper arms aquiver, she virtually made love to the microphone, singing in a husky voice:

> 'In olden days a
> Glimpse of stocking . . . '

On cue she lifted her skirt to reveal a glimpse of black fishnet, complete with saucy red garter.

'Get 'em off!' Fred shouted, unexpectedly roused from his torpor, and quickly hushed by a nurse.

But Carmen, fired by this solitary spark of audience appreciation, made a beeline for his wheelchair and, without interrupting the song, leaned so close her face was within inches of his – a veritable assault by eyelashes.

> '. . . heaven knows,'

she warbled on,

> 'Anything goes.'

Fred made a grab for her boa and again had to be restrained (although not before he'd managed to pull out a fistful of scarlet feathers).

Clearly one for the gentlemen, Carmen next approached Sydney, but even a full-throated rendering of two more verses of 'Anything Goes' elicited no response beyond a dribble.

Lorna admired the woman's valour as she pranced around the room, skilfully avoiding furniture and wheelchairs, and flirting with relatives, male care assistants or indeed anyone who could meet her eye without flinching. What a way to earn a living – putting on a performance for a circle of largely uncomprehending faces, plus an assortment of bored relatives, derisive staff and unashamedly giggling children. Some of the residents looked not just blank but terrified – and, of course, imprisoned in their own private world of dementia, they *would* be frightened by the extra noise and upheaval.

'Wasn't that just glorious?' Rodrigo enthused, again taking centre stage. 'Let's give the lovely Carmen a great big hand. Thank you, ladies and gentlemen! Thank you, thank you kindly. And now I want you all to join in. I'm sure you know this next number – maybe you even danced to it in your youth. Well, let's be young again!'

With a twirl of his hips, he broke into 'Dancing in the Dark' – somewhat inappropriately, since the lights were glaringly bright.

> '. . . till the tune ends we're dancing in the dark.
> And it *soon* ends . . .
> Time hurries by. We're here, and we're gone.'

Too true, thought Lorna, noticing a man near by who looked as if he was gone already, his eyes closed and his skin deathly pale. Still, her heart went out to Rodrigo. He was doing his desperate best, smiling and cavorting and coquettishly ogling the few souls brave enough to join in – among them a tiny, bird-like lady with a bandaged knee and her arm in a sling, who was being minded by a nurse.

'Elizabeth used to sing in a professional choir,' the nurse whispered to Lorna. 'She had a beautiful voice, didn't you, Elizabeth?'

'Used to' must be the watchword here, Lorna reflected as she listened to the old lady's wavering monotone. Used to sing, used to dance, used to work, make love, bring up children, contribute to the community. Strengths and talents could atrophy as much as ears and eyes.

In sudden gratitude for her own powerful voice, she too sang along, and was rewarded with a beaming smile from Rodrigo.

By the end of his performance she was hoarse. They seemed to have worked their way through the collected works of Cole Porter, Irving Berlin and Richard Rogers, finishing with a lacklustre rendition of 'Will You Love Me in December as You Do in May?' (unlikely).

An agitated Val now returned to the microphone to inform the assembled company that, although Father Christmas was expected, she'd just had news that he was unavoidably delayed. 'You know how far it is from Lapland!' she said gamely, rather spoiling the effect by mentioning a hold-up on the A3.

In the air of anticlimax, the care assistants cleared the dirty plates and removed those residents whose brains, bowels or bladders were unequal to any more excitement. Lorna would have gladly sacrificed several thousand brain cells for the chance of leaving too, but she was jammed into a corner and could hardly claim priority treatment with so many valetudinarians present. One of the worst things about old age was dependence on other people for every aspect of life, including motion up and down or in and out.

Still no sign of Father Christmas, much to Val's dismay. Carmen and Rodrigo had departed (with much kissing of hands and a force-nine gale from Carmen's lashes), so to fill the gap she tried to jolly the care assistants into doing a turn or singing a song. No takers: they were all too shy or too busy. Lorna wondered if she should offer – do a one-legged jig, for instance, or recite 'The Charge of the Light Brigade', which she had once known off by heart. Instead she helped herself to the last of the iced fancies – a particularly garish specimen iced in lemon-yellow with puce-pink decorations. She assumed there would be no more food till tomorrow's breakfast, and even that wasn't a certainty on Christmas Day with severe staff shortages.

Val kept glancing at her watch, and every so often would dart over to the window to look for the awaited car (sleigh) or scuttle to the door and peer left and right in a state of high anxiety. Lorna found it distressing that Father Christmas should be so eagerly anticipated when the presents in his sack could never be what these people really needed: health, happiness and hope.

However, Val was now engaged in a long whispered conversation with a young West Indian nurse, who left the room taking several carers with her. A search party for Santa?

'He was late last year as well,' Dorothy One complained.

'And the year before he never came at all.'

'I don't know why they bother. He probably charges an arm and a leg. I'd rather they spent the money on more nurses. I waited half an hour this morning before anyone answered my bell. And then it was a coal-black fellow who couldn't understand a word I said.'

'I won't let the black ones touch me. They've all got Aids, you know.'

Poor Oshoba, thought Lorna, licking icing off her teeth. Nevertheless she joined in the conversation. On Christmas Eve even racist company was preferable to none. 'How long have you all been here?' she asked, resolutely changing the subject.

'Three years,' said Dorothy Two. 'Which is three years too many.'

'Six months,' Dorothy One chimed in. 'I was a fool to give up my house, but my daughter said I couldn't manage. *She* couldn't manage,

85

more like it. And since I've been here she hasn't had to, of course. I scarcely ever see her these days. I suppose she may pop in tomorrow, give me a present I don't want, stay for five minutes and say she's got to rush back for the boys.'

Lorna gave a sympathetic murmur, although a pep talk from Aunt Agnes might have been more effective – a reminder of how lucky they were to have daughters, presents and grandsons at all, and to be waited on hand and foot (well, stretching a point) in a nursing-home.

The next half-hour passed innocuously enough, with the two Dorothys capping each other's complaints about the staff, food and management at Oakfield House, the demise of decent standards in both the monarchy and the BBC, and the deplorable state of the pavements, the countryside, the education system, the present government and the nation in general. No wonder the Monster was lying low – he couldn't cope with the competition.

Dorothy One was just fulminating about the incompetence of the local council when Val bustled in triumphantly to announce Father Christmas's arrival.

'About time too,' said the Dorothys in unison.

In walked not Father Christmas but a scowling tight-lipped Tommy, kitted out in a red velvet dressing-gown and one of the Santa caps. A large quantity of cotton-wool whiskers was affixed to his chin with an even greater quantity of glue, and he carried a bulging pink nylon pillowcase stamped 'Property of Oakfield House'.

'Father Christmas doesn't wear glasses,' a little girl objected.

Val sprang to his defence. 'Oh, but he does! You see, he spoiled his eyesight reading the long lists of presents all you children sent him.'

'Where are his reindeer then?' the girl insisted.

'I'm afraid they're delayed on the A3. But he has brought two of his elves with him.'

'*Where?*' asked the child.

'They're, er, coming.'

'Tommy,' Fred called. 'Why are you wearing a dress?'

'Now, Fred, dear, don't spoil the fun,' one of the nurses chided. 'It isn't Tommy, it's Father Christmas. He's come all the way from Lapland.'

'Like hell he has,' muttered Tommy. 'I'm suffocating in this bloody stupid get-up.'

Val ignored him. 'And here are the dear little elves', she said, 'who help Santa in his grotto.'

'They're Angie's boys,' Dorothy said disparagingly. 'She's had to bring them with her today because their nan went down with flu.'

'Who's Angie?' Lorna asked.

'One of the cleaners. Nice girl, but useless – can't see dirt unless it's under her nose. And the boys are a pair of right little tearaways.'

In fact they looked enchanting, dressed in makeshift crêpe-paper costumes and coloured tights, and seemed a good deal keener on the task in hand than Father Christmas himself, who stood shuffling from foot to foot and glaring down at the carpet, misery personified. Seizing the pillowcase, the boys began pulling out presents and ripping off the paper.

'No! No!' Val shrilled. 'You don't unwrap them, you hand them round.'

The boys' enthusiasm patently dwindled.

'Each one has a label with a name on. Can you read them out, Sam?'

'Sam can't read,' his brother declared proudly.

'Oh dear. Can *you*, Josh?'

'Some words. Not the hard ones.'

'Look, I think I'd better do it. And you can distribute the presents.' Val put on her glasses and peered at one of the labels. '"Dorothy",' she pronounced.

Half a dozen voices piped up simultaneously, all laying claim to the gift.

'We'd . . . er . . . better leave that one for the moment.' Val rummaged in the pillowcase and pulled out another present. '"Ellen".'

'She's not here,' someone said. 'She had to see the doctor.'

'I'll have it then.' The older boy made a grab for the package.

'No you *won't*, Josh.' Val's eyes narrowed in anger for an instant, before her mask of professional geniality returned. 'Right – third time lucky: "Sydney".'

Sydney didn't recognize his name, but Val pointed him out to Josh, who raced across (with Sam in close pursuit) and hurled the present on his lap.

'Gently, boys! Gently. You're not on the football field! Maybe Sydney would like you to help him open the present.'

The boys evidently regarded this as a privilege worth fighting for. Josh eventually won and presented Sydney with a rather battered box of McVitie's Abbey Crunch. Neither boys nor biscuits, however, seemed to impact on his consciousness. His eyes were focused inward, his face totally impassive. And, since he lacked both teeth and relatives, the gift was singularly inept.

'Say Happy Christmas, boys, then come and get the next present.'

'Happy Christmas,' Josh muttered, already charging back to Val.

'Christmas,' echoed Sam.

'This one's for Marjorie,' Val told them. 'The lady in the blue.'

To Lorna's surprise, Marjorie's face visibly softened as Sam and Josh approached. She even reached out a shaky arm and tried to put it round Sam's waist. Was she remembering Trevor as a little boy? Certainly she looked happier than at any time this afternoon, smiling at the children with genuine affection. Yet her withered cheeks and faded, filmy eyes were a chastening reminder of mortality, set against the boys' unblemished skin and penetrating gaze.

Don't grow old, Lorna longed to tell them. Stay as you are, two Peter Pans.

The Peter Pans showed little interest in Marjorie's present – a gift-pack of soap and shower gel. Vi and Cynthia received the same. Presumably it made economic sense to give them things the home should have provided anyway. Lorna hoped her present would be a knife and fork. At lunch she had been supplied with only a spoon, bent so spectacularly out of shape it made her wonder if Uri Geller had ever visited the premises.

'Oh dear,' Val tutted, examining the next parcel. 'This one hasn't got a label. And nor has this. Sharon, weren't you meant to write them?'

'Yeah, sure – and a million other things. I've only got one bloody pair of hands, you know.'

'Ah, here's one with a name,' Val said hurriedly, forestalling further invective. '"Lorna". That's the lady with the bad foot. Take care now, boys!'

But the warning came too late. Sam cannoned into Lorna's footstool, banging her bandaged toes. Tears of pain sprang to her eyes, but she blinked them away, realizing how important it was to maintain the charade of good cheer. Without it they all had cause to weep (more cause than a mere throbbing foot) – overworked staff, underpaid carers, creaking performers, guilt-ridden relatives, and aged residents doomed to a joyless existence.

'Happy Christmas,' the boys recited, oblivious to her pain.

'Happy Christmas!' came the unexpected response – a booming, jolly voice outside the door. And in strode Father Christmas Mark Two, correctly dressed in red trousers and red hooded jacket, and accompanied by a pair of elves in smart green livery.

Spotting competition, Tommy sprang to aggressive life, squaring up to the interloper. 'Sorry, chum' – he sounded far from chummy – 'you're too late.'

Josh and Sam didn't bother with words, they simply set about their rivals with flailing feet and fists.

'Happy Christmas,' Lorna muttered, as a distraught but helpless Val surveyed the mayhem. 'Happy Christmas to us all.'

9

'Not going out today?' Sharon was making Lorna's bed – a perfunctory straightening of the covers, followed by a long, vociferous complaint about her back.

Lorna shook her head, feeling something of a failure. Over half the residents were spending Christmas Day with friends or family. 'My husband's still in bed with a high temperature.'

'I wouldn't be surprised if I had this flu myself. I've got a blinding headache. You could die here and nobody'd notice.' Sharon retrieved a pillow from the floor and gave it a vicious punch. 'Talking of death, we had another this morning. Mr Wilcox – heart attack. His wife's here too. They shared a double room.'

'Gosh, how awful – being widowed today of all days.'

'She doesn't know the difference. Well, she senses something's missing, but she's not sure what exactly.'

'Poor woman.'

'*She*'s not poor. They're rolling. The old man's left her a fortune.'

'Yes, but . . . '

'Do you *need* all these pillows, Mrs, er, Pat . . . ?' Sharon seemed to have trouble remembering even the wrong name, although – small mercy – she hadn't yet resorted to Dorothy.

'Well, I am meant to put my foot up.'

'It's just that we're short, you see, so if I could nick a couple . . . '

'OK,' Lorna conceded. No doubt she could put her foot up on the window-sill.

'Ta ever so much. Enjoy your breakfast.'

Lorna eyed the lumpy porridge and slice of burnt toast. At least there was a knife and a spoon this time. No cup, though. Well, the porridge bowl would have to do, once she'd disposed of its contents. If nothing else, Oakfield House provided a useful training in improvisation.

While she ate, she listened to the rain drumming on the window-panes. It seemed odd to have rain at Christmas, although torrential downpours were forecast for the whole country. She imagined standing in the grounds stark naked and letting wild, wet rain sheet down on her body. She hadn't had a breath of fresh air for ten days. Still, most people here hadn't been outside for years.

Sister Kathy put her head round the door. 'Just thought I'd say Happy Christmas. How are you, Lorna?'

'Fine. Well, my back's playing up a bit, but . . . '

'Haven't you had your pain-killers? I'll fetch them.'

'Thanks. Oh, and could you bring a cup?'

Pills and cup duly arrived; Kathy even poured the tea for her.

'Are you working the whole of Christmas?' Lorna asked, hoping to detain her for a while. (Nothing was scheduled for this morning, and time was already dragging.) Of all the staff, Kathy was her favourite; they'd had a long talk last night and were now on first-name terms.

'Yes, I'm in all week.'

'Bad luck!'

'No, it was my choice. I got divorced this summer and I didn't fancy Christmas on my own.'

'Oh, I'm sorry . . . '

'Don't be. It's good riddance as far as Don's concerned. I should have left him years ago. I didn't even have the excuse of staying for the sake of the children.'

'You mean you haven't any?'

'No. Though not for want of trying. I had every treatment in the book, but – well, we were unlucky, I suppose.'

'I haven't any either,' Lorna admitted.

'Did you want them?'

'God, yes!' She blanked out treacherous memories of Tom and the abortion. Best to stick to marriage. 'I was pregnant three times, but I miscarried.'

'Poor you. That's even worse.'

Certainly Ralph would say so, Lorna reflected. He had been shaken by the messiness of the miscarriages, dismayed by their abruptness. Yet she suspected he was secretly glad that they had never had a family. In her own mind, though, she was still a mother of four; still mourning the unfledged foetuses. 'It's always worse at Christmas, isn't it?' she said, sipping her lukewarm tea. 'No stockings to fill.'

'Don't you believe it! Don and I used to give each other stockings. He was marvellous at things like that. He'd put in fairy bubbles and chocolate hearts and all sorts of crazy stuff.'

'He had his good points then.'

Kathy raised an eyebrow. 'Yes, but he could be violent too. As well as the chocolate hearts I was just as likely to get a beautiful black eye for Christmas.'

'Oh, Kathy, how ghastly.'

Kathy shrugged. 'It happens all the time. Half my female friends have been knocked about at some point. The trouble is, no one likes to say anything. We're all too loyal. Or too ashamed.'

Lorna gave silent thanks that *she* had never been hit. Before Tom, there'd been a string of men who were mostly quite unsuitable but in no case actually violent. However, none of the relationships had lasted, as if the pattern set by her father was somehow inherent in her genes. Any man she was involved with was bound to disappear. Even Tom, whom she'd adored, had upped and left soon after the abortion. Ralph alone had offered permanence.

'Don was a real brute when we were going through the divorce. Instead of alimony I got a broken nose! But this is no subject for Christmas Day,' Kathy said with a laugh. 'And if I don't go and change Mrs Foster's dressing she'll be marching up here to know the reason why. See you later.'

Lorna turned on the television, flipping through the channels to avoid Christmas carols, Christmas cooking or Christmas anything. She finally settled for an old romantic movie – no black eyes or broken noses. Watching the lovers' lips make lingering contact, she wondered if Ralph was thinking about her, even missing her . . .

'I doubt it,' the Monster interjected. 'He'll be dead by now, I imagine.'

'Get lost!'

'People can cop it just like that! Look at Mr Wilcox. He was having a high old time at the party yesterday and today he's a decomposing body in a box.'

'In the interests of accuracy, he won't be in a coffin yet, *nor* decomposing. And I'm not listening, anyway.' Her thoughts were still with Ralph – his own disrupted childhood. When his father waltzed off with another, younger, woman, his mother couldn't cope and he'd been passed from pillar to post. Eventually she remarried, but his step-father rejected him, sending him away to school and to various odd bods in the holidays. Yet whatever bitterness he might feel he kept strictly to himself, seeking solace only in whisky and his pipe.

'Cheers, Ralph darling!' she murmured, toasting him in cold tea and wishing she could make up for his sad and blighted years. But he'd only have said, 'They're over. Why hark back?'

She put down the cup and tried in vain to get comfortable in her chair. Without supporting pillows her foot ached horribly, and the ibuprofen seemed to have no effect on the fierce pain in her back. She had never known time pass so slowly. If she'd had the use of a phone she could have rung those few of her friends not up to their elbows in sage-and-onion stuffing.

'Clare,' she said aloud. 'Jump in the car and come over, there's a pal. If you get here before lunch I'll treat you to a blow-out at the Savoy.'

Loneliness, like violence, was something one didn't admit. The very word dripped with self-pity and personal failure. How could she be lonely when she was married?

'How indeed? You don't know when you're well off. Have you spared a thought for those *truly* on their own? Widows, for example.'

'Yes, Aunt Agnes, I have. But thinking about other people's troubles doesn't always alleviate one's own.' She turned the television up to full volume to drown any tart rejoinder.

'I love you,' the tall, dark, handsome man was saying (bellowing). 'I love you more than life itself.'

She closed her eyes. 'I love you too,' she responded, surrendering to his embrace.

'Everyone's on drugs these days.'

'*Everyone?*' Lorna demurred.

'Oh yes.' Dorothy was adamant. 'And the schools are full of mur-derers. Children carry guns and knives routinely. I blame the parents. There's no discipline. When we were young we were beaten for the tiniest thing. My father had a stick as thick as your arm. It didn't do us any harm.'

'Well, I'm not sure . . . '

'Do you want this?' Hilda pressed her holly-printed paper napkin into Lorna's hand.

'It's all right, I've got one, thanks.'

'Take it! Take it!' Hilda whimpered.

'Oh, well . . . yes, OK.' Lorna was afraid the poor woman would burst into tears. She spread the second napkin on her lap, on top of the first, although both were somewhat superfluous. The food hadn't arrived – and probably never would, since, according to Sharon, the chef had stormed out after an altercation with Matron. His timing seemed a trifle remiss. The residents were sitting at their tables (some in bibs and many perched on waterproof incontinence cushions) waiting for their turkey and Christmas pudding.

Not all had sat in silence. Dorothy Two had been pronouncing on the latest crime statistics and their relevance to the abolition of corporal punishment – a polemic totally lost on Hilda and Sydney. For the past half-hour Lorna had been caught in a three-way conversation on 'Bring back the birch' (Dorothy Two) and the likely content of the Queen's speech (Ellen), with added incoherent musings from Hilda on a certain dearly beloved William. Whether this was her husband, son, dog or budgerigar, Lorna never did discover. In truth, she was finding it hard to concentrate when hunger was her main concern. Presumably the turkey was already cooked, as the chef hadn't been gone long. If they just wanted someone to carve, she would gladly volunteer – although perhaps it would be better minced, given the general dental deficiencies.

A ripple of dread swept the dining-room as Matron strutted in – an imperious character somewhere between Pol Pot and the Empress Catherine of Russia. Lorna, however, perked up when she saw the tray of sherry-glasses: in the absence of food, a liquid lunch would be perfectly acceptable. It did strike her as rather odd, though, that Matron herself and not one of her minions should be distributing the Christmas tipple. On their only previous meeting Lorna had taken a dislike to the thin-lipped martinet with concave chest and cold grey eyes. Today's smiling version was no improvement – in fact positively unnerving. The smile was like the tinsel round her cap: an artificial accessory, to be swiftly discarded after the festivities.

'No, Hilda. Not for you. I'll get Sharon to bring you some fruit juice.'

'I want sherry,' Hilda wailed.

'Alcohol doesn't mix with your pills. You know what the doctor said.'

'I want sherry,' Hilda repeated.

Ignoring her, Matron passed a glass to Dorothy. 'Happy Christmas, Mrs Fleming.'

'I'd like to know what's happy about it.'

'Now, now, my dear – we must make an effort. And how are *you*, Mrs Pearson?'

'Oh, I'm . . . fine.'

'Good! That's the spirit. Sherry for you?'

'Yes *please*.'

When Matron moved to the next table, Lorna attacked her drink with gusto. 'Cheers,' she said to Ralph again, wondering if he was already the worse for wear or too ill to lift a glass.

Sharon bustled up with orange-juice for Sydney and Hilda, in glasses so small they looked more suited to a doll's house. The sherry-glasses, weirdly, were more generous.

'I want sherry,' Hilda persisted.

Sharon made a face. 'Why the hell didn't you say so? It means trekking all the way back to the kitchen.'

'You couldn't get me another, could you?' put in Lorna quickly, 'while you're there.'

'I'll have another too,' said Dorothy. 'Though it's pretty foul, isn't it? I like a decent Tio Pepe, not this British muck.'

Sharon returned with not three but ten more glasses, all brim-full. She looked rather flushed, as if she'd been having a tipple herself. 'I've brought enough to last you – to save my feet. Otherwise I'll be crawling about on my hands and knees by tea-time.'

Lorna felt uneasy as Hilda seized a glass and gulped the contents – suppose it provoked some terrible reaction . . . Yet reporting her to Matron would be sneaky and unthinkable. The only solution was to down most of the sherry herself, to keep it from those on medication. At least Sydney seemed quite happy with his orange-juice (although he had already spilled half of it down his front), and Ellen was more concerned about missing the Queen's speech than with refreshment, solid or liquid. The sixth person at the table, a stone-deaf woman called Irena, stared straight ahead, much to Lorna's discomfiture. Earlier she had tried smiling at her, then addressing her in a loud, clear voice, so that she wouldn't feel left out, until Dorothy said dismissively, 'Don't waste your breath. Even if she could hear, she wouldn't want to talk to the likes of us.'

'Why?' asked Lorna.

'Because she's a countess – so she says. Polish, mind you, and countesses are two a penny in Europe. But it doesn't stop her giving herself airs.'

Even so, thought Lorna, to be foreign and profoundly deaf in this hotbed of prejudice couldn't make life easy. She offered the countess a glass of sherry. The offer was neither accepted nor refused. Irena continued staring at the wall; not a muscle moved in her face or body. Even her eyes seemed disturbingly expressionless, and her hands looked dead, the fingers pale and bloated. Was she genuinely disapproving? Or suffering from depression?

'What this country should do' – Dorothy rapped her fork on the table – 'is bring back the hangman, and quickly.'

Lorna wondered if this draconian measure was aimed at Irena in particular or the lawless population in general. Luckily she spotted Sharon just coming from the servery with a tray. 'Oh, look,' she said. 'Food!'

Not, alas, the turkey, but a starter: melon-boats, each adorned with a glacé cherry and half an orange-slice – the first fresh fruit she had seen at Oakfield House. However, it didn't please Dorothy or Hilda.

'I want soup,' said Hilda plaintively.

Dorothy waved the proffered plate away. 'Melon gives me indigestion.'

'It's a *treat*,' said Sharon, banging down Dorothy's plate in front of Sydney. 'For Christmas.'

'Hardly a treat! It's not even ripe.'

'I want soup.'

'There's no soup today, Miss Chambers. Tomorrow you'll have soup – turkey soup all bloody week, no doubt.'

'Did you say "bloody", Sharon?'

'No, 'course not, Mrs Fleming. I said – '

'I want turkey.' Hilda again, changing tack.

'Yeah, so do we all. Tommy's just carving it – or hacking it to pieces, more like.'

Tommy was clearly versatile, juggling the roles of bath attendant, Santa Claus and chef. Melon-cutter too, perhaps. Each slice had been cut crossways, to form bite-size chunks, although this didn't prevent mishaps on the part of the less dextrous. Soon melon bullets were flying in all directions, landing on the carpet or the tablecloth. Lorna retrieved one from her lap, wondering whether to hand it back to its owner.

A care assistant was trying to feed Irena, who stubbornly refused to open her mouth. 'OK, *be* like that,' the girl said, snatching the plate away. (Peace and good will had reached a depressingly low ebb.)

'I want soup,' Hilda reiterated, in case her previous demands had gone unheard.

Soup would certainly have been a better choice for Sydney, whose lack of teeth made unripe melon hazardous. He did rather ill-advisedly put the orange-slice in his mouth, but then took it out, half-chewed, and offered it to Irena. The countess haughtily ignored him.

'Well, down the hatch!' said Lorna brightly, raising her second glass. She felt better already, in spite of having to sit with her foot propped up at an extremely awkward angle, which sent spasms of pain down her back. One took so many things for granted, like being able to sit four-square at the table, with both feet on the floor.

'Chin-chin!' responded Hilda, also embarking on her second glass. Fortunately there was no sign of Matron nor any obvious change in Hilda's condition, but Lorna kept an eye on her, prepared for emergency measures.

The carers started to clear away the melon plates, and indeed most of the melon. At Oakfield House, serving the food was clearly of more importance than ensuring its consumption. Maybe the recent spate of deaths was due less to strokes and heart attacks than to simple malnutrition.

Lorna refused to relinquish her plate until she had scraped the melon-skin clean and even eaten the orange-rind (to provide a few extra calories). After all, there was no guarantee that any more food was on its way. Knowing Tommy's temperament, the turkey might end up on the kitchen floor.

But no, she was wrong. Sharon and a small, spindly, dark-skinned fellow were approaching with a tray of plates.

'Good God,' Dorothy expostulated. 'What's *this* supposed to be?'

The turkey, anaemically white, was reduced to shreds – a sorry heap spattered with blobs of stuffing and accompanied by a single boiled potato and a mush of disintegrating, greyish Brussels sprouts.

'Where's mine?' asked Lorna anxiously when everyone but her had been served.

'Coming.'

While she waited she sipped yet more sherry. Pure benevolence, of course – to keep the others out of danger. In fact Dorothy must have drunk as much as she had, although her tongue was as sharp as ever.

'If I've told them once I've told them a thousand times. There's no goodness left in vegetables if they're cooked to a pulp like this.'

'I want vegetables.'

'You've *got* them, Hilda,' Dorothy said tartly. 'That disgusting mess there.' She poked it with her knife. 'If you don't mind, Lorna, I'll start. Mustn't let it get cold. A joke, of course! In all the time I've been here I've never known a meal served hot, and I doubt if today's will be any different.' Sampling a piece of turkey, she gave an exaggerated shudder. 'Tough, tasteless and probably swarming with Tommy's germs. Well, if this is Christmas dinner they can keep it. Sharon!' She snapped her fingers at the girl, who was now serving the adjoining table. 'Bring me a round of buttered toast. This food's inedible.'

'I can't be making toast, Mrs Fleming. Not now. I've got all the others to serve.'

'Including me,' Lorna reminded her. Tough, tasteless, germ-infested turkey was still preferable to none.

'I won't be spoken to like that, Sharon. It's high time you learned some respect.'

'And it's time you learned to get off your high horse,' Sharon muttered, marching off in a huff.

Lorna sighed. With Sharon gone she would have to beg a dinner from one of the other carers. She craned her neck to look into the servery, where a couple of girls appeared to be doing nothing. Then she realized to her horror that they were, in fact, helping themselves to the residents' Christmas pudding, apparently unaware they were being watched. They gouged out lumps with their hands, licking their fingers greedily before digging into the pudding again. No wonder Dorothy had talked about germs: she too must have observed such flagrant breaches of hygiene. Their behaviour was outrageous. Wasn't anyone in charge? Surely if Matron saw them she would sack them on the spot. Some of the residents had only just recovered from flu. Now, it seemed, they were in danger of food-poisoning.

Revolted, she turned back to the table. Maybe it was just as well she hadn't any food. But then all at once her stomach rumbled audibly, as if informing her that a stomach upset was preferable to starvation. And at that moment the small, spindly fellow happened to be passing, so, suppressing her scruples, she caught his eye. 'Sorry to bother you . . . ' – she squinted at his name-badge – 'Hashim, but I haven't had my main course yet.'

'You Mrs Clark?'

Oh dear. With his thick accent, there were bound to be more misunderstandings. 'No, I'm Mrs Pearson. Or Mrs Paterson, if you prefer. Either will do fine.'

'You Mrs Fine?'

'No.' (The Monster would die laughing.) 'Mrs . . . Peear . . . sonn.'

'Oh.' He frowned, abandoning further attempts to use her name. 'You like melon?'

'Yes, very nice. But I've had my melon. Now I want turkey.'

'*Turkey?*'

Was it such a peculiar request – on Christmas Day, when everyone else in the room was tucking in? 'Yes, turkey, please. Lots.' Untouched by human hand, she added *sotto voce*.

'I go ask Chef.'

'Chef not there.'

'*He's* not there, if you ask me,' Dorothy put in, removing a black bit from her potato. 'It's always the same with these darkies. God knows what language they speak at home – if they've got homes, which I doubt – but it's certainly not English.'

Lorna sprang to Hashim's defence, regretting her earlier irritation. The poor man might be struggling to support an invalid mother or a brood of under-fives. 'At least he's trying,' she said, crunching a stray orange-pip to fight off her hunger pangs.

'They have to do more than try, Lorna. That's the trouble with this country today: no standards, no national pride. Is it any wonder we're going to the dogs?'

'I want sherry!' Hilda reached for another glass.

'No, that's mine,' said Lorna, alarmed at Hilda's hectic flush and having visions of her keeling over . Would they all be charged as accessories to murder?

'You've had more than your fair share already, young lady!' The words were perfectly enunciated, the voice unmistakably English. Astonished, Lorna looked at Irena – deaf, foreign Irena, who met her eyes with a malevolent glower. The countess said nothing further, although the unflinching gaze was condemnation enough.

'Gosh, yes, you're right. I'm . . . sorry,' Lorna stammered. Perhaps Irena was neither Polish nor deaf. Feigned deafness could be useful here, as an escape from largely pointless conversations. Had she known in advance the vagaries of Oakfield House, she could have come forearmed with a hearing-aid (switched permanently off), a canteen of cutlery, a supply of ready-meals and several rolls of toilet-paper (there had been none this morning, and no one to ask).

Every time she glanced up she met the intimidating Gorgon stare. Again she gave thanks that she wasn't actually eating – subjected to such venomous scrutiny, even a morsel of food would have choked her.

'Goodnight,' said Sydney suddenly – the only word Lorna had heard him utter.

'Er, goodnight,' she replied. Was it wishful thinking on his part, to make the day go faster?

'Goodnight,' he said again.

'Goodnight,' she countered valiantly.

'Goodnight, Madge.'

Madge? Lorna gave a bewildered smile. He was evidently still addressing her, his rheumy eyes fixed doggedly on hers. Another name to add to the collection.

'Goodnight,' he prompted.

Her turn. 'Goodnight.'

'Goodnight.' Would they continue like this till it *was* night? Well, in the absence of other distractions there were worse ways of passing the time.

After a dozen more goodnights, Hashim came to the rescue by bringing her meal – not turkey, not stuffing, not even vegetables, but a small piece of plain white fish marooned on a large white plate. She goggled. '*Fish?*'

'Matron say you on special diet.'

'Special diet? Certainly not!'

'Matron say no meat.'

'Goodnight.' Sydney spluttered bits of stuffing in Lorna's direction.

Dorothy rounded on him in annoyance. 'It happens to be lunch-time, Sydney. I admit you have cause to doubt it, since several of us here have failed to *get* any lunch – or anything worth calling lunch – but it certainly won't help matters if you keep insisting that it's bed-time.'

Her outburst was largely wasted on Sydney, although it did succeed in reducing him to silence. In the lull, Lorna told Hashim again that she wasn't on a diet. In fact in the two days she'd been at Oakfield House she must have lost half a stone. And this was Christmas, for heaven's sake, when the rest of the nation was gourmandizing.

'You *fish!*' beamed Hashim, his comprehension levels roughly simi-lar to Sydney's.

'He's mixing you up with Miss Bagley,' Dorothy explained. 'She eats fish for every meal, including breakfast. It's some religious thing. She's stark staring mad, but they have to humour her. Her husband's a big noise on the council.'

'Where is she? Can't we swap?'

'No, she's in her room. She never comes out except for church.'

'So how could they muddle the plates?'

'Here they can muddle anything. I suggest you eat it, dear. If you ask for it to be changed they'll probably bring you Rodney's meal, and he's a vegan. It's up to you. If you'd *prefer* a plate of sunflower seeds . . .'

'No, no, this'll do.' After removing several bones, Lorna took a cau-tious mouthful and washed it down with sherry. At least fish was mar-ginally better than last year's cheese and deadline sandwiches, even if it was flavourless and semi-raw. No one else was eating. Hilda had hic-cups, Sydney was now serenely dribbling (perhaps imagining that night had fallen at last) and Irena engaged in fisticuffs with a despotic care assistant who had tried to force a fork between her lips. Dorothy was in full flow about over-fishing in the North Sea, presumably inspired by Lorna's minuscule portion of cod. All the while the rain provided a counterpoint, slamming against the windows with gleeful malice.

'Who's that woman with the bad foot?' A loud voice from the adjoining table.

'I think she's Hilda's daughter.' Equally loud.

'She can't be. Hilda's not married.'

'Well, whoever she is, she's no business to stick her leg up like that. It's bad manners. And right in Dorothy's way. If there's something wrong with her she should stay at home.'

Lorna froze. Should she explain the situation? Best not. Judging by their volume, the speakers were deaf, which meant she would have to shout, and she didn't fancy introducing the shameful subject of bunions to the assembled company. (Actually the dining-room was much less full than yesterday, with only the rejects left – those without families, or too ill or decrepit to go out for the day. A few relatives had come for lunch, looking wretched for the most part as they made stilted conversation between mouthfuls of cold turkey.)

'Oh my God!' Dorothy exclaimed, interrupting her own tirade about dwindling haddock stocks.

'What's wrong?' asked Lorna, startled.

Dorothy leaned towards her and hissed in a stage whisper: 'They're about to remove Mr Wilcox.'

'I beg your pardon?'

'Mr Wilcox. Who passed away this morning. They always smuggle the corpses out at mealtimes. They think none of us will notice. But I always know. For one thing, it's the only time they shut the dining-room doors. Look out of that side window and you'll see the ambulance.'

Lorna swivelled in her chair. A long, low, white vehicle was parked by the dustbins, with 'Private Ambulance' in blue letters on the side. The piece of fish in her mouth turned rubbery and dead. She was chewing Mr Wilcox – that same cold, stiffening body being trundled past the firmly closed dining-room doors. 'Where's M . . . Mrs Wilcox?' she asked.

'Over there.' Dorothy pointed to the table in the corner. 'The lady in green.'

The lady in green, sublimely indifferent to the fate of her late husband, was tackling her food with vigour, trying to stuff a whole potato into her mouth.

'Isn't she . . . upset?'

'Not at all. Just before lunch I saw her cuddling up to Rodney. One man's as good as another as far as Edna's concerned. It's OK – all clear now. They're opening the doors again.'

Lorna clutched her sherry-glass. How appalling it must be to live here permanently and watch your fellow residents die off one by one, knowing you might be next. She glanced again at Mrs Wilcox, who now appeared to be choking and had sicked potato down her bib. The others at her table sat in silence, making no attempt to eat. Was the Christmas dinner really worth the effort? Maybe it would have been better, and safer, to have invested in a few dozen jars of baby food; it would have been far less work for the carers, who were now stacking the dirty plates and scraping vast amounts of uneaten food into a plastic pail – whole dinners in most cases. Lorna hoped it would go to the pigs: they at least would enjoy their Christmas.

After an interval punctuated only by Hilda's hiccups, Sharon came slouching back to their table. 'Do you want Christmas pudding or mince pie?'

'Both, of course,' snapped Dorothy.

'Sorry, one or the other.'

'It's a scandal, considering the fees we pay. I shall write to the management, on principle.'

Sharon merely shrugged.

Lorna was surprised there was any Christmas pudding left, after the depredations of the two thieving care assistants. She herself resolved to opt for pie – if she could manage to eat anything, that is. Mr Wilcox was still lodged in her throat, decomposing, as the Monster had predicted.

'Which for you, Miss Bancroft?' Sharon said with increasing exasperation.

'I'm very worried, dear, about missing the Queen's speech. I've heard it without fail for the past seventy-odd years and I wouldn't want to break the tradition.'

'It's not on till three. And it's only five past two now. Do you want pudding or mince pie?'

'They said it was in the lounge, but the lounge television's broken. Do you think I ought to tell that man who – ?'

Sharon raised her eyes to heaven, but finding no help there either she turned instead to Hilda. 'Miss Chambers, pudding or mince pie?'

The only response was a hiccup, and, since Sydney was incapable of choosing and Irena refused to hear, Sharon announced irritably, 'I'll bring three of each, OK?'

'Yes, fine,' said Lorna, to keep the peace.

'It's *not* fine, Lorna. If you don't take a stand, who will? The food's an absolute disgrace. I've complained till I'm blue in the face, but no one ever listens.'

Lorna wondered if she could persuade Aunt Agnes to take up residence here, with the express purpose of inculcating gratitude into Dorothy. But that would require a miracle, and miracles were beyond even Aunt Agnes's capabilities.

Both pudding and mince pie eventually arrived, in the same piecemeal state as the turkey. Tommy's heavy hand again, or had all the carers had a go at sampling them? The choice was between dark crumbs (pudding) and pale crumbs (pastry – mincemeat was practically nil). Sharon slammed the plates down indiscriminately. Lorna got pale crumbs, with a coarse black hair – Hashim's? – draped tastefully across the top.

'Brandy sauce?' Another girl was hovering with a large metal jug of something white and viscous, which looked and smelt like distemper.

'Oh . . . thank you.' Lorna removed the hair before it could be swamped. Fortunately Dorothy hadn't seen it, otherwise she would have summoned the health inspectors on the spot.

'I want brandy,' Hilda hiccupped.

'Well, you won't get it,' retorted Sharon. 'And there's none in that sauce neither. Only starch and chemicals.'

'Sharon, I intend to report you for gross impertinence.'

'Go ahead, Mrs Fleming. Find some other idiot who'll work all Christmas week for a pittance, waiting on ungrateful sods like you.'

Apoplectic with rage, Dorothy tottered to her feet. '*Matron!*' she shrieked.

'Matron go home,' Hashim informed her helpfully.

'Yeah. Me too, if I had any sense.' Sharon turned on her heel and stalked out.

Lorna seized the last glass of sherry and drained it at a gulp. The only way to endure the remainder of this unspeakable Christmas Day was to get completely and utterly smashed.

10

'Mummy!' she sobbed. 'Mummy, where have you gone?'

The room was wrong. Small and strange. And cold. Everything had changed. Different bed, different-coloured walls.

'Mummy,' she screamed. 'Where am I?'

'It's all right, Lorna, I'm here.'

A figure had floated in, all in white like a ghost.

'I want Mummy. I want my mummy.'

'You're living with *me* now, Lorna dear.'

'I want to go home. Take me home.'

'This *is* your home.'

'It's not, it's not,' she wept. She closed her eyes and sank down, down, down, searching for Mummy and Daddy. She was deafened by the silence, blinded by the dark. Everything dark dark dark dark dark . . .

'Mrs Pearson?'

Another voice. She tried to swim towards it, catch it, like a buoy, a raft.

'What're you doing lying in the dark?'

A glaring light snapped on. She blinked, rolled on to her side. In the doorway stood a short, stocky girl in glasses.

'I've brought you a cup of tea. Sorry it's so late.'

She swallowed. Her lips felt dry and there was a foul taste in her mouth.

'Were you asleep?'

'Yes . . . I think I must have been.' She was still trapped in the dream: four years old and newly arrived at Aunt Agnes's. House, meals, surroundings, bath-time were all frighteningly unfamiliar. 'What . . . what time is it?'

'Half past five. Tea's meant to be at four, but I'm miles behind. I'm new here.'

'Oh . . . ' She ought to be friendly, say it didn't matter, but the tendrils of fear from the dream were threatening to shoot up to monstrous proportions, like Jack's beanstalk. She focused instead on her headache – physical pain was much easier to deal with. 'Could you possibly bring me some aspirin? My head's pounding like a sledgehammer.'

'I'm not allowed to give out drugs. But I'll ask Sister if you like.'

'No, it's OK.' She didn't want anyone seeing her like this. Her clothes were creased and she probably stank of sherry. Worse, the commode was disgustingly full, although she didn't remember using it.

The girl put the cup down by the bed. 'There was supposed to be Christmas cake, but it ran out, I'm afraid.'

'Don't worry, I'm not hungry.'

'Too much Christmas dinner, eh?' The girl laughed, not unkindly.

Lorna considered: a sliver of melon, two mouthfuls of fish, a few pastry crumbs and possibly a hair. But the thought of food induced a wave of nausea.

'Well, I'd better be off. I'm Becky, by the way.'

'Oh, right. Becky.' She could barely remember her own name. Back, foot and head all ached hideously. If only she could speak to Ralph. His Christmas Day must have been worse than hers – all alone, with flu. And yet what good would she have been at home? Her natural instinct would have been to bring him drinks and meals; hold his hand literally as well as metaphorically. But illness for Ralph was a slur on his masculinity, a sign of personal failure. He hated the indignity of wearing pyjamas in the daytime or having a thermometer stuck absurdly in his mouth, so everyone, including her, was banned from entering the sick-room.

She hauled herself up in bed to drink the tea. Over-sugared this time but short on milk. Well, it made a change.

'Sorry, Mrs Pearson, I forgot to give you this.' Becky again, with a folded piece of paper.

The first instalment of the bill? No, three messages scrawled in biro.

'*Your husband rang. Sends his love.*'

'*Clare says Happy Christmas. Keep your chin up!*'

'*Aunt Agnes wants to know why haven't you phoned?*'

Three lifelines. Ralph cared, Clare was thinking of her, and even Agnes had rung, if only with a rebuke. She sat fingering the piece of paper as if it were a love-letter. If Father Christmas had given her a mobile instead of a pair of lace-edged hankies (which she had loaned to Hilda yesterday to help staunch a sudden nose-bleed) she could have returned the calls. Being without a phone made her feel marooned, an exile from the outside world.

Gradually she became aware of a moaning sound coming from the room next door – not her aggressive neighbour (who, judging by the quiet, must still be out with her son) but the other side. Slowly it increased in volume to become a keening, desolate wail. In alarm, Lorna glanced around for her crutches, but they were nowhere to be seen. She vaguely recalled coming back from the dining-room in a wheelchair. The crutches must be still down there.

The crying continued unabated. Lorna pressed the bell. Becky seemed a decent sort – surely she would help. But no one came.

As the minutes ticked by with no sign of any assistance, Lorna's agitation turned to panic. What if there was a genuine emergency? The poor wretch next door already sounded desperate, and as for herself she couldn't move a step. Without her crutches she was as helpless as a baby, as helpless as in the dream.

She jabbed the bell so hard it hurt her finger, and almost at once heard footsteps outside. Not Becky but the angry woman, with her family in train. Soon a full-scale row was in progress, which Lorna couldn't avoid hearing through the wall.

'I'm *not* ungrateful. I didn't *want* to go out to lunch. I told you twenty times.'

'Oh sure, and if we'd left you here on your own we'd never hear the end of it.'

'Fay, please, don't provoke her.'

'Shut up, John, I'll say what I bloody well please.'

'Look, why don't we all – '

'I'm sick of kowtowing to your mother.'

'She's old. She doesn't understand.'

'Oh, I'm old, am I? And stupid? I'll have you know I . . .'

In desperation, Lorna turned on the television. However, the manic jamboree on screen was nearly as bad as arguments and sobs. Couldn't they make a special programme for those who didn't enjoy Christmas – the sick, old, lonely and bereaved – something uplifting and consoling? Switching channels, she was assailed by peals of canned laughter. It struck her that Matron might invest in something similar, to give visitors the impression that the Oakfield residents were a cheerful bunch, given to bouts of irrepressible mirth.

Next door, meanwhile, the real-life family were leaving, still hurling accusations in their wake. Once the voices had faded, Lorna turned off the TV. Silence? No. Although the woman on the left had stopped crying, now the other one had started, presumably upset by the quarrel.

Lorna pressed the bell yet again. If nothing else, she had to get her crutches back.

'OK, OK, I'm coming! I haven't got seven-league boots, you know.' Sharon's impatient voice came from down the corridor, although it was some time before she reached Lorna's door. She tottered in unsteadily – as a result more of drink than of exhaustion, Lorna reckoned. (But who was she to talk, with a hangover herself?)

'Yeah, what d'you want?'

'Oh, Sharon, it's my crutches. I think they're downstairs. Could you be an angel and – '

'No, sorry. Can't do nothing now.'

'Well, could you please ask someone else?'

'Who, I'd like to know? There's only Becky. She's about as much use as a fart in a colander. She forgot to give Mr Hall his lunch. He's a diabetic on insulin, so of course he's gone hypo.'

'Oh dear. Is that serious?'

'I should say! He's shaking like a leaf. He could even go into a coma, like he did last month.'

'Good gracious! Shouldn't you call a doctor?'

Sharon yawned hugely, without bothering to cover her mouth. 'It's Sister's problem, not mine.'

'Well, I only hope she can sort it out. And when she's free perhaps you'd tell her that the lady next door sounds terribly upset.'

'Mrs Owen? She always sounds upset. If you bought her bloody Buckingham Palace she'd complain about the neighbours. Did you hear her just now – giving her son what for? If she was *my* mother I'd have throttled her years ago.'

'Yes, but she's crying now. And the lady the other side was crying too, earlier.'

'That's nothing new. Take no notice. It's her sister – died of cancer last August, but she's still banging on about it. They didn't even like each other.'

'But it seems callous just to leave her.'

'Look, it's all we can do to get them washed and fed. We're not agony aunts, you know. I've got enough problems of my own, without listening to theirs. For one thing, I haven't seen Danny all day – '

'Danny?'

'Yeah, my kid.'

Kid? Sharon was no more than a kid herself. 'Where is he?'

Sharon's face crumpled and tears welled in her eyes. Only now did Lorna notice how terrible she looked. Her face was swollen and flushed, and her hair was coming adrift from its ponytail. 'Sit down for a minute,' Lorna said gently, passing her a box of tissues. 'I expect you're just tired out. You've been working such dreadful long hours.'

'It . . . it's not that – I'm used to it. It's Danny. He's only four and I promised him I wouldn't be late, not tonight of all nights.'

Lorna bit her lip. Children of four roused her instant compassion.

'I tried to ring him and explain, but he's obviously shit-scared. He's on his own in the house, you see.'

Lorna was shocked. 'All day, you mean?'

'Oh no. He spent Christmas with his dad. But Steve's no good with kids. By tea-time he'd had enough. So he's pissed off out with his mates.'

'But, Sharon, that's appalling! You must get home and make sure he's all right.'

'How can I? Matron would do her nut.'

'I thought she'd gone.'

'Yeah, but she's back now and raising hell. You see, me and Tommy had a little drink. Well, you wouldn't think they'd begrudge us one on Christmas Day, would you? But Matron didn't see it like that.' Sharon screwed a Kleenex into a tight, damp, lilac ball. 'If anything happens to Danny I'll *kill* her.'

Lorna averted her eyes from the overfilled commode. 'Sharon, I wonder if it would help if I had a word with Sister Kathy? *She* might understand.'

'Yeah, Kathy's OK. But she doesn't like me much. None of the nurses do. Can't say I blame them really.' She gave a hollow laugh. 'I'm not exactly a little ray of sunshine. But then nor would they be if they was trying to bring up a kid on their own. Steve never wanted children. He says it's my fault I lumbered him with Danny.'

Lorna fixed her gaze on the carpet. Exactly what Tom had said. *She* could be in Sharon's position, a single parent struggling to make ends meet. What if Danny were her own child, alone on Christmas Day, likely to injure himself, or maybe venture out in the dark in search of his mother or father . . . ? It didn't bear thinking about. 'We've got to do something, Sharon. You go and find Kathy and ask her to come up here. If I explain the situation I'm sure she'll be able to help. And if she can't I'll tackle Matron myself!'

'Oh no! You'll get me sacked.'

'OK, I'll tell you what. If all else fails we'll send a cab to Steve's place and get them to pick Danny up.'

'I can't afford cabs.'

'Don't worry. I'll pay.'

'But where can he go? There's no one at my place, bar the cat.'

Where indeed, thought Lorna, trying to force her brain to work. There was always Ralph, of course, but even if he were well he would hardly welcome an errant four-year-old. And nor would most of her friends. 'He'd better come *here*, Sharon.'

'Here? They'd have a fit!'

'They won't know. I'll say he's my nephew or something. I'll ask the cab-driver to bring him up to my room, and I'll look after him till you've finished work.'

Sharon stared at her in amazement, evidently not used to being offered help. '*Would* you, Mrs P . . . P . . . ? That's fantastic! Thanks ever so much.'

'Don't thank me yet. We'll try Kathy first, in any case. Now off you go and find her. And no more drinks!' Hypocrite, Lorna told herself, pressing a hand against her aching head. Well, playing social worker was a good way to forget a hangover – *and* dispel the threat of panic. She was also greatly cheered by the thought of looking after a child. For so many years she had longed to have a child around at Christmas. Now her wish might be granted.

11

'Come in,' Lorna said listlessly, flipping over a page in her magazine. It would only be someone to collect her tray.

The door opened to reveal a tall, lean, haggard figure in an impeccable dark suit.

'Ralph!' she exclaimed, 'What a lovely surprise!' Unable to leap up and embrace him, she reached out her arms and drew him down towards her.

For once he didn't resist, and she pressed her face into his chest, inhaling his familiar smell of pipe-tobacco and Silvikrin shampoo. 'I've missed you, darling, terribly.' At Oakfield House she had come to realize how precious a husband was. So many of the residents were widowed, or had no one in the world to care for them or about them. And today she had been feeling bereft, stranded in her room, unwell, with only a new and singularly ungracious carer bringing her meals on a tray. 'Did you miss me?' she dared to ask.

'Mm,' he murmured, embarrassed. 'How *are* you, darling? I couldn't get much sense out of anyone when I phoned.'

'I'm doing well,' she lied. He looked so tired and ashen-faced she didn't want to burden him with more problems. 'More to the point, how are *you?*'

'Fine.'

'Fine? With flu?'

'It wasn't flu.'

She hid a smile. Rather than inflating a cold to flu, as many people did, Ralph was more likely to pass off double pneumonia as simply a sore throat.

'Good God!' he said, alarmed. 'What's that awful noise?'

'Oh, it's only the woman downstairs. She's paralysed, so they have to use a hoist to get her in and out of bed.'

He prowled over to the window, grimacing at a sudden blare of music. 'Do they have to have their televisions so loud? These walls are paper-thin.'

'Mrs Owen's deaf. Sometime she even has it on full volume in the middle of the night.'

'How on earth do you manage to sleep?'

'With difficulty!'

'You can't stay here, Lorna.' He turned to face her, raising his voice above a booming commercial. 'It's absolutely appalling! I couldn't believe it when I walked in – all those fossils sitting around in various states of decrepitude.'

'Oh, come on, Ralph, it's not that bad. We'll be old one day.' You sooner than me, she thought.

'And this room . . . ' He gazed around in disgust. 'It's so small and shabby. And the *smell*.'

'You get used to it in time,' she said, although she had to admit that with Ralph here the room did seem smaller and shabbier. He was too tall for it, too smart. Suits were unknown at Oakfield House. The few male residents she'd met were kitted out in standard-issue sweat-pants to disguise their bulky incontinence pads. Seeing Ralph's tailored trousers, she suddenly remembered their first meeting – how elegant he'd looked compared with Tom: a good deal older, yes, but distinguished. It had been part of his attraction: the crisp white shirt and navy cashmere coat, the quiet silk tie and gold cufflinks, all of which seemed to preserve him in a time-warp – old-fashioned, sober, safe. (And 'safe' was crucially important to her, as much then as now.)

He ran his finger across the television set, leaving a pale pathway in the dust. 'I thought this was a proper convalescent home, not a . . . a mausoleum.'

'I couldn't find a convalescent home. Apparently they don't exist any more. One of the nurses told me. The NHS wouldn't fund them, so they sort of . . . withered away.'

'Well, in any case, it's time you came home. You've been here over a week.'

'Six days.'

'Is that all?' He sank down on the chair and rubbed his eyes. 'It seems like years.'

'So you *did* miss me!'

He gave a non-committal grunt, fumbling for his pipe.

'I'm sorry, darling, you're not allowed to smoke in here. Only downstairs in the Smokers' Lounge.'

'I'm not flogging down three floors again. It was bad enough walking up.'

'Didn't you find the lift?'

'Yes, full of old biddies in wheelchairs. And then the doors wouldn't close.'

'Have you eaten?' she asked, changing the subject.

'No.'

'Do you fancy a couple of cold fish fingers?' She indicated her untouched supper-tray. 'Or there's fruit jelly, if you like. Well, that's what Gary called it, although I can't see any fruit. Still, it seems a shame to waste it.'

'Aren't you hungry?'

'No.'

'Nor me. Just dying for a smoke.' He was sitting cradling his pipe. Suddenly he rooted in his pocket for the matches and struck one defiantly, lighting the pipe with a series of short, coaxing puffs, before inhaling with a sigh of satisfaction.

She prayed Matron wouldn't choose this moment to appear. 'They'll go mad, Ralph! It's a fire risk.'

'Don't worry. I'll hide it if anybody comes.'

'But the smell . . . ' She wafted the magazine to and fro, to disperse the smoke.

'I'll open the window.'

'No, please don't. It's perishing in here.' The manic-depressive radiator was in its depressive phase, which was why she had put on Ralph's old towelling dressing-gown in addition to two nighties and a sweater – hardly alluring nightwear to attract a long-absent spouse. She pulled the sheet up to cover her clothes; and as for the pipe-smoke, she would tell Matron it was the only way to mask the stench of urine. In fact it was working rather well – St Bruno was infinitely preferable to pee. Much as she hated Ralph smoking, she did feel a certain affection for his pipes. They were like his children: endlessly loved and indulged. The downside, of course, was that they provided a wonderful excuse for him not to talk. When an intimate conversation threatened, he would select his most refractory pipe and go through a laborious repertoire of scraping, filling, prodding, poking, puffing, sucking, blowing – ample demonstration that words were out of the question. Now, however, he seemed surprisingly communicative – a result of their week-long separation perhaps.

'So how's the foot?' he asked, disposing of his spent match in the jelly-dish.

'OK. Well, I had a bit of bother on Christmas Day. A little boy ran his toy truck right over my bad toes, and, God, did I yell!'

'Little boy? Whose little boy?'

'Oh . . . just one of the visitors' children.' She knew he would disapprove of her babysitting for Sharon, although, sore toes notwithstanding, Danny's impudent charm had cheered her up enormously.

Ralph exhaled another plume of smoke. 'Look, I don't want to push you, darling, but when d'you think you'll be back in harness?'

The phrase conjured up the image of a horse – a sickly, spavined creature stumbling between the shafts of its cart. She tried to picture instead a young racehorse raring to go. 'Oh, not long now, I hope. How about you?'

'I managed to do a bit today. And whatever happens I must be back full-time on Monday. Things are piling up.'

'It's New Year's Eve on Monday.'

'Oh, God, yes. Which reminds me – the Kirkwoods have invited us out. There's some ghastly dinner-dance at Hugh's golf club.'

'Well, for once we've got the perfect excuse.' She gestured to her foot again, propped on a pile of books in lieu of pillows.

'We're not really in a position to refuse. Hugh's doing us a favour, darling – he's asked his next-door neighbours, who are apparently very taken with the Kirkwoods' low-maintenance garden. Well, the wife is, anyway. *And* they've got a place in the country, so it would be madness to pass up the chance of new business.'

'But, Ralph, I can't go to a dance on crutches.'

'There's no need for you to dance. All you have to do is be charming and look nice. And surely you don't want to spend New Year's Eve in *this* dump? What treats have they in store? Let me guess – bingo and a sing-song.'

'Close! Carpet bowls and Scrabble. Followed by tea at five and bed at seven thirty.'

'Well, there you are.'

'Actually, I was rather looking forward to not having to celebrate. You see, I've come out in a rash and – '

'Like the one you had in hospital, you mean?'

'No, that was nothing much – just a side-effect of the antibiotics. This is rather nasty.'

'Where is it? Let me see.'

She pushed the two nighties down, to show him.

'Strewth! It's awful. And it goes right round your side. Do you think it could be bites – fleas, or bed-bugs, or something? I wouldn't be surprised in a run-down place like this.'

She shook her head. 'It's not just itchy, it's painful. Ow! Don't touch. The slightest pressure hurts. I can't even wear a bra.'

'I don't like the look of it at all. What did the doctor say?'

'I haven't seen a doctor.' Come to think of it, she hadn't ever seen one at Oakfield House. No doubt doctors were rationed, along with pillows, knives, functioning lifts and care assistants with problem-free personal lives.

'Well, the sooner we get you home the better. Then you can make an appointment with Dr Burgess.'

'All right.' She was too dejected to argue. The thought of moving from her bed, packing her stuff here and then unpacking it at home seemed beyond her powers at present, never mind sitting through a dinner-dance till the small hours.

'Would you like me to ask at the chemist's? That place in Park Street stays open late, and maybe they can recommend an ointment.'

'Don't worry. I'm OK.' He made no demands on her when *he* was ill, so it seemed unfair to burden him with shopping trips. Besides, what use would ointment be? Morphine and a skin graft might help, but they, alas, weren't available at chemists'.

'Or how about ice, to cool it down.'

'Ice? I shouldn't think they have any. And even if they did it would be a puddle of water by the time it got up here.'

Ralph sat frowning, his shoulders tense, his fingers drumming on the chair-arm. 'Mind if I just catch the news?' he said finally.

'N . . . no.' He had only been here ten minutes. Still, ten minutes' conversation was quite a triumph compared with home. She had long suspected that Ralph's addiction to news was simply another ploy to avoid talking. Faced with footage of a big London hotel going up in flames and Serbian corpses being exhumed from a mass grave, she could hardly burble on about rashes or bad feet.

She retrieved her magazine and turned to the problem page. *'If your marriage is lacking oomph, you may need to play the seductress. Give your husband a luxurious sensual massage, or share a bubble bath . . . '*

Ralph hated sharing the bathroom, let alone a bath. Should she write in for advice?

'Use a loofah mitt for extra stimulation. And whisper endearments as you soap his . . . '

Ralph would regard it as assault if she approached him with a loofah mitt, and, as for whispered endearments, he'd probably complain that she was interrupting the weather forecast.

The magazine seemed to throb with sex – a piece about multiple orgasm, a picture of a couple in a clinch, and a feature called 'Position of the Month', which looked uncomfortable in the extreme, if not anatomically impossible. Had anyone ever had it away in Oakfield House, she wondered? Perhaps she should set a precedent, bare her breasts and inveigle Ralph under the blankets. But the rash practically covered her left breast, and if she lay on it and exposed only the right the pain would be horrendous.

At that moment he stood up. Had he had the same idea? After all, it was a fortnight since they'd last made love, and she would subject herself even to pain for the sake of knowing he desired her, unglamorous and spotty as she was.

Smiling as he approached, she tried to free her right breast from its layers of clothing, but then realized to her confusion that he was interested not in her but in the empty teacup. He took it over to his chair, deliberately turning his back so she couldn't see what he was doing. However, the splash of liquid and the smell of whisky were unmistakable. Well, what did she expect? Ralph never watched the news without a drink. A pity, though, that Scotch didn't loosen his tongue. There was so much she wanted to know – the latest on the business front; how he was coping on his own at home; who had written; who had phoned.

She suddenly noticed that his eyes were no longer focused on the screen. What was going through his mind? Money worries? What to have for dinner? Steamy fantasies of females in G-strings rather than muffled up to the eyeballs?

'Ralph,' she said tentatively. 'D'you think we might – ?'

She was interrupted by a knock on the door. 'Oh *no!*' she said. 'Matron!'

Ralph sprang to his feet, upsetting the whisky bottle. He rammed the window open and knocked his pipe out on the sill. There was a sudden exclamation, followed by a curse. 'I've dropped my pipe,' he muttered through clenched teeth.

Another knock.

'Just a minute!' she called, and hissed at Ralph: 'Never mind the pipe. Hide that whisky bottle!'

Ralph darted over to pick it up, then hid it behind the curtain.

After a third knock the door opened a crack. 'I'm sorry, Lorna, is it inconvenient?'

'Oh, Frances, it's you. N . . . no – not at all.' Earlier she had asked Frances to pop in, but of course she hadn't known then that Ralph would turn up out of the blue. 'Frances, this is my husband, Ralph.' Or his back, at least. He was leaning out of the window, trying to see where his pipe had fallen. 'Ralph,' she said sharply, 'I'd like you to meet Frances.'

He turned round, visibly shocked at the sight of a totally bald woman with a pronounced facial twitch, dressed in a moth-eaten fur coat. 'Er, how do you do?' he mumbled.

Frances smiled warmly. 'Hello, Ralph. It's a great pleasure to meet you. Lorna was telling me about you just last night.'

'Yes, Frances and I met two days ago,' Lorna said, in the awkward silence. 'We've discovered we've got a lot in common.' Panic attacks, reclusive husbands, an off-beat sense of humour.

'Did you have a nice Christmas?' Frances asked Ralph as silence loomed again.

'Well, up to a point. How about you?'

Lorna winced. Frances had spent Christmas in a psychiatric hospital and had only just returned to Oakfield House.

'I must admit I've had better ones!' Frances laughed.

Aunt Agnes would be proud of her. It took courage to survive years of severe depression, followed by stomach cancer, and still be able to laugh. 'I'll come back later,' she murmured tactfully.

'No, please . . . '

But she had gone.

'Honestly!' Ralph said. 'These people give me the creeps – going around with shaven heads and wearing coats indoors.'

'Ralph, she's got *cancer*. The chemotherapy made her hair fall out. And she feels the cold because she lost so much weight.'

'Oh, I'm sorry. I didn't realize. But that twitch – it's so off-putting.'

'I know, but worse for her. She finds it frightfully embarrassing. But it's a result of some drug they gave her and she can't do anything about it.'

'It's not good for you to be with all these old fogeys. No wonder you're depressed.'

'I didn't say I was depressed. Anyway, Frances isn't that old. She's only seventy-one.'

'Old enough to be your mother.'

'So what? It doesn't mean we can't be friendly. We had a good laugh last night.'

'I can't think what she's got to laugh about.'

'Well, exactly – that's why I admire her. She's jolly brave.'

Ralph shrugged. 'Look, I've got to go and find my pipe. It's my best Dunhill.'

'Will you be able to see in the dark?'

'I'll manage.' He forced a smile. 'Don't run away!'

He certainly seemed on edge tonight. Was it just post-flu gloom, or something amiss with the business which he was keeping from her? Both perhaps.

While he was gone, she leafed idly through the magazine and, coming across the horoscope page, read his: *'Mercury, the planet of communication, meets easy-going and expansive Jupiter, so don't worry about work, just party the nights away! Your animal magnetism will be too powerful to resist.'*

And hers: *'A perfect week for travel – exotic places, new horizons, the promise of romance . . . '*

Yeah, sure.

She tossed the magazine aside, shivering in the blast of wintry air from the window Ralph had left open.

'You'll die of pneumonia sitting in this draught. If the rash doesn't kill you first, of course.'

'Go away!'

'Rashes can be dangerous, you know,' the Monster continued, unabashed. 'It could be scarlet fever. And even measles can lead to serious complications.'

'I'm watching this programme, if you don't mind.'

The news had finished and a romantic drama was now playing to itself – a smoochy couple enjoying a candlelit dinner at home; flowers on the table, wine chilling in an ice-bucket. The sight of any couple sharing a meal always made her envious, especially when it involved lively or even flirtatious conversation. Soon she would be back to separate trays in separate rooms again. In that respect she'd miss Oak-field House. However vile the food, she was beginning to enjoy the company, having recently moved tables and now sitting with a friend-lier bunch. Even Dorothy Two had revealed a less aggressive side and had invited her to her room to see a stack of photo albums. The record of her life fossilized in two-dimensional prints had been oddly touch-ing – one picture in particular: Dorothy sixty years ago, looking achingly young and glamorous at the wheel of an MG.

She would even miss Sharon, who was confiding in her more and more, asking advice about Danny or his father. It was good to feel use-ful and appreciated rather than sitting in her office with only the com-puter for company.

'I doubt if you'll ever make it to the office. I mean, how are you going to cope with the huge backlog of work when you're in such pain?'

'I'm not listening.'

'It's bound to be something serious, and that'll be the last straw for Ralph. The business will go broke and . . . '

Where *was* Ralph, she wondered, doing her best to ignore the Monster. Had he found his pipe and sneaked off home without bother-ing to say goodbye?

'No, he's had a heart attack. And no wonder, careering around in the dark with flu. He may *say* he's better, but did you notice how pale and gaunt he was?'

'There's someone at the door. That'll be him now.'

'Or a police inspector, more like, come to report his death.'

In walked Sister Kathy. 'Hi, Lorna. How's things? Sorry I didn't stop by earlier – we're up to our eyes as usual.'

'Oh, Kathy, *am* I glad to see you!'

'Why, is something wrong?'

'Not really. It's just that . . . ' Should she show Kathy the rash and get some expert advice, or was she making a fuss about nothing? 'You'll probably think – '

The door burst open and Ralph appeared, his hair dishevelled and a rip in the side of his jacket. 'I've had it with this place! I can't *believe* the way I've been treated.'

Kathy slipped out with a conspiratorial smile at Lorna. '*Men!*' it seemed to say.

'Ralph, whatever's happened?'

'I was only looking for my pipe, for heaven's sake! I was groping about among the dustbins when suddenly this crazy woman starts screaming blue murder and saying there's an intruder trying to get into her room. The next thing I know I get grabbed from behind and frog-marched off to Matron. Who clearly thinks I'm lying through my teeth until she checks your name and room number. They're imbeciles, the lot of them. Just look at the state of my suit!'

'Oh, Ralph, how awful.' It was so unusual for him to explode in fury, she realized how upset he was. But of course he'd been humiliated – a reminder of his school-days, when he'd been derided as a scholarship boy. 'Come and sit on the bed, darling.'

Surprisingly, he did, and when she put her arms around him he clung to her like a drowning man.

'Lorna,' he said, softly, into her hair. 'I *do* miss you. Please come home.'

12

'Come on, Hugh, let's dance.' Olive was pushing back her chair. 'Someone's got to break the ice.'

Hugh rose to his feet with alacrity, clasping his wife's hand in his and placing his other bear-paw on Lorna's shoulder. 'I'm just sorry, Lorna, that I can't ask *you* to dance.'

'Please don't worry,' Lorna said, cringing at his touch, which sent shooting pains down the whole of her left side. 'It's fun for me just to watch.' Fun? God forgive the lie.

'Are you sure you're all right, my dear?' Olive glanced at her in concern. 'You've hardly eaten anything.'

'Yes . . . fine, Olive, thank you. The food's superb.' Determinedly she attacked the meringue with her spoon, surprised it didn't shoot all over the place like the granite-hard specimens at Oakfield House. Thank goodness they had reached the dessert. A five-course dinner wasn't exactly a recommended cure for nausea.

'You're not slimming are you, Lorna?' Clarence's simpering little giggle had been getting on her nerves all evening.

'Good gracious no! I love my food.' Ironic then that she had swallowed scarcely a mouthful of the most splendid meal she had seen in years: venison pâté, crab and caviar tartlet, followed by fillet of sole and beef Wellington, and now rounded off by raspberry pavlova with hazelnut ice-cream. Rather different from the five-o'clock Oakfield repast of tinned spaghetti hoops and sago, or fish cakes and jam tart. She'd also had to decline the succession of château-bottled wines, which meant that, while everyone else became more relaxed and garrulous, *she* sat dismally sober. The dinner seemed interminable. Far from anticipating the stroke of midnight, she felt as if the New Year had long since come and gone, and they were now well into February.

Aware that Clarence was still watching, she forced down a soupçon of ice-cream. It was deliciously rich and creamy, so all the more frustrating that she couldn't do it justice. Also it was unlikely to be alive with germs. She had once seen Hashim use his fingers to scoop ice-cream from the carton into bowls, sneezing between portions and wiping his nose on his hands. Funny the way she kept thinking of the home. She should be glad to have escaped, yet in truth she was missing the place – even feeling uprooted and insecure. This evening, while the food was being served, she had half expected to hear Sharon's acerbic remarks, not the obsequious 'sirs' and 'madams' of the golf club's over-attentive waitresses. And it was somehow odd to be eating a meal unaccompanied by a chorus of choking and coughing. The diners here were perfectly capable of feeding themselves without spillages or dribbling and, as far as she could tell, no one yet had wet their knickers.

Ralph cleared his throat. 'Er, Jackie, would you like to dance?'

Poor Ralph. He hated dancing as much as formal dinners, but Jackie must be courted until he'd secured the contract for the garden job. Olive had thoughtfully seated them together, with Alexander opposite. Throughout the fish course Ralph had done his best to overcome Alexander's resistance to the notion of artificial grass. Fortunately, though, Jackie seemed to be the one who made the decisions and she was 100 per cent in favour.

As Ralph approached the dance-floor, he wore the expression of a hapless victim entering a torture chamber. Lorna hoped no one else had noticed. All was well at least below the neck: the elegant black dinner-suit emphasized his tall, slim build. Jackie was wearing a low-cut mini-dress in racy pink shot silk. Lucky for some, Lorna thought, uncomfortable in the high-necked blouse and long, frumpy skirt she had been obliged to wear to cover both the rash on her top half and the bandage on her foot. And there was the added complication of trying on clothes while hopping about on one leg. Even washing her hair had proved a major challenge. Finally she had managed it by sitting on the floor, drenching the bathroom in the process. (A bath itself was out of the question, since she mustn't get the bandage wet.) If nothing else, a bunion operation taught you how valuable two legs were – essential equipment, in fact, for almost every stage of preparing for an evening out.

With a flourish on the keyboard the band launched into 'Some Enchanted Evening'. Rather an overstatement, she felt, scratching her rash surreptitiously while all eyes were on the dance-floor. Despite his lack of enthusiasm, Ralph was an excellent dancer, but the slow foxtrot was not Jackie's forte, alas. She kept tripping over his feet, apologizing and clutching at his arm, until he began to look as grim as someone bent on hara-kiri. Hugh and Olive, in contrast, might have been contestants on *Come Dancing*, whirling around the floor with professional ease and grace, adding sequences of fancy steps and daring spins and turns.

Lorna watched enviously. They were so in tune with each other's movements they could have been one body. Did they achieve the same harmony in bed, she wondered, and in their marriage generally? She had always longed to be fused with another person, coupled in every sense. Life would be less frightening then, less lonely. From the age of four she had been forced to see how precarious things were. Most children's first experience of death involved a goldfish or pet rabbit, not their parents. But why on earth was she musing on death in the middle of a dinner-dance? Besides, thirty-five years on, she should be over it.

Except you never did get over it.

'I wish *you* could dance like that, Clarence,' Caroline said with an irritable shake of her bangles. (She was wearing so much jewellery she clanked.)

'I can't dance at all,' Clarence sniggered.

'It's nothing to be proud of!'

'Well, I can manage the Gay Gordons at a pinch, and my version of the twist, of course.'

Caroline turned to Lorna with a sigh. 'We'll just have to be wallflowers.'

'Oh, Ralph would be delighted to dance with you, I'm sure.' Lies, more lies. She wished Alexander would come to Caroline's rescue, but he was deep in a golfing conversation with a portly chap on the adjacent table.

'Well, that was the whole problem, Paul. You see, I started well enough with a bogey and two pars, but on the sixth I hit a tree, and after that it was downhill all the way. I four-putted on the eighth, and by the time I . . . '

Lorna found golf even more tedious than bridge, a subject Jackie had already covered at exhaustive length, giving them a blow-by-blow account of every hand in every rubber she had played in a recent tournament. Bemused by two-club openings and grand slams, Lorna had taken refuge in fantasies about the rather ravaged-looking but distinctly dishy double-bassist.

'And did you play in the Centurions?' the portly man droned on, now occupying Olive's chair.

'Yes, that was slightly better. But I blew it on the eighteenth when I was looking at a net sixty-eight. What happened was . . .'

Naked in a four-poster bed (and miraculously rash-less, pain-less and nausea-less), Lorna let the double-bassist pluck her quivering strings. His little goatee beard tickled down her thighs, did amazing things between them. And, conveniently, the vocalist had just broken into the perfect number for a seduction:

'I'd love to make a tour of you,
  The East, West, North and the South of you . . . '

'Yes,' she murmured, opening her North and South to his tantalizing lips.

'Lorna?'

She jumped. 'I'm sorry. What did you say?'

'I was asking about your bad leg. Was it a skiing accident?'

If only. 'Well, it's actually my foot. I, er . . . ' She deliberated whether a congenital deformity would sound better or worse than a bunion. Luckily Clarence came to the rescue by asking if he could finish her meringue.

'Please do,' she urged, wishing he had offered to eat all her other unfinished courses, saving her from seeming picky and ungrateful. The nausea had come on only this morning, and she had no idea whether it was related to the rash or was just a consequence of Oakfield catering.

'Did we tell you', Clarence said between enthusiastic mouthfuls, 'that James's school thinks he should try for Cambridge?'

'Yes,' she said. Repeatedly. She remembered their parental pride from the Kirkwoods' dinner party, way back in September. Since then, it appeared, the teenage prodigy had gone from strength to strength.

'He's got his own web site now,' Caroline said smugly. 'He set it up himself.'

'It's had thousands of hits already,' Clarence added. 'We may be the teeniest bit biased, Lorna, but we just *know* that boy's destined for great things.'

'Mm. Yes. I'm sure.' Was it unkind to wish that the little brat had been strangled at birth? 'Is he your only child?'

'Oh no. Didn't we tell you about Amanda?' Caroline at once rectified the oversight with a run-through of Amanda's CV. Although only twelve, she was already a ballet star, an ace skater, a mathematical genius like her brother, and so strikingly attractive that people stopped in the street to stare. Caroline had got as far as her daughter's equestrian skills (copious cups and rosettes for show-jumping *and* dressage) when Hugh and Olive returned in triumph from the dance-floor, followed by a silent Ralph and Jackie.

'Marvellous band!' Hugh mopped his brow and was about to sit down, changing his mind as the music struck up again with '*Quando, quando*'. 'Caroline, do you samba?'

'Yes, I'd love to.' Ear-rings shimmying and bracelets jangling, she let him lead her on to the floor. Lorna stroked her gold-and-diamond bracelet, which (gallingly) was outsparkled by Jackie's diamond clusters – one ring in particular a veritable Koh-i-noor. Still, it was a good omen for the business. If the Prescotts could afford such conspicuous opulence, they could certainly run to a few square metres of artificial grass.

She gripped her left hand with the right to stop herself from scratching. The rash was itching so badly it was all she could do not to wrench open her blouse and rake at her breast with a fork. If only some magic potion existed to assuage it – *and* the music. They had lowered the lights for the dancing, and her natural inclination was to close her eyes and drift off. The lucky Oakfield residents could sleep through practically any din. (Several of them had snored a lusty descant to the Boxing Day accordion recital.)

'Hardly *lucky*, child. They've nothing to look forward to but further decline and death. You'll get better. They won't.'

'Yes, I know, Aunt. But I do envy them, in bed asleep.'

'Asleep? Most over-eighties are plagued by chronic insomnia. Besides, those poor old souls have lost their friends, homes, hearing, sight and spouses. All of which you are fortunate enough to have.'

'Yes, Aunt, you're right.' Nevertheless, she would give anything to be able to stretch out on the carpet, stomach down. Not only would it ease the ferocious throbbing in her foot, it would also take the pressure off her backside. Being immobile for a fortnight, she had developed a sort of bedsore, and the raw skin on her buttocks made sitting absolute torture. In short, she was a dead loss – unable to sit, stand, dance, drink or eat.

'All right?' Ralph mouthed, noticing her flinch as she shifted position.

She nodded stoically. They were on duty this evening, not here to enjoy themselves. Indeed, the vocalist's erotic undulations and rapturous expression were in marked contrast to Ralph's rigid posture and tight-set jaw. Although, to be fair, Ralph *was* putting on a great display of interest in Alexander's shark-fishing expedition – a performance all the more heroic considering he was suffering serious nicotine withdrawal (smoking was forbidden during the meal). Thus chastened, she turned to Jackie with a smile. 'And are you a golfer?'

'Oh, God, yes! It's the love of my life.'

Lorna found it an impenetrable mystery that tramping around in all weathers in pursuit of a silly little ball could arouse such ardour. The only game she had ever excelled in was snakes and ladders, which she had played on her own as a child with two counters – red for her and blue for her imaginary playmate, Susie. Susie was braver and taller than she was and not frightened of the dark or fireworks.

'Do *you* play, Lorna?'

'No, I'm afraid not.' She caught the disdainful eye of one of the portraits on the wall – a past captain, Hugh had said – nursing in his arms an enormous silver trophy. He looked utterly incredulous that anyone should admit to not playing the king of games. Jackie, of course, would gain his unqualified approval, elaborating as she was on a recent marathon: thirty-six holes a day for seven days. In truth it was hard work following any conversation in the general hubbub, especially with competition from the vocalist's spirited rendering of 'All the Things You Are.'

How romantic the lyrics were – a world away from Ralph's monosyllabic grunts.

> 'You are the promised kiss of springtime
> That makes the lonely winter seem long . . . '

Mr Hughes and her father, both in dinner-jackets, had joined the double-bassist in the four-poster and were singing for her personally. The sole memory she had of her father was, in fact, of him wearing a dinner-jacket, when he had come to kiss her goodnight before leaving for some do. The details were still sharp: the sheen of his silver hair against the sombre black of his suit, the mirror-polished shoes and strangely frivolous bow-tie, the soft graze of his cheek . . .

Enough. Or she would cry.

She returned to Mr Hughes, whose usual obsessive interest in her feet had shifted blissfully upward. He was using his thumb to palpate her nipples as he had once palpated her toes, his eyes smouldering with desire, his voice husky with soon-to-be-consummated passion.

> 'You are the breathless hush of evening
> That trembles on the brink of a lovely song . . . '

'Coffee, madam?'

'Oh, er . . . Yes please.' Coffee would wake her up, stop her drifting off into adolescent reveries. And – relief! – it signalled the end of the meal. She had feared there might be a cheese course, involving yet another charade of enthusing over the food while trying to dispose of it anywhere but in her mouth. Liqueurs were also being offered. She prayed Ralph would refuse. Normally *he* drank and *she* drove, but she wasn't allowed to drive for three or four months, and, although he had been remarkably restrained, he must be close to the limit.

'I'd love a brandy,' he said.

She tried to semaphore caution with her eyebrows, but he was still talking to Alexander about barracudas and carbon-fibre rods, and failed (deliberately?) to notice. If he lost his licence the business would grind to a halt. He *had* to use the car. Just this coming week he was due to measure up and give estimates to two prospective clients in Gloucestershire.

'Do try this water, Ralph,' she said pointedly. 'It's from a natural spring and really rather good.' Who was she kidding? Water for Ralph belonged in taps, or puddles, not in his stomach. The alternative was to go home by cab, but that would entail vast expense and probably hours of waiting.

The band was now playing 'Pennies from Heaven' – an unfortunate choice in that it reminded her she needed to spend a penny, entailing a long trek on crutches to the end of the corridor, then down a flight of stairs. Could she last till 2 a.m.? Unlikely.

'Mm, *petits fours* – yummy!' Clarence stuffed a couple in his mouth, then passed her the dish.

The exquisite marzipan creations decorated with miniature glazed fruits only induced in her another spasm of nausea. 'No thanks, Clarence. I'm . . . full.'

'Full? You've hardly eaten a thing. You ought to see Caroline. She can really pack it away – especially when no one's looking!'

'That's very funny, I must say, coming from Mr Greedy Guts himself!'

To forestall further marital discord, Alexander whisked Caroline off for a waltz, followed by Hugh partnering a giggly Jackie, tottering unsteadily. Avoiding Olive's eye (*she* was now the wallflower), Ralph offered Clarence a cigar. Unable to speak with a mouth full of marzipan, Clarence waved it away; evidently he was intent on demolishing the entire plateful of *petits fours* before the others came back. Ralph, however, lit up and, armed with a Havana and a glass of brandy, began to look more his normal self.

Trying not to think of breathalysers, Lorna watched the dancing with a valiant smile. For some reason the music seemed obsessed with water: there'd already been 'Moon River', 'Raindrops Keep Falling on My Head' and 'How Deep Is the Ocean?'– testing her bladder (*not* as deep as the ocean) to the limit. At last she could bear it no longer. 'Ralph, be a love and pass me my crutches. I'll have to go to the Ladies.'

'I'll come with you,' Olive said. 'I need to powder my nose.'

Making her halting way across the room, Lorna attracted curious glances. Wearing the hospital shoe on her bad foot and a high heel on the good, she walked with an uneven, drunken gait. Olive hovered at her side, moving any impediments and helping her to negotiate the stairs.

'Can you manage now, my dear?' she asked, opening a cubicle door.

'Yes, thanks,' said Lorna, inwardly cursing the fact that, bursting bladder or no, it was impossible to rush. You had to rest your crutches against the wall and balance on one leg while struggling to yank your long skirt up and your knickers down, then finally manoeuvre yourself on to the seat.

When she emerged she was struck by a dizzy spell and had to clutch the basin, dropping one of the crutches with a clatter.

'Lorna, are you OK?' Olive clucked, retrieving the crutch and helping to support her. 'If you don't mind my saying so, you really don't look well.'

'I've got this stupid rash, that's all. It's driving me mad.'

'Rash? Where?' Olive was all concern. 'With four children and seven grandchildren I'm an authority on rashes! Will you let me take a look?'

Lorna flushed. Ralph would be horrified at her baring her breast (literally) to business clients, however well intentioned they might be. Reluctantly she unbuttoned her blouse.

'Good heavens!' Olive exclaimed. 'That's *shingles*, Lorna!'

'Shingles?'

'Yes. I had it myself years ago, and the pain was quite appalling. I was working then and the doctor gave me three weeks off. He said it was incredibly debilitating. And I must admit I did feel terrible.'

'But how do you know it's shingles? Mightn't it just be an allergy or – ?'

'No, it's definitely shingles. You can tell by those scaly blisters, and you only ever get it on one side. I had it on the right side. With you it's on the left. You should be in bed, my dear, not out at a dinner-dance! Look, I'll have a word with Ralph and get him to take you home.'

'No, please . . . I've been such a nuisance already.' She paused, fearing she had said too much, yet tempted to go on. 'You see, I . . . I found it a strain leaving the nursing-home. There are so many stairs at home, for one thing. And so much to do, and . . . and . . . I keep getting weepy and pathetic.'

'I was just the same, Lorna, and that was *without* an operation. Hugh was frightfully worried. I'd burst into tears over nothing.'

'And I feel sick, and . . . '

'So did I. I'm afraid you have to take this seriously, my dear. It often lasts for ages. I had it for over three months.'

Lorna stared at her aghast. Three months?

'There you are,' the Monster cackled. 'Told you so!'

'And if you're not careful you can get a secondary infection in the blisters.'

'Yeah – you're bound to, knowing your luck.' The Monster gave a gloating laugh.

Olive patted her hand kindly. 'I really would advise you to go home.'

She remembered Ralph's anger after her panic attack at Olive and Hugh's. Admittedly this was rather different, but she couldn't let him down again. 'I'd feel awkward disrupting the proceedings, Olive. Look, it's not that long till midnight. I'll stay till then, OK?'

Olive was about to protest, but Lorna got in first. 'I'm fine, Olive, honestly. And I wouldn't want to miss the fireworks.'

The worst lie of all. She detested fireworks.

A squall of rockets zipped the sky apart, cascading down in shards of coloured light. Inside, the walls convulsed with more pulsing, jouncing lights, glittering and blinding. A fanfare from the band lasered through her side, disorienting her with pain and sound combined. Faces loomed and receded. Who were they? Did she know them?

Glasses clinked to glasses, their tiny consoling chinks drowned by the war zone beyond the window – bombs exploding blue and gold.

Someone crushed her in a bear-hug. She tried to smile. More pain. A waft of scent and cigarette smoke as another person kissed her. She swallowed, tasting nausea.

Balloons were showering from the ceiling: dangerous silent bombs. Nothing else was silent: discordant voices rising all around her; mouths opening, shutting, blurring; faces split with scarlet grins.

> 'Should auld acquaintance be forgot
> And never brought to mind . . . '

No! she tried to shout, as she was swept towards the dance-floor. Her legs were paper streamers, her voice a burst balloon.

'Don't worry, Lorna, we've got you! We're holding you nice and tight.'

Strong hurting arms on one side, soft hurting hands the other. She couldn't fall; she wouldn't. She was being shunted round and round in an unsteady, drunken circle. Walls and floor and ceiling circled drunkenly the other way, while the frenzied sky outside rampaged red and silver, so loud, so bright, it was shattering the glass.

Then a voice she knew suddenly rose in warning: 'Careful! She's falling! Oh my God, she's . . . '

13

'Lorna, how are you?' Clare hugged her eagerly.

'Ow! That hurts! I'm sorry, I'm a bit like a vestal virgin at the moment – can't be touched. But it's great to see you. I've missed you.'

'Me too.' Clare perched on the end of the bed. 'Christmas was the usual farce, but yours sounds ten times worse. You do look pretty grotty, I must say.'

'Thanks a lot!'

'How's the foot?' Clare peered curiously at the blood-encrusted toes protruding from a now somewhat grubby bandage.

'Not marvellous. I have the stitches out tomorrow, which means I see my darling surgeon.'

'How are you getting there, with Ralph away? Want me to drive you?'

'It's sweet of you, but no thanks. I've arranged an ambulance on BUPA, believe it or not.'

'I should jolly well think so, considering what you fork out. By the way, you know they've got the wrong name on your door?'

She laughed. 'Yes. Mrs Paterson.'

'Shouldn't you ask them to change it?'

Lorna shifted position to reduce the pressure on her bedsore. 'I've grown to like Mrs Paterson. She has certain qualities Mrs Pearson lacks, so it's quite liberating really.'

Clare gave her an odd look.

'As for Mr Paterson, he's a bigamist, I've decided, who lives contentedly in Penge with the *other* Mrs Paterson.'

'You're nuts.' Clare began pulling things out of her carrier-bag. 'Now then – I've brought all sorts of stuff: vitamin C, lemon barley, echinacea, leeks . . . '

'Leeks?'

'I looked up shingles in my *Natural Cures* book and it said apply honey and raw leek juice to the blisters. We really need a liquidizer to extract the juice. Shall I ask in the kitchen?'

'I shouldn't. The new chef's deaf and dumb.'

'You're joking!'

'No, honestly. They've had a succession of agency cooks since Christmas, but none of them would stay.'

'I'm not surprised, after what Ralph's told me.'

'Oh, he's just biased. Though actually he couldn't wait to get me back here after I collapsed at the golf club. I think he was scared I might peg out on their hallowed premises! Of course he had to eat humble pie after saying all those insulting things to Matron.'

'I can't imagine Ralph eating humble pie.'

'Nor me.'

'So is it really as dire as he says?'

'To tell the truth I quite like it, but perhaps I'm just a masochist. They *are* chronically short of staff. And those they've got do seem rather accident-prone. One's slipped on the ice and dislocated her shoulder, another's gone down with glandular fever, and a third's in hospital with appendicitis.'

'And meanwhile you starve. Ralph said you've lost a stone.'

Lorna shrugged. 'It won't do me any harm. I've no appetite in any case. You can have my lunch if you want – if and when it comes. It's meant to be mixed grill, but what they say and what you get are never quite the same. I don't suppose many people notice – very few of them still have a short-term memory.'

'Actually mixed grill sounds rather good.'

'It may be tripe and onions. You've been warned!' Lorna tensed as a sharp pain seared her chest and side. Aunt Agnes used to tell her that the human body was proof of God's omnipotence – the perfect instrument, the cream of all creation. Even as a child, Lorna had doubted it: if God was so wonderful, why did knees get grazed and noses run? Later in life this view was reinforced. Bodies, and minds more so, seemed unreliable, if not wilfully perverse. And as for the present, any deity that might exist had clearly given up on her: apart from the shingles, she had developed a crop of mouth ulcers, calluses on her hands from the crutches and, a final indignity, chronic constipation.

Clare retrieved a pillow from the floor. 'Lorna, I hate to see you like this. Is there anything I can *do*?'

'Just your being here is great.' Dependable, outspoken Clare always made her feel less unreal. Clare was solid in appearance (stocky and broad-shouldered) and solid gold in character. With her no-nonsense hairstyle and unfashionable clothes, she was striking rather than pretty, although she did have a perfect complexion and distinctive slate-blue eyes.

'Let's try this anyway,' she said, unscrewing the honey jar, 'on its own, without the leek juice.'

Lorna made a face. 'I'm not sure I fancy being all sticky.'

'You never know – it might just work. Come on, show me this rash.'

As Lorna unbuttoned her nightdress, Val's head appeared round the door. 'Hope I'm not intruding . . .'

'Er, no . . . come in.' Lorna hurriedly made herself decent. 'Clare, this is Val, the activities organizer.'

'Nice to meet you, Clare,' Val gushed, proffering a hand which, with honey on her fingers, Clare was obliged to refuse. 'I just came to ask you, Lorna, if you'd like to join us for darts this afternoon.'

'I don't think so, thanks all the same.'

'Well, if you change your mind it starts at two. I'll pop in at quarter to, OK?' And she rustled off in a swirl of yellow frills. (Even in the daytime Val tended to favour cocktail-wear.)

Clare frowned. 'Darts on one leg? Is she mad?'

'Oh, I expect you can play from your wheelchair. Most people here have no legs – at least not in working order.'

Clare suddenly giggled. 'I wonder what she thought – you about to strip off and me advancing on you with a jar of honey! It'll probably be all round the place that we're a couple of weirdo lezzies.'

'There's more than a couple here already, from what I've heard.' She might joke about it, but there was pathos in the fact that, deprived of family visits or contact with the outside world, some of the residents cuddled up together for the only comfort they could find.

'You'd better watch it, Lorna. A young, glamorous slip of a thing like you, they'll be buzzing round in droves!'

Young and glamorous? Lorna glanced from her oozing blisters to her unprepossessing feet. If she had a shred of vanity she would crawl under the covers and pull the sheet right up. But even the thinnest blanket pressed against the bandage, as well as aggravating the rash.

'Now lie back and think of England while I get down to business!'

'Ouch! No, Clare – it's agony. I can't bear you touching me.'

'Sorry, I didn't mean to hurt you. Let me trickle a bit straight from the jar, very, very gently. Better?'

'Yes. *No!* It's going all over the sheets. And they never change the beds here, so I'll be gunged-up for the next two weeks.'

'You're not staying that long, surely?'

'The doctor said two weeks.'

'You'll go bananas!'

Lorna wiped a drool of honey from her stomach. 'It's not all bad, you know. I like the other residents, on the whole. They may be a bit peculiar, but some of them are also very brave and I feel a sort of . . . bond with them. Anyway, it was awful being at home. Even two days got me down. It was as if I were seeing the house with new eyes after being out of it. Normally I'm stuck there day after day, and often on my own. It's terribly isolating, Clare, with no neighbours close by and not a sound from another living soul.'

'It beats me why you don't move. You've never liked the place much.'

'Oh, I couldn't. It would break Ralph's heart. That house is his security, in every sense.'

'What about *you*, though?'

'Mostly I'm OK there. I think it was being so immobile and in pain and everything. And I had this strange feeling of Naomi's presence, as if she was still . . . around, and haunting the place. I mean, it's her home really, not mine. She and Ralph chose the house together. And the fact that she died there does make it rather spooky.'

'Does Ralph ever talk about her?'

'Of course not. You know Ralph. He probably felt guilty, not realizing how sudden the end would be. She'd been ill for ages, you see, and I suppose he assumed the situation wouldn't change. It must have been a dreadful shock for him – though perhaps a relief as well. With a full-time job and an invalid wife it can't have been much of a life.'

'Surely he had some help.'

'Well, yes, a nurse came in in the daytime, but he took over evenings and weekends. In fact I'm sure that's one of the reasons he became rather a recluse. You see, it was always just the two of them, and as Naomi got worse she withdrew into her own world. So he would eat alone and sleep alone and – '

136

'Poor Ralph. It does sound grim. You'd think after that ghastly childhood he'd have picked a nice normal wife.'

'She *was* nice and normal, as far as I can gather. The illness came on unexpectedly, which was hard for Ralph as well as her, because above all else he hates being out of control, and you can't control MS. His natural inclination is to try to put things right, create order out of disorder, and when he can't he feels impotent. I suspect that's part of the trouble at the moment – me being laid up much longer than he thought. He does seem incredibly tense. After I'd talked to him on the phone last night I felt completely wrung out. I have to say I don't relish the prospect of going back to work.'

'Well, why not stay with *me* for a while? Come right away if you want, then at least you'd be shot of this dump. I may not be Florence Nightingale, but I would remember to bring you meals.'

'You're an angel, Clare, but I'm probably better off here.' She couldn't explain, even to Clare, her dread of panic attacks, especially in a small, claustrophobic flat. They were a risk wherever she was, of course, but Oakfield did have night staff, whereas she could hardly wake Clare in the early hours and expect her to cope. How fantastic it would be if friends (or spouses) could take things from you literally, endure them in your stead. Perhaps that should be the definition of true love: if they could they would. But would *she* bear Clare's pain, on top of her own, or Ralph's unspoken fears?

There was a tap on the door: Sharon, with the lunch-tray, and as voluble as ever. 'I should be home in bed, Mrs Pater . . . , not dragging myself up and down these stairs. I've got the galloping trots. I spent all night on the loo. Agony it was. No good telling Matron, though. If you'd got terminal cancer she'd still force you to do your normal shifts.'

'Oh dear, I am sorry.' It occurred to Lorna that since her return to Oakfield House she had spent more time commiserating with the carers over their ailments than vice versa.

Sharon was eyeing Clare. 'If I'd known you had a visitor I'd have brought two cups.'

Lorna refrained from saying that even one cup was an improvement on this morning. Breakfast had been cupless, knifeless, porridgeless and butterless. 'What's for lunch?' she asked, craning her neck to look at the tray.

'It was meant to be mixed grill, but . . . '

Clare and Lorna exchanged glances.

' . . . *this* chef's buggered off now, so it's cold meat and salad. And fresh fruit for afters.'

'Well, that sounds nice and healthy,' Lorna said brightly, her sanguine tone faltering as Sharon put the tray in front of her. Marooned on a large white dinner-plate sat an anorexic slice of luncheon-meat, a quarter of a tomato, three cubes of beetroot in a pool of purple liquid and a teaspoonful of coleslaw distinctly past its prime.

'You're lucky to get anything,' Sharon said, noticing Lorna's grimace. 'The cold meat's just run out. God knows what they'll dredge up for the poor sods in the dining-room.' Suddenly she clutched her stomach and let out a harrowing groan. 'Sorry, must dash – need the loo again.'

'I can't believe it!' Clare said, as the door slammed. 'If that girl's got diarrhoea she shouldn't be working with frail old people. It's criminal, Lorna. And, good grief!' – she gestured to the minuscule apple and shrivelled tangerine – 'they have the cheek to call that fresh fruit?'

Any fruit was a bonus, Lorna thought, pouring some tea for Clare into the cup, and hers into the glass.

Clare took a cautious sip. 'Ugh! It tastes of chlorine.'

'Yes, I'm afraid it often does. It'll kill the germs, though!'

'Lorna, you're incorrigible! You ought to complain.'

Clare didn't understand that it took energy to complain and that she was glad to be allowed simply to lie back and do nothing. At home she would have to hop around doing everything for herself – shopping, cooking, cleaning, ironing – plus answering the phone umpteen times a day and feeling constantly guilty about not pulling her weight in the business.

There was another knock at the door and in walked a cadaverously thin man of about thirty, his long, greasy hair tied back with a flamboyant yellow ribbon. More coarse black hair – whorls of it – covered his arms and sprouted between the buttons of his shirt. Lorna stared at him in trepidation.

'Hello. I new nurse, Antonio.'

'Oh, *parle italiano?*' Clare said, proud of her Beginners' Italian.

Antonio looked blank.

'Are – you – Italian?' Lorna asked slowly and clearly.

'Me Spain.'

'Ah . . . ' Neither she nor Clare knew a word of Spanish. What they needed here was a linguist and a team of psychotherapists – these last for the staff as much as for the patients. Last night she had counselled Sunil, a new carer from Sri Lanka, who did speak (basic) English but who was homesick, anxious and apparently alone in the world. Antonio, too, looked far from cheerful as he handed her her pills, and she caught a whiff of cigarettes and beer on his breath. Comfort in adversity perhaps.

On his way out he was steamrollered aside by another visitor – Anne Spencer-Armitage: just about the last person Lorna wanted to see. 'Oh, Anne . . . How nice.' She managed a weak smile. 'Come in.'

A redundant instruction, as Anne was well and truly in already, and her arrival was anything but nice. For one thing, she and Clare detested each other. She also had the knack (amply demonstrated at the Princess Royal) of leaving you feeling ten times worse than before.

'Good gracious, Lorna, you look absolutely terrible! What have they been *doing* to you?' With a curt nod in Clare's direction, she ensconced herself in the only chair and continued her mission of mercy. 'I hear you've got shingles, you poor darling. When a friend of mine had it it affected the nerves of her face. Post-herpetic neuralgia I think it was called. Anyway, the cornea was scarred, which left her sight permanently impaired.'

Lorna blinked nervously. Even the Monster hadn't mentioned eye damage.

'For Christ's sake, Anne,' Clare snapped, 'Lorna hasn't *got* it on her face.'

'It can spread, though. That's the trouble with shingles. Mavis kept having these new flare-ups just when she thought she was cured. The pain went on for years.'

Lorna swallowed.

'Mind you, at least you got out of hospital alive – that's something, I suppose. Did you see the programme last week about medical negligence? I was utterly appalled. Nearly sixty thousand people die every year just from being in hospital.'

Yes, she *had* seen it. And so of course had the Monster, glued to the screen and positively drooling over the figures.

'And another four hundred thousand are injured.'

Five hundred thousand, according to the Monster.

'That's one in twenty-five patients, Lorna. And it said even minor surgery can be lethal.'

Clare shot her a withering look. 'Quite the little ray of sunshine, aren't we?'

Ignoring her, Anne gave Lorna's arm a condescending pat. 'All things considered, I think you're being amazingly brave. I know what courage it takes to suffer in silence. I've been ill as well, with bronchial asthma.' Whereupon she doubled up in a paroxysm of coughing.

'Well, how kind of you to share it with Lorna.'

Anne was still rasping and snorting, and luckily didn't hear.

'Would you like some lemon barley?' Lorna suggested quickly, to pre-empt further sarcasm from Clare.

'Yes please,' Anne spluttered.

'Damn! There isn't another glass.' Lorna was reluctant to call Sharon in case Anne was infected with the 'galloping trots' on top of bronchial asthma. 'Clare, could you be a darling and wash this glass?' In fact she should have thought to wash it before using it herself: Dorothy Two had said that drinking-glasses frequently doubled as receptacles for false teeth. 'The bathroom's just at the end of the passage.'

Clare departed huffily, banging the door with a vehemence worthy of Sharon. Anne meanwhile rummaged in her bag for her inhaler and took a series of urgent puffs, contorting her face into an expression of martyred agony.

Lorna closed her eyes. Her tolerance of other people's afflictions was beginning to wear thin. Besides, the doctor had told her to rest. Little did he know . . .

'Oh my goodness!' Anne shrieked, jumping up from the chair. 'Now I'm having a hot flush.' She wrenched her coat and scarf off. 'Mind if I open the window? I'm sweltering.'

'No, please do.' It was only minus two outside.

Sharon chose this moment to reappear. 'Oh . . . ' She stopped short at the sight of Anne leaning out of the window, gasping for breath and frantically clawing at the neck of her blouse. 'Bit nippy in here, innit?' she said at last, with a histrionic shiver. 'I've brought a cup for your friend. Your other friend. Where's she gone?'

'To wash a glass.'

'You don't say? She wouldn't like a job here, would she? The dishwasher's packed up. As if we didn't have enough grief . . .'

Between anguished fits of coughing, Anne managed to bark an order at Sharon. 'Fetch me some tea please, Nurse. Earl Grey if you have it.'

'Come again?' Sharon looked perplexed, evidently unfamiliar with any classification of tea beyond strong or milky, with sugar or without.

There was a sudden shrill from a phone. Surprised, Lorna reached for her mobile (a present from Ralph). For some obscure reason it had been displaying an 'Out of Service' message all morning. Had it relented at last?

'It's mine,' Anne said, locating the phone in the depths of her bag. 'Hello? . . . Oh, darling, it's *you* . . . No, I'm terrible – coughing my guts up. And the flushes are just vile. I'm having one this very minute. I'm wet through, literally.'

And I'm frozen stiff, Lorna thought, shivering in her thin nightie as the litany of symptoms rattled on. Maybe it was time she got under the covers, not just to prevent hypothermia but also to conceal her distorted right foot. Clare was used to the bunion, but Anne (wearing enviably smart shoes) must find it rather grotesque. Not that Anne had the energy to concern herself with defective feet.

'Sorry, Katie, no can do. We're going out this evening . . . Yes, dinner, then the theatre . . . It's madness, of course, in my condition. There's a risk of complications if I so much as put my nose out of the door. Basil says I should stay in bed, but you know me, darling – even at death's door I feel duty-bound to soldier on. Yes, speak to you tomorrow – if I'm still in the land of the living.'

On the way back to her chair Anne noticed Lorna's cache of pills. 'Good God! What's that lot for?'

'I'm not sure – pain-killers and stuff.'

Anne stood, arms akimbo, hot flush and coughing fit subsumed in indignation. 'Do you mean to tell me, Lorna Pearson, you're taking drugs without knowing what they are? You could *kill* yourself that way.

Only the other day I was reading about people in residential homes being dosed up to the eyeballs with tranquillizers and sleeping-pills.'

Lorna wouldn't have said no to a few tranquillizers, as an antidote to Anne. Perhaps the Monster had lost his voice and sent her in his place. Whatever, she was doing a marvellous job.

'I wouldn't be surprised if that's why you collapsed. Valium affects your sense of balance.'

'Right on the nail, Anne! They're drugging her deliberately, to beat her into submission. No wonder her bowels won't work. It's the morphine, I expect. It bungs you up – then kills you.'

Lost his voice? What an absurd idea! His squawk was as loud and malevolent as ever. 'Go to hell,' she hissed, before turning to Anne. 'I think these are only ibuprofen.'

'That's nearly as bad. It can cause internal bleeding and stomach ulcers and – '

Clare barged back in, minus the glass. 'Sorry I was so long. I got collared by some weird old boy who didn't seem to know where he was. He kept asking me to take him home.'

'Oh dear. That'll be Arthur. He's ninety-six and his wife's just died. They brought him here against his will.' Lorna had stumbled upon the poor old man herself, wandering around in a daze and desperately repeating, 'I want to go home. Please take me home.'

'Heavens, there's my phone again! Hello? . . . Barbara? . . . Good – I was hoping you'd ring . . . No, I'm *dead* at the moment. The asthma's worse. In fact they've made me an appointment with a lung specialist – best in the country, they say.'

Clare shut the window with a bang. 'You'd better get his name, Lorna. You'll need it if she's given you pneumonia.'

' . . . well, Harley Street, naturally. He got an OBE last year. And he's frightfully well connected. He's married to the Duchess of Kent's second cousin. And his son-in-law's the . . . ' Anne momentarily halted her name-dropping to call out, 'Come in!' in response to a knock on the door.

'Bloody cheek,' Clare muttered. 'Does she think she's taken up residence here?'

'Get *rid* of her,' Lorna mouthed.

'Gladly. Just give me a gun.'

142

'Come in!' Anne carolled again.

And in came bald, fur-coated Frances with the twitch. 'Oh, I'm sorry, Lorna, you're busy.'

'No, please stay!'

Lorna had been touched at how gratefully, even joyously, Frances had greeted her return to Oakfield House. Some of the others, too, had welcomed her back with genuine warmth. They had become her friends, in a sense – Frances especially. 'Sit here, Frances,' she urged, patting the bed and wishing (not for the first time) that there was more than one chair – which Anne, of course, was monopolizing. Clare, meanwhile, stood leaning against the wall, bemused by all the comings and goings.

'Barbara, I'll have to ring off – I can't hear myself speak . . .Yes, I'll keep you updated, darling, but prepare yourself for the worst. He's already said my lungs are in a shocking state.' Anne coughed again, authoritatively.

'Good gracious!' Frances clucked. 'You do sound bad.'

'Yes, I was plagued with bronchitis in childhood. And now' – Anne adopted a wistful, consumptive tone – 'my lungs are affected.'

'How dreadful. Poor you.'

Lorna fumed silently. If anyone deserved compassion it was Frances, who since her early twenties had been in and out of psychiatric hospitals where the regime was not only ineffectual but brutal into the bargain. Anne, however, revelling in the sympathy, continued to elaborate on her parlous condition. 'I can't breathe at night,' she confided. 'And' – lowering her voice – 'I'm going through the change, which is a nightmare, I can tell you.'

Frances doesn't *need* telling, Lorna wanted to shout. Some cretin of a doctor yanked out her womb when she was only twenty-nine, as a cure for her depression. And when she complained about hot flushes they silenced her with years of electric-shock treatment. *That's* a nightmare, Anne.

'I get these fearful sweats. Sometimes I have to change my nightie half a dozen times a night.'

Gingerly Lorna tried to ease her own nightie away from the blisters. The honey had made it stick, while doing nothing to alleviate the itching. Yet, whatever her problems, talking to Frances had made her realize what a lucky escape she'd had. In her twenties she, too, had been unstable and depressed and might well have been incarcerated like Frances in some horrendous institution, had Ralph not come along and saved her.

'It's been going on for years. My GP can't understand it. He says most women of my age – '

'Anne,' said Clare with undisguised hostility, 'I'm sure Frances would like a private word with Lorna. I think it's time we left.'

'Oh, please,' Frances looked dismayed. 'Don't let me drive you away.'

'It's lunch-time,' Clare persisted. 'We're holding everyone up.'

'No, really,' Frances assured her. 'They've told us lunch won't be until two. It seems there's some trouble in the kitchen.'

Just as Lorna was wondering whether a single slice of luncheon-meat might somehow divide into four, Clare pulled the leeks out of her carrier-bag and brandished them in the air. With the other hand she held the honey jar aloft. 'If they're desperate, they're welcome to these. Leeks with honey sauce.'

'It's no laughing matter,' Anne said disapprovingly. 'I consider it gross incompetence, messing the residents about like this.'

'Ye gods! She's finally thinking about someone other than herself.'

'*Clare*,' Anne all but spat at her, 'I find that remark abusive.'

'Me abusive? And what about your . . . '

Frances, caught in the crossfire of insults, hung her head in embarrassment. Then all at once both phones rang, affording a brief lull. *Very* brief. Anne pounced on her mobile and began an animated conversation, raising her voice above the shrilling of the second phone.

'Blast!' Lorna muttered, not yet familiar with the buttons. 'Ah – hello! . . . Ralph! Where are you? . . . Tewkesbury? . . . Stuck where? . . . Outside his house? But surely . . . No, of course I haven't got the address here, Ralph. They're on the database at home. Anyway it *is* Holly Tree House. I remember the name distinctly . . . Darling, I can't go home and look it up, not on crutches. Just a minute . . . Clare's offering to drive me. But there's no point, Ralph. I remember checking the address before you went. And we've no record of him moving . . . '

Ralph's next words were lost in a new spate of coughing from Anne. Undeterred by Clare, she appeared to be demonstrating the critical state of her lungs to yet another friend. Strange she *had* so many friends, Lorna thought uncharitably.

'What, Ralph? I can't hear.'

'Shut up, Anne, for Christ's sake!' Clare's patience had reached breaking-point.

'Do you imagine I'm coughing on purpose?' Anne retorted, dissolving into further gasps and wheezes.

'I'm sorry, Ralph, could you speak a bit louder? . . . No, it's *not* the woman next door – not this time . . . Why don't you ask in the Post Office? . . . Yes, do ring me back. It's worrying. Good luck!'

'What's up?' asked Clare.

Before Lorna could utter a word, the door opened once again. This time it was Dorothy Two, armed with an ancient photo album. And Dorothy Two meant more trouble. She and Frances were almost as incompatible as Clare and Anne: Frances was cowed by Dorothy's abrasive manner, while Dorothy regarded Frances as weak-willed and eccentric. 'I'll come back when you're free, Lorna,' she said, with a disdainful glance at the bald head.

'No, it's OK, honestly. We're just a bit short of chairs. But sit here on the bed.'

Dorothy sat, stiffly, putting as much distance as possible between herself and Frances's fur coat (which had a distressing tendency to moult). As well as the photo album, she was holding a sheet of vellum notepaper covered with spidery writing. 'I came to ask you, Lorna, if you would sign this formal letter of complaint. Someone needs to make a stand. It appears we're not going to eat today at all.'

'Oh, we are!' said Frances earnestly. 'At two o'clock.'

Dorothy ignored her. 'It also happens to be my birthday, and I was promised a birthday cake. But of course there's no hope of that now. In fact I doubt if any more meals will materialize until someone gets to grips with the problems in the kitchen. No wonder all the chefs give notice, when the equipment doesn't work and they have an infestation of woodlice.'

'Woodlice?' Frances cried.

'*And* worse,' Dorothy added darkly.

'Well, happy birthday!' Anne said, off the phone at last.

'Anne, Clare, this is Dorothy,' Lorna mumbled, realizing she had neglected the social niceties in the general mayhem. 'And Frances.'

Once greetings were exchanged, Dorothy took centre stage again. 'I'm not concerned about the cake – it's of no consequence. People of my age shouldn't have birthdays anyway.'

'The older you are, the more reason to celebrate,' Anne declared, herself approaching sixty.

'It's just another year closer to death,' Dorothy countered morosely. 'And death costs a fortune these days. It's a scandal. You can't even buy a plot in advance. I enquired about it recently, and it seems you have to wait until you're dead. A bit late then, wouldn't you say?'

'I only hope they don't cremate me,' Frances put in nervously. 'It's so upsetting, isn't it, when those velvet curtains come across?'

Dorothy gave her a look of contempt. 'You'll hardly be aware of it, in your coffin.'

Frances shuddered. 'It's not natural, being cremated. Jesus wasn't cremated.'

With an imperious gesture, indicating that the subject was now closed, Dorothy handed the vellum sheet to Lorna. 'Could you please sign your name just there, under mine.'

'Er, I'm not sure that . . . ' Lorna was ashamed to realize that in a conflict between principle and personal convenience it was principle she would sacrifice. If she made trouble she might be turfed out, and she wasn't ready to face the brisk, pitiless pace of the able-bodied world. Oakfield House, whatever its deficiencies, had become a sort of refuge. With a look of entreaty at Clare, she mumbled something about not having a pen.

Before Dorothy could produce one, Clare evinced a sudden curiosity in the contents of the photo album. 'Wow! This looks fascinating. May I have a peep? I adore old family photos. Oh, it's holidays – even better. Where's that? Hawaii?'

'Yes. Honolulu.' Dorothy was gratified by Clare's interest. 'I brought them to show Lorna, but you're welcome to look at them too.' She positioned the album for Clare and Lorna to see, excluding Frances deliberately. 'I don't think we got round to these last time, did we, Lorna?'

'No.' Lorna had, however, seen the whole of Dorothy's extensive family, stretching back three generations (plus their various servants, houses and assorted dogs and cats). She had been saddened by the thought that the once attractive Dorothy, with her big house and garden and busy social life, should now be cooped up in one room for much of the day, with little diversion beyond the occasional game of darts or visit from the mobile shop.

'Some of these are spectacular.' Dorothy sighed nostalgically as she leafed through the pages. 'Especially the world cruises.'

'Oh, do you like cruising?' Anne chipped in.

'I did, in the old days. I'm afraid I'm past it now. My husband and I went winter-cruising for many, many years.'

'We love it too,' Anne enthused. 'Have you been on the *Oriana*?'

'Yes, a beautiful ship. Although Henry and I did find the cabins marginally better on the *QE2*.'

Clare and Lorna were displaced as Anne and Dorothy vied in superlatives, comparing exotic destinations, exquisite six-course meals, bewitchingly handsome captains, and sensational sunsets, seascapes, scenery. Which meant that the letter of complaint was conveniently forgotten – much to Lorna's relief.

The relief was short-lived, however, as Oshoba put his head round the door and she blushed scarlet in confusion. She knew he wasn't on duty and had come specifically to see her, to hold her hand, flirt with her outrageously. And as he met her eyes she felt sure that all her visitors could see into her mind, where he was naked and gloriously rampant. Such fantasies had become her nightly fix, but she hardly dared imagine what the racist Dorothy might say about them, or censorious Anne, or lifelong celibate Frances.

'You're busy,' Oshoba said, in his thrilling basso-profundo voice.

Yes, she thought, busy with you, ecstatically entwined . . . 'Mm, I am a bit.'

'I come back later. OK?'

'OK.' Fortunately Clare alone seemed to have witnessed the exchange. Dorothy and Anne were still in the South Pacific.

'Isn't Easter Island out of this world?'

'Yes, absolutely divine. Did you visit the moai statues?'

'But of *course*. And our next stop was Papeete. Mount Orohena just took my breath away.'

Poor Frances looked mutely on, quite out of her depth – *her* travels were confined to brief shuttlings between mental institutions. However, Dorothy's account of an active volcano on Bora Bora was cut short by a rather different kind of eruption: Arthur, bursting in with his flies undone.

'I want to go home,' he wailed. 'Can somebody please take me home?'

'This *is* your home,' Dorothy said sharply, annoyed that her tropical odyssey should be disrupted in full flow.

'No it's not, it's not. Me and Winnie live in Cranbrook Close.'

Clare patted the old man's arm. 'Why don't I take you back to your room instead?'

Thus encouraged, Arthur suddenly thrust a hand up Clare's skirt, using the other hand to manoeuvre his limp and shrivelled member out through his open fly.

'Steady on, old chap!' Clare said, showing remarkable equanimity in the circumstances.

Dorothy, however, sprang to her feet with a yelp of alarm. 'The man should be locked up! We're all in danger of our lives.'

'I quite agree.' Anne rallied to the support of a fellow cruise-enthusiast. 'He should at least be reported for sexual harassment.'

'Come off it, Anne. He's ninety-six and he's just lost his wife. I'd say a little TLC would be more in order.' Clare coaxed the recalcitrant member back into the folds of Arthur's baggy white underpants, then deftly zipped up his fly. Whereupon he, possibly seeing her as Mother, clung to her pathetically, reiterating his former pleas.

'I must go home. I must go home. There's things need doing there. The gas man's coming to see about the boiler.'

'I'd better ring for a nurse,' Lorna said. But, before she could press the bell, her mobile shrilled again. 'Oh, Ralph! Have you had any luck? . . . But surely someone must know? What about the next-door neighbours?'

'I want to go *home*.' The word became a howl of pain.

'What, Ralph? . . . No, I'm OK. It's just someone who's . . . I'm sorry, I don't know what to suggest . . . Why don't you cut your losses and come home?'

'Home. Please take me home.'

'Ralph, can I ring you back? I can't hear a word you're saying. Shit! Who's this?'

Yet another knock, heralding the return of the yellow frills. 'Oh, Val . . . Hello. Just a sec . . . Ralph? Are you still there? . . . Fuck! The phone's gone dead.'

As 'Fuck!' succeeded 'Shit!', Anne and Dorothy turned to her with deeply shocked expressions. 'Sorry,' she murmured wretchedly.

'Take me home!' Arthur quavered.

Val seized his arm with unnecessary force. 'That's quite enough from you, Arthur! Now, Lorna,' she said, trying to make herself heard above his sobs of protest, 'lunch has been postponed again, till three. So we're starting darts early – in five or ten minutes. I wondered if you'd changed your mind about coming?'

Lorna surveyed the assembled company: Arthur cringing and weeping under Val's Gestapo grip; Clare spitting invective at such crass bullying; Anne and Dorothy combining in righteous indignation about tardy meals and sexual perversion; Frances apologizing to all and sundry for being in the way. A game of darts suddenly seemed a most inviting prospect. 'Yes,' she said, 'I'd love to come.'

'Ah, Mrs Pearson – do come through.' Mr Hughes stood smiling at the door of his consulting-room. 'How are you?'

'Fine,' she lied, hobbling in. It was essential that he saw her as attractive, not a mass of blisters and bedsores.

But, as usual, he was interested only in her feet. 'You don't seem to have got the hang of walking on those crutches. Didn't the physio show you?'

'Well, yes, but – '

'You appear to be holding your toes up rather stiffly. Are you in pain?'

'Mm. Quite a bit, actually, but I suppose that's only to be expected.'

He frowned. 'Not at this stage, no. And the foot's been bandaged incorrectly, I see. The big toe should have been held away from the others with adhesive tape.'

She doubted if Oakfield House could run to anything as arcane as adhesive tape. Just asking for a safety-pin was a severe test of their resources – and of Antonio's English. In fact the pin had never materialized, and two hours later, when her bandage unravelled itself completely, Antonio's nursing skill proved to be no better than his linguistic ability.

'Would you sit up here on the couch, please.'

Oh *yes*, she thought, but lie beside me. Hold me. Stroke me. Baby me.

She met his disturbingly dark eyes and looked away in confusion. Her *father* – alone with her and loving her, his face taut and finely chiselled, his hands cool on her throbbing foot.

She had become blasé about the sight of the foot: still swollen like a boxing-glove, but gradually turning from puce to yellow, and mottled with dull reddish-purple streaks.

Mr Hughes was examining the third toe, which, she now noted with alarm, was not only blood-encrusted but oozing a sort of pus. He shook his head in concern. 'I don't like the look of that. It appears to be slightly infected.'

'*Another* infection?' She had only recently finished the antibiotics for the first one.

'I'm afraid it's a pin-tract infection this time, Mrs Pearson.'

'I beg your pardon?'

'The toe's infected around the tip of the wire.'

'What did I tell you? It's one thing after another, just like poor old Job. It'll be a plague of boils next.'

She ignored the Monster's hoot of derision. 'But how on earth did it happen, Mr Hughes?'

'These things do, unfortunately. I'd put it down to bad luck.'

Bad luck or bad nursing? Antonio, she'd noticed, hadn't washed his hands between fingering the boil on his neck and rebandaging her foot. 'So will you have to take the wire out?'

Mr Hughes pondered for a moment. 'No,' he said. 'First we'll try another course of antibiotics. If we remove the pin at this stage we may lose the good position we've achieved.'

Good position? She stared disconsolately at her toes. The big one in particular seemed to have already started curving to the left again. 'I have to say, Mr Hughes, I did hope this toe would be straighter.'

He coaxed the toe back to the right and held it gently but firmly in place. 'I'm afraid we haven't got quite as satisfactory a result as we might have wished.'

She noted the 'we'. Was he suggesting that *she* shared the responsibility? Or did he work in partnership with God? Yet in a way she felt sorry for him. He seemed genuinely disappointed, whereas if she had addressed such critical remarks to Ralph in his present frame of mind he would be instantly on the defensive. When he had phoned last night from Gloucestershire he sounded so tired and tetchy she was almost glad he was too far away to visit her.

'And I am a little worried that the second toe may stiffen,' Mr Hughes observed in his Courvoisier-and-honey voice, handling her foot like a piece of priceless Venetian glass. 'Are you moving it as I asked you?'

'Yes, but it hurts.'

'Nevertheless, it's imperative that you do it every hour. Move it really vigorously, back and forth, back and forth. But otherwise I'd like you to rest as much as you can, with the foot elevated on several pillows. And please only use the crutches for going to the bathroom. I don't want you trying to walk long distances. Is that quite clear?'

'Er, yes.' But how could she lie around with her foot in the air when Ralph needed her to hold the fort at home? Work was getting out of control, he'd said: invoices not sent, quotes not followed up. The travelling was bad enough, without all the paperwork. Yet it was unlike him to complain. In fact he didn't seem his normal self at all. She was used to him being morose, but not downright acrimonious.

'Right, Mrs Pearson, I'd like to see you again in three or four days, to review the situation. Meanwhile Nurse will take the stitches out.'

Don't go, she pleaded silently. All we've talked about is failure. I want to tell you other things – intimate, important things.

But he had already closed the door.

A couple of minutes later, in bustled a pretty young nurse. Lorna envied anyone blessed with two fully functioning feet and an absence of blisters on their breasts, but this girl, with her big blue eyes and cascade of ash-blonde curls, could have sprung from the heaving pages of Mills & Boon. That Mr Hughes might succumb to such charms was almost more than she could bear.

'Hello, Mrs Pearson. I'm Samantha.'

Yes, you would be, Lorna fumed, disliking her even more. Why couldn't she be plain Jane or two-a-penny Susan?

Unabashed, the nurse perched on a stool at Lorna's feet, displaying long, shapely, sun-tanned legs. 'I'd better warn you, this may hurt.'

'What she means', the Monster cackled, 'is that it'll be sheer, bloody purgatory! Just you wait and see.'

There wasn't long to wait. Samantha set about gouging at the stitches with an array of vicious-looking instruments. 'I know it's painful,' she said cheerily, 'but this type of stitch is rather difficult to get out. Your skin's so thin, you see, that Mr Hughes couldn't use absorbable stitches.'

''Course he couldn't, the stupid oaf! And *she*'s no better, is she? Call herself a nurse? She's making a real pig's ear of it. I bet she's not even trained.'

For once the Monster seemed to be right. Despite her strenuous efforts, Samantha hadn't yet managed to remove a single stitch. Lorna had to agree that she must indeed have been chosen purely on the strength of her looks. Image and appearance were, after all, major considerations in private medicine.

'Oh dear' – Samantha sat up suddenly, her baby-blue eyes growing ever bigger as a realization dawned – 'I forgot to give you any painkillers.'

'Typical!' the Monster sneered. 'I expect she's just an ex-model, playing at doctors and nurses until a nice, rich, gullible consultant comes along.'

'Would you like some paracetamol now?' the ex-model enquired.

'Well, yes, I would. But won't they take a while to work?'

'Grab them while you can,' the Monster advised. 'She's so cack-handed you'll be here all day – all night as well, I shouldn't wonder.'

Lorna gulped the tablets down, grateful for the interruption (albeit brief) in the gruesome process of stitch-removal. Samantha continued her digging and delving, and eventually succeeded in extracting the first stitch. One down, thirty to go. Lorna gritted her teeth, hoping the paracetamol would take effect before she expired from the trauma.

After a great deal of sighing and tutting to herself, Samantha finally gave up the struggle. 'I must confess', she giggled, 'I'm not the world's best when it comes to removing stitches – especially brutes like these. I think I'd better ask Mr Hughes to take over. The trouble is, he's seeing another patient, so it might be a bit of a wait.'

'No problem,' Lorna murmured in relief. However long the wait, she knew it would be worthwhile, in every sense.

She closed her eyes and drifted back to childhood. She had fallen over and cut her foot, and her father was bathing the wound in warm water, applying soothing cream. Then he dried her tears, held her close and whispered into her mane of tawny hair, 'Who's the most beautiful, precious girl in all the world?'

'Good gracious!' Val exclaimed as Lorna was wheeled through the front door by two burly ambulancemen. 'Are you all right, my dear?'

'Yes thanks.' Again Lorna felt somewhat embarrassed about the manner of her arrival at Oakfield House. Being ferried by ambulance was all very well if you were in the throes of a heart attack or about to give birth to twins, but it did seem over the top for a minor procedure like having a few stitches out. (Or not out, as the case might be. Even Mr Hughes had failed to dislodge the last two.)

'Shall I take you back to your room?' Val offered. As usual, there wasn't a nurse in sight.

'That's kind of you, Val.' Lorna fumbled in her purse for some change, wondering how much to tip the men. They hadn't been exactly friendly. In fact they had spent the entire journey discussing Chelsea's chances against West Ham (leaving the field free for the Monster to dispense dire warnings about the near-certainty of her being a lifelong cripple). Still, better to be generous. She'd need another ambulance for next week's visit to Mr Hughes, when Ralph would be in Colchester. Infections came expensive.

Val wheeled her down to the lift. 'I do hope you'll come to our next session of darts. It's Thursday again, at two. You were brilliant yesterday. I've never known anyone get a bull's-eye and a triple seventeen the very first time they've played.'

'Oh, it was only beginner's luck,' she demurred.

'Not at all. Darts requires a steady eye and good coordination, both of which you obviously have. And lots of natural talent.'

Lorna smirked at the Monster. 'Hear that?' she said. 'Crippled maybe, but a darts champion in the making.'

15

'Darling, I got another bull's-eye! This afternoon. Everybody clapped!'

'Well done,' Ralph muttered abstractedly. His pipe kept going out – bad-tempered, like its owner.

'It's a marvellous feeling, you know, being good at something without even trying. I'd never have dreamed of playing darts before, but it's actually great fun.'

'I don't know how you do it, with all those ailments you're supposed to have.'

She chose to ignore his sarcasm. 'But that's the point. It takes my mind off things.'

Ralph struck another match, heedless of Oakfield's no-smoking rule. 'And as for the old crocks around here, it's ridiculous for them to play any kind of game in their condition.'

'They enjoy it, Ralph. And some of them have the guts to overcome their condition, as you call it. There's one old chap with Parkinson's whose hand shakes so much he can barely hold the darts. But he insists on having a bash. And there's a lady who's blind, for heaven's sake, who got two darts on the board today. Think what an achievement that is.'

Ralph snapped the spent match in two. 'With any luck euthanasia will be legal when I'm their age.'

'Well, it's a good job *they* don't feel like that. Mostly they have a tremendous will to live. I sat next to a man who's new – Alistair he's called. He used to teach at Oxford and he's had half a dozen books published. He's stuck in a wheelchair with osteoporosis, but it doesn't stop him working. He's writing a sort of thesis on whether machines can ever be conscious. He seemed to take a fancy to me and kept telling me how young I was.'

'I suppose it's all relative.'

Did he have to be so grudging? Alistair had actually taken her hand and held it affectionately in his, and told her she was as pretty as a picture (even though she was dressed in her baggiest, rash-friendly clothes). It did her a power of good to feel appreciated. Compared with the other residents, she *wasn't* bad-looking and certainly a mere baby in their eyes. 'Stay young, stay young!' a woman of ninety-three had urged. And she'd heard Ellen remark wistfully to her neighbour, 'That young Lorna's very fortunate. She'll get out of here. We never will.'

She repositioned her air cushion (provided by Oshoba to reduce the pressure on her bedsore). 'It's funny, Ralph – the darts seemed like an analogy for life. I mean, some people tried so hard and put their heart and soul into doing well. And others got annoyed and carped about the scoring, or accused Val of favouritism. And a few just slumped in their chairs and refused to have a go. Poor Sydney wasn't with it at all. He kept looking out of the window and saying, "There's the bus! Quick, catch the bus!"' She laughed. 'There isn't even a road outside, let alone a bus route. I expect he was harking back to his earlier life. But it struck me as rather symbolic – how important it is not to miss the bus. I've been thinking about it a lot. *They're* too old to make changes, but I'm not. Ralph, are you listening?'

'Mm.'

'Well, can't you say something?'

He got up and paced restlessly about. 'It beats me how this place can call itself a nursing-home when there isn't any nursing. Someone should have *noticed* the wire was getting infected.'

'Oh, Ralph, don't start that again.'

'You just told me to say something.'

'Yes, but not about my foot.'

'And that surgeon! Fancy him admitting he's not pleased with the result. You'd better think seriously before letting him loose on your other foot. You don't want *two* botched operations.'

'Can we change the subject?' She had no wish to be reminded of the second operation – weeks of sitting around immobile again, guzzling pain-killers like Smarties, and, knowing her luck, probably another crop of infections.

He glanced at his watch. 'There's a thing I want to see on *Future World* – a faster type of modem.'

End of conversation.

She lay miserably, watching him take surreptitious sips of Scotch.

Today it was in a hip-flask, no doubt so she couldn't see the level going down. His attempts at cover-up were pathetic. This morning she'd found a whisky-smelling empty Lucozade bottle stuffed down the side of the chair. Ironic, she thought, that although they were not at present under the same roof they did spend an hour together most days – a rare occurrence at home. But these shared hours were becoming increasingly stressful. If only they'd had a child, to make them a proper family. Her failure to carry a baby to full term had never been satisfactorily explained, although she did sometimes wonder if it was connected with her parents' death: because they had died so young, *she* couldn't be a parent. A totally irrational idea, yet . . .

Irritably, Ralph zapped the remote-control. 'The programme doesn't seem to be on.'

'Well, that means we can talk.'

'What d'you want to talk about?'

'Nothing in particular. Just – you know . . . chat.'

'But you can't hear yourself speak with that racket next door.'

'It's only the old girl's television. Surely you're used to it by now.'

'I'll never get used to this place.' He rooted in his pocket for the pipe-cleaners. 'If you want to know, it really gets me down.'

'Gets *you* down? Come off it! You're here for less than an hour a day. And then we never communicate. Every time I open my mouth you snub me.'

'Well, I'm sick of hearing about illness and old age. Can't you lighten up?'

Hurt, she lapsed into silence. She had recounted plenty of funny stories as well as distressing ones, but Ralph was being completely vile for some reason. She had never known him so cantankerous, so lacking in compassion. In fact the thought of returning home filled her with dismay. No more communal meals or companionship, no more reminiscences about pea-soupers, gaslight, Zeppelins, coach-built prams, wedding-dresses made from parachute silk, rice pudding with brown skin on top. For all Oakfield's faults as an institution, just being with the people here had made her think more deeply about life, health, marriage, death. Yet Ralph showed not the slightest interest in such things. It occurred to her that perhaps he was missing sex. If even Arthur, at ninety-six, could make overtures to Clare, then Ralph might well be frustrated. But what was she meant to do about it? Stripping off to reveal a suppurating rash would hardly turn him on. And if she gave him what the professionals called private hand-relief someone was bound to barge in – Frances, maybe, who would die from sheer embarrassment, or Matron, who would eject them both on the spot.

'Darling, come and sit beside me.' She edged over to make room for him on the bed.

The invitation was ill-timed. He was sucking out his pipe to clear a blockage and could only answer with a series of phlegmy gulping noises. How she envied the love and attention he lavished on that pipe! She watched him unscrew the stem and probe it with a pipe-cleaner, finally removing a dollop of black, malodorous gunge. While he was thus preoccupied she wished that, like Anne, she could have phoned her friends on the mobile, but the wretched thing was again displaying an 'Out of Service' message. Out of service, like her and Ralph of late.

All at once he put the pipe down and gripped the arms of his chair so hard his knuckles protruded like a row of marbles. 'Lorna, I . . . I've something to tell you. Something serious.'

The blood drained from her cheeks. The house had burnt down. He'd crashed the car. He had cancer.

'I . . . I don't know what you'll say. I've been lying awake night after night, trying to decide how to break it to you.'

Don't, she begged. I can't take any more bad news.

But that was thoroughly selfish. If Ralph was in trouble he needed help. She studied his face: grim, and grey with tiredness. He was staring down at his lap, unable to meet her eyes. The fact that he had broached the subject yet couldn't bring himself to continue meant it *must* be serious. Lesser concerns he would hide.

'Ralph, what . . . what is it?' She forced the words out, her voice sounding shrill and strained.

He was about to speak when Kathy put her head round the door. 'I'm just going off duty, Lorna, so I thought I'd . . . Oh, sorry, Ralph, I didn't see you. How are you?'

'OK,' he muttered, seizing his pipe and stuffing it in his pocket.

'Did Lorna tell you what a star she was at darts today?'

'Mm.'

'I'm sorry, I'm in the way. I'll make myself scarce.'

'No. Don't.' Suddenly Ralph was on his feet. Grabbing his coat and the hip-flask, he strode to the door. 'I've got to go. I'm late.'

'But Ralph, you were in the middle of – '

'It'll have to wait. A client's ringing at nine and it's already twenty to. I'll phone you tomorrow.' And he hurried out, shouldering Kathy aside. No goodbye. No kiss.

Hesitantly, Kathy came back in. 'I don't want to interfere, Lorna, but what on earth's going on? You look absolutely shattered.'

'Ralph's in a bit of a . . . state.'

'So I see. And last night he was as bad. He nearly bit my head off just for asking if he'd like a cup of tea.'

'You should have offered him a double Scotch!' It wasn't easy to joke when her mind was in such turmoil. She longed to confide in Kathy, but it would be disloyal to Ralph, and she'd said far too much already about their peculiar marriage. Ralph preferred to maintain the pretence that they were a conventional couple, sharing meals and a bed.

Kathy settled herself in the chair. 'I've nothing to go home for, so if you want a chat, feel free.'

'Thanks, Kathy, you're a darling. But I don't actually know what's wrong. He seems awfully tense. And preoccupied. And drinking even more than usual.'

Kathy kicked off her shoes and curled her feet underneath her. 'I'm not sure if I ought to say this, Lorna, but d'you think he might be having an affair?'

'Oh *no* – not Ralph.'

'How can you be certain? You say he's always travelling. Well, you wouldn't even know.'

'He's . . . he's not the type. He believes in marriage and fidelity and all that sort of stuff.'

Kathy gave a snort. 'That's the line Don used to take. He swore blind there was no one else – until I found her photo in his wallet.'

'Kathy's right. He's met someone on one of his trips and fallen madly in love. And now she's pregnant.'

Lorna closed her eyes. She couldn't cope with the Monster on top of everything else. Surely Ralph wouldn't cheat on her – it just didn't seem in character. But perhaps he was beginning to weary of her panics and all her medical problems recently.

'Yes, he's sick to the back teeth of you. He's found a girl in the pink of health, with nerves of steel and a huge bank balance.'

She pressed her hands against her head. If she were to lose Ralph, as she had lost Tom, and her father . . .

'Lorna, are you all right?'

She nodded.

'I didn't mean to upset you. I just hate to see you so cut up over Ralph. Is he really worth it? Forgive me being blunt, but I don't know why you stay with him.'

'Oh, I couldn't function without him.'

'But you could, Lorna – that's the whole point. You keep telling yourself he's strong and you're weak, but it's not true. If you ask me, he's the weak one, relying on booze and nicotine just to stop him falling apart.'

'You don't understand. When I met him, it was *me* who was falling apart. God knows where I'd have ended up if he hadn't come along and saved me.'

'But don't you see? – that was the myth he wanted to create: the great protector, keeping you from harm. How marvellous for his ego! Don was the same – the great protector who beat me black and blue.'

'But Ralph isn't violent. He's never laid a finger on me.'

'Yes, but he's such a grouch.'

'Only because he's stressed.'

'That's no excuse. *We're* stressed, you and me, but we don't go round snapping at everyone.'

Lorna winced as a pain skewered through her chest and side. 'He doesn't normally snap. He's just not himself at the moment. And he has good points, don't forget. When he came on Sunday he wheeled me round the grounds for a whole hour. And he takes my dirty clothes home and brings them back washed and ironed.'

'Big deal! You wouldn't say that about a woman, would you? It'd just be taken for granted that she'd do her husband's laundry.'

'Exactly. That's why Ralph's the exception. Loads of men are useless around the house. In any case, look what he has to put up with – my stupid fears, and being stuck here out of action, and – '

'Yes, but most of the time he gets a wife who's extremely capable, and more or less runs his business.'

'I don't, Kathy! I'm just a glorified secretary. In fact I *was* his secretary to start with.'

'Really? I didn't know that.'

'Well, it was ages ago. We both worked at Atlantic Plastics. He was one of their top engineers, and I was his general factotum. But the company went bust in the recession, so we found ourselves out of a job. That's when he decided to set up his own business and he asked if I'd like to come and work for him.' How amazed she'd been that Mr Important (Inscrutable) Pearson should require the services of the scatty and self-conscious Miss Maguire with her ponytail and bitten nails. 'So I swapped my grotty bedsit in Staines for a four-bedroomed house in Queen's Hill Drive.'

'You married for money, you mean?' Kathy said with a complicit grin.

'Certainly not! I may have been naïve, but the thought never even occurred to me. Besides, we weren't married at that stage. I just moved in to save the hassle of travelling. I didn't have a car and the buses were practically non-existent, especially at night. We often worked till nine or ten, you see, and – '

'And when did he first swoop?'

'Oh, it wasn't like that. His wife had recently died and he was terribly cut up about it.'

'You mean the two of you shared a house and he never laid a finger on you? Don't you think that's odd?'

'No, I think it was rather decent. I was at a pretty low ebb myself. I'd just been ditched by a guy called Tom, and . . . You don't want to hear all this.'

'I do. I'm interested. It sounds to me as if you both married out of need. He was bereaved and you were dumped, so it was a good solution at the time. But maybe now you ought to look at things more critically. It's a bit like your crutches, if you'll pardon the analogy. You rely on them at present to get about, but soon you'll be able to do without them.'

Lorna was too shocked to answer. Do without Ralph? What a glib, unfeeling remark!

'I mean, what's in the marriage for *you*?'

'A lot! Love, and sex . . . And security.' She broke off. Kathy *wasn't* glib or unfeeling.

'It doesn't sound as if you're secure. You told me you're always worried about the business.'

Yes, *and* the bills, Lorna thought. And sex was so sporadic. But perhaps only because he was involved with someone else.

'Dead right!' the Monster chortled. 'Why d'you think he dashed off just now? Not to take a client's call but to jump into bed with his fancy-woman.'

'Anyway, Ralph's ancient. He looks more like your father than your husband.'

Lorna flushed. It was a comment that never failed to wound and invariably made her defensive. 'You've got the wrong idea about our marriage, Kathy. On the whole it's worked out well. But two years ago the business ran into a bad patch, and that put us under pressure. It just seemed to be one thing after another. For instance, we quoted for a big council project – a leisure complex, with tennis-courts, bowling-greens and an all-purpose pitch and running-track. It would have been a fantastic job and brought in masses more work. We spent ages planning it, attending endless meetings with surveyors and local councillors, but then the budget was drastically cut and they cancelled – just like that. And not long afterwards one of our best clients went bankrupt and he owed us thousands of pounds. We never recovered any of it, even though we . . . I'm sorry, Kathy, I'm boring you.'

'Not at all. But the way I see it, you're using the business as an excuse for more deep-seated problems between you and Ralph.'

Was Kathy right? She couldn't tell, couldn't think coherently. She was too worried about the bombshell waiting to drop.

Kathy got up to pull the curtains. She was the only nurse to bother with such details – small things but significant, like making sure the water-jug was filled, or asking how you were each morning and wishing you goodnight. 'I shouldn't really tell you this, but quite a few of the male carers have got the hots for you. You're so attractive you could get any guy you wanted.'

'Don't be ridiculous, Kathy! I look an absolute fright.'

'There you go again – putting yourself down. Don't you see? – that's part of it. When I was married I lost every shred of confidence. I let Don walk all over me. But I'll never allow it to happen again.'

Lorna scratched miserably at her rash. Because Kathy had escaped a destructive marriage, she saw everything in terms of herself and Don. The situation with Ralph was more complex. Admittedly the relationship left a lot to be desired, but they did have things in common – negative things, maybe, but no less important for that. They had each started out with a mistrust of life, an experience of grief and loss that had left them nervous yet longing for commitment. They had both lain awake at their respective boarding-schools, wishing they were less different from the others, with proper parents and a house that felt like home. And, although it was so long ago, it had forged a bond between them – one Kathy could never fathom.

'Some bond!' the Monster sneered. 'He's leaving you. Tonight.'

'Don't be silly. He wouldn't just walk out.'

'It may be something worse, of course. They've discovered a tumour on the lung. I mean, he can't expect to smoke and drink without –'

The Monster's words were drowned by a sudden crash outside the door, followed by a cascade of breaking china.

Kathy jumped. 'What's that, for heaven's sake? Your hot drink gone for a burton by the sound of it.'

'What hot drink? I never get one. Well, apart from tea at four.'

'Really, Lorna? That's bad! You should have Ovaltine or Horlicks every evening. I'll make sure it's sorted out.'

'Don't worry, I'm not fussed. I can't stand Horlicks anyway.'

'That's not the point. It's my job to see that the care assistants do what they're paid to do, which includes offering every patient a bedtime drink. In fact I'll go and have a word with someone now.'

'But you're meant to be off duty.'

'It doesn't matter. The night nurse may not realize. She's a new girl, from an agency.'

Kathy must be dead on her feet. She'd been rushing around since half past eight this morning, combining the roles of nurse, carer, administrator and even activities assistant: she had sat through the whole of the darts session, helping those with the shakes, removing a lady who'd soiled herself, bringing pills for Sydney, and comforting a poor old thing who was convinced she'd been sent away from home as a punishment for stealing sweets – although in Kathy's eyes no patient was ever a 'poor old thing'. She treated them all with the utmost respect – which couldn't be said of most of the other staff.

Kathy slipped her shoes back on. 'In any case, I must leave you to rest. I've been talking far too long. You look exhausted.'

'I'm . . . fine.' Never had 'fine' seemed so insincere. Her entire world could be in ruins. As soon as Kathy had gone she planned to ring Ralph, to confirm he was in fact at home. No, she couldn't – the wretched mobile didn't work. Had he given her a faulty one on purpose, so she couldn't check up on him? Now she was being paranoid.

'Goodnight,' Kathy called from the door. 'Sleep well. I'll get someone to bring your pills.'

Sleep well? No chance. True, she *had* been sleeping better (with the aid of ear-plugs and stronger pain-killers) but tonight a thousand new fears would conspire to keep her awake. Kathy didn't realize how vulnerable she was. She needed Ralph – needed him alive and healthy and faithful.

'He's probably unfaithful *and* dead,' the Monster sniggered. 'You know what happens when men of his age start shagging a new bird. The excitement's too much and they cop it on the job. A few groans of ecstasy and bingo! – their heart gives out.'

'Look, will you kindly leave and not come back?'

'No way! I want to be here when they break the news. I wonder who'll come first – a policeman or a reporter from the *Sun*? Or maybe the other woman's husband, brandishing a carving-knife.'

The Monster had barely finished speaking when there was a knock at the door. Lorna closed her eyes. Was it one of them already?

'Hello, dear. I've brought your sleeping-pills.'

Lorna looked at the nurse in surprise. She had been written up for antibiotics and pain-killers, but not for sleeping-pills.

'You are Mrs Murray, I take it?'

Couldn't the woman read? It said 'Mrs Paterson' clearly on the door. Unless they'd got it wrong again.

Decisively she sat up. 'Yes,' she said, 'Mrs Murray – that's me.' She held out her hand for the pills and swallowed them at once. Whatever the deception involved, she damn well *would* get some sleep tonight.

16

Lorna scrabbled at the earth with her bare hands. She must get them out. They were under the ground, in a box. But the soil was so hard it broke her nails.

'Mummy!' she shouted. 'Daddy! Where are you? I can't find you.'

'Stop that noise at once! You'll wake the other girls.'

Suddenly she was lying in the dormitory with Miss O'Donnell looming over her bed. Miss O'Donnell's breath smelt like dead chrysanthemums; her eyes were tiny, dangerous points of fire, glinting in the darkness; her voice was a nutmeg-grater.

'Every night the same – it's high time you pulled yourself together.'

She opened her eyes. Miss O'Donnell vanished. And it wasn't even dark. She had gone to sleep with the light on. She looked at her hands – not a trace of mud, although she had been digging for her parents all night. And she seemed still ensnared in that terrifying childhood confusion about where her parents were. Aunt Agnes said in heaven, Uncle Neil said underground. But Uncle Neil wasn't her real uncle, so maybe he was lying.

There were other puzzling things. Why didn't she have grandparents, like most children? Were they, too, underground? And why would no one answer when she asked where babies came from, or why you couldn't see God?

She peered at her watch: 1.15. What use were sleeping-pills if they only put you under for three hours? Put you under. She shuddered. It was years before she saw her parents' grave. And then her first reaction was surprise that they should have so many names. Not Mummy but Margaret Anna Martha Rose. And her father's names took up two whole lines: Garret Michael David Alexander. Their ages were there too. She knew it was rude to ask people how old they were, so it seemed odd to write their ages on the gravestone for everyone to see. And Daddy's age was wrong. He couldn't be fifty-two. Fifty-two was terribly old and Daddy wasn't old. In fact, gazing at the headstone, she'd felt more and more uneasy. Parents didn't live in boxes underground. They had run away, more likely, but no one dared to tell her.

None the less, most nights she continued digging. Even after marrying Ralph she'd had dead-parents dreams. He'd been kind when she woke up screaming, despite his months of disrupted sleep.

Yesterday's conversation suddenly flooded through her brain like a tide of dirty water. She sat up with a start. *Ralph!* Where was he? In his bed or someone else's? If he left her she would be orphaned again – although at least she would be spared his gloominess. She tried to imagine being married to a man who laughed and joked, confided in her, cuddled her; who loved parties, outings, fun. No, not possible: she had too many fears. Except Kathy disagreed. Kathy regarded her as strong.

Strong? Just now she felt as helpless as a child without a mother, as bewildered as the man at darts who'd kept saying, 'I don't know.' Every question put to him received the same response: 'I don't know.' 'I don't know.' 'I don't know.'

Lorna had recognized the fear in his eyes. It was terrible, not knowing. When the girls at school had asked her where her parents were, she often said, 'I don't know.' It was safer than saying dead. Dead was like damn – a word that got you into trouble.

'*Help!*' she whispered, tempted to press the call-bell. But then that agency nurse would come and there'd be more trouble about pretending to be Mrs Murray.

She clenched her fists. She *would* be Mrs Murray. Happy, calm, content. And inseparable from her husband after sixty years of marriage, still deeply in love.

Nonsense! Mrs Murray was probably a widow, alone, depressed and ill. Anyway, *she* was stuck with Ralph's name: Mrs Ralph Pearson. Ralph's creation – his lackey, Kathy would say, trapped in a marriage based on weakness. Yet without him she would crumble. Already a roller-coaster of panic was heaving through her stomach. She levered herself out of bed and, not bothering with her special shoe, seized her crutches and made for the door. She couldn't stay a moment longer in this claustrophobic room; the walls were closing in around her, the ceiling pressing down. She must get out and speak to someone – anyone, just to make contact with reality.

In the corridor, she steadied herself against the wall. The sleeping-pills had left her feeling hung-over and with a foul taste in her mouth.

It was deathly quiet as she limped along the passage. Were all the patients drugged? And where were the staff? Normally at night you heard them moving about and chatting, or answering patients' bells. Terrified, she doubled back to the staircase and tried to negotiate the steps. The second floor had twice as many rooms; surely she would find a nurse down there.

No one. The same morgue-like quiet prevailed. Perhaps this was another nightmare and she was in the realm of the dead, still seeking her lost parents. She glanced up at the windows: blank black squares like the gaping mouths of graves.

Heart pounding, she hobbled along the corridor. Most of the doors stood open and she could see ghostly white shapes in the beds. That could be *her* one day, lying helpless, awaiting death.

Suddenly there was a shout of 'Nurse!' from a room a few doors down.

Thank Christ, she thought – now someone will come: someone living, able-bodied. But there was no response at all.

'Nurse! Nurse!' The cry grew more insistent, increasing her own panic. She had become one with the unseen patient, begging for a lifeline. But still no nurse appeared.

She paused outside the room, listening to the frantic voice. In the absence of staff, *she* would have to help. Timidly she knocked, and ventured in. 'Is there anything I can do?' she asked.

The bundle in the bed stared at her in fright and she realized how peculiar she must look: an apparition in a long white nightdress, hair awry, and stumping about on crutches, one foot bandaged, one bare. 'I'm sorry,' she said gently. 'I didn't mean to alarm you. I'm a patient here too, and I wondered what was wrong.'

The woman looked shame-faced. She was a shapeless creature, with rheumy eyes and straight grey hair clipped back in a plastic slide. 'Well, I've wet the bed, you see. I'm sorry – I didn't mean to, only I can't get out on my own, and when I ring no one ever comes. It's gone cold now. It feels horrid. Do you think you could change the sheets?'

Not a practical proposition on crutches, even if she knew where the clean linen was kept. 'I'll . . . get someone,' she said, wondering who and how. At least her panic attack had been halted in its tracks. Fear had turned to anger – that the residents should be so shamefully neglected. Along the entire length of the corridor she didn't find a single member of staff. Then suddenly there was a sound of giggling from behind a closed door. Opening it a crack, she saw a buxom black nurse lying on a sofa in the arms of Sunil, the male carer from Sri Lanka. Her gaze strayed to the carpet, littered with incriminating objects: a wine bottle and two glasses, an ashtray studded with fag-ends, and a pair of white lace knickers – presumably the nurse's. Brilliant! While the patients called in vain for help, the staff spent their time smoking, drinking and shagging. She coughed loudly and they sprang apart.

'There's a patient needs you,' she said curtly.

The nurse had the grace to look embarrassed as she smoothed her crumpled uniform, but her tone was aggressive in the extreme. 'And what are *you* doing down here, may I ask?'

'I couldn't sleep.'

'That's no reason to go prowling about.'

'I needed some pain-killers and there's no one on duty up there.'

'Excuse me but there most certainly is. Oshoba's on duty. And Janet. Go back to your room and I'll phone through for Janet to bring you some aspirin.'

'I don't want aspirin. I want an explanation. What's the point of patients having bells if you never take any notice? There's a poor lady along the passage getting cold in wet sheets. And yesterday Sydney fell out of bed and it was over two hours before anyone discovered him. He could have been lying unconscious for all you lot cared.'

The nurse drew herself up to her full height. (Sunil had already fled.) 'How dare you speak to me like that?'

'Because I'm utterly disgusted! This place is a scandal. Kathy's the only decent member of staff, and she's rushed off her feet. *You'*ll be old one day, and then you'll know what it feels like to be stuck in a cold, wet bed.'

'Stop shouting, Mrs Pearson. You'll wake the patients.'

'They're already awake, some of them, calling for help, but you're so busy necking on the sofa, you – '

'That's outrageous! I shall tell Matron what you said.'

'Please do. I'm sure she'll be interested to know what her staff get up to.'

The nurse turned on her heel and stalked off.

Lorna stood trembling, with triumph, anger, fear. She had spoken up for Kathy's sake. Kathy was too professional to admit that Oakfield House was badly run, but it was obvious to anyone. And the patients were mostly too ill or confused to know their rights, let alone demand them.

She steadied herself on her crutches, overcome by a wave of dizziness. What the hell had she done? They would probably expel her now, as they had tried to do at school. (And, unlike school, she didn't want to leave, whatever the abuses.) It was only her word against the nurse's, and Matron was duty-bound to support the staff, especially after that business with Ralph's pipe.

God! She had forgotten about Ralph, and that she didn't know what was happening in his life. If they sent her home tomorrow she might find him already gone.

'Ah, Lorna, *there* you are!'

Hearing the familiar deep voice, she looked up in relief. 'Oh, Oshoba!' she said, and clung to him. He put his arms around her and she realized with a jolt that Ralph would never hold her so close. Often when she tried to hug him he would back off or pull away, as if such contact was emasculating.

Oshoba was even stroking her hair. 'I saw you were missing from your room,' he said, 'so I came downstairs to find you. What's wrong, my lovely lady?'

'I've just shouted at a nurse and – '

'That's not the end of the world!'

'No, but the reason I was angry is that no one here seems to . . . care.'

'I care. I care about you especially. You know that. Remember, I brought you the chocolate. And the bar of lavender soap.'

She wiped her eyes. 'Yes, you did.' A succession of little treats. Treats that had meant a lot.

He took her elbow and guided her towards the stairs. 'And the cream for your bedsores.'

'Yes. You're an angel.' She leaned on him gratefully as they made their slow way up.

'How *are* the bedsores?'

'Not good.'

'Maybe we should bandage them.'

She smiled, despite herself. A bandage on her bum?

'You're smiling! That's better. You have a very beautiful smile, Lorna.'

Pathetic how his flattery could cheer her. Yet he seemed a genuinely decent person – in fact he and Kathy were the only two unfailingly compassionate staff.

'And is the rash any better?'

'Not really. Still itching like mad!'

In her room, he took the crutches from her and rested them against the wall, then lifted her bodily on to the bed.

'No, Oshoba,' she protested. 'I'm too heavy.'

'Not at all. You're as light as a feather.' He peered intently at her foot. 'And how are those poor toes of yours?'

'A bit messy, I'm afraid.'

Unexpectedly, he leaned over and planted an ardent kiss on the blood-encrusted toes. Lorna was dumbstruck. Here was a man she scarcely knew, who had not only embraced her but was now performing an intimate act of devotion more suited to a parent or a spouse. Yet Ralph, her husband of eleven years, would no more dream of kissing her foot than of stripping naked in Hyde Park. The gesture was so potent it was as if Oshoba had healed her foot – instantly, miraculously; made her feel that, even with the infection and the scar, she could climb a mountain, run a marathon.

'Now, before I leave you to sleep, I'm going to bring you a cold compress for the blisters.'

'No, really, Oshoba, don't bother. I know how busy you are.'

'It isn't any bother. I want to make you comfortable, and it'll help cool the irritation.'

He returned with a small metal bowl of water, a folded piece of gauze and a bottle of calamine lotion. He placed them on the bedside table, then dipped the gauze in the water and wrung it out.

'I'll do it,' she said, embarrassed. Surely an untrained male care assistant wouldn't presume to bathe the rash himself.

'OK.' He plumped the pillows behind her and helped her sit up.

'Thanks, Oshoba. That's fine.'

But still he made no move to leave – indeed, his broad, burly figure seemed to fill the room. Below his smart white tunic he wore patched blue jeans: a strange combination of the professional and the casual. The jeans were very tight, she noticed, defining every muscle of his legs, and the musky scent of his hair-oil lingered in the air, overlaying the usual Oakfield smell of urine.

'Use the compress while it's cold,' he urged.

'Yes . . . of course.' Self-consciously she picked up the gauze and dabbed it on her throat.

'No, not like that. I'll show you.' He sat beside her on the bed and eased her nightdress down, to expose her left breast. She knew she ought to stop him, yet she was intrigued by the sight of his black, black hands applying the compress to her pale, pale skin. The coldness of it made her gasp.

'Yes, it is a bit of a shock,' he smiled.

A shock in every sense. Here she was, half-naked and alone with him, as she had been in her fantasies. Those fantasies had become daringly erotic. Every night and morning she would draft him in to pleasure her.

He pressed a little harder – pain and pleasure mixed: the rash still smarted, but the texture of the gauze was wonderfully sensuous against her breast.

'Nice?' he said.

She nodded. Did he need to ask when he could see her nipples were erect? Yet his face betrayed no emotion as he moved the compress back and forth, in slow, deliberate circles. Was he aware of the effect he was having? Far from being cooled, her whole body was on fire. And she was still fascinated by his hands: the size of them, the breadth; the contrast of the paler palms and the pinkish sheen of the nails.

'Now I'll pat it dry and put some calamine on.'

The soft graze of the towel was tantalizing, his velvet fingers more so as they glided around the nipple, rubbing in the lotion. Don't stop, she wanted to plead. Keep doing this all night.

But he stood up, wiped his hands and pulled her nightie back over her breast. 'There – that should feel better. Now where's that cream for the bedsores?'

'Here. In the drawer.'

He uncapped the jar and coaxed her on to her side.

Cheeks flaming, she made a token show of resistance, although her emotions were a turmoil of excitement, shame, desire.

He, however, remained detached and simply said, 'It's easier if I do it. You can't reach.'

As he drew aside her nightdress and began to apply the Vasocrem, she could only surrender to the sensations: the exquisite contrast of warm hands and cool cream. The soft pads of his fingers brushed across her skin and she let her breath out in a guilty, moaning sigh.

'I'm sorry. Did I hurt you?'

'No . . . no.'

He used just the right amount of pressure, massaging in the cream yet causing no discomfort. His touch was assured but leisurely, as if she were the only Oakfield patient and his sole concern was to serve her.

Or was it more than service? She was becoming disturbingly aware that his fingers were straying ever further, until they reached the crease between her buttocks. Nor did they rest there, but explored the crease, idling to and fro, across it and between. She tensed against him, making a desperate effort to stop – stop herself, stop him.

'Oshoba, we mustn't . . . This is wrong.'

Wrong. And magical. He seemed to know by instinct just how to stir her senses, work her up to such a pitch that she had to bite her lip to keep silent. It was imperative to maintain the charade that they were patient and carer engaged in a medical procedure.

Yet Oshoba must be aware that she was responding – indeed he was inflaming that response as he inserted just one finger and probed gently, deeper, deeper. She shut her eyes and pictured him stretched naked beside her: the gleaming expanse of blackberry-coloured skin, the springy pubic hair, the penis . . . Black? Pale-tipped? She longed to turn and face him, cup the penis in her hands, make this encounter mutual, total, real.

No . . . it was already real enough. He was driving her to the ecstatic point of almost-no-return, only to withdraw his finger teasingly, then slip it in again. Her back was arching up beneath his hands, her breathing fast and fractured. Nothing else existed save the pressure of that finger, so intense and yet so subtle that any moment, any moment, she was going to explode.

'Oh, Oshoba,' she gasped. 'Oh, *Oshoba*.'

II

17

A pity, Lorna reflected, that humans hadn't been created with double the number of hands. She could do with them just now – to carry her stick, umbrella, suitcase and bag, and a couple more to stop her hair blowing across her face and dab her eyes, watering in the wind. March had come in like the proverbial lion, roaring its defiance with hail, snow, sleet and storms. Still, whatever the weather, it was a relief to escape to the countryside and leave everything behind for one weekend. There were even signs of spring: waterlogged catkins nodding at their reflections in the swollen sludge-brown stream; rooks flapping overhead with unwieldy cargoes of sticks. Years ago, at the time of the miscarriages, she had envied the birds building nests for a whole clutch of young . . .

She put down her case to give her arm a rest. There was no rest from the wind, however, which had seized her coat and scarf in its teeth and was trying to wrest them off. The stick made walking difficult, as did the clomping boots Mr Hughes had advised her to wear, even though they made her feel like a navvy, and also hurt the scar, which had gone red, ridged and uncomfortably hard. She had asked him if it would fade.

'A scar is for ever, Mrs Pearson.'

Ralph had said diamonds were for ever, although for all she knew he might have bought some other woman diamonds. She still had no idea what his 'serious' problem was. Seven weeks had passed since his first mention of it, yet he'd made no further effort to explain. Nor had she pressed him – partly out of fear of being told bad news and partly from guilt about Oshoba.

Even thinking about Oshoba brought her out in a cold sweat. She should never have set foot in his flat. 'Just come for a coffee,' he'd said, and admittedly they hadn't moved from the kitchen. But she had let him kiss her, let him half-undress her, and if his brother hadn't barged in God knows how far they might have gone. Whatever Ralph was up to, she was in no position to adopt a high moral tone when she had behaved so badly herself.

She walked on, past the village church, where an elderly man was sheltering in the porch. Her stint in the nursing-home had made her more aware of the old. Before, they'd been invisible; now she saw them everywhere: dithering, tottering, fumbling their way through a world that valued youth and strength over experience and maturity. She still missed Oakfield House. Things were so fraught at home she sometimes wished she could return there as a patient, instead of struggling to hold a business together, look after a big house and cope with Ralph's strange moods.

The rain had started again as she reached the familiar gate, which, she noticed with surprise, was loose on its hinges and hanging at a perilous angle. It wasn't like Aunt Agnes to allow a gate to sag. In fact the cottage looked shabby altogether. The paint had blistered on the window-sills, several tiles were missing from the roof, and the garden was neglected: the once sternly pruned rose-bushes now gangling and unruly.

She rang the bell and heard a protracted bout of coughing before the door was opened. She stared in shock at the whey-faced, stick-thin woman with hair like straw and deep shadows beneath her eyes. Agnes looked years older and had lost at least two stone. The voice, though, was as brusque as ever.

'Good gracious, Lorna, you're soaked to the skin! Where's the car?'

'I came by train. I'm still not allowed to drive.'

'Why on earth didn't you say? I'd have ordered you a taxi from the station.'

'Look, a bit of wet won't hurt. What matters is how are *you*?'

'Fancy walking all that way. *And* on a stick. Come in and get dry.'

'Aunt . . . are you all right?'

'Never mind about me. Take off that wet coat and put this woolly on.'

The habit of obedience was so deeply ingrained that Lorna meekly slipped into the home-knitted yellow cardigan Agnes was holding out. Well, an extra layer would be useful – the house was cold and smelt of damp.

'Cup of tea?'

'Yes please. *I*'ll do it.'

'You will not. In my house I make the tea. Anyway, I don't want you in the kitchen under my feet. The fire's on in the sitting-room. It should be warm in there.'

Tepid. And the room, like its owner, was clearly in decline. It was neat, of course, and clean, but long, mouse-coloured fingers of damp were seeping through the wall, the blue carpet had faded to grey, and even the gas fire was wheezing and complaining. As she sat down in a saggy chair (draped with a rug to hide a tear in the cover), Lorna realized to her shame that it must be a year since she had last visited. She had meant to come before the operation, but she and Ralph had been so incredibly busy. And then she'd been immobile for weeks and . . .

Agnes appeared with a towel. 'Here, dry your hair on this. I see you haven't had it cut.'

'Ralph likes it long.'

'Well, I *don't*. Frankly, it's a mess, Lorna.'

'I know. But in this wind . . . '

'How *is* Ralph?'

'OK.' Silent, brooding and more tense than ever.

'And how's the foot?'

'Fine.'

'Then why are you walking with a stick? The operation was months ago.'

'Eleven weeks. But . . . various things went wrong.'

'After paying all that money?'

'Yes. In fact the surgeon says he won't know until my six-months check how well I'll be able to walk in the end.'

'Disgraceful! Those doctors should be shot.'

Lorna winced at the thought of her precious Mr Hughes meeting so brutal an end. 'We ought to have been made with skateboards for feet, instead of all these complicated bones.'

Her attempt to lighten the tone was wasted on Aunt Agnes, who said simply, 'Sit up *straight*, Lorna. No wonder you've got a bad back. Is it any better?'

'Mm, a bit. But that's quite enough about me. How are you?'

'I'll tell you when I've made the tea. I baked a cake – the one you like, with the chocolate butter icing.'

'Oh, Aunt, you shouldn't have.'

'And why not, pray? It's not often I see you these days.'

Lorna stifled another pang of guilt. It wasn't just 'these days': her visits had always been sporadic. She tended to excuse herself on the grounds that Agnes lived in the back of beyond – a pathetic excuse.

'Do you still take all that sugar in your tea?'

'Only two.'

'It's bad for you. I've been telling you for years.'

'Everything's bad for you, so they say. Coffee, tea, red meat, and certainly cake with chocolate butter icing!'

Agnes had the grace to smile. 'I'll cut you a nice big piece. It's only cold meat for supper. I don't find it easy to cook these days.'

'Yes. What's wrong? You don't look well. Is your arthritis worse?'

'Oh, that's a minor detail.' Agnes dismissed two hip replacements and stiff, distorted finger-joints. In silence, she cut the cake, poured the tea and eventually settled herself in her chair. 'I've got cancer, Lorna. They diagnosed it in January.'

'*Cancer?*' The very thing she had feared for Ralph – still feared, in fact, among a host of other possible reasons for his malaise.

'Yes, lung cancer. Serves me right for smoking.'

'But you never smoked.'

'That's what you think! I took it up when you first came to live with me.'

Her previous guilt was nothing to this. Had she given her aunt a terminal illness? 'Was I *that* bad?'

'Oh, it wasn't you, my dear. It was the shock.'

'You mean the accident?'

'That and everything else. But never mind – we muddled through. And I kept my little vice a secret. I smoked mostly at school, between lessons, although I did retreat to my bedroom for the odd illicit cigarette while you were playing downstairs or outside.'

'But how was it I never knew? – later, at least.'

'There's a lot you never knew. Understandably. You were very much locked in your own world. It was partly my fault. I didn't tell you anything. Perhaps I should have been more open. But at the time I was trying to spare you.'

'Spare me?'

'The cancer's inoperable, Lorna. They give me six months at the most.' Agnes spoke as matter-of-factly as if she were reading out a shopping-list. 'And now that I'm at the end of my life I've been looking back and seeing where I made mistakes.'

Lorna glanced at the photo on the mantelpiece: a dark-haired, strapping Agnes holding by the hand a timid five-year-old – both doing their best to smile. Her only relative was going to die. Horribly. Painfully. She might even be dead by the summer. 'Is there no treatment you can have? Radiotherapy? Or chemo?'

'What's the point, at my age?'

Agnes had always been old. Older than other children's mothers. Older than her real mother. Old in her ways, her dress. 'You're not even eighty yet. Some people at Oakfield House weren't far off a hundred.'

Agnes gave a shudder. 'I've no intention of going on that long. And as for ending my days in a nursing-home, it would drive me to distraction. No, I've lived quite long enough.'

'Don't say that.'

'It's perfectly true. What good am I to anyone? It was different when I was teaching, or trying to bring you up. I had a sense of purpose then. Your father was very ambitious for you, which is why I had to be strict. Mind you, I wonder now if that was wise.'

'Look, forget about me. What we need to – '

'Forget about you? How could I? You're the most important person in my life.'

'I am?'

'Well, who else, for heaven's sake?'

'Your . . . your pupils, maybe. Or Celia.'

'Celia died last month.'

'Oh, I'm sorry. How awful.' Celia was Agnes's closest friend, the companion of many holidays.

'As for my pupils, how on earth could they mean more to me than my sister's only child? I adored my sister, Lorna.'

'Yes, I know.'

'You don't know. As I said, you know very little. In fact these last few weeks I've been trying to decide how much I ought to tell you.'

'What d'you mean?'

'Drink your tea before it gets cold.'

Mechanically, Lorna picked up her cup. What was all this stuff she didn't know? The cancer itself was a terrible shock. And that it had been diagnosed in January yet Agnes hadn't mentioned it until now. How badly that reflected on *her* – the busy (selfish) niece who mustn't be bothered. The smoking was also a bolt from the blue, although it made Agnes seem more human and it was surely understandable in the circumstances: a single woman with a demanding job being suddenly landed with a traumatized orphan.

Agnes was coughing again – a racking cough deep in her chest.

'Can I get you a glass of water?'

'No, for goodness' sake sit still. It's difficult enough talking about your father, without you jumping up and down like a jack-in-the-box.'

'We're not talking about my father, are we?'

Agnes muffled another cough in her handkerchief. 'We have to, Lorna. There's something I feel you ought to know.'

Lorna tensed. Agnes's forceful voice had become unexpectedly flat and forlorn. 'Yes?' she prompted uneasily.

Agnes sat bolt upright in her chair. 'He killed your mother.'

'*What?*'

Agnes gave a mirthless laugh. 'Oh, I don't mean deliberately. But the night he crashed the car he was blind drunk.'

'You're lying! I don't believe you.'

Agnes remained silent, although she couldn't disguise the hurt on her face. Agnes never lied. She was the only person Lorna knew who would never tell even the tiniest untruth.

'I'm sorry, Aunt. That was rude. But . . . but I just can't take it in.'

'No, of course you can't. Perhaps I shouldn't have told you. It's not easy to know what to do for the best. Though one thing I *am* clear about – I owe you an apology.'

'What for?'

'Sending you to Grange Park. I knew it was wrong and I knew you were unhappy there. I should have taken you away.'

'But I thought my father –'

'Yes, he chose it. Silly man.'

'Silly? Why? You always told me what a good school it was.'

'Not good for a motherless child. And not good for you to be so far away. Your father was a romantic, Lorna, and also, I'm afraid, something of a snob. He fell in love with the place because it was ancient and historical and had once been the home of the Earl of Stockwood. He and your mother toured the country looking for the perfect school. He did love you, Lorna, and he certainly wanted the best for you. The trouble was, he lived in a dream world. For instance, you might think they'd have consulted me about your education, as a trained teacher with twenty years' experience. But because I worked in a village school he thought I was the lowest of the low. My opinion counted for nothing.'

'Look, why are you being so horrible about him? It's jealousy, I assume – because my mother married and you didn't.' OK, it was hurtful, but Agnes had hurt her first, practically accusing her father of murder.

Agnes took a slow, reflective sip of tea. 'It's true I wished that Margaret hadn't married him. I'm not talking about the age difference. That needn't be a problem, as you and Ralph have found. But Garret was so wild – a crazy, starry-eyed Irish fantasist, who swept the poor girl off her feet and then gambled away all the money.'

Lorna gripped the arms of her chair. Her father a *gambler* as well as a drunk? Could she be hearing right? 'That isn't true. It can't be. He paid for my schooling, didn't he?'

More protracted coughing from Agnes, which angered Lorna suddenly. Was it a convenient way of blocking out what she didn't want to hear?

'Well, *didn't* he?' she repeated, louder.

'He certainly intended to, my dear. He was obsessed with schools from the moment you were born – probably because his own education was . . . well, sketchy, shall we say.'

'Stop rubbishing him, for God's sake!' An ignoramus now, on top of all the rest.

'Lorna, please . . . I'm trying to explain. He put your name down for Grange Park when you were only tiny. Your mother wasn't keen on you boarding, but he could always charm her into doing what he wanted. He set up an endowment fund to cover the fees, so you could go there from eight to eighteen.'

'Well, that was decent of him, wasn't it? And generous. At least he was thinking ahead.'

'No, it wasn't quite like that. The money ran out when you were ten. I'm sorry to say he had a chronic drink problem, and it often clouded his judgement. So when he made his investments – '

Lorna sprang up from her chair. 'I'm not listening to any more of this. You're determined to run him down. I'm leaving!'

'Don't be silly, Lorna. You've only just arrived.'

'Oh, silly, am I? Like him, you mean. Except he *wasn't* silly – he was wonderful. You're just too eaten up with jealousy to see it.' Lorna slammed out of the room and wrenched open the front door. How dare Agnes turn her beloved father into a feckless alcoholic?

She blundered out into the lane, heedless of what she was doing or where she was going. Horrific images curdled in her mind: her father lolling drunkenly at the wheel, or flinging his last £50 note on the gaming-table, or risking all he owned in crackpot schemes. She sobbed aloud with frustration – and with pain from her stupid foot. Without her stick every step was difficult and she kept tripping on the wet ground. Vicious as ever, the wind continued to harry her, whipping her hair across her face, shaking trees as if they were frail poppies, ripping the storm-clouds to shreds. She understood its fury. Fury at her aunt's vindictiveness; fury at her father's criminal negligence. No, she didn't believe it, couldn't. It was a lie – a colossal lie.

Agnes didn't lie.

She stumbled to a halt. Flurries of rain were spitting in her face, drenching her thin skirt. She sheltered in the lee of a hedge, trying desperately to suppress the allegations and instead summon up convincing, concrete memories of a good and honourable father. In truth, she barely remembered him. He was little more than a fantasy, concocted from hints and dreams. For all she knew he *might* have been wild and feckless – like her, now, storming out in the rain because Agnes had shattered her dreams so cruelly.

Agnes wasn't cruel.

Bewildered, she brushed the rain from her hair. There had been such a web of secrecy over the past. *Had* her father been a drunkard – the man she'd imagined as a hero? Agnes's remarks were surely prompted by spite.

Agnes wasn't spiteful.

Strict, yes, curt, yes, bossy and opinionated, but not deliberately unkind. It was *she* who was unkind: perpetually too busy to visit, and thus unaware until today that her aunt was ill or that Celia had died. The two friends had spent Christmas together in a second-rate hotel – a joyless time, no doubt, with both of them in the shadow of death and reliant on each other in the absence of any relatives. Agnes never made demands; if she was neglected for a year she didn't complain. She was used to coping on her own – it was what she had always done.

On impulse, Lorna turned back towards the cottage. Hunched against the wind, she hobbled on, scarcely able to see in the leaden, murky light. Dusk had fallen, although it was only four o'clock. The day had lost heart, as if it no longer had the will or strength to keep the night at bay.

The cottage, too, stood unlit. Lorna felt a surge of panic. Normally Agnes switched the lights on at the first sign of darkness. Suppose she were dead already? It would be like her parents' death again – no goodbyes, no last words.

Ignoring her painful foot, she strode up to the front door. Although the bell shrilled loudly, no one came. Frantic now, she darted round the side of the house to see if the back door was unlocked.

Yes, thank God. She hurried in, not daring to think what she might find. Nervously she peered into the sitting-room. Agnes was still in her chair – not dead, not even asleep, just staring at the wall with expressionless eyes. A scum had formed on her cup of tea; the gas fire had gone out. The room was dim and chilly. Lorna groped her way over to the chair. 'I'm sorry, Aunt. I'm so sorry.'

Agnes shook her head, unable to speak. Tears were sliding down her face.

Agnes never cried.

Lorna took her hand. The swollen fingers were cold. 'I shouldn't have run out like that . . . '

Agnes rubbed her eyes vigorously with a handkerchief, as if angry that they had betrayed her. 'It's I who should apologize. I made a grave mistake. I thought you'd prefer to know the truth, but I was wrong. I didn't realize how upset you'd be.'

'It's OK. It was . . . just the shock.'

'I know. I understand. But I'm not sure *you* do, Lorna.' Agnes got up to turn on the lamp by the window and stood supporting herself on the sill. 'I've been going through all my possessions, turfing out as much as I could. The clothes were no problem. They're too big for me now and Oxfam were glad to take them off my hands. But, when it came to the other things, I was faced with a dilemma. Some of them I felt sure you'd want – your drawings and letters and school reports and so on.'

'You kept all that?'

'Well, naturally I did. It's your history in a way. You were my *child*, Lorna, and a mother keeps everything.' Agnes folded her handkerchief and tucked it back into her sleeve. 'But, as well as all your handiwork, I'd saved the newspaper cuttings of the car crash, and the details of the post-mortem. And your mother's letters to me when she and Garret were having financial troubles. So I had to ask myself, "Do I throw all this away and say nothing, or hand it over as your legacy, unwelcome or no?" After much deliberation I decided on the latter – mistakenly, it appears.'

Lorna sat in silence. Press cuttings, post-mortems . . . Brutal facts damning her poor father. But didn't he deserve it? Killing her mother, leaving her an orphan? If he hadn't crashed that car, her whole life would have been different. And Agnes's too.

'I have to admit, Lorna, that there was another, more selfish, motive. I wanted to justify myself for not being able to leave you more in my will. This house is yours, of course, but I'm afraid it's riddled with dry rot, so I doubt you'll get much for it except the value of the land, which won't exactly be a fortune in this neck of the woods. No, please don't interrupt, and on no account thank me. I'd have left you a good deal more if I hadn't got myself into debt.'

Another shock. Debt was anathema to Agnes. It was one of her maxims in life that what you couldn't afford you didn't have.

'It wasn't easy to pay the Grange Park fees on a teacher's salary. I remortgaged the house, which of course was bigger than this one. That helped, but it wasn't sufficient. I took out a loan at an extortionate rate of interest, and the payments continued for years.' Agnes shook her head impatiently. 'But that's quite enough about financial matters. I don't want the subject mentioned any more. The important thing is that we both survived.' She went back to her chair, coughing again and breathless. Taking a sip of cold tea, she gave Lorna an affectionate glance. 'I can tell you, my dear, I was very proud when you left Grange Park with the Sixth Form Prize.'

'A prize for Effort, wasn't it?' Lorna said acidly. 'I suppose that was the only prize they could possibly award to a dunce like me.'

'You weren't a dunce. And there's nothing wrong with effort. That's what life's about.'

'Is it?'

'Definitely.'

'Well, in that case I'm a dunce at life.'

'Nonsense. You've always done your best, from childhood on. Look at your drawings and letters, and read those school reports. I'll get them out for you now and you can decide what you want to keep. Then I'm going upstairs to rest.'

'Oh, I'm sorry, Aunt – I've worn you out.'

'Not at all. It's the cancer that makes me tired. Anyway, I need to use my nebulizer.'

'Your what?'

'It's a machine to help my asthma.'

'I didn't know you had asthma.'

'It's of no consequence. Don't fuss.'

'But all these ghastly illnesses . . . it must be hard to bear.'

Agnes shrugged. 'More a nuisance than anything else. The tumour's pressing on my oesophagus, so I can't eat much except slops. But there's a kind soul in the village who keeps me supplied with Complan. Her husband's a builder, conveniently. He installed a shower for me at a very reasonable price. I can't get in and out of the bath, you see, but that's due more to the arthritis. And as for the asthma, it just makes me wheeze a bit. But enough of this dreary talk. We all have to die of something.'

'But how will you cope? I mean, later – if . . . when . . . '

'I'll cross that bridge when I come to it. Now for goodness' sake get out of those wet clothes. You don't want rheumatism, do you? You can change upstairs in your room. I put the fire on there at lunch-time to take the chill off. And while you're getting dressed I'll go and fetch your drawings and things.'

'I can do that.'

'I'm not completely incapable, Lorna! And once I'm dead I'll have plenty of time to sit around and do nothing.'

Lorna couldn't help smiling. If there *were* an afterlife, she was sure Agnes would be bustling about, instructing the angels to sit up straight or set to and polish their haloes.

She took her case upstairs and unpacked, putting her presents for Agnes on the bed – a box of chocolate truffles, when her aunt could eat only slops; Radox herbal bath salts, when she could no longer get in or out of a bath; a Treasures of the National Gallery calendar (meant to have been posted in December), when she had less than six months to live. As well as inappropriate, the presents seemed rather stingy. After a life of financial struggle, didn't her aunt deserve a king's ransom? Yet she had never spoken of the struggle, nor had she cast the slightest aspersion on her brother-in-law before. How tragic that her adored sister Margaret should marry a man who would kill his bride within five years. Agnes had every right to be bitter.

Except she never was.

Having changed her clothes, Lorna went down to the sitting-room. On the table lay a pile of folders, each clearly marked: 'Lorna's Drawings', 'Lorna's School Reports', 'Lorna's Letters from Grange Park', 'Lorna's Baby Teeth' . . .

Teeth! Had Agnes kept even those? She opened the folder and drew out a series of small envelopes, inscribed in her aunt's neat hand: 'Lorna's left front tooth, November 2nd, 1969', 'Lorna's bottom right tooth, February 23rd, 1972', and so on and so on – all her milk teeth, chronicled and dated. She slit open the first of the envelopes: the tooth inside was still white and pearly, and scarcely bigger than a grain of rice. She had been rewarded for each one with a silver sixpence under her pillow, left by the Tooth Fairy. Tooth Fairy Agnes; Father Christmas Agnes – so many roles her aunt had played. She leafed through the certificates for piano and recorder, swimming and cycling. It was Agnes who had made her practise, walked with her to lessons, bought her the bike, taught her how to ride it, supervised her sessions in the pool. A life's work; a labour of love.

In the folder marked 'Lorna's Cards', she found a sheaf of home-made creations coloured in garish crayons or decorated with pressed leaves and flowers: Birthday, Christmas, Mother's Day – all made for

Aunt Agnes. 'Thank you for being my Mumy' was written on one of the Mother's Day cards in a smudged and childish script. 'I hope you will never leve me.'

Agnes never had.

Next she read the letters. Letters to her parents, begging them to come back; a letter to Father Christmas asking for a paintbox (which, she recalled, had duly appeared). And countless notes to Agnes, all stressing the same theme. 'I love you more than anywon else', 'I will love you for ever and ever', 'I love you as much as this' – with a picture of a tree so tall its topmost branches soared right off the page. Had it been genuine love or simple insecurity, a child clinging to the only adult left?

There was also a drawing of a fairy queen with silver crown and wand, surrounded by a retinue of elves. Underneath was written, 'Daer Fairis, please please please bring my Mumy and Dady back please.'

She sat looking at it for a few moments, then returned everything to the folders, fetched a tray from the kitchen and started clearing away the tea things. Better to keep busy than indulge in pointless self-pity. As Agnes would say, the devil finds work for idle hands.

Her slice of cake lay untouched. Every year Agnes would make her a birthday cake, with candles on the top and icing-sugar animals. Yet in spite of such devotion, and her own protestations of love, she had come to regard her aunt as a harridan. Why, she wondered now, had she turned hostile in her teens? To cast herself as a victim? To idealize her parents? Or was it just adolescent spleen (another burden poor Agnes had to bear)?

Without bothering to sit down, she ate the slice of cake – ravenously, feverishly, devouring every crumb. Then she cut a second piece and stuffed it into her mouth, scooping up the last stray fragments and licking the icing from her fingers.

'*Manners*, child! You're not a monkey. Monkeys cram their food in like that. Little girls eat nicely.'

Agnes's voice had been sounding in her head for thirty-five years. Would it be silenced when her aunt was dead? Ironically, she suspected she might miss it.

In the annexe off the kitchen she found the table laid for supper:

embroidered cloth and napkins, best rose-printed china, ivory-handled butter-knife. 'Use the proper knife for the butter, Lorna, not your greasy one. And a napkin isn't a plaything. Put it back on your lap.'

She drew out a chair and seated herself at the table. There was chutney in a cut-glass dish, fruit in a porcelain bowl. Glass and china contrasted sadly with the dire state of the walls. Tendrils of grey mould sprouted upward from the skirting-boards, imprinting an alien pattern on the wallpaper. Damp was bad enough; worse was the dry rot, eating like an unseen cancer into the fabric of the house. Which would crumble first – Agnes or her cottage? Clearly there was no money for repairs.

She closed her eyes, remembering childhood meals. Thousands of times she and her aunt had eaten together: she learning the weighty business of manners and the necessity of clearing your plate. Disgusting things like ox-liver and swede had to be completely finished before you were allowed syrup sponge or red jelly in a rabbit mould. Strange how she'd forgotten Agnes's food: fat, floured, comforting rissoles; knobbly bacon joints served with pickled beetroot and pease pudding; home-baked soda-bread with a tough crust and a soft heart.

These days her meals were solitary. Ralph would be slumped in front of the television with a plate on his lap and a whisky at his elbow, while she nibbled bits and pieces in the kitchen.

She heard Agnes coming down the stairs, not at her usual brisk pace but laboriously, taking the steps one at a time, like a child. In the old days her aunt would never have dreamed of having an afternoon nap. Honest toil was the norm, from dawn to dusk.

'Lorna? Where are you?'

Quickly she got up from the table and started rinsing teacups in the sink. 'Here, in the kitchen.'

'What *are* you doing washing up? You ought to be resting that foot of yours.'

'Listen, Aunt – '

'No, you listen to me – this is important. Before I die I want to know I'm forgiven.'

'Forgiven?'

'Yes. For upsetting you just now. And for getting so much wrong when you were small. I don't believe in excuses, but I think it's true to say that I wasn't cut out to be a mother. I never intended to have children myself, nor even to get married, despite what you said about my being jealous of Margaret.'

Agnes was never jealous. 'I . . . I'm sorry, Aunt.'

'That's all right. It was a misunderstanding on both sides, like others in the past. When Margaret died I didn't know how to deal with my grief. Or yours. You used to have nightmares and wake up screaming, and sometimes you'd sleepwalk, which was a dreadful worry for me. And another thing – if ever you found a dead bird you'd pick it up and put it in a bush or tree, as if that would restore it to life. You even did it with dead leaves – you'd try to stick them back on the branches and cry when they fell off.'

She remembered almost nothing of this. Had she blanked it out on purpose in order to survive? Yet what a trial it must have been for Agnes.

'And I'd often find you talking out loud to your parents, or writing them letters. Before their death you'd been an adventurous child, but you began to develop all sorts of fears. You were frightened of the dark, and ghosts, and dogs, and even feathers. And when I took you swimming you wouldn't put your head under water even for a second. I wasn't sure how to handle it. What I did know was that *one* of us had to be strong. So I tried to establish order and regularity, and provide boundaries, to make you more secure. I probably went too far and overdid the discipline, but you see I feared you might inherit your father's . . . wildness. In your teens you did show signs of it.'

'Did I?' She recalled only surly disobedience and private sulks in her room. Although when she'd left home there had of course been the long succession of men (before Tom appeared on the scene) – mostly older and married and mannerless, sometimes even cruel. Why had she let them near her? Perhaps she did take after her father. The new unreliable father could well have had affairs.

'Yes, and I reacted badly. I hope you understand.'

Lorna nodded. She did understand. At last. She had been wrong about so many things: criticizing Agnes as parsimonious when she had been saddled with a legacy of debt; blaming her unfairly for the horrors of Grange Park; resenting her brusque manner, which, like Ralph, she adopted purely as a defence weapon. And, again like Ralph, she never gave way to self-pity, nor expected gratitude. Yet her strength had held the home together, provided continuity.

She went over and clasped Agnes in her arms. She was shocked by the feel of the scrawny body, the lack of flesh to cover the sharp bones. She said nothing. There was too much to say.

18

'Ralph, I wish you'd listen!'

'I am listening.'

'No you're not.' Lorna kicked off her slipper and massaged her toes. 'I've been away the whole weekend. Surely we can talk for five minutes.'

'You've been talking non-stop since you got in.'

'That isn't true.' She had been too tired to talk after the journey: hours and dismal hours on cold, late, crowded trains. Only now, after a hot bath and a hot toddy, was she reviving. 'And I doubt if you've heard a single word. What did I say last?'

'That Agnes was mending a sock – '

'A stocking. Oh, I know it sounds trivial, but it was so pathetic, Ralph – all that effort darning a thing she might only wear a few more times. It reminded me of when she used to mend the sheets, turn them sides to middle to give them an extra lease of life. I kept wishing I could do that for *her*.'

'I can't understand why you're so fond of her all of a sudden. I thought she treated you so badly.'

'No, she actually treated me well. It's just that I didn't see it. Admittedly she was strict – she still is. But she's strict with herself too. I mean, she must be in a lot of pain, but she didn't mention it once.'

She watched Ralph prowl around the room, focused, as usual, on his pipe. Was he listening even now? The time she'd spent with Agnes, talking, sharing confidences, had made her realize how long it was since she and Ralph had communicated in any sort of depth. 'You don't seem interested in anything I've said. I might as well have saved my breath.'

'I *am* interested, but what do you expect me to do? I can't work miracles or change the past.'

Lorna pulled off the other slipper. Her feet were sore and throbbing. 'Actually, there *is* a way we can help.'

'Mm?' Ralph was staring morosely out of the dark uncurtained window. It was still raining half-heartedly, occasional spits and gusts spattering the glass.

'Draw the curtains, will you, and sit down. Then I'll tell you.'

'I'll just get a drink.'

'You're drinking an awful lot these days.'

'Not quite in your father's league,' he grunted.

'Ralph, that's . . . *vile!*' Surely he knew how devastated she was. Now that she'd read the pathologist's report, there was no denying the facts: 320 milligrams of alcohol per hundred millilitres of blood. Criminally high. And the injuries were unspeakable: her father's skull smashed to pieces and gaping lacerations on both legs; her mother's thigh and pelvis fractured, along with seven ribs. Yet Ralph could use it as a way of scoring cheap points.

Eventually he sat down, in the chair furthest from hers. 'Well?'

'I've got a sort of . . . plan,' she said, trying to dispel the gory images of her parents' mangled bodies. 'I know you'll probably come up with all sorts of objections. But it wouldn't be for long. Only a few months. And I'd do everything . . . '

'For heaven's sake get to the point. What are you trying to say?'

'I'd like to invite Agnes to come and live here. With me – with us. I owe it to her, darling. She brought me up. I can't let her die alone.' She glanced at Ralph apprehensively, but his face was expressionless. 'We've got plenty of room – it's the obvious solution.' The house seemed huge after Agnes's poky cottage, and luxuriously warm. 'It's terribly bad for her lungs to be living in all that damp. But it's not just that. I want to make her feel that someone cares. And *wants* her. She wouldn't be a nuisance. You know how independent she is. And if . . . when . . . she gets worse I can arrange for a nurse to come in. It would mean so much to her to be offered a home. And she's always liked you, Ralph. Remember how relieved she was to see me marrying a successful, sensible businessman and settling down at last?'

He gave a bitter laugh.

'What's funny?'

'Sensible. Successful.'

'Well, you were, darling.'

'*Were* being the operative word.'

'Getting back to Agnes – I admit it's a lot to ask, but please would you consider it? Honestly, Ralph, you'll hardly know she's here. She'll stay in her room most of the time. And meals won't be a problem because she only eats things like soup and Complan. And at least she'll be warm and dry, and feel less . . . ' The words petered out in the face of Ralph's continued silence. His mouth was set in a thin line, his hand clamped tightly around his glass. 'I don't know why I bothered to ask. You've no intention of agreeing, have you? We swan about in this great barn of a house, yet you'd let a poor old woman die alone.'

Silence. Except for the rain. And the measured ticking of the grandfather clock. And little muffled gasps from his pipe.

But all at once he put the pipe down. He even put his glass down. 'We haven't *got* a house, Lorna.'

'What?'

'Well, not for much longer.'

'What on earth are you talking about?'

He refused to meet her eyes. 'I'm sorry, I don't know how to tell you.'

Oh my God, she thought, he's selling up, going to live with another woman . . .

'I've been trying to spare you, all these weeks.'

'Spare me?' Just what Agnes had said. The familiar stirrings of panic began to take a grip: a steel cordon clamping her lungs, a piece of granite lodged in her throat.

'It didn't seem fair to worry you any more, when you had so much to cope with already – the foot and the infections, then the shingles and . . . '

Ralph was gazing at the ashtray. In her mind she saw lipstick-tipped cigarette-ends nestling amid the ash and broken matches from his pipe. Yet she was no Goody Two-Shoes herself. She had responded with alacrity when Oshoba had invited her to his flat. 'I'm worried anyway. I . . . I've suspected for ages something's going on.'

'So why didn't you say?'

'I suppose I was scared to hear it confirmed. But now I've got to know. You *have* to tell me, Ralph.'

He picked up his pipe again and sucked on it briefly, seemingly unaware that it had gone out. 'Remember that Shropshire job, about a year ago – the private tennis-court?'

'Oh, you mean in Lydbury.' She wondered why he was changing tack. 'Derek Bowden. Wasn't he a car dealer?'

'A used-car salesman. Anyway, he's injured himself playing tennis. One of the seams on the Astroturf came undone and he tripped and fell very awkwardly. He fractured his wrist and ankle and twisted his back.'

'That sounds nasty. Poor man!'

'Poor *us*. He's threatening to sue.'

'Sue? Christ, no!'

'For shoddy workmanship.'

The panic spiralled. She was breathing not air but tar. 'I don't understand. Len and Matthew are normally so reliable. They've never botched anything before.'

'That's just it – it wasn't Len and Matthew. Don't you remember when we were snowed under with work last March? We had to get different fitters for that one job. And evidently they used substandard glue. You know how expensive glue is – well, they obviously thought they could get away with using inferior stuff. Not only that – they skimped on the amount, so naturally the seams didn't hold.'

'Well, why doesn't he sue *them*?' Her voice was shrill with fear.

'They've disappeared. I tried ringing them scores of times, but the number's unobtainable. It struck me as rather odd that they only had a mobile, but I assumed it was because they're on the road so much. In the end I went round in person to the address they gave on their letterhead and found it was just a front. Some poor old duck lives there, who said they'd rented her garage for a while but had cleared off months ago. The bastards have done a bunk.'

Lorna put her hand to her throat and tried to swallow. The fitters had seemed so professional, so eager to please on the phone. How could they have conned her like that? 'But if it's *their* fault, Bowden can't hold us responsible.'

'He can, and he does. And legally he's right. We hired them, don't forget.'

'But you inspected the court. I remember you driving there in that dreadful storm.'

'Yes, of course I inspected it, but faulty glue wouldn't have shown up at that stage. Anyway, whatever the rights and wrongs of it, Bowden's claiming for a massive loss of earnings as well as the physical injuries. Apparently he was planning a trip to Japan to import a load of cars, and he had to cancel it. And a similar trip to Portugal. He can't fly or drive, you see. In fact he's still on crutches even now.'

'On crutches, with a broken wrist?'

'*One* crutch. According to his solicitor, walking's so difficult he often has to rely on a wheelchair. The ankle was a compound fracture and there were a lot of complications, so he says. Three weeks after the accident he developed an infection, and the doctor was worried it might get into the bone.'

Lorna bit her lip. With first-hand experience of infections and complications, she could imagine the difficulty of hobbling around on one crutch. 'I can't help feeling sorry for him.'

'Don't waste your sympathy. We've no proof it's as bad as he's making out. Clearly it's in his interest to inflate it for all it's worth. He's already claiming medical expenses and chauffeuring costs and for the disruption to his social life and God knows what else besides. Plus he insists on having the tennis-court resurfaced, but he won't let our men touch it. He says he'll get it done elsewhere – *another* fifteen grand. I bet you anything you like he gets it patched up on the cheap and pockets the difference. I wouldn't trust him further than I could throw him, and his solicitor sounds a nasty piece of work. At the start of all this he said Bowden was after a hundred thousand in damages.'

'A hundred *thousand?*' The figure was like a physical blow: a fist smashing into her face.

'Yes, I was appalled too. I went straight to Philip and told him the whole story. I said I intended to fight Bowden every inch of the way. But Philip didn't think I had much of a case. Rogue fitters or no, at the end of the day I'm the one responsible. To put it bluntly, he said I'm likely to be flayed alive in court.'

'Flayed alive?' She could only repeat Ralph's phrases – each more alarming than the last.

'I suppose it was decent of him to warn me. Most solicitors would be rubbing their hands in glee at the prospect of a fat fee. But that's the trouble. He said the fees could amount to thirty grand by the time both sides have brought in medical experts. Orthopaedic specialists don't come cheap.'

Her heart was beating so wildly she clasped her hands across her chest in an attempt to slow it down. 'Ralph, I . . . I can't believe this is happening.'

'I know – I've hardly slept for weeks. I did everything I could to keep it from you. I made sure the correspondence went through Philip and told him only to call me on the mobile.'

Would it have been worse to have known earlier? She couldn't judge; couldn't think coherently at all. 'What can we *do?*'

'Well, just this week Philip phoned to say he had good news. Hardly good – it's all relative, of course – but Bowden's willing to settle for forty grand, so long as it's paid by the end of May. And that includes the cost of resurfacing the court.'

'Forty grand? But we'll still never be able to pay!' She rose shakily to her feet, clutching the back of the sofa to steady herself. If only she could escape – not just the appalling facts but the turmoil in her body. She felt sick, feverish, frighteningly unreal. She tried to control the shaking – she was no help to Ralph in this state. 'Why would he cut his damages so drastically? Isn't that rather suspicious? What d'you think's going on?'

'God knows. But Philip had a phone-call from Bowden's solicitor, off the record or whatever they call it. It seems Bowden's not keen on going to court. You know what used-car salesmen get up to – clapped-out old bangers with a miraculously low mileage on the clock, stolen cars with switched number-plates . . . He's bound to have something to hide. And he's desperate for the cash by May. Again I don't know why. But reading between the lines I'd say the VATman or the Inland Revenue are breathing down his neck. Or he may have less kosher creditors – the criminal fraternity demanding money with menaces: pay up or the showroom gets torched.'

She couldn't take it in. This was the stuff of nightmare: criminals, blackmail, arson. 'But if he's such a crook, or involved with crooks, why don't we call his bluff?'

'We haven't any proof, Lorna. And he's the injured party – literally. He'll milk the situation for all it's worth, hobbling into court on crutches and claiming to be half-paralysed. He says he's in constant pain from his back and that the bones in his ankle haven't knitted properly and he may still not be able to drive for a whole year.'

'But that *is* awful, Ralph. Not driving for only three months has been incredibly hard for me.'

'Stop being so gullible! The man's an out-and-out liar. Philip thinks so too, although he's sure Bowden will produce a tame doctor or three to swear he's falling apart.'

She glanced at the wedding-photo on the sideboard. She and Ralph were smiling, raising champagne glasses in a toast. Another era, another life entirely. 'So why should we let him get away with it, if you say he's such a liar?'

'Because we haven't any choice. If we fight him it could drag on for a couple of years at least, and the legal fees would be astronomical. And think of the adverse publicity. He's already made veiled threats about exposing the hazards of Astroturf if we don't agree to settle by May. Apparently he knows this bloke on the *Daily Mail*, and you can just imagine the line they'd take: a death-trap for children, a danger to life and limb – all that sort of emotive stuff. He's got us by the short and curlies, Lorna.'

'That's blackmail.'

'Maybe. Unfortunately he's the one calling the shots, so we're in no position to argue. I mean, if we lose – which Philip says is likely – we'll be liable for Bowden's costs as well. And the strain of a court case would probably kill us both. Remember poor old Michael Moore – he ended up with a heart attack and costs of two hundred grand.'

Lorna dug her nails into her palm. The figures kept rising and rising.

'Philip said it might not even *get* to court for a year or more, what with all the legal rigmarole that has to be gone through first. And with every month that passes you can bet your bottom dollar Bowden will suffer more convenient complications and lose thousands of pounds' more business until he's dunning us for Christ knows how much.'

She sank down on the sofa again. How could one weekend produce so many shocks? She was still struggling to come to terms with the violence of her parents' death and her father being the cause of it, and now this new revelation.

'We have to face the facts, Lorna. If we don't pay Bowden by May we're finished.'

'We're finished anyway. How on earth can we find forty grand? We just haven't got that sort of money.'

'We'll have to sell the house.'

Suddenly it seemed unutterably precious – the house she had always thought of as isolated, gloomy and too big. Nevertheless it was home: the place where she felt safest, the place where she belonged. 'We can't do that in two months.'

'I'll ask the bank for a bridging loan.'

'They won't agree, with the enormous mortgage we've got.'

'They will if Philip undertakes with them to repay the loan from the proceeds of the sale. The trouble is, without a house I don't see how we can run the business.'

No house. No business. She closed her eyes, saw a snail without its shell, a tent collapsing in a hurricane. Was it any wonder that Ralph hadn't been able to sleep? He had had to bear this on his own. And, far from giving him support, she had let herself believe that he was involved in an affair. Desperately she cast around for a solution. 'What about Agnes's cottage?'

'What about it?'

'It's ours – or soon will be. I know it isn't worth a lot, but Agnes says we'll get the value of the land.'

'That won't be much where *she* lives. She moved to Lincolnshire precisely because property was cheap.'

More guilt. Unwittingly *she* had been the cause of Agnes's financial difficulties and hence her move to a benighted village.

'Besides, we can hardly turf her out of her own home.'

'Maybe *we* could live with *her*, instead of the other way round.' She was clutching at straws.

'Oh sure! With the cottage crumbling around us. And what would we live on?'

'We still have clients – a few. And there's that golf-club job in Dorset. They're debating about whether to go ahead. The estimate's only just over their budget, so if we could trim it slightly I'm pretty sure we'd get the contract.'

Ralph shook his head wearily. 'It'll be months before they make up their minds. You know what these committees are like, squabbling over their own petty interests. And the other clients are as bad – ditherers or penny-pinchers, or both. We work ourselves to death and there's sod-all to show at the end of it. It's hard enough when things are going well, but with that little shit holding us at knifepoint the situation's hopeless.'

'No, it's *not!*' she said, astounding herself. Never before, in the grip of panic, had she managed to fight back. It was Agnes who had inspired her. If a woman of seventy-nine could show such courage in face of a terminal illness then she too must take a stand. 'We've got to be positive, Ralph. I know you're feeling down at the moment, but once the house is sold we'll have *some* money. Then we can rent a place and keep the business ticking over. We don't need a vast amount of storage space. The material's usually delivered direct to the site, and we can keep the tools in the van and . . . '

'The van's not big enough.'

'We'll *make* it big enough.'

'What's the point? It's clapped out anyway.'

'Ralph, for pity's sake! Are you determined to wallow in gloom?'

'I've told you, I've had it up to here with bloody Astro-Sport. I'm sick to death of having to be polite to clients who shilly-shally about and then won't pay on time. And arguing the toss with tinpot little surveyors who think they're God and – '

'OK, we close the business down and find jobs somewhere else. That's the only alternative. Where do we start?'

'I've started,' Ralph said bitterly. 'I've already approached various people, but no one's the least bit interested. It's my age, obviously. They think I'm past it, but they're too polite to say.'

'Past it? At fifty-three?'

'I'm nearly fifty-four. Anyway, in some jobs you're past it at *thirty-four.*'

'Well, that's me done for too.'

'Oh, *you're* all right. With your computer skills you'd be snapped up in a trice.'

Did she detect a note of jealousy? 'But surely that's an advantage, Ralph. One wage is better than none.'

Ralph knocked his pipe sharply against the ashtray. 'I don't intend to be kept by my wife.'

'You may not have much choice.'

'There's no need to rub it in.'

'I'm only trying to help.'

'There isn't any help. Not now.'

'I'm sorry, Ralph, I don't agree. I admit the Bowden thing's a terrible setback, but if I can keep working that'll tide us over.'

'And where are we going to live?'

'I've told you – we'll rent a flat.'

'Great! Ending our days in a grotty little bedsit.'

Lorna tried to draw on Agnes's vigour, her refusal to exaggerate. 'Come off it, Ralph, we're hardly ending our days! You're still twelve years away from your pension. And I didn't say a bedsit.'

'That's all we'll be able to afford.'

She went over to the window and peered out at the garden. Everything was shadowy, wet, depressing, dead. She could feel herself capitulating already. Ralph's relentless negativity was too much for her to withstand. The panic was surging back, Agnes's determined voice drowned by the craven bleating of her fears.

She heard Ralph strike a match, then another and another. Each one fizzled out, followed by a muttered curse. His failure to light his pipe seemed to symbolize their predicament. She remained standing at the window, watching drops of rain snail down the glass. Shapes in the garden came gradually into focus: the wooden bench, the laurel-bush, the dark stump of the beech-tree. It had fallen last year in a gale and crashed through the roof of the shed. Luckily the insurance had . . .

'Ralph!' She wheeled round. 'We're mad, stark staring mad! We've forgotten the insurance. How could we be so stupid? *They*'ll pay.'

Ralph's expression didn't change. He was sitting with his shoulders hunched, one hand fidgeting on the chair-arm.

'*Ralph?*'

'Yes.'

'Did you hear? The public-liability policy. End of panic – we can relax! I'm just amazed we didn't think of it before. But I suppose with all the upheaval of Agnes and my father . . . Oh, darling, I'm so relieved! Come and give me a hug.'

He didn't move. The muscle in his cheek was twitching.

'What's wrong?'

'Nothing. Leave it, can't you. I'm tired.'

'Leave it? With a solution staring us in the face! I'm beginning to think I'm married to a masochist.'

He drained his whisky. His hand was shaking as he put the glass down. 'They . . . won't pay,' he grunted at last.

'Why ever not?'

'I can't explain.'

'Look, I've read the policy enough times, and there's no reason why they shouldn't.'

He put his head in his hands and let out a muffled groan.

'Ralph, what *is* all this? I don't understand. We should be jumping for joy.'

'We haven't any insurance,' he mumbled.

'*What?*'

'I . . . didn't renew it.'

She stared at him, incredulous. The efficient, prudent businessman letting his insurance lapse? There must be some mistake. 'You can't mean you forgot it?'

'No.' His voice rose querulously. 'But money was so damned tight. The renewal came at the worst possible time. There was a tax demand, a VAT demand, that big repair on the car. I did intend to renew it, Lorna, every day, I swear, but whenever any money came in it was swallowed up by yet another bill. Besides, we've been shelling out on premiums for ten years without putting in a single claim on the business. Then I make one mistake and all hell breaks loose.'

'Stop feeling so bloody sorry for yourself. *You* landed us in this mess.' How weak he looked suddenly, and shifty, deliberately avoiding her eye, and that stupid muscle still twitching in his cheek. Kathy was right: he wasn't her great protector – he was a bungler and a fool. 'I can't *believe* you didn't renew it, Ralph. You must be out of your mind.'

'Look, you're the one who sees to all that side of things. You should have –'

'Don't you dare blame me! I distinctly remember telling you it had to be paid in December and did you want me to do it before I went into hospital. And you said no, you'd take care of it yourself this year. But I see now – you'd already decided not to renew it, hadn't you? You didn't even have the decency to talk it over with me. I slave my guts out for the business, and then you go behind my back and land us both in the shit.'

'Slave your guts out? You've been sitting on your arse for three months.'

'If I can't even have an operation without you begrudging me the time to – '

'I don't begrudge you anything – you know that. You're just determined to put me down. But if *you* had to cope with the pressure I'm under you'd crack up in half an hour.'

'Thanks very much! At least I wouldn't be idiotic enough to cancel the insurance – the one thing that's absolutely crucial. No wonder you don't dare go to court. They'd make mincemeat of you, running a business like ours with no insurance cover. And don't give me that spiel about never having needed it before. If you used *that* as a defence you'd be laughed to scorn.'

'It's easy for you to criticize. What else could we have economized on? We've already cut out new clothes, new cars, holidays, painting the house, repairs . . . '

'Couldn't you have discussed it with me first, though? That's what really hurts. We're supposed to work in partnership, but when it comes to the crunch it's *your* business – like this house is yours, and all the important decisions are yours. I'm just a minion, too lowly to be consulted.' Her cheeks were flaming, her heart racing – with fury now, not panic. She seized his whisky glass. '*This* is what's wrong with you,' she shouted, slamming the glass on the sideboard. 'You keep telling me we have to economize, but think of all the money that gets pissed down the drain every day. How can you expect to run a business when you're always half cut?'

He sprang to his feet, his right hand clenched in a fist. She cowered, terrified he was going to hit her, but he just punched the fist into his other palm. 'That's rich, I must say, coming from you. At least I haven't managed to kill us both through drunk-driving.'

Without another word she turned on her heel and marched out. Grabbing her coat, car-keys and a pair of battered shoes, she wrested open the front door.

'Goodbye!' she whispered. 'Good riddance!'

19

She sat shivering in the car outside Clare's flat. Where *was* Clare at five past midnight? The street seemed deserted except for a skinny black cat crouching under the hedge. The lamp-posts cast an amber glaze across pavements glistening with rain and trembling with the shadows of gaunt and naked trees.

She counted the lighted windows in the flats: fewer now than half an hour ago. People were going to bed – normal, solvent people, cuddling up companionably; husbands and wives safe, at peace; children who had living, breathing parents.

Was Clare away, perhaps? They had spoken only two days ago, but if her mother's flu was worse she might have had to rush off to Wales. Alone, she was prey to ominous visions of the future: she and Ralph thrown out of the house, living on benefit, pitied by their friends. Or she back in some lonely bedsit, jobless and despondent.

Listlessly she traced a series of noughts on the misted-up window. The panic had burned itself out, leaving the usual dregs of dejection, shame, fatigue. Her earlier attempts to rouse Ralph from his pessimism now seemed crass and superficial. His gloom had seeped into her bloodstream like a virus and was killing off all hope.

On an impulse she started the car. Driving – somewhere, anywhere – would serve as a distraction, despite (or even because of) the throbbing in her foot. Also it would give Clare time to return. Only Clare would take her in. True friends were rare.

As she turned into the main road, she passed a guest-house with a Vacancies sign outside, and was tempted for a split second to stop and book a room – human contact, a friendly welcome . . . But, in a strange place on her own, the Terrors were bound to strike again as soon as she closed her bedroom door. Besides, she would seem suspicious, arriving so late and dressed in an old gardening coat over a nightie.

Perhaps she should just go home, admit defeat.

No, dammit. For once in her life she had stood up to Ralph. She would *not* go grovelling back.

She continued past the golf-course into a more prosperous part of the town. No poky little houses crumbling with dry rot or large ones about to be repossessed. Stone lions stood guard outside colonnaded porches, flanked by bay-trees in smart tubs; carriage-lamps gleamed on gold-tipped railings designed to keep out ne'er-do-wells and bankrupts.

A car overtook her, followed by another. Each time she glimpsed only the anonymous back of the driver's head before they were swallowed up in darkness. This was how it would be when she and Ralph had gone their separate ways: a world inhabited by faceless strangers.

She glanced at her watch: ten to one. Clare *must* be back by now.

But, as she drew up outside the flats again and switched off the engine, silence closed around her. The world had shut down for the night. Only the sky was restless: menacing clouds besieging a sliver of moon.

She got out of the car, pulling her coat around her. The wind knifed between her bare legs, ran cold, taunting fingers through her hair. She pressed Clare's bell. No answer.

She stood wretchedly in the shelter of the porch, listening to the rain drumming on the balconies. Her thoughts kept circling back to Ralph. Had he drunk himself into a stupor or was he, too, awake? Perhaps he was out searching for her, sick with remorse.

Unlikely.

Returning to the car, she drove on aimlessly, wondering what to do and where to go. Even if she found an all-night café, she had no money for food or drink, and in any case she shouldn't really be driving at all. It was her first time since the operation, and her foot was registering its protest. She also felt uncomfortable without socks or underclothes, her rain-spattered nightdress clinging soggily to her legs. If only she could stop thinking about the future. *Was* there any future? – with Ralph? In some new job? The past, too, had changed grotesquely from her cherished vision of it: her parents' happy, stable marriage before the crash . . .

Preoccupied with thoughts of death and debt, she lost track of her surroundings. Trees and buildings flashed by – mere shapes and shadows; the road itself a strip of sleepy black until startled by her headlamps. But suddenly one building sprang into focus: a red-brick church on a corner. Why did it seem familiar? And then she remembered: she had noticed it a fortnight ago on her way to . . .

She must stop. At once. Turn round and go straight back. She had resolved never to come here again. It was dangerous. Indefensible.

But what did it matter at this hour? – he wouldn't be in. He worked five nights out of seven. She'd simply drive past, not even turn her head to look.

Or perhaps she'd just slow down, to see if the lights were on. That couldn't do any harm.

The place was in darkness. Well, what did she expect? He'd be at Oakfield House, as she'd thought. No point getting out of the car – it would mean braving the wind again, and she was cold enough already. And why ring the bell when no one was there?

She got out.

She rang the bell.

Silence.

She rang again, louder.

Scuffling footsteps crossed the hall. The door was flung open and she stood face to face with a stocky black man wearing garish purple pyjamas.

'Oh, gosh, Olu . . . I'm terribly sorry.' She had forgotten Oshoba's brother. Forgotten caution, common sense.

'You woke me up,' he snapped.

'I'm sorry,' she repeated, not daring to look him in the eye.

'What d'you want?'

'Nothing. I . . . I was just passing and . . . '

He startled her by yelling over his shoulder, 'Oshoba! That woman's here.'

She froze. So Oshoba *was* in. He mustn't see her. 'No, really, Olu, I'll leave. I'm going now.'

But Oshoba was already emerging from the bedroom, draped in an old grey blanket. Beneath it he was naked. She could see his long black legs; the skin gleamed smooth and hairless, and instinctively she took a step towards him. 'I'm sorry to disturb you. I happened to be driving past your door.'

'I like to be disturbed.' He gave her a dazzling smile. His voice was hoarse and scratchy, little more than a whisper. 'Come in, beautiful lady.'

'He's not meant to talk,' Olu complained. 'He's recovering from laryngitis.'

'Oh, if you're not well, I'll . . . '

'I *am* well,' Oshoba croaked. 'Now you're here I'm very, very well.'

With a sniff of annoyance, Olu strode back across the hall and dis-appeared into the bedroom, slamming the door.

Oshoba shrugged and took her arm. 'We'll go into the other room. I'm so glad you managed to get away. Did they tell you I was off work?'

'Who?' she asked, confused. Seeing her strange garb, he had evi-dently assumed that she had sneaked out expressly to see him, leaving her husband asleep.

'Oakfield House.'

'Er, no.'

'I thought you might have phoned them?'

'No.' His voice – lack of voice – was mesmerizing. The throaty rasp imbued every word with emotion.

He led her into the sitting-room, turning on just one dim light. The room was small and stiflingly hot and contained a few shabby pieces of furniture: a table, a couple of wooden chairs and a low-slung, battered sofa. He didn't invite her to sit down but simply stood, swathed in the grey blanket, looking at her intently. He seemed to be drinking her in, assuring himself of her presence. The room was uncannily quiet, hold-ing its breath, as she was. The blustering wind was shut out; even the rain had stopped.

'Lorna' – he spoke with effort – 'are you OK? You look upset.'

'Well, yes, I . . . '

'What's wrong? Do you need help?'

'Yes . . . No . . . I can't really discuss it.'

'But I don't like to see you sad.'

'I'm not sad.'

'You are. I can tell from your eyes. And you're shivering. Are you cold?'

'Mm. Freezing, actually.' She forced a smile.

'Then I must warm you.'

She felt his arms latch around her and the blanket graze her cheek. She inhaled its musty smell – and *his* smell, of heat and sleep. He seemed so big, so solid, a bulwark, a protector. His very calmness and composure were already beginning to soothe her. She could feel her-self thawing in his heat, blurring with the soft shadows from the lamp.

A car passed in the road outside. The noise rose and died away, lost in the pooling silence – a silence that seemed to enter her, fill her veins, her mind.

'Better now?' he whispered.

'Yes.'

'I'm *too* hot.' He stepped back and let the blanket slip. His naked body was only inches away – the pubic hair tight-curled and fiercely black, blacker even than his skin; the penis long, thick, erect.

One step forwards and the tip of that erection would nudge against her stomach. '*No*, Oshoba. We mustn't. It's . . .'

He placed a finger on her lips. 'Shh, shh. My brother says I'm not allowed to talk.'

He eased the coat from her shoulders. It fell to the floor with a soft, surrendering swish. He moved his face towards hers. The kiss was simple, chaste.

She closed her eyes – she had no need to see. Feeling was enough: first the pressure of his hand as he pulled her nightie up, then the gradual sensation of warmth and breadth inside her, of being filled and fused. He used no force; indeed he hardly moved, just stood pressed against her, as if he had slowed the night down, transformed its churning nightmares into a sensuous reverie. She too stayed motionless: if she took no active part it was all a dream, and in dreams you had no choice but to submit.

Gently he withdrew a fraction, and then pushed back, repeating the sequence in a slow, tantalizing rhythm. She was amazed at his restraint. Most men would slam and thrust. There was no urgency, no haste – she could simply *be*, savouring the feeling of him rooted in her. His hands were clasped tightly round her waist, his body so hot, the room so hot, she was liquefying, melting. A tiny sound escaped her, a sharp intake of breath.

Aware of even her slightest response, he pressed more deeply into her. She let it happen. If he succeeded in arousing her it was not of her volition. She no longer owned her body: it was part of his, joined to his, moving to the same dream-like rhythm – deep and slow, deep and slow.

Languorously he slid out. 'Lie down. I want to look at you.'

He led her to the sofa, turned her round so that her back was against his chest, and slipped the nightie over her head. For a moment she was blinded, trapped in a billow of nylon before he lowered her carefully down. She watched his gaze travel from her eyes to her mouth, down to her breasts and belly, down further to her groin and thighs. The tiny golden hairs on her arms were standing up, not from cold but from the fierceness of his scrutiny. In turn, she looked at *him*, intrigued by the contrast in their bodies: hers fleshy and milk-pale; his long, broad, solid, muscly, black. And his hair, a close-cropped frizz, was joltingly different from her tawny, tangled mane. Even their navels were individual in shape – his a tiny swelling; hers a tiny cavern.

'Your skin's so smooth,' he murmured. 'I could spend the rest of my life kissing it and still want more. I'm going to kiss every single part of you.'

He would expect her to kiss him in return. Instead, she lay passively, her only role to acquiesce.

He bent to kiss her eyelashes, with the lightest, teasing touch, and ran his tongue along the lids. The sensation was exquisite, but she gave no sign of pleasure – no one should accuse her of encouraging him. She simply registered the feelings as he kissed her neck and throat: the deftness of his tongue; the slow, voluptuous pressure of his lips.

He took her hand and pressed it into his, his broad, chunky fingers straddling her slender ones. Then, turning it palm upward, he licked between each finger, lingeringly, deliciously, and along the base of the thumb. His lips moved from her hand to nuzzle the length of her arm, from the inside of her wrist to the soft hollow of her elbow and up to the ridge of her collar-bone. He took his time, relishing the texture of her skin, its smell, its taste, the blue tracery of each vein. Then he stroked the curve of her breast and, cupping it in his hand, touched the very tip of his tongue to the very tip of her nipple, flicking to and fro across it in the subtlest of caresses. His mouth made gradually widening circles around the nipple until he reached her belly.

'I can hear your secret sounds,' he whispered, laying his head against it. 'I'd like to bury myself in your flesh and stay there for ever and ever. That would be my heaven.'

His extravagance, in word and deed, astonished her. No one had ever worshipped her body like this.

Now he was exploring her navel, probing the tiny cavern, licking a slow pathway to the top of her pubic hair. 'In Nigeria we call this toco-hair,' he smiled, letting his fingers brush teasingly across it. His voice sounded painfully hoarse.

'You mustn't talk, Oshoba.'

'No, I mustn't talk – I must kiss.'

He eased her legs apart, but before using his tongue he gently fingered every fold and cranny, making a minute examination, as if she were the first woman he had ever seen. Perhaps he had never made love to a white woman. The thought was pleasing – to be his first.

'Your labia are wonderfully long. And one's just slightly bigger than the other. I love that – it's exciting.'

He stretched them gently between his teeth, as if to make them longer still, then he kissed them, kissed between them, pushing his tongue swiftly in and out.

The tension was unbearable. She was forbidden to respond, yet her body was betraying her, aching to move as he used a finger as well as his tongue, alternating one with the other, setting up tiny shock-waves from the friction of his knuckle.

She bit her own knuckle in an effort to keep silent, but her body was arching under him and she knew she was losing control. Pushing his hand away, she suddenly cried out, 'Oshoba – make love to me. *Now!*'

Without a word he stood up and eased her body to the very end of the sofa, until her feet were resting on the floor and her neck and head were arched back. Then he knelt on the carpet, between her legs, and insinuated himself into her, centimetre by centimetre, as if the slightest haste or roughness might upset or alarm her. And he was right – this must remain a dream, a delicious lassitude, a dawdling drift to ecstasy.

Time itself seemed suspended as he moved rhythmically back and forth, back and forth, letting her feel the length of him, spinning out her pleasure in slow motion. She knew she would come, eventually, extravagantly, and that he would come with her, thrillingly, exquisitely, and then they would come again, together.

And again.

Again.

There were no limits in a dream.

20

'Good afternoon, Mrs Pearson. How are we?'

She bridled at the 'we'. *He* was probably fighting fit, judging by his sleek appearance. 'Never been better,' she said.

The sarcasm was lost on Mr Hughes. 'Splendid!' he smiled. 'So I take it the foot's improved?'

'No. It's worse. A lot worse. I've been getting a pain just here.' She indicated the underside of her foot. 'A sharp, searing pain. It's difficult to walk.'

He gave his professional frown, combining dismay and concern with a hint of incredulity. 'We'd better take a look at it. Would you remove your shoe and sock, please.'

He placed her naked foot on his pin-striped thigh. His hand was hot, her foot was hot, and all at once she felt herself melting in the heat of Oshoba's embrace – a pin-striped Oshoba with silver hair, shafting her so wildly the sofa-springs were gasping in shock.

'Good job you don't live somewhere like Iran. You'd be stoned to death for adultery there, or at the very least have your hands and feet cut off.'

'I wouldn't mind my feet being cut off,' she retorted to the Monster, wincing as Mr Hughes pressed hard against the ball of her foot.

'Is this where it hurts, Mrs Pearson?'

'Yes. Ouch!'

'If Ralph finds out he'll divorce you.'

'We may as well *be* divorced. We're hardly speaking to each other any more.'

'It'd be far worse on your own. Mega-panics every night – you'd soon be hauled off in a strait-jacket.'

Mr Hughes was still squeezing her foot – a form of third-degree torture. 'Mm,' he said, shaking his head, 'I'm not quite sure what's going on here . . . I suspect you either have a transfer metatarsalgia or you've developed a plantar digital neuroma. Possibly both.'

'I'm sorry, I don't understand.' Couldn't he speak plain English?

She stifled a scream as he touched a particularly tender spot.

'A neuroma is a swelling on the nerve, Mrs Pearson. You can't see it, but it does give rise to acute neural pain. As for the metatarsalgia, I'm afraid we, er, may have shortened the bone a fraction too much, which means you're now taking the weight on the second toe. That causes pain in the ball of the foot. We call it a transfer lesion.'

'In other words, he's made another balls-up. Nice pun, eh?' the Monster cackled.

'So what can I . . . *we* do about it?'

'Well, temporarily, I'm afraid you'll need more pain-killers.'

'I'm already gulping them in handfuls.' And not only for the foot. The shingles had returned with a vengeance – a stress reaction, no doubt.

'Probably a stronger variety would be better. I'll write you up for some Distalgesic. And we'll arrange to make you a pair of orthoses.'

'A pair of what?'

'Anti-pronatory devices.'

She looked at him blankly.

'Special insoles for your shoes. I'm afraid they're not a cure, but they can help in the short term. They work in the same way as, say, a pair of spectacles, accommodating a problem without actually correcting it. We'll make an appointment for you with Mr Weekes, the podiatrist I use.'

Podiatrist? She was in need of a medical dictionary.

'I'm afraid his practice is in Plumstead, which is rather a trek for you.'

He was right about that, especially when she wasn't supposed to drive and had to walk with the aid of two sticks.

'But why I recommend him is that he's just invested in a state-of-the-art scanner which shows exactly where your feet are taking the pressure. It measures the transference of your weight through the feet as you walk. And another thing Mr Weekes can assess is the articulation between your ankle and your knee, your knee and your hip, your hip and your pelvis, the whole of your spine, and . . . '

She was reminded of 'Dem Bones, Dem Bones' and wondered if he was about to break into song:

'Your thigh-bone's connected to your hip-bone,
Your hip-bone's connected to your . . .'

'Then they take a plaster-of-Paris impression of your feet, and the orthoses are moulded over the cast. But of course with all those different processes they do tend to be rather expensive.'

Forget it then, she bit back. 'How expensive?'

'Oh, four hundred pounds. Five hundred perhaps. Somewhere in that region.'

'Five hundred pounds for *insoles?*'

'And all because he did a crap job in the first place.' The Monster was flexing his own feet, demonstrating their innate superiority.

'Well, they are custom-made, Mrs Pearson. And Mr Weekes is extremely sound. He's made some first-class orthotic devices for many of my patients.'

'Would BUPA cover the cost?'

'BUPA?' jeered the Monster. 'You can't afford those luxuries now. You'll have to wait your turn on the NHS like everybody else. Which means you'll get your insoles by 2010 – if you're lucky.'

'Unlikely, I'm afraid. Most health-insurance companies are unwilling to fund such devices.'

Well, what was another few hundred pounds compared with forty thousand? Perhaps she could sell her gold-and-diamond bracelet – or her wedding-ring, come to that.

She stared glumly at the wall. Oshoba's bare black body was superimposed on the stark white paint. If Ralph were ever to hear of it . . . Was a casual affair worse than letting the insurance lapse? Had she any right to be angry still? Had he?

Mr Hughes was now examining her toes, palpating each in turn. 'I'm not completely happy about these second and third toes. I think I'll send you along to X-ray. They should be able to fit you in within half an hour or so. Then if you come back here with the plates we can look at them together and see what's going on.'

She watched apprehensively as he scribbled something on her notes. It wasn't just her feet that were distorted: her whole life was a disaster. 'Yes, the second toe is terribly stiff. I can hardly move it. And I'm rather worried about the scar. That hurts too, especially at night.

Just pressure from the sheet or blankets seems to set it off.'

Mr Hughes ran his finger along the horny red ridge. 'Mm, I'm afraid it's somewhat hypertrophic.'

Another word she didn't understand. What she had noticed, though, was how often he kept repeating 'I'm afraid'. She, too, was afraid – truly afraid: of more expense, more pain, more complications; of what might happen with Ralph, and with Oshoba. What if Oshoba had made her pregnant, or she'd caught some ghastly infection from him? It didn't bear thinking about. With difficulty, she resumed the conversation with Mr Hughes. 'You said the insoles were only a short-term solution. Isn't there anything else you can do?'

'Certainly, Mrs Pearson.' He flashed her a reassuring smile. 'When you have your second foot done, we can make some minor adjustments to this one.'

'Minor my arse! It'll be major, that's for sure – another major cock-up. And another major fee. Don't let him near the other foot or you'll be left with nothing but a pair of stumps.'

'Look, Mr Hughes, about the second foot . . . I'm not sure if I really want to go ahead with . . . '

'I quite understand. You've had a bit of a rough ride with the left one, so it might be advisable to allow a little time to elapse before we proceed with the right.'

'Rough ride? Let's face it, you're crippled.'

'Yes, I think that would be best. I am very busy at the moment. We're . . . moving house, you see.'

'My goodness, that is an upheaval, isn't it? I hope it doesn't mean you're overdoing the walking. You still need to rest that foot as much as possible.'

Rest didn't figure on her current schedule – only estate agents and prospective purchasers. She wasn't sure which breed was worse. The brash young men from Gascoigne-Pees and Mann & Co. (reeking of aftershave and breath-mints) had mercilessly exposed every defect of an elderly house and every deficiency in maintenance, but at least they didn't have children in tow. The first people who had come to view brought obnoxious eight-year-old twins who had upturned a potted plant and smashed her favourite vase.

As well as hobbling up and down stairs showing round other families from hell, there was the task of finding somewhere else for her and Ralph to live. They would probably end up in a block of flats similar to Oshoba's – imitation clapboard, covered in graffiti, and with the odd syringe or used condom littering the stairwell. Or would they still be together? Although they had reached an uneasy truce, Ralph didn't know about Oshoba, of course, and were he to find out it would blow everything apart.

She must stop dwelling on Oshoba. But each time she looked at Mr Hughes the two men seemed to blur together, despite the enormous physical contrast. Closing her eyes she imagined their penises side by side: one long and black, one pale and slender, both brazenly erect.

'Are you all right, Mrs Pearson? Not feeling faint or . . . ?'

'No, I'm fine. Just thinking.' She returned to the matter in hand. 'I do really need to be mobile, so it's an awful nuisance not being able to drive, or walk far. When do you think the foot will improve?'

'Well, the orthoses will certainly help.'

'Could you make me an appointment now to see the podiatrist?'

'I'm afraid that won't be possible. I was talking to him only yesterday and it appears there's a problem with the scanner.' He gave a rueful smile. 'It seems the more complex these machines are, the more temperamental they become.'

'And the more expensive these surgeons are,' the Monster put in contemptuously, 'the more useless *they* become.'

'Well, when – if – it's mended, how long does it take from the scan to the finished product?'

Mr Hughes smoothed his silver hair. 'It depends on how busy Mr Weekes is. He'd have to give you at least a couple of fittings once the prescription's made up. And I'm afraid there is another factor. The devices are manufactured in the States, so they have to be sent by post. There can be quite serious delays. One pair I ordered went permanently astray.'

'So are we talking about a month? Or longer?'

'Let's say six to eight weeks.'

So she'd be stuck with the pain for another two months, and just when she was hectically busy. Apart from anything else, she wanted to spend time with Agnes and also arrange some permanent help for her at home. (In fact she had planned to phone Kathy this evening to ask advice about live-in nurses.) 'Is there no chance of this transfer meta-whatever-you-said getting better on its own? What I need to know is when I can drive again and when I'll be able to walk at least as well as I could before the operation. Surely that's not asking much.'

Mr Hughes clasped his hands together.

'He's *praying*, look!' chortled the Monster. 'He's so inept he needs divine intervention.'

'As far as the driving's concerned, I wouldn't advise it at present. And as for the foot in general, it's difficult to say. You see, Mrs Pearson, with any bunion operation there's no guarantee that there won't be complications. Normally, whatever improvement there's going to be would happen in the next three to six months. If you find you're not free from pain and not walking well by, say, September, I'm afraid you probably never will be.'

She stared at him aghast. Never? After all she'd been through?

The Monster was smirking. 'Strange he didn't tell you that at the outset. These surgeons can't wait to get their grubby little hands on your money, but if you're left a cripple it's never *their* fault, is it? Well, they're hackers and slashers, aren't they, so why should they give a damn about a piddling thing like being able to walk?'

'I do feel you could have warned me, Mr Hughes.'

'But I did, Mrs Pearson. Several times. I made it absolutely clear that – '

'You never said I might end up worse than before.'

'*Far* worse,' the Monster sneered. 'In fact why not call it a day? I mean, what have you got going for you? No house, no business, crap feet, a failing marriage. And I doubt if Oshoba will still fancy you when you're permanently in a wheelchair.'

'Come, come, Mrs Pearson, let's not be pessimistic. We may see a considerable improvement in the next three months or so.'

'Bollocks! Suicide's the answer – get shot of all the problems in one fell swoop.'

'And there *are* measures you can take to help yourself – for instance, continue with those foot exercises I gave you, and be sure to wear good supportive shoes.'

'But I *am* doing the exercises, and they don't seem to help at all.'

'We must have patience, Mrs Pearson. These things take time, I'm afraid.'

'Oh, for God's sake stop saying you're afraid!'

Mr Hughes flinched as if she'd struck him. 'I'm sorry . . . I don't – '

'You're not afraid in the least. It's just a stock phrase with you, isn't it? You couldn't give a shit.'

Visibly shaken, Mr Hughes tried to regain his composure. 'Well, Mrs Pearson, I suggest you, er, pop along for your X-ray now and – '

'That's another of your stupid words – 'pop'. You medical people use it all the time. You talk to us as if we're children. "Pop up on the couch." "We'll just pop a little bandage on." "Pop the thermometer under your tongue." "Pop in and see me if you're worried." Well, I'm not popping anywhere, is that clear? I've had enough of X-rays. And pain. And *these* stupid things.' Seizing her sticks, she blundered out of the door.

'*And* bloody useless fathers,' she muttered, stumping along the corridor. 'I suppose you were blind drunk when you did the operation and that's why you lost the saw. Three hundred and twenty milligrams of alcohol per hundred millilitres of blood. That's criminal. That's evil. Don't you understand?'

She turned right, past X-ray, and out through the main exit. 'I don't need you any more,' she shouted, hurling one of the sticks against the hospital sign and the other into the street. 'Fathers, surgeons, lawyers, husbands – you can go to hell, the lot of you.'

21

'Kathy! Come in. Lovely to see you.'

'I say!' Kathy was gazing up at the gabled roofs and ornamented chimney-pots. 'Nice place you've got here!'

Lorna was more conscious of the house's state of disrepair – not as bad as Agnes's cottage but hardly up to the pukka standards expected in Queen's Hill Drive. 'You should hear some of the rude comments we've been getting. All people seem to see is missing roof-tiles or chips in the paint. Thank heavens I haven't got to show you round.'

'Oh, but you *have*, Lorna! I'm terribly nosy about people's houses. I insist on the grand tour.'

'Well, let's have a drink first, to give us strength!'

'Yes, I could do with one – I'm knackered. We're so short-staffed, this is the first day I've had off in weeks.'

'How *is* Oakfield?'

'Falling apart at the seams.' Kathy unbuttoned her grey gabardine, revealing a red sweater and tight black skirt. Lorna had rarely seen her out of uniform and was again struck by how different she looked: slimmer and more elegant. Her shoes were the kind Lorna could only dream about – narrow and low-cut, with spindly heels.

'How's the foot?' Kathy asked, as if reading her mind. 'You're still limping, I see.'

'It's my own silly fault. I threw away my sticks.'

'Threw them away? You're joking.'

'No, it's true. And I don't regret it. The house is decrepit enough without me hobbling around like an old crone. The foot's actually more painful than it was before the op. But I've got used to it, and' – she shrugged – 'at least it's not terminal! In fact I've just started driving again. I'm not meant to, of course, but frankly I'd rather put up with the pain than be stranded here without transport. Now, tell me, Kathy, what can you smell?'

'*Smell?*'

'Yes.'

Kathy cocked her head and sniffed. 'Coffee, and sort of . . . honeysuckle.'

'Not pipe-smoke?'

'No.'

'Good. The estate agent said that nice smells are a useful selling-point. Freshly baked bread is supposed to be best, followed by freshly brewed coffee. I draw the line at baking bread, but I do try to keep the coffee on the go. The honeysuckle's the bottled sort. I hope I haven't overdone it.'

'No, it's fine. And I love your staircase. Very grand!'

'Faded grandeur,' Lorna said with a smile, ushering Kathy into the sitting-room. Looking at the room through Kathy's eyes, she found it oppressive and unwelcoming. Even after eleven years of marriage, practically everything in it was Ralph's – not only the sombre colour scheme but the furniture, the pictures, the stern-faced grandfather clock with its ponderous tick, the stubborn wine stains on the carpet. (And memories of recent quarrels added their own dark tinge.)

'God, you're tidy!' Kathy remarked.

'You have to be when you're selling a house. You've no idea how fussy people are. The couple who came yesterday must have had X-ray eyes. They spotted cracks in the ceiling that weren't even there.'

Kathy moved to the window. 'Maybe you could cut those bushes back? They do tend to block out the light.'

'Ralph won't let me touch them. He likes that gloomy laurel.'

'Honestly, Lorna, you shouldn't let him be so domineering. Where is he, by the way?'

'In Salisbury. We're in the middle of a job there' – she grimaced – 'another tennis-court.'

'I thought you were closing the business down.'

'Yes, but we still have to look after our existing clients. And actually I'm not sure what he's decided. He seems to change his mind from one day to the next.'

'Surely *you* have a say?'

'Yes, of course, but – '

'I'm amazed you're still around. I'd never have forgiven him for stopping the insurance. I'd have walked out there and then and left him to rot.'

'Let's not talk about it, please, Kathy. Do you mind?' She had no wish to be deflected from her new serene persona. She was reading a book called *Conquering Panic*, which suggested role-playing the type of placid character you'd ideally like to be and repeating the exercise until it became automatic. So today she was Ms Unflappable. (The only problem was, she and Ms U kept splitting off from each other.)

Kathy took a sip of wine. 'OK. Let's talk about Agnes. That's what I'm here for, after all. I've brought you some bumf about Marie Curie Nurses.'

'Thanks. That's sweet of you. But first I want to hear your news. You said it was exciting, so I presume it's about a man.'

'No fear! I'm better off without men just now. No, it's about work – I'm leaving Oakfield and going to help a friend manage a brand-new residential home.'

'*Really*, Kathy? Well, that should be a good career move.'

'Yes, definitely. You should see the place! The Cedars, it's called, and it's incredibly luxurious. There's a library and a health spa and landscaped gardens with four huge cedar-trees. They're two hundred years old, would you believe!'

'It sounds fantastic!'

'Oh, it is. Straight out of *Homes and Gardens*. I'm going to be in charge of the residents and Chris'll handle the business side – well, her and Jeremy, her brother. He's providing the financial backing. In fact the house belongs to them – a great, rambling mansion their father left them in his will.'

'Where is it?' Selfishly, she hoped Kathy wouldn't move too far away.

'Weybridge. They badly need somewhere in that area. Hayes Court is due to close this year and Belmont's closed already. Homes for the elderly are disappearing at a rate of knots, you know. Mostly because they can't meet the new government regulations. I wouldn't be surprised if Oakfield goes under too.'

'But what will happen to the residents?' Lorna had a vision of poor Frances turfed out into the street, Dorothy Two fulminating about such iniquitous treatment.

'Well, I suppose we could take one or two at The Cedars – those who can afford it, and are relatively fit. It's not a nursing-home, you see, only residential. Chris was clear about that at the outset. It means you don't need so many specialist staff. And she's aiming at the private market, to avoid hassle with local authorities. Chris is in it for the money – she doesn't pretend otherwise. And her brother even more so. He's something big in the City. He made his first million before he was twenty-five, and God knows what he's worth now.'

'It doesn't sound like *you*, though, Kathy, all this talk of profit.'

'No, but the great thing is they're giving me a free hand to run it the way I want. Which means the highest possible standards of care. And that isn't incompatible with profit. If you offer the best, you'll get customers. It's a growth industry, after all. We're all living much longer these days. There are nine million people in Britain now who are over sixty-five, but by 2030 there'll be fifteen million. And three million of those will be over eighty-five, compared to only nine hundred thousand at the moment. So if you take – ' The front-door bell interrupted her. 'Are you expecting anybody?'

'It's probably the toner for the fax machine.' Lorna went to the door, to find not the expected courier but a gaggle of people on the step – six in all (or seven counting the massive black Alsatian, growling in a threatening manner).

One of their number stepped forward – the only man, as far as she could see. He wore a royal-blue blazer, a yellow-spotted cravat and several chunky rings. 'Hello, love. We saw the For Sale board and wondered if we could look round.'

Lorna quickly summoned Ms Unflappable, who spoke in calm but resolute tones. 'I'm afraid it's appointments only. If you phone the estate agents I'm sure they'll – '

'No can do, darlin'. It's now or never.'

'I'm sorry but it's not convenient.'

'Oh, come on, just a dekko. You'll hardly know we're here.'

Doubtful, thought Ms U, eyeing the dog's raised hackles, the squalling babe-in-arms and the truculent-looking toddler. 'I'm sorry,' she repeated. 'I have someone with me at present.'

'Not much point advertisin' if you don't want buyers.' The thin-faced woman curled her lip. 'Let's not waste our time, Ed. It looks a dump, anyway.'

'Phew,' said Lorna, returning to Kathy. 'We nearly had company for lunch! And, talking of lunch, you must be starving. I just need to check if a fax has arrived and then we can eat. Come into the office. I won't be a sec.'

'So this is where you work. Goodness, *two* computers! I'd never cope. Put me in front of a VDU and I turn into a gibbering wreck. Mind you, I've got to do some training – Chris insists. Perhaps you could give me lessons!'

Lorna wasn't really listening. She was annoyed that the promised fax hadn't come. Why were clients so unreliable?

'Are these all the jobs you've done?' Kathy was studying a large framed map hanging on the wall, stuck with a scattering of different-coloured pins. 'I never realized the business was so big.'

'It isn't really. Only the green-headed pins are completed jobs. Red means jobs in hand, and pink we've quoted for but haven't had the go-ahead.'

'You *are* efficient.'

Lorna laughed. 'Hardly. It just helps me keep track of things.'

'Oh, and this must be your publicity stuff.' Kathy picked up a brochure from the desk. 'It's quite a work of art, Lorna.'

'I'm glad you think so. I designed it myself. It's not bad, I suppose, although Ralph and I look horribly smug. We decided to put our picture on, to make it more personal.'

Kathy scrutinized the photo. 'Ralph's so much younger here.'

'Actually it was taken not that long ago. The business has worn him down, poor soul – especially the past two years. It isn't easy being self-employed.'

'Nothing to it,' Ms Unflappable put in. 'I could run a business in my sleep.'

'You're not exactly short of phones,' Kathy remarked, continuing her tour. 'No wonder you're so busy.'

'Luckily they're quiet at the moment. I daren't turn on the answering-machine in case a prospective buyer rings. Let's just hope we can get through lunch without too many interruptions. By the way, do you mind eating in the kitchen? The dining-room's a bit like a morgue.'

'It's a treat to be invited to lunch at all. I've been up to my eyes this month, what with Oakfield House and making plans for The Cedars.'

'Won't you miss Oakfield in some ways?'

'I'll miss the residents, but nothing else, I assure you. That home's so badly run it makes my blood boil! I couldn't say anything when you were there, Lorna, but the amount of abuse that goes on is scandalous. They don't pay the staff enough, so of course they get the dregs.'

'*You're* hardly the dregs,' Lorna observed. And nor was Oshoba. He was continually on her mind – the kick of desire countered by the brake of guilt. That was one thing she couldn't tell Kathy, dared not even tell Clare. He had phoned again last week and begged to . . .

'Well, some of us do try. But the general apathy is terribly frustrating. I've hated it for the last eighteen months, so when Chris offered me the job I was over the moon!'

Lorna dragged her thoughts from grey blankets, black fingers on white breasts. 'You must feel rather daunted, though. It sounds a pretty big undertaking.'

'Yes, but Chris has done the donkey-work. She started ages ago, as soon as probate was cleared. All the building work's completed. We've got thirty en-suite rooms in the main house and ten assisted-living apartments in a new block in the grounds. And the health spa's finished. And they've converted the old stables and the coach-house to make staff living-quarters.'

'Oh, the staff will live in?'

'Some of us. *I'll* be in the coach-house. I fell in love with it at first sight. It's got such character. And you know how boringly fifties my flat is.'

'When are you moving?'

'Four weeks from today.'

'So soon?'

'Yes, I'll be free of Oakfield by then. The Cedars isn't opening until June, but Chris wants me on hand to help interview staff and do various bits and bobs. She's planning a swanky launch party to publicize the place – inviting local dignitaries and GPs and what have you. It'll be a kind of open day, with food and wine and tours of the house. Anyway, enough of me and my news! Let me show you the bumf for Agnes.'

'We'll look at it over lunch, shall we? I've made some carrot-and-orange soup. And beef Wellington to follow.' Yes, Ms Unflappable had pulled out all the stops – quite a contrast with her own efforts in the past, when part of her job had been to entertain business clients. (Was the menu right? Suppose the cream sauce curdled? Would Mr A and wife get on with Mr B and mistress?) It was easy for her to blame their current peculiar eating habits on Ralph's anti-social temperament, but in fact his suggestion that she stop cooking hadn't been entirely selfish. True he hated long, elaborate meals, but he also wanted to reduce the stress on her.

'You shouldn't have gone to so much trouble,' Kathy said, as Lorna led the way into the kitchen. 'Just a sandwich would've done.'

'No, I wanted to make something special,' Ms U responded airily. 'I don't often get the chance to cook.' Well, that was true at least. In the last few weeks Ralph seemed to be surviving on whisky and tobacco, while she grabbed an apple or a hunk of cheese when time allowed. It certainly made a change to sit down to a proper meal.

'The table looks pretty.' Kathy unfolded her gingham napkin. 'Those tulips are gorgeous.'

'It's another house-selling ploy – flowers everywhere, to create a good impression. But these I bought for us.'

Kathy took a spoonful of soup. 'Mm, delicious. Bit different from the Oakfield variety!'

'Yes, I remember the lumps!'

'You must have found Oakfield awfully noisy compared to this place. I can't hear a sound. Don't you get lonely, though, stuck here on your own?'

'Not now, with all the comings and goings. But I used to, yes. When Ralph was away, sometimes I didn't speak to a soul for days.'

'Well, you'll soon be able to change all that. Have you thought about what sort of job you want?'

'Not really.' She'd hardly had time to job-hunt and anyway would need to enlist the help of Ms Unflappable to combat the apprehension she felt about working for an unknown boss and possibly having to deal with office bitchiness. To say nothing of having to travel on public transport. There'd be more choice of jobs in London, but that would mean being wedged chin to chest in claustrophobic trains and, worse, descending to the dreaded tube, fearing she might never re-emerge. 'Let me have a look through this stuff,' she said, purposely changing the subject. 'What I'd like to arrange for Agnes is – Damn!

223

There's the doorbell again. It must be the toner this time. Excuse me a second.'

'We've *made* an appointment – eight o'clock tonight. But Kylie here's busting for a pee. Can she use your toilet?'

'Well, I . . . ' Ms Unflappable had chosen just this moment to disappear.

'Please. It's urgent. She's only three and she can't hold on.'

The child pushed past her father into the hall, a hand clamped over her crotch.

'It's through here,' Lorna said, judging it safer to agree than risk a puddle on the carpet. She opened the cloakroom door for the child, whereupon the rest of the party, including the muddy-pawed Alsatian, trooped into the hall.

Lorna seethed inwardly. It was clearly a ploy to gain entry. Indeed the man was already peering into the sitting-room, while his wife inspected the stair-carpet and the two other women (sisters? friends?) fingered the ornaments on the table. Seeing this invasion of her home by strangers gave her a dismal foretaste of the future: being uprooted, losing all her possessions, having to start again from scratch in some alien little flat. Yes, Ms Unflappable had deserted her completely.

'If you're quite finished,' she snapped, as the man sauntered down the hall, 'I'll see you this evening.'

Back in the kitchen with Kathy, she exploded. 'Honestly! That wretched dog's tramped mud all over the carpet.'

'You shouldn't have let them in. You're too soft – it's time you stood up for yourself. Take Ralph. It's obvious to me he's losing it, yet you still let him make all the important decisions. What about *you*, for heaven's sake? I mean, this new job and everything – you don't seem to have even considered what you actually want to do.'

'Well, yes, I . . . have. As I said, I don't like being so isolated, so I'd change that if I could. To tell the truth, I rather envy *you*, working in a community.'

Kathy stared at her for a minute, then clutched her arm in excitement. 'That's *it*, Lorna – of course! You must come and work with us. As it happens, Chris is looking for an administrator. The one she had lined up got pregnant and cried off. You'd be perfect for the job.'

'Oh, I don't know . . . I've never done anything remotely like that.'

'You run your business, don't you? Do the accounts and bookkeeping?'

'Yes, but – '

'Well, that's what Chris wants – someone to deal with the residents' fees and staff salaries. And chase debts. And judging by the office here you're a model of efficiency. You can even design brochures, which would be jolly useful in the future, should Chris need help with marketing.'

'But ours is the only one I've ever done.'

'Doesn't matter. It has the professional touch. Also you're tremendously good with people – I noticed that at Oakfield. You got on well with everyone. A lot of them still miss you. Sharon and Frances, and Val especially. She says whenever you helped with darts or painting you'd get the others interested and bring them out of themselves. That's a rare talent, Lorna. We want all our staff, even on the admin side, to relate well to the residents. And by the way, I heard about that time you gave Speranza what for.'

'Gave *who* what for?'

'The Kenyan nurse you found carrying on with Sunil in the lounge.'

'God, I'd forgotten about that. I made an utter fool of myself.'

'Not at all. It showed you had ideals. And courage. Those are exactly the qualities we need.'

'But how on earth did you hear about it? It was the middle of the night – you must have left hours before.'

'Oh, these things get around. And walls have ears, you know. Anyway, I was impressed.'

Was Kathy just being kind? No, she *did* have courage – she had stood up to Mr Hughes and lived to tell the tale.

Kathy seemed to have forgotten lunch, and Agnes. Her soup sat untouched as she continued eagerly, 'You'd be working with me, as manager, and because we're friends already things would be so much easier. OK, the pay isn't marvellous, but at least you'd be getting a regular salary without the worry of keeping a business afloat. Besides, staff get lots of perks, and it's a beautiful place to work. Honestly, Lorna, it's time you made a new start – like I'm doing. We're both coming up to forty, you know. We need to take stock. I've been battling on at Oakfield when I knew deep down it wasn't right for me. Then one day I decided that I must do something about it and that if I didn't make a move this year I never would.'

'Yes, but it's easier for you, Kathy. You're not married. You've nobody else to consider.'

'God! We're back to bloody Ralph again! Why should *he* mind? He wanted you to find a job. Well, now you've as good as found one. Surely he'll be pleased.'

'There's the phone – that might be him.' Lorna took the call in the office, glad of a chance to be on her own and digest all that Kathy had said. The phone-call was fortunately brief: the estate agent again, arranging to show more people round.

She rang off and stood by her desk, looking at the framed map on the wall. Each of the coloured pins represented weeks of hard work, and often angst and arguments as well; yet, in spite of all that effort, her heart had never been in Astro-Sport. She *was* good with people – Kathy was right – and working at The Cedars she would be part of a team, part of a community. At Oakfield she'd enjoyed being needed: befriending Frances, counselling Sharon, helping Val with activities.

She leaned against the desk to rest her foot – that was another factor to be taken into account. She could hardly start a new job if she was going ahead with the second operation. But, since there was no guarantee that the second op would be any more successful than the first, she could simply decide to live with the pain and to hell with it. In fact it would make her a more sympathetic administrator, dealing with elderly residents who might themselves be in pain.

She walked slowly back to the kitchen and sat down. 'I am tempted, Kathy, I must admit. Obviously I'll have to discuss it with Ralph, and you and I will need to talk in more detail.'

'Yes, and Chris has the final say, of course. But I know you'll like each other. She's very honest and direct, and though profit's her main concern she shares a lot of my ideals. Oh, Lorna, I'm so excited! Shall I ring her now and tell her?'

'No, wait until tomorrow. Ralph's due back later this afternoon and I'll discuss it with him then. I'll give you a buzz tonight.'

'OK, but let's drink a toast. To us – a new start for both of us!'

*

226

'It's madness, Lorna,' Ralph said vehemently, getting up from his desk. 'You can't turn on the radio these days without hearing about another old folks' home going down the tubes. The boom's over – well and truly. This Chris or whatever her name is will be bankrupt before you know it, and *you*'ll be left high and dry.'

'At least get your facts right, Ralph. Most of those homes had to close because the local authorities wouldn't pay enough for their residents. But Chris's aiming at a different market entirely. Her place will be more like a five-star hotel, except people can buy in services as and when they need them, like nursing, or help with bathing and dressing.'

'Yes, and there's the problem. How does she intend to find halfway-decent staff? You've only got to look at Oakfield House to see how impossible it is.'

'But that's the point. They're deliberately setting out to avoid abuses, by – '

'Fine talk in theory. But once the place opens its doors Chris'll realize what she's up against. Hell, we think we have problems with *our* clients, but at least they're not gaga or incontinent.'

'And nor will most of hers be. I'm sure she knows what she's doing. Kathy says she's had years of experience. She used to run a group of specialist hotels.'

'That's different altogether. Hotels don't have the government breathing down their neck with endless petty regulations and miles of red tape.'

'I bet they do,' she said irritably. He was standing right behind her and she was trying to finish a complicated report.

'Well, they certainly don't have the social services turning up on the doorstep every five minutes to do spot checks.'

'OK, according to you the venture's doomed before it starts.' Lorna jabbed at the keyboard with unnecessary force. 'What do you suggest I do instead?'

He leaned over and took her hand. 'Continue as my partner in the business.'

'*What*?'

'I've been reconsidering, Lorna. We'd be crazy to wind it up when we need every penny we can get. Last night, when you were showing people round, I rang George at the Sherborne golf club and he said he thinks we'll get the contract.'

Indignantly she shook his hand off. 'I *told* you that a fortnight ago, and you said you were sick to death of the business and there wasn't a hope of running it without a house.'

'OK, I over-reacted. I was very low at the time. But that job's worth a heck of a lot. And it's pretty straightforward stuff. In fact I could do the fitting myself at a push, to save on costs. They want pathways, tee-tops, cross-overs, a practice putting-green and –'

'I know exactly what they want, Ralph. But you can't keep chopping and changing like this. I mean, I've more or less accepted this job of Kathy's, and now you say we're back in harness.' She already sensed the heavy straps pressing down again, the bit hurting her mouth as Ralph yanked on the reins. 'Besides, we need money in hand for a big job like Sherborne. How are we going to pay for the materials?'

'By juggling things very carefully. We delay paying the suppliers until our cheque from the golf club is safely in the bank. George is a decent enough chap. If I tell him we need payment on the nail I'm sure he'll sort it out.'

'That's taking an awful risk, though. What if he's off sick or gets the chop? They might not pay up for months.'

'Now who's being negative?'

'Ralph, for goodness' sake, we can't *afford* to juggle things, as you put it. We're in enough trouble as it is.'

Dejectedly he returned to his desk. Their chairs were back to back. She had often thought it significant that at work they should face in opposite directions, never meeting each other's eyes. She heard him strike a match.

'Ralph, please don't smoke. We've got those people coming later.'

'They won't smell it in here.'

'Of course they will.'

'Don't change the subject. What I'd like to know is, if you take this job with Kathy at the princely sum of £8 an hour, how are we meant to live?'

'You get a job too.'

'I've told you, no one wants me. Including my own wife it seems.'

'Oh, Ralph . . . ' He sounded so forlorn. 'I just can't bear to lose this chance. It's the sort of thing I'd really love to do. And Kathy and I get on so well . . . '

'All right, go ahead. It's not fair for me to stop you.'

She swivelled round to look at him: his shoulders were hunched, his head bowed. He had spoken not with bitterness but in a tone of utter desolation. This year he had lost so much: his financial clout, his pride, his self-esteem. And soon he would lose the house, which he had owned for half a lifetime. She went over to his chair and put her arm round him. 'Can't you run the business without me – get an assistant perhaps?'

'And how do I pay her? In any case, it's *you* I want. You know the business inside out. You're brilliant at it. I'd never train anyone else to your standard.'

'You . . . you've never said that before.'

'I'm sorry, darling. I've taken you for granted. I realize I haven't been at my best these last few months, what with all the strain and worry. But I love you, Lorna, and it means a tremendous lot to me that we work together. I'd hate that to change.'

'Ralph, you told me we were finished.' She looked wearily at his cluttered desk. 'Don't you see how confusing it is if one day you say one thing, and the next you – '

'I'm sorry,' he repeated. 'You've every right to be annoyed. But I've come to the conclusion that our only chance of staying solvent is to carry on as we were. We've got one decent-sized contract in hand – two, including Sherborne – and the Salisbury and Lewes tennis-courts in the pipeline, and at least six other jobs we've quoted for.'

'We can't count on getting more than two of those six – if that. You know how much undercutting goes on. That new team, Art-Grass, can hardly be breaking even at the ridiculous prices they charge, never mind making a profit.'

'Yes, but they won't survive. And we will. Anyway, if only two of the six come back to us it's something.'

'And how do we pay for materials?'

'On credit.'

'That's risky too.'

'No more than trying to exist on one piffling wage.'

She sighed in exasperation. 'I just don't believe you can't get a job of some sort.'

'Oh, stacking shelves in Tesco's maybe. Except even they probably don't employ the over-fifties. Anyway, that's not the point. We've built up this business between us, darling. It's our child, if you like, and we can't simply give it up after nurturing it all this time.'

Their child, she thought with a shudder. Another miscarriage, another aborted mess flushed down the sluice. 'I don't think we're very good at children, Ralph. They've cost us too much emotionally.'

'You're forgetting how well things went in the beginning. We lived comfortably for years.'

No, she hadn't forgotten – nor ever would. When she had moved here as Ms Maguire she was skint and also in debt. She had brought nothing to the marriage except depression, insecurity and panic. Yet a few months later, as Mrs Pearson, she owned a joint share in a substantial house and a potentially profitable business, a snazzy little car, a wardrobe full of clothes, and private health insurance.

'Let's give it one more try. We'll find out soon enough if it's going to work. *Please*, Lorna.' He squeezed her hand. 'You don't know how much it means to me.'

Never before had he pleaded with her – he was too proud. His pride was part of the problem. If, as he feared, he didn't manage to get a job, how would he feel queueing at the dole office – the once successful engineer and company director?

'Remember on our honeymoon we promised to stand by each other, whatever happened?'

She nodded, thinking of her previous relationships: brief, reckless couplings, desperate, ill-advised. But Ralph was completely different: a man who valued fidelity and trust, and who would neither hurt nor leave her. It was *she* who had ruined the honeymoon, with her nightly panics, her fear of drowning and shipwreck. Yet Ralph had talked her through them, steadied her, consoled her.

She glanced down at his hand, clamped over hers. It was all very well for Kathy to say leave him to rot. No outsider could ever be privy to the intimate balance sheet of a marriage. Besides, when you married someone you took on the child as well as the adult, and how could she abandon that vulnerable boy? She had seen photos of him at school: a thin, pale child with frightened eyes.

In the ensuing silence the pressure of his fingers increased – a form of wordless plea. Then suddenly he cleared his throat and said with an embarrassed air, 'There's something I want to tell you, Lorna.'

Oh, God, she thought, what now?

'I've . . . decided to stop drinking.'

'Ralph, surely you don't expect me to believe – '

'I mean it. Last night I poured every drop of Scotch in the house down the sink.'

'Down the sink?' she echoed.

'Yes. As a gesture. To prove that you can trust me.'

'But, Ralph, don't you think that's rather extreme – giving up altogether?' He'd be restless, sleepless, impossibly bad-tempered. 'Why not just cut down?'

'No, I want to do it properly. For your sake.'

She was touched, despite herself. He must value her more than she'd realized if he was willing to make such a sacrifice – or at least value her help in the business.

'Don't fall for it, Lorna,' Kathy's voice warned. 'How long do you think he'll last? A couple of days? Remember when he tried to give up smoking? He's just using every trick in the book to stop you taking the job with us.'

Lorna looked at his dead pipe. Normally if she asked him not to smoke he ignored her. Might he genuinely want a new start? There was a side of Ralph that Kathy didn't know: he was stoical, and loyal; he took flowers to Naomi's grave every year, on her birthday. And every year he sent cheques to various multiple-sclerosis charities, even when money was tight. Nor did he bear grudges. Indeed, he had supported his mother financially after she was widowed, despite her former neglect of him.

'I . . . I think I'll make a cup of tea.' She needed a moment to herself. She was being pulled in all directions and hardly knew what to think any longer, except that Oshoba was somehow the key. If she hadn't betrayed Ralph she would feel morally justified in taking the job at The Cedars. But to betray him twice . . .

She stood by the hob, twisting her wedding-ring round and round on her finger. For better or worse, she had vowed. Forsaking all other . . .

Forlornly she walked back to the office, hearing the four cedar-

231

trees crash headlong to the ground. 'OK, Ralph, we'll give it one last go. And I'll do my utmost to make it work.'

He said nothing, simply took her in his arms. Pressed close to him, it was Oshoba she could feel, the hardness and heat of his body, the polished gleam of his skin.

'Let's start again,' Ralph murmured. 'I'll never touch another drink, I promise.'

'It won't be easy.' Any more than giving up Oshoba would be easy. Or The Cedars.

'Doesn't matter. I owe it to you. I know I've been a disappointment.'

'Don't say that, Ralph.'

'It's true. I wanted to give you everything. I couldn't even give you a child, and now – '

'I didn't know you minded about . . . the child.'

'Well, more for your sake than mine. But I still feel that I failed you.'

'We both failed. It was me as much as you.'

'Let's make love,' he whispered suddenly.

'What, now?' Was he about to break the rules of a lifetime, strip naked on a busy afternoon?

'Why not? It's been so long.' He gave a nervous laugh. 'I was beginning to think you'd gone off me.'

'No, of course not.' Could he somehow tell she'd been unfaithful; see the imprint of Oshoba's kisses branding her body? Yet she *wanted* to make love. It would be a way of renewing her marriage vows, negating that exquisite, dangerous, amazing night on the sofa.

Ralph unfastened the top button of her blouse and gently kissed her throat. Normally he wouldn't make a move to undress her, and if he kissed her at all it was never in such a devoted, lingering way. This was not the Ralph she knew.

Which meant anything was possible.

As she slipped off her blouse the phone rang. Her first instinct was to ignore it, then she realized it might be George. 'Yes, hello?' she said, mouthing 'Don't go away!' to Ralph.

'. . . *Who?*' she said, confused. 'Oh, my God! Yes, of course I'll come. I'll leave at once.'

22

'Your aunt's in here. We moved her from the ward to give her more privacy.'

Privacy to *die*, Lorna thought, gazing at the motionless body in the bed. Or was Agnes dead already? The eyes were closed, the mouth gaped open, the skin of the face was dry and brown, like the petals of a shrivelled flower. Almost more shocking was the ugly gash on the forehead. Around its blackened edges the hair had been cut away; purplish bruising had spread beneath the left eye.

Lorna started at a sudden rasp of breath. No, Agnes wasn't dead; yet nor was she alive. She was caught between the two, in an unknown void.

'Sit down,' the nurse said kindly. 'You can stay with her all night if you wish. I'm afraid we can't provide proper beds for visitors, but you'll find that chair quite comfortable.'

Visitors? She was Agnes's *child*, and she hadn't said goodbye. 'Do you think she'll last the . . . ?' Pointless question. Hadn't they told her already that the cancer was worse, and that the fall had shaken her up considerably.

'Can I get you a cup of tea, Lorna?'

'No thanks.' Lorna bristled at the use of her Christian name by a person she'd only just met. Unfairly, she resented everything about the hospice – the cloying friendliness in a place of death, the calm matter-of-factness with which they reported terrible news. 'A neighbour found her on the floor, unable to get up. No one knows how long she'd been there . . . ' ' . . . and I'm afraid the cancer's spread to her bones. But we're doing all we can to keep her comfortable.'

Comfortable? What did this chit of a nurse know? Her peachy skin and lustrous hair seemed insultingly healthy, given Agnes's pitiful condition.

'Well, if you'd like a drink later there's a kitchenette along the passage, with a kettle and a fridge and so on. Just help yourself. And if you see any change in your aunt, press this bell and someone will come at once.'

'What sort of change?'

'Well, if she has trouble breathing, for instance.'

How could her breathing be any worse? Every few seconds a fierce, wheezing spasm contorted her face. The difference between life and death was reduced to that grotesque yet reassuring sound. Without it Agnes would simply fade to nothingness.

'I'll see you later, Lorna. I'm on duty all night, so I'll be popping in every now and then.'

Once the nurse had gone, Lorna pulled the chair closer to the bed. It was hard to recognize this almost-corpse as Agnes. For one thing, she had never seen her aunt without her teeth. It seemed disrespectful, an invasion of her privacy – indeed, wrong to be looking at her at all when Agnes didn't know that anyone was there.

'Come back,' she begged. 'Open your eyes.'

No response. Just more racking breaths.

She reached out to take her aunt's hand. It wasn't cold, surprisingly, but hot and clammy, as if she were running a fever. Yet she was wearing only a flimsy nightie, puff-sleeved and sprigged with turquoise flowers. Agnes's nightgowns were sterner in style – high-necked and virginal white. This must be hospice property.

'It's Lorna,' she whispered. 'I'm here. I'm with you. I came the minute I heard.'

Too late, though. If she had only stayed with Agnes in the cottage she could have prevented the fall. Stupidly, she had assumed they would have months more. She had been trying to arrange home nursing, planning little treats, for someone who was beyond all help, by the looks of it. She longed to hear Agnes's irascible voice saying, 'Take me home at once, Lorna. You know I hate these places.'

Yet the hospice was pleasant enough: nicely furnished, homely, surrounded by attractive shrubs and trees. And the room had all mod cons: en-suite bathroom, telephone and television, adjustable bed with enough control buttons for a jet plane. But what was the use of any of it when Agnes was incapable of opening her eyes?

Lorna squeezed the scrawny hand. It was curled in her palm as trustingly as a baby's, yet the veins were those of an old woman, standing out like gnarled blue cords. And the arms were pathetically thin, as if all the flesh had fallen away, leaving only skin and bone. Lorna caressed the ringless wedding-finger. How hard it must have been for a lifelong spinster to bring up a child. The balance was so unequal – what she had done for Agnes, what Agnes had done for her. 'Please don't die,' she murmured. 'Not yet. There are things I need to say.' With her free hand she touched Agnes's face, traced the hollows in her cheeks, carefully avoiding the bruise. 'Can you hear me? Do you know who I am?'

Another shuddering gasp.

She let go of the hand and sank back in her chair. The curtains were only half drawn and through the window, behind the silhouette of a leafless tree, hung a cheese-paring of moon. Agnes had taught her about the moon and stars – told her the names of the constellations, explained the rise and fall of the tides. Nearly everything she knew had come from Agnes: kings, queens, fairy-tales, poetry, hymns, nature lore.

'Aunt,' she said, 'remember the stories you used to tell me? Once upon a time . . . '

She glanced at her watch. Ten to midnight. How long might Agnes last? And would she simply slip away, or suffer horrendous death throes?

'Hello, Lorna. I'm back!'

It was the young nurse again, maddeningly pink and plump. 'I won-der if you'd mind just popping outside for a moment. I need to give Agnes an injection.'

'Yes, of course.' Lorna got up reluctantly, though at least it would give her a chance to phone Ralph – if he was still awake.

Walking along the corridor, she caught glimpses through open doors of ghostly inert figures, heard sounds of coughing or retching, or people crying out in their sleep. The lights had been dimmed for the night, which gave her an eerie sense of being in an underworld, an antechamber of death. Yet all along the passageway there were vases of spring flowers: pert daffodils, new-fledged narcissi, brazenly red tulips. Were these the flowers of the dead? Ephemeral blooms outlasting ephemeral patients?

'Are you all right, my dear?' asked the nurse at the desk – a solid, grey-haired woman with a soft Lincolnshire accent.

'Yes,' she lied. 'I'm looking for a quiet corner where I can phone my husband. I've got my mobile with me, but I don't want to disturb any-one.'

'I'm sorry, mobile phones aren't allowed inside the building. They interfere with our electrical equipment. But there's a public call-box you can use. It's a little further down, on the right.'

She had to reverse the charges as she hadn't any change. It was a relief to hear Ralph's voice when he came on the line at last – an anchor in this unfamiliar world.

'How is she, Lorna? Did you get there in time?'

'Yes. Well . . . I hope so. I just wish they'd phoned me earlier. She had a nasty fall two days ago and was taken to Casualty. They did X-rays and God knows what. There was no serious damage, fortunately, but they kept her in because of the cancer. She was in a big noisy ward, which she absolutely loathed. In fact she was so desperate to go home she tried to get out of bed and nearly killed herself in the process. So they rang her GP and told him she was far too ill to be living on her own. Apparently he's been saying the same himself for quite some time, so he took the chance to get her into a hospice.'

'And is she any happier?'

'Impossible to say. She's drugged up to the eyeballs with morphine. It's controlling the pain, which is something, I suppose. Oh, darling, I'm so glad I got you. I thought you might be asleep.'

'I can't sleep. I was worrying about you. And actually without the old nightcap I don't expect I'll ever sleep again!' He laughed mirth-lessly. 'I can't say I'm enamoured of Ovaltine.'

'Ralph, you *are* good. I'm impressed.'

'There's no need to be sarcastic.'

'I'm not. I can't tell you how much it means to me that you've decided to give up.'

With an embarrassed cough he changed the subject. 'Is there any-thing I can do? I could join you, if you like: come up there in the morn-ing and – '

'Let's wait and see, OK? I'm not sure how she'll . . . be.'

'Well, ring me again tonight if you want. I'll be up.'

'Thanks, darling. Love you.'

'Love you, too.'

She did love him tonight – her newly sober, insomniac Ralph. Now he was off the drink, perhaps it would be more like the old days: instead of communing with his whisky in the evenings, he might converse with her.

On the way back to Agnes's room she heard the sound of anguished sobbing. A patient? A bereaved relative? She stopped to listen. Shouldn't *she* be crying? She felt drained, unreal, out of touch with every emotion, even fear. Fear had been ousted by anger – anger with herself for neglecting Agnes; anger with old age, illness, death. Agnes had always been so strong. How could she be reduced to this?

She stood looking at the emaciated body, then suddenly leaned over the bed until her face was almost touching Agnes's. 'Now listen to me' – she used her aunt's own brusque tone – 'you've got to hang on a bit longer, do you hear? I want to say I'm sorry. And thank you. And . . . and goodbye. You can't just disappear without a word. That's what my parents did. Don't you see how cruel it is to leave me high and dry? Agnes, I'm your *child*!'

At that moment Agnes opened her eyes. They stared at each other in shock. Then Agnes licked her lips and made an attempt to speak. 'M . . . Margaret?'

'No, not Margaret. Margaret's daughter.'

'Margaret's daughter?'

'*Your* daughter. Your little Lorna.'

'My little Lorna?' Agnes repeated wonderingly. 'Come . . . back?'

'Yes,' she whispered, 'come back.'

'Can you manage another spoonful, Aunt?'

'Yes please.'

A miracle, Lorna thought – Agnes sitting up and eating. Admittedly it was a struggle. Each mouthful took time to go down and was followed by a deep, shuddering sigh, as if the effort had exhausted her. And her breathing was just as laboured as before. Lunch had been punctuated by the convulsive spasms that seemed to shake her frame.

Again Lorna held the spoon to her lips and again felt a glow of triumph as a thimbleful was swallowed. She had never fed a baby, but now she was feeding Agnes, and with a baby's food: semi-liquid scrambled egg, semi-melted ice-cream.

'It's pretty, isn't it?' Agnes said in her new hoarse, drunken-sounding voice. 'The pink and white.'

'Yes, raspberry ripple.'

'I remember it was one of your favourites when you were little.'

'It still is!'

'Well, you have some, dear. There's far too much for me.'

'Certainly not. We've got to build you up. Come on – try a little more.'

'Careful,' Agnes said. 'Don't spill it on the carpet.'

'It's all right, Aunt, there isn't a carpet.'

'Yes there is. It's blue. I used that left-over bit for the spare room.'

Lorna said nothing. Evidently Agnes was muddling her room here with the cottage. A result of the drugs no doubt. Most of the time she was perfectly coherent, then her mind would wander.

'Do you want a sip of juice to help it down?' Lorna held the plastic beaker to Agnes's mouth. It had two handles, like a child's cup, but Agnes was too weak to hold it herself. Eating and drinking were major undertakings, demanding patience and fortitude on both their parts, but together they had succeeded. At least a quarter of the scrambled egg had gone, half the ice-cream and a good part of the drink.

'That's enough, Lorna dear. I'm tired.'

'OK. I'll get Pam to take your tray. I can hear her outside.'

'You've done well, Agnes,' Pam observed as she stacked the dishes.

'That's because my niece is here. She's an angel. You're all angels. I must have died and gone to heaven.'

It was a still greater miracle, Lorna reflected, that Agnes should be so grateful and contented – indeed, positively benign. Far from complaining or wanting to go home, she seemed to be relishing life in the hospice. She didn't even mind being addressed as Agnes by everyone from cleaners to doctors. Instead of the anticipated rejoinder – 'Miss Hoxton, if you *don't* mind. My Christian name's not public property' – Agnes simply smiled. Was it an effect of the morphine? Drug-induced euphoria? Lorna didn't care. Whatever the cause, it was welcome, if extraordinary.

'Shall I draw your curtains? The sun's quite bright today.'

'No, I like to see it. And the garden's very pretty.'

'When you're strong enough I'll wheel you out there for a nice breath of spring.'

'We'll see. Now, before I forget, there's something I want to give you, Lorna.'

'Give me?'

'Yes. Your mother's wedding-ring. It was returned to me by the . . . the . . . Oh dear. I can't think of the word.'

'Coroner?'

'No.'

'Mortuary?'

'No.' Agnes tutted in frustration. 'It doesn't matter anyway. They gave me all her jewellery in a small brown-paper packet. I'm afraid I had to sell the necklace and the . . . the . . . what d'you call it. But the ring I kept for you. I intended to give it to you on your wedding-day, but I thought Ralph might . . . ' Her voice tailed off.

'Be hurt?'

'Yes. He bought you such a lovely ring.'

'Mm.' Lorna glanced at it. 'Victorian.' Ralph had chosen it for the inscription: 'For ever'. How sad that his romantic soft centre got submerged so often beneath a prickly carapace.

'Now, if you open my top dressing-table drawer . . . '

Lorna frowned. 'You mean at home?'

'Yes. Over there.' Agnes was pointing in the direction of the television. 'Be careful. It tends to stick.'

'Aunt, dear, we . . . we're not in the cottage.'

'Where are we then? I get muddled.'

'We're in the hospice. Together. You and me. We're doing well. We're fine. I'll get the ring later and bring it in to show you. All right?'

Agnes nodded.

'Now you settle down to sleep.'

As Agnes obediently closed her eyes, Lorna recalled the few occasions when she had seen her ill in bed – invariably chafing at the enforced inaction which she deplored as sinful sloth. Yet she now happily accepted that even the simplest procedures such as being fed or washed required a recovery period afterwards.

'You won't go away?' she murmured, groping for Lorna's hand.

'Of course not.' Lorna clasped the arthritic fingers. 'You don't get rid of me that easily. I'd better warn you, Aunt, you'll soon be sick of the sight of me!'

'Come in,' Lorna called.

Agnes was still dozing, but she opened her eyes as a short, black-suited man in a dog-collar entered the room. 'Good morning, Agnes. I'm Simon Taylor, the vicar of St John's.' He included Lorna in his friendly smile of greeting.

'Do sit down.' She indicated the second chair.

'No, thank you. I won't stay. I just came to ask if you'd like to take Communion, Agnes?'

'I'm not a Christian, Mr Taylor.'

Lorna wondered if she'd heard right. What about the God of her childhood – Agnes's vengeful, all-seeing God? Every Sunday, she and her aunt went dutifully to church, to confess their sins and sing His praises – the very model of good Christians. Had Agnes only been pretending to believe, to give an orphaned child something to cling to? It had proved effective, certainly: she *had* found comfort in the thought of her parents strolling hand in hand in heaven, among gambolling bunnies and flowers that never faded.

'Well, if you'd like me to pop in at any time I'd be happy to oblige. It doesn't matter if you're not a formal believer. We welcome all religions and none.'

'I'm afraid I'm beyond help, Mr Taylor. The doctors say there's nothing more they can do for me.'

'No one's beyond help, Agnes.'

'I doubt that, Mr Taylor.'

Lorna looked at her anxiously. Had the euphoria passed, or was she simply resigned to the prospect of death?

'What's the date?' she asked suddenly.

Lorna tried to remember. Time was so hazy she couldn't even think how long she had been here.

'It's March the twenty-first,' the vicar put in. 'The first day of spring! And if you'll forgive me, dear ladies, I'd better be on my way.'

'He reminds me of your father,' Agnes remarked when the door had closed behind him.

The drunkard and the gambler? Surely not.

'Too charming by half,' Agnes continued, with a touch of her old acerbity. 'Dear ladies, indeed!' She counted on her fingers. 'Now let me see – Margaret died on the twenty-fifth of March. Wouldn't it be strange if I went on that day too?'

Lorna outstared the callous sun. Not strange. Horrific. Spring or no, it would become the darkest day of the year, blighted by three deaths. It had been bad enough in childhood, especially if Easter was late and she was still cooped up at boarding-school. The other girls didn't understand why, on that black-edged day, she couldn't eat or concentrate and often hid in the grounds and howled her eyes out. 'You're getting *better*, Aunt,' she insisted, to convince herself as much as Agnes.

But Agnes didn't seem to have heard. 'You're not to worry about my funeral, Lorna. It's all been taken care of. I've been paying for it in instalments, so you wouldn't have the expense.'

'Oh, *Aunt* . . . '

'I don't want anything fancy, mind. I've left strict instructions. I'm not wasting money on coffins that only get burnt. But there's one thing you could do, when you find the time – take my ashes and scatter them near Margaret's grave. I miss her.'

Lorna frowned against the glare of the sun. The two sisters had been apart for thirty-five years. A lifetime of missing.

'And if it's no trouble, dear, I would like a little funeral tea, for the people in the village. They've all been exceptionally kind. You can have it in the cottage, to save expense.'

'Yes, of . . . course.'

'As you know, I'm very partial to ham sandwiches. Would it be a bother to arrange it?'

Lorna got up and put her arm round Agnes's shoulder. 'You shall have a *ton* of ham sandwiches. And egg, cheese, tongue, chicken – every sandwich under the sun.'

'Extravagance! The food's paid for, anyway. It's included in the funeral plan.'

'Look, if I can't afford a few . . . '

'It's not a question of affording – it's a question of what's right. I've always paid my way, and I don't intend things to be different just because I'm dead.'

Lorna smiled, despite herself.

'And you won't forget to thank people for coming.'

'No, Aunt, I won't forget.' How could she, when Agnes was the one who'd taught her the common courtesies? 'Oh, look,' she said, 'here's Carole, come to do your manicure.'

It was perhaps the greatest miracle of all that plain, no-nonsense Agnes, who all her life had trimmed her nails with a pair of clippers and considered nail varnish a frippery beneath contempt, had agreed to submit herself to Carole's ministrations.

Lorna watched with bemused pleasure as her aunt lay back against the pillows and allowed Carole to apply cuticle-remover while instructing her on the latest fashion colours: Sizzling Scarlet, Think Pink, Strawberry Crush. If things went on like this, she would no longer recognize her. There were other volunteers who visited the hospice: hairdressers, beauticians. She tried to picture Agnes with Barbara Cartland eyelashes and a shimmering blue rinse, but her imagination failed to make the leap. 'Agnes, I'm going to phone Ralph. I'll leave you in Carole's capable hands.'

'Yes, you get some rest, child. I'm perfectly all right. I don't need looking after.'

On her way to the phone, at least half a dozen people stopped her to chat. The hospice had become her substitute family as well as Agnes's. And she too felt a certain euphoria (even without the benefit of morphine) such was the sense of community here, embracing not just each patient but all their relatives. She hadn't experienced a single stirring of panic or heard a squeak from the Monster. Ms Unflappable she couldn't be when Agnes was facing death, but Ms Courageous, yes. Courage came more easily in this supportive atmosphere, where she'd already received a wealth of tiny kindnesses. Jane, the house-keeper, had supplied a pile of blankets for the night and managed to wangle her a lavender pillow; Emma, one of the volunteers, had brought her in a home-made chicken pie; Sue, the physiotherapist, had given her a shoulder massage; and Angela, the cleaner, always made sure she had plenty of change for the phone. ('You mustn't neg-lect your hubby, dear.')

She slotted two of Angela's coins into the slot. 'Ralph, it's me. Do you feel neglected?'

'No, but I miss you. How's Agnes?'

'So cheerful you wouldn't know her.'

'Cheerful, on her deathbed?'

'Yes. It's a bit spooky, actually. This is the first time I've ever seen her so upbeat, and I'm not sure if it's . . . real.'

'Well, she wouldn't be pretending, would she?'

'I'm not sure. I'm beginning to wonder if I know her. Anyway, how are *you?*'

'OK.'

'Not drinking?'

'No. Though it's a hell of a strain. I feel restless and sort of jumpy. And as for sleeping, forget it!'

'Give it time. You'll soon be over the worst. And, Ralph, I want you to know I really do admire you – having the guts to stick at it. To be honest, I never thought you would.'

The usual embarrassed silence.

'In fact it helps me cope with what I'm doing here. If I get tired sitting on a chair all night, I think of you awake as well and it stops me feeling sorry for myself.'

He laughed morosely. 'Well, I have to say I'm feeling sorry for myself just now. I've got several different people coming to view the house this afternoon, and a whole lot more tomorrow. Then the dentist at six – I've lost a filling and it's giving me gyp. And what's left of my birthday I'll probably spend doing the VAT return.'

'Oh, Ralph, your birthday! I'd completely forgotten!'

'Doesn't matter. You know my opinion of birthdays.'

'It *does* matter. What would you like? I can buy you something at the hospice shop, if you don't mind Yardley's lavender water or home-knitted bedsocks.'

'There's only one thing I want.'

'What's that?'

'*You,*' he said sheepishly. 'All night.'

All night hadn't happened for years. This really was a new model Ralph.

'Don't worry, I'm only joking. Being off the booze makes me – well, amorous. And the nights seem . . . lonely without you.'

'Oh, Ralph . . .'

'I'll survive. By the way, are you OK for clothes and stuff? I could drive up first thing tomorrow if there's anything you need.'

'With all those people coming to see the house?'

'I'll put them off.'

'No, Ralph, we've *got* to sell. Time is of the essence, otherwise think of the interest on the bank loan.'

'OK.'

'Look, I'll phone again this evening and say happy birthday properly.'

'Forget the present, though. Bedsocks aren't quite my thing. I'll have what I asked for – on credit.'

She laughed. 'All right, I promise! Love you, darling. Bye.'

As she rang off, Megan, the day sister, happened to be coming round the corner. 'Ah, Lorna, could I have a word with you?'

Lorna felt a twinge of fear. Surely Agnes couldn't have suffered a decline in the few minutes she'd been gone.

Megan ushered her into the office. 'Do sit down. Take that comfy chair. All I want to say is that we're a bit worried about you, Lorna.'

'Worried? About *me?*'

'Yes. You're doing too much. You haven't had a breath of fresh air or a wink of sleep since you arrived. You really need a good night's rest. We do have a couple of put-you-ups for relatives, but they're not particularly comfortable and I'm afraid you wouldn't get much peace. Agnes is in no immediate danger at the moment. She appears to have plateaued out, which means there probably won't be any change for the next few days. So I suggest you take the chance to catch up on your sleep. I presume you could stay in her house.'

No, she thought, aware of Ms Courageous shrivelling to a husk. However well she was coping in the hospice, alone in Agnes's damp, dark cottage she would be beset by instant panic.

'Or there's a guest-house up the road. It's very reasonable, and of course we'd phone you immediately should the need arise.'

She smoothed her crumpled skirt. The Monster might be silent now, but he'd be back at the first opportunity. And what better place for an ambush than an anonymous guest-house?

'Perhaps you feel you shouldn't leave Agnes, even for a moment. It's a natural reaction. But you have to think of yourself too, you know. You'll be more help to your aunt if you recharge your batteries.'

'Well, would it be OK if I went home? Just for tonight, I mean.'

'Mm, that's a long drive when you're already tired. Are you sure you're up to it?'

Her foot most certainly wasn't – on the journey here it had hurt badly – but pain was always preferable to panic. 'Oh yes,' she assured Megan. 'And I know my husband would be pleased. It's his birthday today, you see.'

'Well, in that case it seems a good idea. I'll get the doctor to take another look at Agnes, and if he feels she's still reasonably stable you could get off straight away.'

'Fine. And I've got a mobile, so if anything should . . . happen, phone me, please, and I'll turn straight back.'

'Of course.'

Lorna got up, then half sat down again. 'Megan, there's something else. My aunt seems so different – much more positive and sweet-tempered than normal. I'm sorry, that must sound awful. I'm not meaning to be critical, but I can't work out if it's really *her* or if it's just due to the drugs. Can morphine change your personality?'

Megan smiled. 'No, but what it can do is take away fear. There are certain sorts of people who are unable to be themselves because they're paralysed by worry, or plagued with irrational fears – fears that last a lifetime in some cases. And if those fears are suddenly removed the person may blossom in an unexpected way. Often they find they can say things they were too inhibited to say before. And you could argue that the new person is *more* real than the old one. I suppose another way of putting it is that morphine occasionally frees people to be their true self.'

Lorna stared at her in surprise. Could Agnes, her intrepid, indomitable aunt, have been a prey to irrational fears or tormented by a Monster as gleefully spiteful as her own? No, impossible.

Or was it? When Margaret died, Agnes's world had crashed around her ears – the shock of losing her only sibling followed by the second shock of having an orphan child dumped on her. Who would *not* be terrified at having to cope alone? Agnes's parents were already dead and Margaret had meant so much to her: not just a beloved sister but her closest friend and confidante.

'You look a bit concerned, Lorna. I hope I haven't upset you?'

'No. Far from it. I'm just thinking about what you said.' And remembering Agnes's remark when they were talking in the cottage: 'One of us had to be strong.' Had Agnes merely fabricated that strength, laid it on top of the fears, as she used to place rugs over worn patches in the carpet? The worn patches were still there, of course, and so might her fears have been – till now.

Megan glanced at her watch. 'Well, I'd better get back to the ward. The doctor won't be long. I'll let you know what he says, and all being well you should be on your way within the hour.'

'Yes. Thank you, Megan.' Lorna spoke mechanically, her mind still fixed on Agnes. What she had said to Ralph was true: she had never really known her aunt, only the brave façade.

'See you soon, then.'

'Right.' Lorna wandered along to the kitchenette and made herself a cup of coffee, to give Carole time to finish.

'Just look at me!' Agnes spread her hands on the coverlet, nails uppermost.

'Fantastic!' Lorna sat on the bed and gently stroked each strawberry-red nail. 'And *you*'re fantastic, too, Aunt, for being so . . . so brave.'

'Brave? There's nothing to be brave about. These wonderful people have taken away the pain.'

Lorna said no more. If Agnes had gone to so much trouble putting rugs over the worn patches, she wouldn't want anyone, perhaps least of all her niece, lifting them up and peering underneath.

23

'Delicious Norfolk turkeys – plump, tender and ready to carve.'

'Delicious Norfolk turkeys – plump, tender and . . . '

'Fuck turkeys!' Lorna muttered, sick of sitting stationary for a couple of hours behind that stupid slogan. And the picture above it was even more absurd: a cartoon red-wattled bird with a knife and fork tucked under its wing and a jaunty grin on its face. The lorry towered claustrophobically over her small car, blocking her view of the road ahead.

Her successive attempts to tune the radio had produced nothing but blasts of static. The fates were clearly against her – the one time she needed the travel news the radio refused to work. Not that she particularly wanted to hear the gory details of whatever accident was responsible for the hold-up. An hour ago she had watched the sun set over the distant trees: a blaze of gold and scarlet, providing a temporary distraction from being stuck in a horrendous jam, nose to tail and three abreast. Now it was dark – and cold.

She switched the engine on again, with an anxious glance at the shopping on the passenger seat. Ralph's birthday strawberries were wilting and the non-alcoholic bubbly would be tepid by the time she served it – if she ever did. The irony was that if she hadn't stopped in Lincoln to buy the ingredients for dinner and a few bits and pieces for Ralph she might be home by now.

She was tempted to ring him, just to hear a voice, except it would spoil the surprise. Yet, as time dragged by, the whole idea of turning up unannounced to give him the present he'd so bashfully requested seemed more and more nonsensical. She had forgotten quite how far it was to drive home and what a toll it took on her foot, and the thought of having to make the same journey tomorrow (especially on this hated stretch of motorway) filled her with dread.

If only she could relax, like other people. The Citroën-driver on her right had been chatting and laughing on his mobile for the last half-hour, so maddeningly cheerful he probably wouldn't turn a hair if the entire motorway network shut down. And to her left the family in the Volvo estate also seemed to be coping. Admittedly the children were getting restive and the boisterous black Labrador was steaming up the windows, but the parents hadn't yet murdered either each other or their brood. At first she had exchanged occasional smiles with them, but now she stared miserably ahead, resenting their forbearance.

' . . . plump, tender and ready to . . . '

Turkeys meant Christmas, and Christmas meant uncertainty. Where might she be by then? Would the business be solvent? Would her foot be better at last?

Judging by how much it hurt at the moment, the answer would seem to be no. And her back was aching hideously after sitting cramped up for so long. Also she was plagued by a vision of the rear end of the lorry expanding before her eyes, looming over her car and about to descend and crush it to a pulp.

Quickly she ran through her anti-panic techniques: breathing, relaxation. Apart from anything else, she owed it to Ralph to keep calm. In her absence he'd been working all hours, and without his usual whisky to sustain him. She tried to drum up Ms Unflappable for moral support, but the character kept guttering like a candle in a draught, and although Ms Courageous proved slightly more substantial her voice was soon lost in another gale of mirth from the Citroën-driver.

Ha ha ha ha ha.

Angrily she reached for her mobile. She *would* ring Ralph. Not for a laugh – little hope of that – but just to feel less alone.

' . . . cannot take your call at present. Please leave a message after the tone.'

He couldn't still be at the dentist's, could he? If so, he'd be in no state to enjoy a celebration dinner. Nor, for that matter, was she. And as for sex, she simply wasn't in the mood. She had planned to feed him steak and strawberries to an accompaniment of soft, romantic music, then coax him up to bed. Now all she wanted was to go to bed to sleep.

She leaned across and helped herself to a couple of the strawberries. If only Oshoba were here he could lift her spirits: he would stroke her gently all over, kiss away her tiredness. But she was on her way to

Ralph and had no right to be even thinking about Oshoba. She hadn't caught an infection, thank God, nor had he made her pregnant, but she still went hot with shame recalling the night in his flat. Yet the memories persisted – indeed, became increasingly erotic as she imagined the two of them back on that sofa (no guilt, no sullen brother) and Oshoba crushing strawberries against her lips, trickling wine from his mouth to hers. Yes, she *was* in the mood, willingly surrendering as his tongue made . . .

There was a peremptory hooting behind. She opened her eyes. The traffic had begun to move, as unaccountably as it had ground to a halt a century ago. Hustling Oshoba out, she turned on the engine, determined to concentrate on the road.

Expecting only stop-start progress, she was heartened when all three lanes gradually picked up speed. Soon the traffic was flowing freely and, with a triumphant toot of her horn, she overtook the loathsome turkey. Without further delays she might be home by ten – a bit late for dinner, but perhaps she could persuade Ralph to crush strawberries against her lips, trickle wine from his mouth to hers. Unlikely in the extreme. But then so was his suggestion that they spend all night together. Ralph rarely asked for a present – however exhausted she might be, this was one he must have.

It was ten past ten when she rang the bell. Rather than let herself in, she had decided it would be more of a surprise for him to find her on the doorstep with an armful of presents and food and wine. She took a breath, preparing to sing him 'Happy Birthday'.

No one came. Surely he wasn't out. He loathed going out in the evenings. Besides, the lights were all on downstairs and Ralph didn't waste electricity.

She rang again. Still no answer. Perhaps he was in bed already. But he never went to bed before midnight, least of all when he had trouble getting to sleep.

She found her key and unlocked the door. 'Ralph?' she called.

Silence.

She put the shopping down and looked around. The carpet hadn't been hoovered, the hall table was cluttered with newspapers, and there was an unpleasant smell of pipe-smoke. Ralph knew all about the psychology of house-selling. OK, he might not remember the extras, like fluffy towels in the bathroom and gleaming kitchen tiles, but the least he could do was keep the place reasonably tidy.

Snatching up the papers, she went into the sitting-room. Ralph's chair was empty, but on the table beside it was a glass half full of . . . No, it couldn't be – not after all he'd said. She picked it up and sniffed. Unmistakable.

She stalked out to the kitchen. He wasn't there, but a bottle was poking out of the bin, a full-sized whisky bottle.

'Ralph?' she called again, as she stumbled up the stairs. The lights were on there too.

His bedroom door was ajar. She found him lying on the bed, fully clothed. His eyes were shut and his mouth gaped open, emitting phlegmy little snorts. A drool of saliva had dribbled from his mouth and there were stains on the front of his jacket. On the bedside table stood another glass, again half full of whisky. An ashtray had been knocked on to the floor, scattering black gunge and broken matches.

'Ralph,' she said, more sharply.

His eyelids flickered and he muttered something indecipherable, then turned his head away.

She walked over to the bed and stood motionless a minute, looking down at him. His suit was creased, his hair clung limply to his forehead; there were dark rings beneath his eyes, a grey scurf of shadow on his jaw. He smelt of sweat and booze.

This was her husband. Her protector.

'Ralph,' she said, 'how *could* you?' Her voice sounded unnaturally loud in the silence. 'Were you lying to me on the phone?'

As he shifted on the bed, she noticed a tiny brown-edged hole in his shirt, where a speck of hot ash must have dropped from his pipe.

'How can we go on living together if I can't trust a thing you say?'

The hypocrisy suddenly hit her. She had conveniently forgotten that he couldn't trust her either. And breaking a promise to give up drinking was nothing compared to sexual betrayal. Shouldn't she off-set his offence against hers?

She leaned over to loosen his tie. He looked uncomfortable trussed up in his business suit, but when she tried to remove the jacket he was a dead weight in her arms. Instead, she unlaced his shoes, placing them side by side on the carpet: well-polished leather brogues now showing their age. 'Ralph, what are we going to do? I love you. And I'm terrified of being on my own.'

He grunted and his hand groped out as if reaching for her, before flopping uselessly back.

She was on her own already. More alone than ever. He hadn't heard a word she'd said.

She picked up the scattered matches and put them in the ashtray; took the glass of whisky and poured it down the basin in the bathroom. She refilled the glass with water and left it by the bed. The counterpane lay jumbled on the floor. She shook it out and spread it over him. Then she drew the curtains and turned off the main light – the glare would hurt his eyes when he awoke.

'I'm sorry', she told him, 'for what I did. And for what I'm doing now. But it's over, isn't it? I don't want to hurt you, darling, but we can't go on like this. I'm leaving, and I'm not coming back this time. Do you understand?' She smoothed his hair from his forehead, kissed the palms of his hands. 'Don't forget I love you. I always have. I probably always will. Goodbye, Ralph.'

She closed the door, switched the downstairs lights off and went out to her car.

24

'Vicky, may I help this time? I feel I shouldn't leave my aunt – not even for half an hour, in case . . . '

'Of course you can help.' Vicky wrung out the flannel from the plastic bowl beside the bed and passed it to Lorna. 'We usually start with her face and hands.'

Lorna dabbed the flannel tentatively against the sunken cheeks. Agnes could no longer speak and the veins on her forehead were bluer and more pronounced, perhaps from the strain of her laboured breathing.

Lorna cradled each claw-hand in hers and gently sponged it clean. The skin on the hands was also bluer, with similar rope-like veins. As Gwen lifted her from the pillows, Agnes put her thin arms around Gwen's neck and clung to her like a baby. She looked troubled, startled, as if unsure of what was happening. Just being washed must be something of an ordeal for so limp and helpless a body, and even having her nightdress removed was a difficult manoeuvre, requiring Gwen's and Vicky's joint efforts.

Lorna averted her eyes from the flabby breasts, the sparse wisps of pubic hair and the incontinence pad spread above a waterproof sheet. It seemed a terrible intrusion to see her fastidious aunt in this naked, pitiful state. On previous occasions when Agnes was being washed and changed she had tactfully withdrawn and waited outside; now, though, she was desperate to be included in these last intimate rituals.

While Gwen washed Agnes's legs and back, she went into the ensuite bathroom to scrub her aunt's false teeth with the denture brush and paste. She had never known that Agnes wore false teeth, just as she had never known about her money worries or her grief and fear. Throughout her life her aunt had hidden pain. Lorna cleaned the teeth without revulsion – indeed with the utmost care and tenderness. Then, returning to the bedroom, she slipped them back into Agnes's mouth, hoping she would forgive this further encroachment into her privacy.

Gwen and Vicky were unfolding a clean nightdress. To avoid the distress of pulling it over Agnes's head, they slit it up the back with a pair of scissors and slipped her arms into the sleeves from the front. Her eyes were fogged and unfocused, but Lorna could imagine her appalled reaction were she aware of what they were doing: 'Cutting up good clothes? Whatever next!'

Lorna no longer resented the nurses' youth and vigour; indeed, she had come to admire their strength – not just their physical dexterity in handling and lifting patients, but their emotional strength generally in caring for the dying. Over the past two days she had watched them tending Agnes, invariably calm and loving as they did everything – and nothing. Nothing could save her now. In fact several members of staff who'd gone off duty had said goodbye and given her a kiss in case it was the last chance they had. Already she seemed to have retreated to some distant place, as if desiring to be rid of her burdensome body: the stick legs and skeletal feet, the loose sack of a stomach and shrunken ribs.

Lorna helped make the bed, lifting her arms in tandem with Gwen's as she smoothed blankets and tucked sheets. She had learned so much from the nurses: a slow, calm rhythmic way of working, accompanied by a simple explanation in case the patient could hear and understand.

'We're making your bed now, Agnes. It's nice and fresh, with clean sheets. That's it, lie back and rest.'

While Vicky cleared away the basin, Lorna took the baby's brush and drew it through Agnes's straw-like hair, careful to avoid the cut on her forehead. 'That's better, isn't it, Aunt? I know you like to be tidy.'

Gwen and Vicky peeled off their rubber gloves. 'See you tomorrow, Lorna.'

Lorna nodded. All three knew perfectly well that Agnes might not be here tomorrow.

'Goodbye, Agnes.'

'Goodbye, Agnes.'

Lorna bit her lip as each nurse kissed the withered cheek. There could hardly be a greater contrast between the Oakfield House regime and this haven of love and affection.

When the nurses had left, she sat on the bed and held both Agnes's hands. 'Aunt, I'm still here. I want you to know that I'll be with you . . . all the time.'

Agnes half opened her eyes. She looked startled again, bewildered. 'I'm here, Aunt,' Lorna repeated. 'You're not alone.'

A lie. Agnes had to pass that final barrier totally alone. No one could die with her.

She licked her lips several times, as if thirsty. Lorna reached for one of the tiny sponges on sticks, moistened it in a glass and slipped it between her lips. Agnes was surviving on nothing but a few paltry drops of water. It was two days since she'd eaten, and then only a couple of mouthfuls of soup.

Lorna settled herself in the chair. Yesterday they had brought a put-you-up into the room for her, so she could get some proper sleep rather than dozing intermittently. But it seemed wrong to lie down when she was here to keep vigil. There would be time enough to sleep.

Strange, though, how slowly the hours passed, especially as everyone else was so busy. She was aware of constant activity outside: Pam with the tea-trolley, Carla with the mobile shop, Dr Stevens talking to a relative, Megan on her rounds. Even Agnes was occupied with the business of dying. As Lorna listened to her jagged breathing, she was struck by the thought that dying was in some ways akin to childbirth. In each case you were impervious to anything beyond the confines of your own body and consumed by immense physical changes you were powerless to resist. Eating and excreting shut down as you lay in thrall to nature's whim. And, however many people might be on hand to help, none could really 'come near' as you struggled to expel the baby or to expel your final breath.

Looking at Agnes, who had never gone through childbirth, she remembered her own first miscarriage: the terror (and outrage) she had felt at the fierceness of the pain. It had lasted eighteen hours – agonizing contractions whose only outcome was a mutilated foetus. Ralph had brought her flowers, a bowl of white gardenias, whose heavy scent was for ever after linked in her mind with bloody, half-formed limbs.

She got up and walked to the window. Whatever happened she mustn't think of Ralph, or she would unleash a tide of anger, pity, worry. She needed all her strength for Agnes.

In the garden squirrels were darting about beneath the trees, an aggressively energetic one chasing its smaller rivals. And a pair of wood-pigeons rustled among the branches of the holly-bush, foraging for the last of winter's berries. All creatures seemed to be busy. She alone had nothing to do.

Except wait.

The click of the door woke her. It was Emily – the softly-spoken night nurse.

'I'm sorry to disturb you, Lorna, but I need to check the syringe-driver.'

Lorna nodded, watching as the morphine was topped up – a drug she both blessed and loathed. It prevented Agnes feeling pain, but the increased dose made her nauseous and so prevented her from eating: killing her while keeping her alive.

'Were you dozing?' Emily asked after she had settled Agnes down again.

'Yes,' she admitted guiltily. Now that Agnes could no longer truly wake, she felt she had no right to truly sleep. They were both existing in a limbo where night and day meant nothing. 'What time is it?' she asked.

'Ten to three. Would you like me to sit with you for a while? Things are fairly quiet just now.'

'It's kind of you, but I'm OK on my own. Honestly.'

'Well, ring the bell if you change your mind. And please do call me if Agnes's breathing becomes shallower, or there are longer gaps between her breaths. All right?'

'Yes, of course.'

'And how about a cup of tea in the meantime?'

'Lovely. Thanks.'

As she sipped the tea, she noticed Agnes making tiny movements with her lips. Was she thirsty again, or could she be about to speak – the first time since yesterday? She put her cup down and placed her ear close to Agnes's mouth. 'What is it, Aunt? What are you trying to say?'

'I . . . I want to go home.' The words were little more than a whisper.

'Home, Aunt?'

'Home to . . . Margaret.'

'Yes. Of course. You'll . . . see her. Soon.'

'Be sure to wake me when we get there.'

'You are awake, Aunt.'

'Am I? I can't tell.'

How disorienting, Lorna thought, to confuse the boundaries of wakefulness and sleep, of life and death. Was Agnes frightened of dying? Should she ask, offer words of comfort? But she had none – the very notion was arrogant. Besides, fear was a subject she dared not broach: the terror of her present homeless, husbandless existence was coiled like a snake, ready to rear up and strike. 'It's all right, Aunt. You're safe now.'

Another lie. But how could she not lie? Just as Agnes had done – reassuring an orphan child that everything was fine. Had it ever been?

Agnes gave a sudden feeble cough.

'Aunt, are you OK?'

Agnes coughed again and tried to swallow, then said with obvious difficulty, 'I've got loud . . . noises in my throat.'

'I'd better call Emily.'

'Emily? Are there other people in the room?'

'No. Just us.'

'Us? Who do you mean? I can't remember names.'

'Do you remember Lorna?'

For a moment Agnes seemed puzzled, then she gave the ghost of a smile, 'My little Lorna?'

'Yes. She's here.'

'Well, she ought to be in bed. It's very late. Has she finished all her homework?'

'Yes, all done. You don't need to worry about her any more.'

'I'll always worry about my little Lorna.'

She smeared a dab of Vaseline on Agnes's dry, chapped mouth. As she leaned over, she saw her aunt's lips move again and strained to hear the slurred, drunken-sounding murmur.

'Is this the day that Margaret died?'

'Yes. Just dawning. I'll draw the curtains, so you can see. There, look at the sky – it's beginning to lighten and the birds are singing already. It's going to be a lovely day.' She stood listening to the bold notes of a thrush bidding the world awake as the last stars faded and a faint ochre haze on the horizon gradually encroached on the darkness. Soon she could make out the forms of trees – trees still bare but promising spring leaf, magnolia in bud, the gold gleam of daffodils. A flight of rooks wheeled across the roof-tops on their way to the fields to begin their busy round.

The grey gauze slowly lifted, to reveal streaks and flecks of pink. The day was struggling into existence, the sun heaving itself from sleep. Clouds marched across the sky, dispersing, changing shape; starlings circled and chattered; a magpie swooped from the sycamore and strutted across the lawn. Such exertion everywhere, and she passive, only waiting.

But then something made her turn. Agnes's breathing was different: shallower, with longer pauses. She counted the seconds between each breath. Ten. It had been six before.

She didn't ring the bell. She just sat on the bed and took the sagging body in her arms. 'I love you,' she whispered. 'Mother.'

And then an extraordinary thing: Agnes's clouded blue eyes seemed to light up for an instant, becoming not just brighter but bluer – luminous points of light against the brown parchment of her skin. There was joy in her face, ecstasy almost, as she fixed Lorna with a piercing stare. Was it Margaret she was seeing?

No, it was Margaret's child – her child. And she was gazing at her with an expression of utter intensity, as if rallying her last shred of strength to pass on a profoundly important truth, communicate wordlessly things never said before.

Lorna strove to comprehend. Agnes was speaking of fear, and of love that overcame fear, of courage and devotion.

Then suddenly the eyes went blank, the harsh breaths ceased, and there was silence in the room.

Outside, the birds were singing.

III

25

'Happy birthday, Kathy!'

'Happy birthday!'

Chris was lighting the candles on two pink-iced cakes in the shape of a 4 and a 0. 'If you can blow this lot out in one go it's free champagne for a week.'

'You might live to regret that offer!' Kathy expelled her breath in a dramatic burst, extinguishing all forty candles. Amid the clapping and cheering, Jeremy stepped forward with the cake-knife.

'Wait a minute,' Kathy said. 'Let's light them again for Lorna. It's her birthday next week.'

All eyes turned to Lorna, who was sitting on the edge of the jacuzzi, a glass of Bollinger in her hand.

'Oh, Kathy, no! This is *your* party.'

'Come on, I insist.'

Lorna approached the table and looked nervously around at faces, faces, faces. The guests had blurred to a patchwork of colours, punctuated by the odd detail: a gleaming bald head, a wide-brimmed velvet hat. She took a deep breath and blew. A dozen candles went out; the rest blazed perversely on. Everybody laughed – she too. 'Oh, lord!' she said. 'I can't laugh and blow at once.'

''Course you can,' urged Kathy. 'Have another go. That's it – brilliant. Now we both get a wish.'

Lorna shut her eyes. 'I wish that the Monster burns in hell!' Mercifully he hadn't turned up this evening, but there was still a long time to go. 'Marvellous party,' she told Chris, who was handing round the cake.

'Oh, it's hardly started yet. There's skinny-dipping at midnight, don't forget!'

Lorna glanced at her feet. Would she dare expose the scarred left and bunioned right? And what about the shingles scars on her breast, which had now faded to an unflattering mud-brown?

'I don't think we've met,' said a voice behind her. 'I'm Jason Carter, a friend of Jeremy's.'

She recognized the name although not the man: he was small and slight, with fair, floppy hair and blue eyes. Kathy had been talking about Jason Carter only yesterday – a millionaire (multimillionaire?) who had started his first business when he was a schoolboy of fifteen. 'Hello, I'm Lorna.' She didn't give a surname, preferring to divest herself of both Pearson (Ralph's) and Maguire (her father's).

'Are you a friend of Chris's?'

'No, Kathy's. I only met Chris and Jeremy this evening.' They, in fact, were hosting the party as a birthday present to Kathy, and had invited many of their own friends too.

'And what's your line of work?'

Tricky question. Her work in the last month had consisted of spring-cleaning a cottage and preparing to put it on the market, clearing an overgrown garden and disposing of Agnes's pathetically few possessions. 'I'm . . . between jobs at the moment. How about you?' Or was that a silly thing to ask? *Did* millionaires work?

Jason flicked back a lock of hair. 'I have fingers in a number of pies. But mainly I deal in shares and currencies on the Internet.'

'That sounds exciting.' Anything but.

'Well, yesterday it was. I made fifty grand on the euro taking a dive. And I'm praying that the Nasdaq will bomb tomorrow. I've been forward-selling all week, so I might cream off another hundred grand.'

'Really?' She hadn't a clue what he was talking about but supposed she ought to look impressed.

Jason held out his glass to be refilled by a passing waiter. (Champagne was flowing in torrents, and the lavish amounts of caviar in the buffet must have seriously depleted world stocks.) 'Do you live around here?'

Another awkward question. She didn't actually live anywhere just now. After three weeks in Agnes's cottage, she (and the Monster) had decamped to Clare's flat, where she was sleeping on a mattress on the floor. 'I'm staying in Woking with a friend temporarily. I'm looking for a place of my own . . . '

'Ah, I can probably help there. I'm joint owner of a property company in town.'

Mansions in Mayfair, penthouses in Canary Wharf – the very thing. 'Here's my card. Give me a bell.'

'Thanks. That's kind.' She imagined a tramp being subjected to such questions: 'Where do you live?' 'On a sheet of cardboard on the pavement.' 'What do you do?' 'Drink meths and beg.' She could identify with tramps at present. The Monster frequently suggested begging and cardboard as a solution to her job and housing problems.

Jason raised his voice above the music. 'Also I'm into vintage sports cars. I've just picked up an E-type Jag in mint condition. And last week I managed to lay my hands on an Aston Martin DB4.'

'Really?' she repeated. Her responses must seem woefully inadequate. Luckily he didn't enquire about *her* car – an elderly Metro suffering from chronic engine-knock.

She felt a hand on her arm. 'Lorna, you promised me a dance.'

It was Paul, a friend of Kathy's. His polo-neck and old chinos looked gratifyingly shabby. (Jason's cream suit and matching silk shirt had probably cost half the price of Agnes's cottage.)

'Do excuse me, Jason,' she said as Paul took her hand and negotiated an obstacle course through groups of chattering people, assorted bronze statuary and glossy-leaved giant plants. Finally they made it to the far end of the pool, which opened out into a glass-domed annexe already crowded with dancers.

'I'm afraid I'm not exactly John Travolta,' Paul admitted.

Lorna smiled. 'Don't worry, nor am I. All we need do is jig around.' The champagne had dulled the pain in her foot and she *could* jig around – just about – hoping her unglamorous shoes would be hidden beneath her long scarlet dress (bought specially for the occasion at Déjà Vu, a second-hand fashion shop).

'Great number, this,' Paul mouthed, singing along.

She nodded, letting the music take her over and mesmerized by the coloured lights spangling the fronds of ferns, gilding the mosaic floor and stippling the birds of paradise on the exotic hand-painted murals.

A slower song came on and Paul held her close, nuzzling her neck with his lips. She liked the feel of his warm, solid body pressing into hers. No need to pull away. She was free now, available.

She lost the rhythm, tripped. Of course she wasn't free, shackled by guilt and marriage vows. Ralph was distraught at her leaving and kept begging her to return.

'I . . . I'm sorry, Paul. I need a breather.'

She threaded her way back to the pool between the swirl of dancers, Paul stumbling in her wake. She managed to shake him off by saying she was going to the loo, and escaped from there into the garden. The night air was a relief after the sultry heat indoors, and the earth, dampened by a recent shower, smelt refreshingly cool. She ventured along a path, unsure of her bearings in the gloom. Although the grounds were floodlit, swathes of light alternated with strips of shadow. She passed the tennis-courts and bowling-green, and came upon the sensory garden, where she sat on a bench amid perfumed flowers and shrubs: honeysuckle, wallflowers, mahonia, viburnum. There were sounds as well as scents: trickling water, recorded birdsong, the muted sound of the music. How marvellous it would be to work in this idyllic place . . . But how could she take *any* job when she was a prey to fear on such a scale? She couldn't even cope with Paul's innocuous advances, let alone embark on a new life. Indeed, now that the person who had loved her most in the world was reduced to a box of ashes, she seemed to be more vulnerable than ever. Her mind kept harking back to the shamefully cheap coffin, which she had tried in vain to upgrade; the sparse attendance at the tea. Her piles of crustless sandwiches, made with lashings of butter and the most expensive ham, had finally been fed to the birds.

She plucked a petal from a wallflower. She had piled the coffin with flowers so that Agnes should be celebrated with glorious extravagance, at least in one small way. And she had put an obituary notice in *The Times* – 'Beloved Aunt and Mother' – wanting Agnes's role (and passing) to be publicly commemorated.

Tossing the petal away, she crossed the lawn towards the cedars, envying their sturdy strength. For two hundred years they had withstood gales and storms; she was matchwood in comparison. Ms Unflappable and Ms Courageous had both faded into oblivion, leaving the field free for the Monster to renew his gleeful bullying. At Agnes's cottage she had got up more than once in the middle of the night and driven round the country lanes in a futile attempt to evade him. And at Clare's she had to sleep with all the lights on, and still woke every hour. Sleep itself had become frightening, and not only because of the nightmares. There was an aspect of death about it, going down, down, down into a void, alone, with no control. Yet staying awake was little better. From midnight to dawn was a prison stretch of solitary confinement. And just looking at the night sky could induce a fit of terror: the vast, incomprehensible distance from earth to even the nearest star; the sense of being abandoned in a callous universe.

For God's *sake*, she told herself, you're neither imprisoned nor alone – you're at a fantastic party, so stop this ridiculous introspection and go back indoors to Paul.

But Paul, too, made her nervous. She wasn't ready to play the field, both because of her ambivalent feelings for Ralph and also through fear of repeating past mistakes. She'd been involved with enough obnoxious men in her time. Even Oshoba was a problem, sweet-natured as he was. During the last month he had written to her twice, asking why she hadn't been in touch.

Yes, why? Was it only guilt, or fear again? Fear was so restricting. It stopped you being your true self, blighted pleasure, shattered confidence.

Miserably, she wandered back the way she'd come, returning to the lee of the main house, with its weathered brick and reassuring solidity. If she turned down this job, what would she do instead? Temp in a dreary office? Join the ranks of commuters? Every area of her life seemed full of question marks.

She shivered in the night air. Her shoes were getting wet; her dress was damp around the hem. This was Kathy's night – party night. She should never have left the others and come out here alone.

Then suddenly she *saw* Kathy, standing on the lighted porch, peering into the garden.

'Oh, Lorna, there you are! Paul said you'd disappeared.'

'I . . . I felt a bit hot. I thought I'd get some air.'

'Well, come and cool down in the pool. We've just started the skinny-dipping.'

Inside, the pool was crowded, although not everyone was naked. The velvet hat was still in evidence but now worn above a minuscule bikini; another woman was topless, and the plump, bearded man beside her was down to his boxer shorts. Jason Carter stood on the side, clad in black Speedo trunks and holding a pair of goggles, as if intent on serious swimming. Paul, in contrast, was larking about in the water, his dark hair plastered to his head. He spotted her and waved.

'Strip off and come on in! It's fantastic.'

She hesitated. Her feet, the scars, her age – only eight days away from forty.

And then, with a whoop of defiance, she kicked off her shoes and jumped in fully clothed. As she surfaced among a cluster of guests, Paul grabbed her round the waist.

'How about finishing that dance!' he shouted above the noise.

Treading water, she clung to his bare chest. Her worries and indecision began to dissolve in the ripples of turquoise water, then subsided even more as he ran a sensuous hand from the base of her neck to the bottom of her spine, tracing the curves of her clinging dress. What a waste of a party to be mooching around demoralized when everyone else was enjoying themselves. Hell – she *would* let rip, if only for one night; *would* be free and flirtatious and of course utterly, blissfully fearless.

The sitting-room door was ajar. Ralph, in black, was kneeling on the floor, flanked by two shadowy figures. He looked gaunt and very old. She called to him, but he didn't hear. He seemed intent on the service and was gazing at the coffin – a cheap plywood thing, with no flowers to brighten its blunt purpose. There was no hint of colour anywhere: all was mournful black – black walls, black windows, black-shrouded furniture . . .

Quickly she closed the door. But the minister's voice still sorrowed through the hall: 'Ashes to ashes, dust to dust . . .'

She sat up with a start. Where was she? Not at home – the bed was unfamiliar. Not at Clare's – the mattress wasn't on the floor. Panicking, she groped for a bedside light and switched it on, to reveal a pleasant, freshly painted room with striped curtains, a thick-pile carpet and new furniture in country pine. And then she recognized it: the spare bedroom in the coach-house. Kathy had insisted she stay the night, wouldn't hear of her driving to Clare's at three a.m.

Still shaky after the coffin dream, she lay back against the pillows. She dreamed of funerals almost every night – funerals held in their house, as if it had become a house of death. Sometimes the coffin was empty – *her* coffin, in waiting. Once, she had dreamed she was getting married, but the ceremony was conducted by an undertaker and her wedding-dress was black.

She noticed with surprise that light showed through the curtains. Normally the dreams woke her in the early hours, but it must be well past dawn. She reached for her watch: twenty-five to twelve.

Unbelievable! She had slept for nearly nine hours. And, in spite of the dream, there was still no sign of the Monster. In her borrowed nightie she went down to the kitchen, glancing nervously about in case he should be stalking her. She found Kathy at the breakfast bar, leafing through the *Sunday Times*. 'Happy birthday again!' she said.

'Yes, I'm well and truly forty now. On the slippery slope.'

'I thought you said forty was the prime of life.'

'Oh, I'm just a bit morning-afterish. Did you sleep OK?'

'Yes, fine.'

'Good. Help yourself to toast and coffee. It's still hot.'

'Thanks. And thanks for a great party, Kathy.'

'Thank Chris, not me. She's always been frightfully generous.'

Lorna poured a mug of coffee. 'Yes, it was decent of her to let you use the health spa. Wasn't she worried something might get damaged?'

'Well, even if it did, I suppose it could be put to rights easily enough. I mean, we don't open for another six weeks. Talking of which, have you decided about the job yet? I must give her a definite answer by Friday.'

'I'm tempted, Kathy, certainly.'

'You keep saying that, but you never actually commit yourself. I know you've had a hard time of it these last few months, but this would be something positive in your life.' Kathy folded the newspaper and put it on the table. 'I've come to see that, although some things might seem vile at the time, they can turn out to be blessings in disguise. For instance, you and I not being able to have children. Well, I couldn't take the job here if I had a couple of bolshie teenagers on my hands. And imagine how *you*'d feel if you'd lost your house and left your husband but had two or three kids to look after. We're free and unencumbered, Lorna, and we should make the most of it.'

Lorna spread marmalade on her toast, playing for time. Whatever the delights of last night, she knew she wasn't free, either of Ralph or of panic. Kathy didn't appreciate the full horror of the panics and had once talked about her 'throwing a wobbly' – a phrase that struck her as both flippant and inaccurate. In the grip of fear it wasn't *her* throwing anything, but being thrown, hurled, flung, crushed, by some malevolent outside force. But perhaps, as with childbirth or falling in love, people couldn't really understand unless they'd experienced it for themselves.

'And we share the same ideals, Lorna. I'm determined to make a go of The Cedars. I want to motivate the staff – get the best out of everyone. I'm sure it can be done.'

'Yes, I saw it at the hospice. I felt quite inspired by the way they treated Agnes.'

'There you are! We can do the same, pass on that sort of love and care to our residents here.'

Lorna picked up a piece of toast and put it down again. They had told her at the hospice how brilliant she was with Agnes and that she obviously had a special rapport with the elderly. She could use that gift, develop new-found strengths.

'Quite honestly, I can't see what's holding you back.'

'It's . . . partly Ralph. I feel awful leaving him with so much on his plate – selling the house, settling things with Bowden, winding down the business . . . '

'Lorna, you've got to leave Ralph out of this. Now you've made the break, it would be madness to go back.'

'But he's in such a state.'

'Too bad.'

Lorna couldn't be so heartless. Or was she just a hypocrite, blaming Ralph for her own indecision? 'I . . . think I'm a bit shell-shocked after Agnes's death. I mean, I ought to be looking for somewhere to live, but instead of doing anything about it I'm just sleeping on Clare's floor.'

'I've *told* you – if you come here you can live in, share this place with me.'

Lorna glanced around the kitchen, a cheerful, airy room with primrose-yellow walls, a rustic dresser and a window overlooking the orchard and the tennis-courts. The coach-house and its neighbouring buildings formed a community, a haven. So different from the dour, isolated house in Queen's Hill Drive. And this would be *her* home, not Ralph's; *her* job.

'And no cleaning or gardening. It's all done for you. You don't have to cook if you don't feel like it. The staff dining-room provides three good meals a day. And just a stroll across the lawn to get to work.'

Lorna stirred her coffee. She had always found it a struggle tending a too-big house and garden single-handed, and it was certainly dispiriting eating on her own. Couldn't she say yes?

She sat holding her cup, seeing in her mind the small, battered suitcase she had taken from the hospice: all that remained of Agnes. A white flannel nightgown, a pair of threadbare slippers, a plastic comb, a tube of denture-cleaner and a photo in a frame – not Margaret, not Agnes's mother, but a child of seven wearing a pink ballet-dress, every frill and flounce hand-sewn by her aunt. That was why she was afraid to take the job: without Agnes and without Ralph, the two props in her life, she might crumble to nothing. And she couldn't risk letting Kathy down.

There was a loud ring on the doorbell.

Kathy got up. 'Now who can that be?'

'Chris, maybe, come to read the Riot Act. Shouldn't we be clearing up or something?'

'Absolutely not. She's booked a firm of cleaners and said I'm not to lift a finger.' Kathy went to open the door.

Lorna could hear male voices – one she recognized. She tugged her nightie down over her knees and tried to hide her misshapen right foot with the hardly less unsightly left. Too late. In walked Paul and a man she didn't know.

'Hi, Lorna! Great to see you again. This is Nick, my flatmate. We're just going out for a drink and wondered if you and Kathy fancied coming.'

'I said yes,' Kathy's head appeared behind him. 'Is that OK with you, Lorna?'

'Well, it would be if I had something to wear. Apart from a red dress that's still soaking wet!'

'Come as you are,' Paul quipped.

Kathy laughed. 'Did I warn you about this guy, Lorna?'

Lorna began to feel better. The sun was shining, Paul had sought her out, and she did find him rather attractive. Once she'd drowned her fears in the pool last night she had become almost a different person – carefree and relaxed. Perhaps it would continue. And if she could just stop being so negative she might even make a decision.

26

Lorna looked up expectantly as yet another white-coated figure emerged from one of the doors. Mr Weekes at last?

No. Or at least not yet ready for her. Whoever it was summoned another patient – a young lad with a fledgling moustache who had been here a scant ten minutes. She'd been waiting half an hour.

Despondently she continued flicking through her magazine. Her eye was caught by a headline: 'First Date: How Far Should You Go?' The article advised restraint – a sure-fire way to make your man feverish with desire. But did she *want* Paul feverish with desire? It was just her luck that the clinic had offered her a cancellation on the very day they were meeting. She was nervous enough about the evening, without the added complication of a foot-scan. And she was bound to be late if the return journey from Plumstead proved as bad as the one there. (Signal failure, litter on the line and a driver pursuing his own personal go-slow.)

'Lorna?' The booming voice made her jump. 'I'm Bertram Weekes. How do you do?'

She winced as he shook her hand. Forget foot problems – her fingers felt as if they'd been crushed in a mangle. And where was his white coat? The man was wearing a hound's-tooth-check suit and a yellow-spotted bow-tie.

'Sorry to have kept you, Lorna.'

'That's OK.' He was not at all as she'd imagined. The name Weekes suggested a frail, wispy type, whereas his bull neck and broad shoulders were more suited to a rugby prop forward than to a podiatrist. A prop forward who toured a lot: he was tanned a deep mahogany. Sunlamps? A time-share in the tropics?

'Do come this way, Lorna.'

She followed him into a poky room whose dimensions seemed further reduced by his bulk. It was furnished with a desk, two chairs, a couch and, unnervingly, a model of a skeletal foot standing on a table in the corner.

'Sit down, sit down. I hope you don't mind me calling you Lorna.'

A little late to ask.

'And please do call me Bertram. We don't want to stand on cere-mony. If you can stand at all – ha ha! Just my little joke.'

She smiled politely.

'Sorry to have kept you. I've just come back from a fortnight in Antigua and I'm trying to catch up with the backlog of patients. Won-derful trip though – scuba-diving, snorkelling, kayaking, sunfish sail-ing . . . ' He continued enumerating the myriad water sports on offer, before launching into the marvels of Caribbean bird life.

No wonder he ran late if he gave all his patients a run-down of his holiday. There must be money in feet: in the few months since her operation Mr Hughes had been on three expensive trips abroad.

Mr Weekes rummaged among the papers on his desk. 'I've got a let-ter somewhere . . . From Mr Brownlow, wasn't it?'

'No, Mr Hughes.'

'Ah yes, of course. I'm all over the place today! Blame it on the jet-lag. It always flattens me. Don't you find the same?'

'Mm.' It was years since she'd been on a plane, or indeed anywhere much beyond Lincolnshire. And as for flattening *him*, that would take a ten-ton truck.

'Damn! I can't seem to find the thing.' He was still riffling through piles of paper. 'I could have sworn I had it here. Let me buzz my secretary . . . Polly? A letter from Mr Brownlow regarding Mrs Lorna Pearson.'

'*Hughes*,' said Lorna.

'Sorry. Mrs Lorna Hughes.'

'No, *Mr* Hughes. My surgeon.'

'Lordy, lordy!' Another throaty laugh. 'We'd better start again. Polly, I need a letter from Mr Hughes regarding Mrs Lorna Brownlow.'

Shades of Oakfield House, she thought, as she corrected him yet again.

'While we're waiting I'll take a look at your X-rays. You brought them with you, I hope.'

'Yes, here they are.' A good job *one* of them was efficient. 'These were done before the op, these just after, and these latest ones six weeks ago.'

'Dear, dear,' he muttered, as he examined them in detail. 'I'm afraid things don't look too good.'

The very phrase 'I'm afraid' now made her fear the worst.

'I'm afraid he hasn't achieved any reasonable degree of correction. The great-toe joint is still very much enlarged. Have you been wearing unsuitable shoes since the op?'

'No, not at all.' Normally she clumped around in the walking-boots advised by Mr Hughes, but today – in Paul's honour – she had put on a pair of just-about-passable (although highly unglamorous) lace-ups. 'And actually Mr Hughes did admit that he hadn't got the toe as straight as he'd have liked.'

There was a tap on the door and in sauntered a girl wearing a tight mock-leopardskin top that barely managed to contain her ample bust. 'There we are, Bertie,' she said with a suggestive smile, handing him the letter as though it were a *billet-doux*.

'Thanks, Pol.' He scanned it briefly, mumbling the odd phrase: ' . . . extensive synovitis . . . pin-tract infection . . . metatarsalgia . . . plantar digital neuroma . . . Dear, dear, *dear*,' he repeated. 'Quite a chapter of accidents. But tell me, Lorna' – he tossed the letter on to the pile – 'where are you having pain at the moment?'

Where *wasn't* she having pain? Wearily she recounted her symptoms. 'Also, just this week a new sort of . . . bump appeared on the other side of my foot – not where I had the op, but near my little toe. It hurts a lot when I walk.'

'We'll take a look at that in a second. First of all I'd like to see you walk. Could you take a few steps, please, up and down the room.'

She did so, feeling clumsy and somewhat foolish under his hawk-like gaze.

'Yes, as I thought, your whole gait is wrong. I'm not surprised. The operation has changed the balance of your foot and that has caused new problems. Take your shoes and socks off and get up on the couch.'

Well, at least he didn't expect her to put her feet on his plump hound's-tooth thighs.

His hands felt hot and moist as he manoeuvred her toes this way and that. She had become inured to the pain of such examinations. What concerned her more was that the bottoms of her best cream trouser-suit were splashed with mud – a result of the torrential downpour that had started as she stepped out of the train. She wanted to look her best for Paul. At this rate he would think her clothes were permanently wet.

'Well,' Mr Weekes said cheerfully, 'in my opinion your feet are worse now, Lorna, than they were before the surgery.'

The Monster swooped in with a triumphant cackle. 'At last! Somebody's admitted it.'

'For one thing, you've developed a second bunion, or bunionette. This bump you've been complaining about' – he fingered the outside of her little toe, almost the only part of her foot not scarred – 'is what we call a tailor's bunion. Tailors used to get them from sitting crosslegged, which built up pressure in this area. And the second toe is extremely stiff. It should have been made much shorter. As it is, you've lost the flexibility in the joint. In fact I'd go further and say that you've had completely the wrong operation.'

The Monster executed a jubilant dance.

'I would never have recommended a Scarfe osteotomy. Or an Aiken shaft, for that matter. Not on a foot like this.' He pointed to the pre-operation X-ray, which he had put up on a screen above his desk. 'I don't want to criticize Mr Hughes, of course, but let's face it, Lorna, none of us gets it right all of the time.'

'Do any of you get it right *any* of the time?' the Monster asked scathingly.

Lorna tried without success to move her rigid second toe, which since the operation seemed to have turned from flesh to wood. 'With all these complications, Mr W . . . er, Bertram, do you think the orthoses will be any help?'

'They may give you some temporary relief, but frankly you'll never sort out that left foot without further surgery. And the right is grossly deformed. Which means radical procedures. And I wouldn't advise you to leave it too long. With every month that passes, the deformity will increase, until – '

'Top yourself,' urged the Monster. 'Less bother. Cheaper too.'

'What I'd suggest is a base wedge osteotomy on the first metatarsal. I'd secure it with a screw and possibly insert a titanium joint implant – '

'*You?*' said Lorna, confused. 'You're not a surgeon, are you?'

'But of course I am. Without wanting to sound immodest, I think I can fairly claim to be one of the best podiatrist surgeons in the country. And quite honestly, Lorna, podiatrist surgeons are a far better bet than orthopods. With all due respect to Mr Hughes, orthopaedic surgeons spend most of their time doing hips and knees, whereas we concentrate on feet, and feet alone. You might have spared yourself a lot of trouble by coming to me in the first place. In fact if you're asking me if you could sue for negligence . . . '

Sue? She stared at him in shock. First her father and now Mr Hughes – criminally negligent.

He gestured dismissively at her left foot. 'Well, frankly this is a mess, and I can't pretend it'll be easy to put right. It's going to entail a great deal of surgery.'

She'd already *had* a great deal. 'Mr Hughes did, um, lose his saw, which meant he had to postpone my operation. For hours. He told me afterwards how furious he was. Do you think that might have affected his work?'

'It wouldn't surprise me. Only last month one of my former patients was operated on by an orthopaedic surgeon, and believe it or not the chappie found he didn't have the right sort of screwdriver to remove a special screw I'd put in. His secretary rang me when he was actually in theatre and I had to send my own personal screwdriver by courier from here to St Mary's, Paddington.'

'Saws? Screwdrivers?' the Monster scoffed. 'These surgeons are a load of cack-handed carpenters. Don't trust him an inch, however good he says he is. If his surgery's anything like his dress sense you're in dead trouble – and I mean dead.'

Lorna dragged her mind from the hapless patient lying anaesthetized all day on the operating-table while the courier fought his way through heavy traffic. It was a fair distance from Plumstead to Paddington. 'So what would you suggest?'

'Well, you'll need four osteotomies in all, if we include the tailor's bunion. And that ridge of bone on the fourth toe needs to be excised. And I would definitely advise redoing the . . . '

She suddenly felt like Red Riding Hood confronted by the wolf: Mr Weekes was positively drooling as he gazed at her feet, enraptured by the prospect of hacking into them.

'Why I'm so successful, Lorna, is that I'm extremely careful to fit the procedure to the individual. There are a hundred and fifty different operations that can be performed on the feet, but if the surgeon gets it wrong . . . '

'The patient never walks again,' the Monster smirked.

'Mind you, it's only fair to warn you that, although the base wedge osteotomy gives a much higher level of correction, it is less stable during the healing period. Which means that instead of a bandage you'd have to be in plaster for six weeks. And it may take longer to heal than last time.'

'You'll be in hospital for *years* then. Well, at least it'll save you looking for somewhere to live.'

'But everything depends on the surgeon, Lorna, and his particular skills, or lack of them. If you'd like testimonials, I can put you in touch with some of my grateful patients.'

'For Christ's *sake!*' the Monster interjected. 'He sounds like a double-glazing salesman.'

'One or two had similar experiences to you, Lorna – surgery made matters worse. But speak to them now and you'll find they're all delighted.'

'Those that can still hobble to a phone.'

'And you won't have all the trauma of a general anaesthetic. I use just a local.'

'You mean I'd still be . . . awake?'

'Yes, but it's nothing to worry about. You'd hear a bit of crunching and grinding' – he gave a jovial grin – 'but I'd talk you through it. I always chat with my patients, tell them a few good jokes. Sometimes they're laughing so much they hardly notice what I'm up to.'

She sprang off the couch with as much dexterity as she could manage. 'I'm sorry, Mr Weekes' (to hell with Bertram), 'it's out of the question. And I don't think I'll even bother with the scan. What's the point of orthoses if you say I'm, well, practically crippled?'

'Come, come, my dear, I said no such thing.'

'That's what it sounded like to me.' And I'm *not* your dear.

'Well, I'm sorry if I alarmed you.' He patted her hand condescendingly. 'Perhaps you're not quite ready for such a major procedure. What I could do instead is remove the fibular sesamoid bone in the inside of the great toe. That would loosen the joint.'

'Yeah, loosen it so much you'd probably collapse in a heap.'

'Alternatively, we could do just the tailor's bunion. That's a simpler option altogether. And you don't have to live with that neuroma. If the pain-killers aren't working I can perform a neurectomy. You need to think of the future, Lorna. After all, you've got years of active life ahead.'

'He obviously needs the business. You'd better agree to *something* or you'll never get away.'

'No, Mr Weekes, I'd rather avoid any surgery at all – at least for the present. I have a few . . . personal problems.'

'A few?' The Monster counted on his claws: 'Ralph in terminal decline, the house still on the market, Bowden not paid off, no job and nowhere to live, and – '

'Well, we can't let you continue in all that discomfort. If you're unwilling to have surgery, then I'd definitely recommend orthoses.'

'Which is why I came to you in the first place,' she pointed out irritably, with a surreptitious glance at her watch. At this rate, it would be midnight before she and Paul had dinner. 'But what I'm still unsure about is whether they'll do any good.'

'Of course they won't,' the Monster sneered. 'He's just out to make money. He's lost his five grand for carving bits off your feet, but he'll settle for five hundred for a pair of mingy insoles.'

'Good gracious yes!' Mr Weekes enthused. 'I wouldn't invest in a state-of-the-art scanner unless it gave damned good results. Ours is the only one of its kind in the whole of the UK, you know. We're extremely fortunate to have it. Or perhaps I should say foolish – ha ha! It set me back sixty thousand pounds.'

'No wonder he needs cash fast. Get out while you're still solvent.'

'Why it's so useful is that it allows us to examine the motion of the joints while the patient is actually walking. And, from what I've seen so far, you definitely have problems with your gait. Just take a few more steps for me, will you, Lorna. Mm . . . you're turning the left foot out more than you should. It may be that the left hip's displaced.'

'Is there *any* part of her that's normal?' the Monster asked derisively.

'It's my back that hurts, not my hip. I had it X-rayed in hospital and they said I had degenerative changes in my spine.'

'Well, in that case I think you should see our osteopath, José Carlos.'

'Now, you mean?'

'Oh no, no, no. We've booked you in for the scan today, as Mr Brownlow suggested.'

'Hughes.'

'What?'

'My surgeon's name' – she enunciated carefully – 'is Mr *Hughes*.'

'Yes, I know. We've been over that already.'

'So why did you call him Brownlow?'

'I didn't, Lorna. I'm talking about José Carlos – José Carlos Carrero. His English isn't brilliant, but he's first-rate as an osteopath. You could book to see him on a subsequent visit. We also have a splendid acupuncturist who might be able to help.'

'He's touting for business again,' the Monster warned, 'for his pals this time. I bet they're all in it together – inventing symptoms for every patient, to make sure they each have a go. It could even be a pan-European racket: José Carlos from Spain, the acupuncturist from Bulgaria.'

'But wait till we have the results of the scan. That'll be a help to any practitioner you see here. I'll just check up on Charlene – she's the one who operates the scanner . . . Ah, Charlene, how are you placed? . . . Half an hour? . . . Don't worry, I'll ask her to wait.'

Lorna groaned inwardly. Should she phone Paul and warn him she'd be late?

Mr Weekes shook her hand again, threatening to reduce it to pulp. 'It's been a great pleasure to meet you, Lorna.'

If only she could say the same.

'And don't worry, my dear. We'll sort you out one way or another. I'll be in touch again when I have the results. Meanwhile would you mind going back to the waiting-room and Charlene will call you when she's ready.'

With an irritable glance at her watch, she took a seat between a mother with a dribbling baby and a man with his arm in a sling. She could hardly digest all Mr Weekes had said – the wrong operation and the outcome bad enough to *sue*, for God's sake! She'd be hopeless company for Paul, with her mind on osteotomies rather than romance. But if she postponed tonight it would mean enduring another bout of nerves, like a teenager on her first date. Would he kiss her? Did he mind that she was older than him? Did he sleep around? Besides, she was all prepared: she had shaved her legs, varnished her toenails, bought sexy new knickers. Why, when they were just going out for a meal? Perhaps next time though . . . If there *was* a next time. Yet Sunday had gone well. He'd made her laugh, taken her out of herself – exactly what she needed, Kathy said: a good-humoured guy, not a misery like Ralph.

But she didn't want to think about Ralph, least of all him pining on his own. She picked up a copy of *Vogue*, as a diversion, and tried to decide which shoes to buy once Mr Weekes had 'sorted her out': the scarlet stilettos with four-inch heels (£650) or the snakeskin slingbacks (£800). No use. The absurd prices only made her worry about the house sale (and Derek Bowden), and the model wearing the slingbacks had her arm round a black man who bore a marked resemblance to Oshoba. Oshoba had written to her again, asking what had happened to her and had he failed to please his beautiful lady?

Oh no, he hadn't failed. She would never forget that session on the sofa. But how could she admit to Kathy that she had let one of the Oakfield staff make passionate love to her? Indeed, if she was in the process of divorcing Ralph, it would be dangerous were *anyone* to find out.

'Divorce? Are you out of your mind? You'd never stand the strain – busybody lawyers, court appearances . . . '

'Go away,' she said feebly.

'Anyway, coming on top of Bowden it'll bankrupt you both.'

'Is there a Lorna Hughes here?' An angular woman in a navy skirt and sweater was surveying the people in the waiting-room.

'Yes, I'm Lorna.' She didn't bother correcting the Hughes; after all, at one time she would have felt a ripple of erotic excitement at being invested with the name of her beloved surgeon.

'Hi, I'm Charlene. We're ready for your scan now.'

Charlene led the way to a dimly lit room dominated by a gleaming black machine which ran the length of one wall. 'This is the Beast. We call it that because it's always causing mayhem.'

Not a good advertisement for a machine costing sixty grand.

'Right, if you'd like to change into your shorts I'll set up the computer.'

'Shorts?'

'Didn't you bring them? Oh dear. You should have been told. We need to see your knees, so we ask you either to come in a very short skirt or bring a pair of shorts.'

'I wasn't told to bring anything except my X-rays.' And a hefty cheque, she didn't add.

'Damn! Polly must have forgotten again. Well, you'll have to wear your knickers. I hope they're reasonably substantial.'

A few wisps of black lace. 'I'd rather not. Haven't you any shorts I could borrow?'

'I'll go and see,' Charlene said dubiously.

While she was gone, Lorna scrutinized the Beast. It (he?) looked rather like an elongated treadmill with two steps leading up to it, a handrail along each side, and cameras at either end. A small video screen was mounted on a bracket above.

'No shorts, but I did find these.' Charlene was brandishing a pair of men's underpants so big and baggy they would have fitted Mr Weekes twice over. 'You're in luck – they're even clean!'

There was nowhere to undress, so Lorna had to remove her trousers in full view of Charlene. Hastily she concealed the skimpy black lace with the acres of off-white interlock. The waistband came up to her armpits, while the legs dangled below her knees. 'Have you got a safety-pin? Otherwise they'll fall down.'

She was rather taken aback when Charlene hitched up her skirt and began fumbling with her underclothes. 'The elastic on my waist-slip went this morning. I'll take it off and you can have the pin.'

Watching Charlene wriggle out of her slip, Lorna felt something of a bond with her. This was very much all girls together.

Charlene stuffed the slip in a drawer and sat down at her desk. 'Now I need to enter your details into the computer. Full name?'

Lorna had to think. Hughes? Brownlow? Pearson?

'Address?'

She gave Clare's. Tomorrow was the deadline for deciding about the job at The Cedars, and she still *hadn't* decided. The main draw-back was –

'Medical history? Any drugs you're on?'

Not Ecstasy, that was for sure. 'Only pain-killers.'

'Do you suffer from diabetes? . . . varicose veins? . . . . epilepsy? . . .

rheumatoid arthritis? . . . cardiovascular disease? . . . respiratory problems?'

After six noes it was clearly blessings-counting time, although if Charlene was obliged to list every ailment in the book they'd still be here tomorrow morning and Paul's romantic dinner would have to be breakfast.

'Now I'm putting up a picture of a female body on the screen – first front view and then back view. I want you to point to any part of it where you're experiencing pain in *your* body . . . Both feet? OK, how severe is the pain on a scale of one to ten?'

'Eleven,' said the Monster.

'Er, three,' Lorna muttered, trying to emulate Agnes's stoicism. She kept it three for all the various pains, ignoring the Monster's interjections of ten, twenty, ninety-five.

'Now, sports. Do you play tennis?'

'No.'

'Go jogging?'

'No.'

'Squash, athletics, badminton, hockey, netball?'

All noes again, and each increased her feeling of inadequacy. To restore a vestige of self-esteem she said yes to swimming. She had swum, once, last year.

'Olympic standard? Competition standard?'

'Occasional,' Lorna mumbled.

They proceeded through surgery and post-op complications to lifestyle habits – smoking, drinking, stress levels (which must surely be sky high by now).

Finally, miraculously, they were ready for the scan. 'We do eighteen tests in all,' Charlene explained, moving from the computer over to the Beast.

Eighteen? Forget breakfast. With luck she might make it for dinner *tomorrow*.

'Take your shoes and socks off, please, and get up on the platform.'

The hard surface was painful to stand on and she was self-conscious about her appearance: smart cream linen jacket atop thermal bloomers and bare feet.

'Before each test, you watch it done on the screen.' Charlene switched on the video and a gorgeous Thai nymphet sprang into view, dressed in a fetching mini-kimono patterned with blue butterflies. (No doubt she'd have looked equally good in voluminous men's underpants.) Her feet, of course, were perfect – small and shapely, with shell-pink nails. As she demonstrated the test, a male voice-over intoned the instructions – *Oshoba's* voice: deep black velvet. Lorna promptly overbalanced, and when it was her turn to do the test she muddled her left foot with her right, looked down instead of up, and eventually collapsed against the rail.

'Start again,' said Charlene. 'No, bottom *in*, bottom *in*. Back straight. Damn! One of the cameras seems to be playing up. I'll see if I can get hold of Kevin.' She reached for the phone. 'Kevin? This is Charlene . . . Yes, another tantrum, would you believe? Can you come as soon as possible?' She turned to Lorna. 'The woman who did this job before me had a nervous breakdown. Apparently when it first arrived the Beast refused to work at all, and yet patients were coming from miles away – Truro, Aberdeen, all over the place. Kevin's quite handy, bless his heart, but we really need a properly trained technician, and there isn't one in Britain. It's an American machine, you see.' Charlene ran a harassed hand through her poker-straight grey hair. 'While we're waiting I'll run the video again.'

Lorna gave the supple, poised Thai female a withering look, and received a simpering smile in return.

'OK if I come in, ladies?'

Kevin. Built on Mr Weekes's scale, although dressed rather differently – in jeans and a T-shirt saying, 'I'm so wonderful I amaze myself.' Perhaps not an idle boast, since he managed to fix the camera in less than fifteen minutes. However, he then peered with some concern at the power point on the skirting-board. 'This is very hot,' he frowned. 'There's a bad connection somewhere. Sorry – I'm going to have to shut everything down.'

'Oh *no!*' Lorna and Charlene groaned in unison.

'Well, I suppose I could come back later . . .'

'Much later,' Charlene begged. 'I have two more patients to scan this afternoon.'

'I don't like to leave it, though.' Kevin scratched his stomach. 'It could be dangerous.'

'I'll take that risk,' said Lorna.

'Yeah, do,' the Monster urged. 'Electrocution could be a blessing in disguise.'

'But how do *you* feel, Charlene?'

'If it's not one thing it's another' was Charlene's only response.

Exactly Lorna's sentiments. In fact the phrase summed up her entire philosophy of life.

'Well, call me if you need me.' And, with a last anxious glance at the power point, Kevin lumbered out.

'I hope to God we won't,' Charlene grumbled, returning to the scanner. 'Now, where were we?'

Lorna couldn't say. Her mind had strayed to Ralph again. She still felt awfully guilty leaving him with the house to sell – guilty leaving him at all, now she'd discovered that he had only got drunk because they'd lost the Sherborne job, which meant the business would fold. So perhaps she'd been too hasty in . . .

'*Lorna?*'

'Sorry, yes?'

'Do watch the screen. See, she's got her left foot out in front, with the weight on that foot and the knee bent, and she's holding her knee with both hands and pushing it across the body.'

Yes, but her knees aren't draped in this lot, Lorna thought crossly, heaving aside swathes of interlock. She couldn't seem to concentrate: the dim light was soporific and the deep male voice kept reminding her of Oshoba – his luscious, pink-lined lips; the exquisite feel of his tongue against her nipples. Luscious or no, she really ought to end things with him or he'd continue writing, which could be risky for them both. Ralph was forwarding her letters, but what if he chanced to open one? Clearly she had to avoid entanglements just now. But in that case why was she seeing Paul? Should she cancel tonight, or at least . . . ?

'Lorna, roll the heels inward, not outward. And keep the weight on the left foot.'

Outside, the rain was sheeting down as they proceeded wearily through tests 4, 5, 6, 7 . . .

By the time they reached the last, she was beginning to feel not just physically inadequate but intellectually challenged, as if she'd taken eighteen GCSEs and failed every single one. She stepped off the scanner with aching feet and great relief. 'Is that it? Can I get dressed and go?'

'Dressed, yes. Go – mm, better not.' Charlene had returned to the screen. 'The computer's flashing a message: "Error 900 Joliet tree sort failed." What on earth does *that* mean?'

'No idea, I'm afraid.' Lorna released the safety-pin and the underpants flopped swiftly to the floor. 'Would Kevin be able to help?'

'No. He hasn't a clue about software.'

'Or Mr Weekes?'

'Bertram? You must be joking! He doesn't know a mouse from a modem. Of course I'm hardly an expert myself. I've only been doing this job a fortnight.'

God – Lorna yanked her trousers up – you'd think they could afford a state-of-the-art operator to match their state-of-the-art scanner. 'Or how about his secretary?'

'Oh, Bertram doesn't employ Polly for her computer skills.' Charlene gave a knowing smirk. 'She has *other* talents.'

'So what do we do now?'

'Well, whatever happens, stick around until I've sorted out this glitch. The error message keeps flashing and I can't get rid of the bloody thing.' Charlene pressed various buttons, muttering expletives that grew more and more obscene. In the end she banged both fists on the desk, making the keyboard bounce alarmingly. 'There's nothing for it – I'll have to phone Seattle. Let me see, what time is it over there? Yes, they should be in the office – just. Sit down and rest your feet, Lorna. This may be a lengthy business.'

Lorna remained standing. 'Charlene, I've got an appointment in Weybridge, which will take me a good two hours from here, given the unreliable trains. And I'm already very late.'

'I'm sorry, I'm doing all I can . . . Hello? Hello? Could you speak up? Is Sinclair in yet? . . . He's not. Shit! Is anyone in? . . . Randy? Yes, OK. . . . Hi, Randy. Look, can we cut the pleasantries? It's this sodding machine – it seems to be frozen . . . It's no good you saying press the Enter key when it just won't . . . Are you positive we can't lose the tests? . . . You're *not* positive . . . Yes, I've got the patient here . . . No, I won't let her go . . . Of course I don't understand. Why the hell would

I be phoning you if I could work it out for myself? . . . Nothing happens – just an arrow. It still hasn't changed . . . Wait, everything's gone blue. Should it have? Now it says, "Are you sure you want to delete?"'

'Don't delete!' Lorna gasped. This was farcical. Should she offer to take over herself? In fact she could probably run the whole clinic more efficiently than this crew. She'd sack Polly for a start, and all practitioners with sub-standard English, limit staff holidays to one week per year (to be taken in the British Isles), get rid of the clutter on Bertram's desk and, last but not least, ship this useless scanner back to Seattle.

'Randy, I haven't time to discuss your peanut allergy. I've got two other patients waiting . . . No, I didn't know that chicken marsala contained nuts. Is Sinclair in yet? . . . Ill? . . . What, nuts? . . . Oh, *mumps*. I see. I'm sorry. When he does come back to work, tell him Mr Weekes will want a refund on his phone-bill. And *I'm* claiming compensation for the stress of the last two weeks . . . I know it's not your fault, Randy. That's the trouble, it's never anybody's fault . . . Oh, God, hold on. Now it's saying, "Please insert blank CD." Which means it must be about to start at the beginning again. In that case has it lost the tests? . . . You think it has . . . Do them all again? You *are* joking, I assume . . . You're not joking. But how do we know it won't go wrong a second time? . . . We don't. OK, I'll tell the patient . . . '

All at once there was an ominous noise: a fizzing sound like a small firework going off. It was followed by a blue flash, and suddenly the lights went out.

'Bloody fucking hell!' Charlene had dropped the phone and was staring at the wisp of smoke curling out of the socket.

'Armageddon!' shrieked the Monster. 'Prepare to meet thy doom!'

Lorna picked up her coat and made her way in semi-darkness past the now blank computer screen. For once the Monster had been right: she was never *meant* to have orthoses. 'Goodbye, Charlene,' she said, tight-lipped, then added a little more kindly, 'Good luck!'

After all, she had just saved herself £500.

27

'Don't stop! Don't stop! It's wonderful. Fantastic. Go on, go *on*! Harder. Yes. Oh yes . . . ' Lorna collapsed back on the bed. Her pounding heart seemed to shake the room, the whole flat. She closed her eyes. Deep black velvet plush behind the lids – Oshoba's skin, Oshoba's feel, Oshoba's touch. She worshipped him. Who cared what Kathy thought? Or Ralph? She had been *born* for this. Her life before meant nothing. 'Oh, Oshoba, I . . . '

'Don't speak.' His lips moved towards hers again.

The kiss travelled down and down, alchemy turning her base cells to gold. Then he drew back a little and looked at her. The gaze was like the kiss: passionate, intense. She could see herself reflected in his eyes: a tiny surrendering figure lost in deep black pools. As he must be in *her* eyes. They were part of one another, skins and bodies exchanged. She was black now; he white. Even their smells had fused, the tang of coconut hair-oil overlaying her rose scent.

He picked up a strand of her hair, ran it through his fingers, pressed it to his lips. Then he took her hand and kissed her broken thumbnail. Every part of her became precious when he kissed it: the sole of her foot, the tiny bruise on her left thigh, the space between her shoulder-blades. Their faces were so close she could see the pores of his skin and the individual hairs in his eyebrows. She adored each pore, each hair.

He sat up at last, disentangling his body from hers. 'I'll fetch the wine.'

'No,' she said, wrapping her legs round his again. 'I want you just . . . here.' She put her arms around his neck and drew his head down, to her breasts. He was the bulwark against her fears. If he moved they would flood back.

Gently he loosened her arms. 'I'll only be two seconds.'

When he'd gone she pulled the nylon sheet up to her chin. What was she *doing* lying naked in this bed? She had come to tell him it was over and that he mustn't get involved now she was thinking of leaving Ralph for good.

But who need ever know? Ralph was hardly likely to track her down to a shabby council flat. No, not shabby – resplendent. The grey walls seemed to glow, and the saggy single divan had become a damask-hung four-poster. Even the balding hairbrush on the dressing-table was an object of fascination. Just because it was his.

The door opened softly and he came in with the wine. 'See? I'm back already.' He handed her a glass – a cheap thing, with garish coloured fruits stencilled round the rim (Waterford crystal once he'd touched it). It was she who had brought the wine, to ease their parting, but now it was for celebration.

He leaned forward and held his glass teasingly between her breasts, cold against her flushed skin. 'To my beautiful lady,' he whispered.

'To my beautiful man.'

'You look happy now.'

'I am.'

'Not sad and stern like when you first arrived.'

'Was I stern?'

'Terribly!' He moved the glass against her nipple.

His voice was so languorously caressing, just hearing it made her want him again. And his penis was still stiff, she noticed with surprise, with pride. She pulled him down beside her, moving over to make room for him. 'Is this your brother's bed or yours?'

'Oh, mine. I wouldn't dare use my brother's. He might find a wisp of your toco-hair lurking in his sheets.' He kissed his fingers and leaned forward to plant the kiss on her bush.

There was a sudden awkward silence. He seemed embarrassed all at once, for no reason she could fathom. He was no longer looking at her, but staring down at his glass. 'I . . . I have to speak to you about my brother,' he said, in a completely different tone – defensive, almost terse.

'Oh dear. Is he cross that I'm here? I know he doesn't like me.'

'It's not that. He has a . . . problem.' Oshoba put his glass down on the wooden box that served as a bedside table. 'He has to go back to Nigeria. Our sister is ill.'

'I'm sorry. What's wrong with her?'

'I'm not sure. Except it's serious. The thing is, he hasn't any money for the fare. He keeps saying I've got to pay.'

'You? Why?'

'Because he's lost his job.'

'Heavens! When did that happen?'

'Last week. They gave him the sack.'

'But you said he was working – tonight, I mean. You told me to come at seven, so he'd be gone.'

Oshoba looked confused for a moment. 'That's . . . only a temporary job. Just for a day or two. He has to fly out as soon as he can.'

'But if you haven't got the money, Oshoba . . . ' She wondered why *he* wasn't going. Surely a carer in a nursing-home would be of more practical use than a chef? 'Why does Olu have to go, not you?'

'He's the eldest and we can't afford two fares. We can't even afford one unless . . . '

'How much *is* the fare?'

'Seven hundred pounds return.'

'That sounds a lot. Can't he get something cheaper from one of those bucket shops?'

'Maybe. But he'll need money while he's there as well.' Oshoba seemed increasingly nervous. He went over to the window and stood fiddling with the curtain. 'I was wondering, beautiful lady, whether you . . . you might be able to help.'

'*Me?*'

'Well, I know you're selling your house.'

She stared at him, incredulous. Was he trying to turn their sex into a sordid cash transaction? 'But it's not sold yet. And most of that money's earmarked anyway.'

'What do you mean? It's a big house, isn't it? It must be worth a lot.'

Don't say any more, she pleaded silently. Don't spoil things.

They were already spoiled. Irredeemably. As they were between her and Paul. (Paul hadn't demanded cash in return for sex: he had demanded sex in return for dinner. And as he'd admitted having several other girlfriends she wasn't keen to join the harem.) 'Oshoba, the money's tied up, mine and Ralph's. We have a joint account.'

'But you said you were divorcing him.'

'Not yet. Things are very . . . uncertain.' Uncertain all round. They did have a prospective buyer for the house, but he had put in a depressingly low offer. Should they accept and get Bowden off their backs, or hold out for the asking price?

Oshoba looked thoroughly wretched, his brow creased, his fingers drumming on the window-sill. Perhaps she was being unfair. If he was genuinely worried about his sister's health he might be forced to take desperate measures. And yet it did seem an awful cheek to expect *her* to shell out. 'I'm not working at the moment myself. Money's very tight.'

'But your aunt's house – the one she left you in her will. That should bring in a good bit.'

All the things she had told him in good faith were now being turned against her. She heard her voice, listless and dejected. 'We have to wait for probate to be cleared.'

'I don't understand.'

No, he didn't understand – only the needs of her body. Had he planned it all deliberately? Shag the woman till she's stupefied, then stand over her while she signs the cheque? But how could he have faked his own excitement? That noisy, shuddering climax? And what about the last time? He hadn't asked for anything then. In fact he had always been gentle and caring; a giver, not a taker. She sipped the wine to allow herself time to think – expensive Chardonnay that tasted flat and sour. 'Oshoba, I'd like to help but I . . . I can't. Things are very difficult financially.'

'My brother says your house is worth a million.'

She flung the covers aside and stood up. 'Well, he's wrong – completely and utterly. And what does *he* know about it? Unless you've been talking, of course.'

He grasped her arm, so tight it hurt. 'You know I wouldn't do that. But he's always asking questions, and then I found that he's been checking up on you.'

'He's been *what?*'

'Don't be angry, beautiful lady.'

'I've every right to be angry.' She wrested her arm away. 'It's a bloody cheek!'

'But he's angry too, you see.' Again he tried to touch her, clutching at her hand this time, as if by maintaining physical contact he could overcome her resistance. 'Because I slept with you.'

'What the hell's it got to do with him?'

Oshoba bit his lip, said nothing.

'Is it because I'm white?'

'Maybe. He's had some bad experiences over here. So now he's prejudiced. And perhaps he's jealous too, a bit. He's never had a girl-friend.'

'Well, that's his problem.' She was already struggling into her clothes – the clothes Oshoba had removed so sensuously and slowly, kissing the insides of her thighs as he drew down her lacy tights, tonguing her breasts as he unfastened her bra.

'Please don't rush off. I hate it to be like this when before we were so close.'

Torn all ways, she sank down on the bed. Perhaps he simply wasn't strong enough to withstand his brother's demands, his dislike of her, his prejudice. For all she knew, Olu could be a brute. And yet the story didn't quite ring true. Why had the sister never been mentioned before? And why was he avoiding her eyes? 'Oshoba, I didn't even know you *had* a sister. How come she's suddenly ill?'

'We only heard last night. My father rang.'

'I'd have thought you'd have been more upset then. If I'd just heard my sister was at death's door I don't think I'd feel like jumping into bed with anyone, even you. And it certainly didn't affect your perform-ance.'

He slipped his hand between the buttons of her blouse. 'That's because I find you so exciting.'

'I don't want flattery, Oshoba. I want the truth.'

'It *is* the truth. When I see you naked, everything else goes out of my head.'

Could she believe him? Or had the whole thing been a sham from the start? Perhaps he had latched on to her at Oakfield in the hope of financial gain, sensed her vulnerability, seen her as a soft touch. According to Kathy, some of the carers did blatantly tout for cash. But Oshoba hadn't seemed the mercenary type. Unless he'd been biding his time, of course. The problem was, she would never know – which meant that things between them could never be the same. Even now, while his thumb caressed her nipple, her body was responding while her mind warned, 'Stupid fool! He's only after your money.'

'Lorna, you don't seem to realize it's *you* I'm worried about.'

'What d'you mean?'

'Well, Olu says if you won't help he might have to ask your husband.'

She sprang up from the bed. 'Oshoba, if you or Olu *dare* say a word to Ralph . . . '

'But how can I stop him?'

'Oshoba, this is blackmail.'

'No, of course it isn't. I just want to save you from trouble. But I'm worried for myself as well. I don't want your husband knowing that we've . . . '

'A pity you didn't think of that earlier.' She seized her jacket and buttoned it with shaking fingers. 'And you can tell Olu that he won't get a single penny from either me or Ralph. Is that clear?'

'No, wait, please. We have to talk.'

'We've talked quite long enough.'

'At least let's finish the wine.' Desperately he pushed the glass into her hands.

She hurled it to the floor. 'It's over, Oshoba, don't you understand? Buy your own wine in future. And pay your own bloody fares.'

28

'An absolute disgrace!'

Aunt Agnes's voice exploded in Lorna's head as, nervously, she approached the grave. It was overgrown with weeds, the headstone cracked and leaning to one side as if drunk, like her father. And the graves around it were similarly out of kilter, some half sunken, some tilted at perilous angles, many crumbling or broken. A marble angel lay helpless on her back, one wing snapped off, her face streaked with green. Groundsel and chickweed had invaded the stone slabs; coarse tufts of grass sprouted between cracks. Was her father so powerful that even after death he could leave this trail of devastation? When she'd visited as a child, the plot had been well tended, the gravestones upright, the whole churchyard neat and trim. Agnes would never have allowed insolent weeds to encroach or rapacious ivy to choke her beloved sister. Instead, pristine white lilies or sprays of scented lilac would be arranged in vases and forbidden to droop. Lorna used to wonder why the dead should even want flowers, when they could no longer see or smell them. As an adult she had avoided the place and all its traumatic associations, preferring to keep her father exuberantly alive, not confined in a box, shackled by a stone.

On impulse she put down the heavy carrier-bag, knelt on the ground and started grubbing up the weeds with her bare hands. How could she leave Agnes's remains in such a wild, disorderly spot? Soon her nails were filthy and her wrists scratched, so she searched for a piece of flint to dig out the obstinate roots. Then she used it to scrape the lichen off the headstone and finally sat back on her heels and stared at the formal names: Garret Michael David Alexander; Margaret Anna Martha Rose. She had never known her parents as they really were. And perhaps the few memories she had of them were coloured by her craving for a perfect, problem-free family.

She shivered, although the day was unseasonably warm – the fields and hills beyond the churchyard shimmering in a heat haze, the recent rain and gloom purged in a convulsion of new growth. Polished celandines carpeted the ground, interspersed with young, keen, sappy nettles, and a white bridal veil of cow-parsley foamed along the hedgerows amid a luminous gauze of green. All around, trees and plants were uncoiling, budding, sprouting, while swifts and swallows painted darting black hieroglyphs on the becalmed blue sky. Living here as a child, she had been too forlorn to notice the beauty of the countryside. Her focus was on her parents (where might she find them? In heaven? Under ground?) and on her hated boarding-school. Nor did she remember the place being as lonely as today. There had always been people – grown-ups mostly, telling her what to do; not just Agnes but busybody villagers. Now, however, the area seemed abandoned, tenanted only by the dead.

She took the heavy cardboard box out of the carrier-bag. How grotesque it was that the person who had brought her up and had loved her most in the world should be reduced to a bagful of ashes. At Clare's, she had kept it under the bed, unwilling to confront it, and indeed the very sight of the oblong box brought back an image of Agnes in her coffin, her nails still varnished strawberry red, in contrast to her old-fashioned clothes. She had kissed the stiff white brow, repelled by its marble coldness and by the vase of artificial flowers standing on a plinth beside the corpse – dusty roses in a hideous shade of mauve. And at a time when daffodils and tulips were running riot in every garden, on sale in every florist's. Were the undertakers too mean to buy a bunch or two? The artificial had no place in Agnes's life.

Ignoring the sick feeling in her stomach, she peeled off the tape that sealed the cardboard box. Inside she found a tall, screw-topped jar, and inside that a polythene bag of silvery cinder-dust. Box, jar and bag all bore identical labels, giving Agnes's name, the date of her cremation and the cremation number: 804. But no, this *couldn't* be Agnes – in a plastic bag in a plastic jar . . .

She drew the bag from the mouth of the jar and undid its plastic tie. Never before had the difference between life and death seemed so chillingly stark. A corpse was at least recognizable as human – clothed and three-dimensional, the person you had known – whereas this gritty grey stuff might just as well be the debris from a bonfire or the sweepings from a grate.

She had no idea how to proceed. The scattering of ashes surely required some form of ritual – a priest intoning solemn words, backed by organ and choir. But, like the village, the churchyard was deserted, basking in Sunday lunch-time stupor. Birds provided the only choir: raucous jays, brash thrushes, a cacophony of rooks.

Kneeling in a respectful posture, she held out the bag and slowly trickled the ashes on to the grave. Some settled there; some lifted in the breeze, dispersed. Was she reuniting the sisters, or simply casting Agnes to the winds?

Tears slid down her face. She wiped her eyes with her sleeve, knowing her aunt would disapprove. Coming out without a clean cotton handkerchief was a capital offence. (Agnes couldn't abide paper tissues.) 'Dearest Aunt,' she whispered, 'I promise not to sniff. There's no need to worry about me any more. Your work is over now.'

She pressed some of the fine granules into the engraved letters of her mother's name. 'Rest in Peace' was written underneath in Gothic script. Had her mother ever known peace?

Suddenly she saw her father coming down the path. She and Mummy had been watching for him, waiting on the doorstep. She ran to meet him, her summer sandals hurting on the ruts. Her head was level with his legs. Pin-striped legs. Unsteady legs, lurching towards her. He bent to kiss her. A dribbly, nasty-tasting kiss.

'Look what I found, Daddy!' She held out the feather. A magpie's feather, blue-glistening-black.

He didn't take it, though. He didn't even seem to see it. His eyes were funny, with little streaks of red in them.

'Don't bother me, Lorna. I'm tired.'

His voice was wrong: a fuzzy growl. Her mother's voice was wrong as well. Scared and shrill. And her face too tight.

They went inside. He sat at the table, but he didn't eat his meat or apple pie. He just drank some brown stuff from a bottle. Mummy tried to stop him, but he banged his fist on the table and the cups and glasses shook. Mummy cried. He laughed. No one noticed *her*, so she slid down from her chair and hid behind the door. She'd lost her magic feather. She wished she had feathers too, to fly away.

She screwed her eyes tight shut. Better not to look. Or make a noise. If she wasn't quiet he'd bang the table again.

'I will *not* be quiet!' she yelled, wheeling round to face the grave.

'Not any more. To hell with you, Daddy! You ruined our lives. Smashed yourself up. Killed Mummy.' She kicked out at the headstone, hurting her foot on the granite. 'I was born brave and you destroyed that, you selfish, drunken pig . . . '

The rooks' voices mocked in echo, but she shouted louder still. 'And that awful school . . . It was like another death. You and your pretensions! You can't imagine what it was like, being treated as if I *smelt*. Just because I had no parents. And all the time I kept thinking, What if Agnes dies too? Nothing was safe. Or permanent. How dare you be so . . . '

Her voice was getting hoarse. What was the point of ranting? It was *over*. Her father was dead. Her mother was dead. Even Agnes was dead. She had to accept it, let them go. Life *wasn't* safe, not for anyone. It was full of risk and uncertainty. So be it – she'd survive.

Somewhere in the distance she heard the throb of a tractor. People working, purposeful . . .

She stood looking out across the patchwork fields, although the combed brown furrows and the green glaze of wheat remained a featureless blur. Her attention was on the past, flashing by in fast-forward: her childhood here, first with her parents, then with Agnes; the prison years of school; the wild affairs; the breakdown; the safe harbour of marriage; the recent squalls and shipwreck.

It hadn't been all bad. At least she'd not been consigned to a mental home like Frances; nor had she become an agoraphobic. In fact she had reached the age of forty able to function more or less normally.

So what now? Did she flounder on in futile indecision, knowing that no choice *was* a choice, then waste the rest of her life in regret?

'No,' she said aloud, punching her fist into her palm. 'Dammit, I *will* take the job at The Cedars.' She repeated the statement, as if requiring her decision to be witnessed and official, heard by the whole county. 'I won't be ruled by panic any longer. Or by Ralph. Or my father. I don't *need* protectors. I don't need men at all. Agnes got by without them, and so will I.'

She tore up a fistful of celandines and flung them over the ashes. No more fake flowers or artificial grass. She wrenched a clump of cowslips from the ground, threw it on to the grave, and added dandelions and buttercups – the flowers she'd loved as a child. That courageous child had died when her world was overturned. But she could resurrect her. And she'd do what they did in fairy-tales: slay the wicked Monster.

She grabbed the box and carrier and broke into a run, thudding down the churchyard path and out into the lane. Her feet hurt terribly – but too bad. She'd finished with doctors, operations, crutches. Pain or no, she refused to be a patient from now on.

Suddenly, up loomed the Monster, breathing fire and blocking her way. 'Slay *me*? Are you kidding? I'll be with you till you die.'

'No you won't. You're nothing – a spectre from my childhood, that's all. I was frightened then, with reason, but – '

'Nothing, am I? Just you wait and see. I can wreck this new job for a start. An administrator prone to panic attacks? – you'll be fired within the week.'

'I'm not listening! You don't even exist.'

'Oh really? Then why's your heart pounding nineteen to the dozen? And why are you short of breath?'

'Just . . . habit,' she gasped. 'But I'll fight you. You can threaten all you like, but I'll win in the end. I'll stand up to you. Like Agnes did. *And* my mother. Everyone has Monsters. Even my father. Obviously.'

'Yeah,' the Monster cackled. 'And we know where *he* ended up!'

She pushed past him, although his taunting voice pursued her along the lane. 'And what about Ralph? You'll never cope with the guilt. Think you can swan off to The Cedars while he hasn't so much as a roof over his head?'

She clamped her hands across her chest. The Monster always sussed out her weak spots: she did feel crushing guilt on Ralph's account. 'I . . . I'll give him the money from the sale of Agnes's house – every penny of it. Then he can buy a flat.'

'Don't be stupid – he's too proud to take your money. Anyway, you'll need it yourself when you get the sack. You can't honestly believe they'll keep you on at The Cedars. Or in any job, come to that. You only survived in Astro-Sport because Ralph was holding your hand. Without him you're unemployable.'

'In that case why did he say he wanted me back and how brilliant I was at the business?'

'He'll change his tune once Olu's been round demanding money with menaces. All hell will break loose.'

Her heart was hammering in her chest. The very thought of Olu made her sweat.

'You won't stand a chance in the divorce court when they hear you jumped into bed with the first available male at Oakfield.'

Desperate to escape, she ducked into the pub. 'Please . . . ' she panted, practically throwing herself on the bar, 'could I use your phone?'

'Help yourself.' The barman jabbed a thumb over his left shoulder. 'It's in the corner.'

It was some minutes before she was calm enough to dial. 'Kathy? It's Lorna.'

'Where are you, for heaven's sake?'

'In the wilds of Sussex.'

'What on earth are you doing there? I rang you at Clare's to wish you happy birthday and she said you'd – '

'Look, never mind that. I'm phoning to see if the job's still open. I know the deadline was Friday, but – '

'Well, actually Chris is in Paris this weekend with her boyfriend, so I don't imagine she's interviewing staff!'

'I could still apply then?' She was nearly deafened by the Monster's bray of contempt.

'Honestly, Lorna' – Kathy let out an impatient sigh – 'that's what I've been begging you to do for weeks. Thank God you've come to your senses at last. What made you decide?'

'My father,' Lorna murmured to herself. 'Kathy, I'm sorry, I can't talk for long. I'm down to my last two coins.'

'Wait! What about your birthday? You can't spend it on your own. Are you coming back tonight?'

'Oh yes.'

'And have you something planned?'

'Only a nice long soak in the bath!'

'Let me take you out to dinner then. I'll book a table at Gianni's.'

'But, Kathy, it's terribly expensive . . . '

'The food's great, though. And after all it's a double celebration. Would seven thirty suit you?'

'Perfect. See you there.'

As she put the phone down she realized how loudly she'd been talking, in an effort to drown the Monster. The pub wasn't crowded, fortunately, but half a dozen locals were staring at her with interest. Apart from her shouted conversation, she must look a sight, with dirty hands and grass-stained clothes. She was tempted to leave, but it would be rude just to walk out without buying a drink.

And she *wanted* a drink – something fizzy and sparkling. This morning she had woken with a leaden weight on her shoulders – forty, and nothing to show for it. No job, no home, no husband or child. But now the weight had disappeared and she felt as light and effervescent as the bubbles in champagne. At last she had made a decision; at last left the past behind. Even the Monster had vanished – for once she'd got the better of him. He'd be back, of course, but she'd show him who was boss. Like Agnes, she must forget her own fear and concentrate on those in her care: the residents at The Cedars.

At the bar she waited her turn behind a doddery old man fumbling for change and slopping beer from his glass. The average age of the customers must be seventy at least. *She* was in her prime and about to embark on a new life.

'Yes, Miss, what can I get you?'

She was amused by the Miss, though in reality she *was* Miss – in Kathy's words, free and unencumbered. 'Mm, I'm not sure . . . ' She scanned the various drinks, her eye lighting on a row of small bulbous bottles the colour of a sunburst, with enticing gold-foil tops. 'One of those, please,' she said, unfolding a £5 note. Then, with a flash of inspiration, she put it back and took out a twenty instead. 'Drinks all round,' she smiled at the barman. 'It's my birthday.'

Re-birth-day.

IV

29

'Hi, Lorna! Come and join us.'

Lorna put her tray on the table and sat down next to Rowan. 'Gosh, I'm glad to take the weight off my feet! Have you two finished lunch?'

'Yeah,' said Rowan. 'We only had salad.'

'Salad, in this weather?' With an exaggerated shiver, Lorna eyed the frenzy of snowflakes that obscured the view from the window. 'Is it ever going to stop?'

'It better had,' said Julie, 'or I won't get home tonight. Michael and me are going clubbing.'

'I don't know how you have the energy on top of a long day.' Lorna forked in a mouthful of Stroganoff.

'Oh, the music wakes you up. You forget everything. It's fantastic.'

'You're lucky,' said Rowan. 'Rob's always down the pub with his mates.'

'Give him the push then.'

Julie was nothing if not forthright, even though she'd only just turned eighteen. Her looks – frail figure, delicate features and wispy ash-blonde hair – belied her acerbic character. Rowan was dark and chubby and gentle.

'Do you think I ought to, Lorna?'

'Goodness, what a question! I suppose it depends on what you want.'

'A big white wedding and twins.'

Lorna laughed. 'And what does Rob want?'

'No commitments. And an Audi TT.'

'In that case Julie's probably right.'

'Lady Tate used to drive a sports car,' Julie said. 'She was telling me about it yesterday. And she never took a driving-test. Apparently in them days you didn't have to.'

'She's a game old bird, isn't she?' Rowan said to Lorna.

Lorna flushed. Any mention of Lady Tate made her instantly self-conscious. James Tate, the youngest son, had been chatting her up for the last month. They had been out once or twice, but although he was a good-looking thirty-seven (and seriously rich) somehow the spark had failed to ignite – on her side, anyway. He was still pursuing her, and every time he visited his mother he came to seek her out. Had Rowan noticed? she wondered. The care assistants didn't miss much.

'Do you want a coffee, Lorna?' Julie asked.

'No thanks. I've got to dash.'

'But you haven't finished your lunch.'

'I'm expecting a call.' Lorna glanced at her watch. Today she was filling in as activities organizer on top of all her other jobs. 'Don't worry. I'll grab a mince pie later.'

On the way back to her office she paused for a second to look out at the grounds. Despite the disruption the snow had caused – blocked roads, cancelled trains and general Christmas chaos – she couldn't help admiring the beauty of the scene. The plump yew-bushes sat like a row of Christmas cakes covered with white frosting, the stone lions sported ermine muffs, and the dead heads on the hydrangeas had become luxuriant white flowers. The sun sparkled on the white lawns, between slate-blue shadows cast by the four cedars.

The phone was ringing when she reached the office. 'Lorna Pearson . . . Oh, hello, Neil . . . You *can* come? Marvellous . . . I'd say about an hour in all . . . Mainly popular music. They like the old tunes, really – songs from the musicals, that sort of thing . . . Yes, sounds great. See you Boxing Day.'

She sat down at her computer, hoping to catch up on some invoicing. There had been various interruptions during the morning – the vicar on a social visit, the woman running the carol concert apologizing about depleted numbers, a long phone-call from Anne Spencer-Armitage (bewailing her own worsening condition and her new consultant's 'criminal negligence') and two or three of the residents, worried about the weather or just wanting a chat.

And now another shrill from the phone. 'Lorna Pearson. May I help you? . . . Oh, *Clare* – lovely! How are you?'

'Stranded! In Portmadoc. And if we don't have a thaw soon I'll be stuck here for New Year as well as Christmas.'

'Oh dear. Poor you. I am sorry. And we were going to that play. I've already booked the tickets.'

'Well, I'll move heaven and earth to get back. But if not you'll have to go without me. Why not take James instead?'

'No fear! I'm trying to extricate myself.' Was it a sign of failure that she had planned to spend New Year's Eve with a woman friend? During the last six months there had been overtures from several men but sadly none she was inclined to encourage. Her thoughts still occasionally strayed to Oshoba, veering from lust to hurt to fear to indignation. She'd half hoped he might contact her again, if only to apologize, but it was obvious he'd just used her.

'You used *him*, you mean! And don't think you're out of the woods yet. If he decides to tell Kathy that you seduced a poor, defenceless care assistant then your job's on the line, no question.'

'Down!' she ordered, and grudgingly the Monster came to heel. It was little short of a miracle that she now had him on a collar and lead, and that for the most part he obeyed her commands.

Clare laughed suddenly. 'Well, whatever you end up doing, my love, it couldn't be worse than last year.'

True. And recalling last year she was immensely cheered by the contrast – she had dispensed with her crutches in all senses. 'So, Clare, is your mother behaving herself? Or is she still insisting – ? Damn! There's somebody at the door. Can I ring you back this evening? . . . Eight o'clock's fine.' She replaced the receiver and called, 'Come in.'

This time it was Kathy, carrying a large, red Father Christmas sack and a dozen rolls of gift-wrap. 'I know you're up to your eyes already, but could you be an angel and wrap this lot? Rita was meant to do it, but I've had to send her home.'

'Flu?'

'Need you ask! That makes it ten off sick. Still, the agency staff are doing reasonably well for a change.'

'I should hope so at the price they're charging.'

Kathy shrugged. 'That's Chris's headache, not ours. We've got quite enough to cope with as it is. Did you know that Mr Palmer had a fall this morning and broke his wrist? We're waiting for the ambulance. I'm just praying it'll get through. I've left Vanessa with him, but I must get back and see that he's all right. Sure you don't mind about the presents?'

''Course not.'

'Winifred's offered to help. It'll be good for her to have something to do. Her son phoned half an hour ago to say he can't come. They're snowed up, apparently.'

'Yes, and Doreen's upset because she can't get to her daughter's. She popped in earlier.'

'With so many disappointments we'll just have to make Christmas extra special for them. I've had a word with Marco and he's going to pull out all the stops. He's concocting a rather ritzy stuffing for the turkey, with truffles and *foie gras* and goodness knows what else.'

'Doreen won't approve!'

Kathy grinned. 'Don't worry, we'll make sure she gets her rabbit food. Must dash – Ah, Winifred, hello. It's so kind of you to help – Lorna's pleased to have an extra pair of hands.'

'Well, you know I hate to be idle.'

'We certainly do.' Kathy relieved Winifred of her walking-frame and helped her into a chair. 'It's a pity you're retired, otherwise I'd rope you in to do some nursing! Anyway, I'll leave the pair of you to it. I'm needed upstairs.'

Lorna placed a small table beside Winifred and laid out scissors, labels, Sellotape.

'I may be rather slow, my dear.' Winifred held up her arthritic fingers, even more distorted and swollen than Agnes's.

'Don't worry. There's no rush.' Lorna piled the presents on the desk. She and Kathy had gone to a lot of trouble finding more interesting gifts for the residents than the usual toiletries or boxes of biscuits – small framed prints of Victorian Weybridge, indoor-garden kits, aroma-therapy oils, books on the old masters for members of the art class.

'Beautiful paper, isn't it?' Winifred was unrolling a length. 'It seems a shame to cut it up.'

A sentiment Agnes would have shared. Lorna often seemed to hear her voice, and in some strange way felt that her aunt was keeping a benevolent eye on her – protecting her from flu, for instance, when a virtual epidemic was raging across the country. Chris and Jeremy were laid low, as well as the maintenance man, both the gardeners and thirteen of the residents.

Winifred cut a strip of Sellotape, with difficulty. 'Are you working tomorrow, Lorna?'

'Well, I wasn't really meant to be, but it's all hands on deck at the moment. I've been doing a weird mixture of jobs. Yesterday I was peeling potatoes, would you believe! It made me realize how spoilt I am here, never having to cook.'

'Yes, I feel the same.' Winifred reached for another present to wrap, a glass paperweight housing a real dandelion clock. 'Good gracious! Look at this. I wonder how they got it inside?'

'You mean without it all blowing away?'

Winifred nodded. 'When I was little I used to love dandelion clocks.' She pursed her lips and blew. 'Three o'clock, four o'clock, five o'clock – that's how quickly time goes now. One puff and an hour's gone. Another puff and a year's gone.'

Another puff and *you're* gone, Lorna thought sadly. Winifred was eighty-nine and suffered from angina. 'If you like it, Winifred, why not have it as your present? I'll put your name on the label.'

'Oh no, dear, that wouldn't be fair. We should accept whatever we're given.'

Lorna hid a smile. Agnes and Winifred were so alike – in their stoicism and diligence, and even in their thick lisle stockings and tweedy skirts. Since starting work at The Cedars, she felt she had acquired a number of mothers among the residents, and even daughters, too, among the staff. Winifred was her favourite mother; Rowan her favourite daughter.

'And how are your poor feet, Lorna?'

'Not bad,' she said, with a glance at her misshapen shoes. Her feet hurt a good deal in fact, but she accepted the pain as simply part of life, along with risk and uncertainty. She wouldn't go as far as Winifred in accepting whatever she was given (too passive a philosophy), but when it came to factors beyond one's control it was best to acquiesce. The trick was to achieve one's aims and enjoy life *despite* pain and insecurity. Besides, she could hardly whinge about bunions when Winifred had leg ulcers, and arthritis in both knees. Working at The Cedars made her grateful for the most basic things: mobility, memory, hearing, eyesight and a remaining life-span measured in decades rather than years. 'What's your son planning to do for Christmas,' she asked, 'now that he can't be with you?'

Winifred's reply was lost in the shrilling of the phone. Lorna picked

305

it up, mouthing an 'Excuse me.' 'Yes, speaking . . . Oh, I see. They're very early, aren't they? . . . OK, I'll sort it out. Goodbye.' She replaced the receiver with a frown. 'I'm sorry, Winifred, the carol singers have just arrived. They seem to have got their timing wrong, so I'll have to give them tea or something.'

'That's all right, dear. Off you go. I'll carry on here.'

'But I can't expect you to . . . '

'Honestly, I like to do my bit. There's nothing worse at my age than feeling you're no use.'

Lorna leaned down and squeezed her hand. 'Winifred, we couldn't do without you.'

'Welcome to The Cedars' first carol concert!' Lorna felt distinctly nervous at addressing such a large gathering: residents and their relatives ranging in age from ninety-eight to nine months. Summoning Ms Unflappable, she raised her voice above the tail-ends of conversations. 'We're very privileged to have the King Edmund School Choir and their teacher, Miss O'Brien. As some of you may know, they won a cup in this year's Cheltenham Festival. And Miss O'Brien is a distinguished singer in her own right.' As Lorna paused for breath, Ms Unflappable reminded her not to gabble and to speak loudly enough to be heard at the back. 'Unfortunately, what with the snow and the traffic hold-ups, some of the children couldn't manage to get here, so I'm afraid we haven't quite as many as we'd expected. But we're delighted to see those who *did* make it today'– she smiled at the seven boys and eight girls standing in a group by the piano – 'and we're most grateful to them for coming out in this weather. Later in the proceedings we'd like everyone to join in, so we can have a nice rousing chorus. Have you all got song-sheets? Rowan, some are needed over there. And, Eric, could you bring more chairs from the dining-room for Mrs Bartlett's son and his family?'

A pity there weren't more staff, to deal with late arrivals, or (better still) a clone of Ms Unflappable to remove the squabbling Bartlett children. 'Well, shall we start? Our first carol is "See Amid the Winter's Snow" – very appropriate for today!'

There was a ripple of laughter, then Miss O'Brien seated herself at the grand piano and began to play.

Lorna took a seat beside Mr Forbes, whose wife had died a month ago. She could imagine how alone he must feel, even in a crowd. She took his thin hand in hers, at the same time keeping a watchful eye on everyone and everything. The Bartlett children were giggling now and Eric was still fetching chairs for latecomers, but on the whole things were going well. The singing was exquisite, especially a solo verse sung by a girl of nine or ten, who looked suitably angelic with long, fair hair and a gauzy white dress. And the Chesterton Room was the perfect setting. Not only were the acoustics good, but the oak-panelled walls and high, ornate ceiling lent an air of gravitas. She and Kathy had been choosy about the Christmas decorations, limiting the colours to midnight blue and silver – the house was too elegant for tinsel and balloons. She herself had arranged madonna lilies in a vase on the piano. Real flowers were important.

There was another solo, 'The First Nowell', this time from Miss O'Brien, whose rich contralto voice more than compensated for her drab appearance: limp brown hair and baggy frock. Giggling and coughing subsided as the pure, liquid notes filled the room.

'. . . Nowell, Nowell,
Born is the King of – '

Then suddenly, without warning, the room was plunged into darkness. The piano and the singing stuttered to a halt. There were screams from the children, cries of alarm from the residents.

Lorna stood up. 'Please, everyone, keep calm. It must be a power cut, but the emergency generator will take over within twenty seconds and the power will come back on.'

There was an expectant hush, but, as the seconds ticked by and the power *didn't* come back on, the general hubbub increased.

Ms Unflappable took over. 'Please stay where you are – it's safest for us all. Rowan, could you look after everyone while I go and sort things out.' At the door she collided with Kathy, armed with a torch.

'Why the hell hasn't the stand-by generator cut in?' Kathy hissed.

'God knows!' Lorna whispered back. 'I'll phone Eddie. I know he's off sick, but he'll just have to come in.'

'OK. Take this torch. I'll find another.'

'We do have candles, Kathy.'

Kathy shook her head. 'Too dangerous. Anyway, with luck we won't need them. Eddie should be here in five minutes.'

Guided by the torch-beam, Lorna made her way along the passage, trying to ignore the knot of fear rising in her throat. The bright, cheerful house had become menacing. Shadows flickered around her, and nothing was visible through the windows save a waste of snow swallowed up in a black void. She steadied herself against the wall, horrified that her symptoms had returned. Far from being Ms Unflappable, she was on the verge of a panic attack. It was months since she'd had this sick churning in her stomach, this sense of her body veering out of control. It must be the strain of the last week – snowstorms, staff sickness, the build-up to Christmas Day. She forced herself to take slow, deep breaths. She must not give way to the sensations – not in the middle of a crisis, when she was meant to be in charge, for heaven's sake.

Somehow she managed to reach her office and with shaking fingers dialled Eddie's number. His wife answered. 'No, he *can't* come out. It's Christmas Eve, I'll have you know. And he's got a temperature of a hundred and two.'

'I wouldn't dream of ringing, Mrs Elliott, if it wasn't an emergency. But we've lost all the power – not only the lights, the heating too. And some of our residents are extremely frail.'

'Sorry, nothing doing. If you think I'm going to drag him from his bed just because – '

'Wait, *please!*' She fought for breath. Power cuts could last hours. There would be no hot meal for the residents tonight, and those with flu might develop pneumonia lying in unheated rooms. The house would be cold for Christmas Day, relatives would complain, maybe even write to the authorities or refuse to pay the fees . . . 'At least could you ask him if there's anybody else I can ring about the generator?'

'Try Frank.'

'He's away. In Ireland.'

'Sorry, he's the only one I know.'

'But Eddie's bound to have more names.'

'He's just dropped off to sleep. I don't want to bother him when – '

'I beg you, Mrs Elliott! Otherwise we're sunk.'

With a muttered curse and a clatter of the phone, Mrs Elliott went off to wake her husband. There were various noises in the background: children's voices, a dog yapping, an announcer on the radio. Finally she returned, sounding slightly less hostile. 'He says there's an emergency number on the side of the generator. If it breaks down they have to come out, he says. It's in the contract.'

'Oh, thank you. What a relief!'

'While you're there, Mrs Pearson, I may as well tell you, Eddie's not coming back. We've been talking about it. He's had enough, and so have I. The hours are too long. And unsocial. It puts paid to family life. So you'd better tell your matron or whoever that she'll have to find a replacement.'

'Look . . . why don't we discuss it when Eddie's up and about again?'

'No, he's leaving. And that's final.' And Mrs Elliott slammed the phone down.

Lorna hadn't time to worry about the Elliotts – the first priority was light. She snatched up a pen and paper and groped her way to the cellar, feeling more and more panicky as she descended the steep stone steps. Suppose she was trapped for the whole of Christmas in this dank, cold, spooky place? The torch was shaking in her hand as she flashed it on the blue-grey bulk of the generator, which loomed like a monstrous steel coffin, clammy to the touch. She eventually found the phone-number, printed on a label on the far side at the bottom. She copied each digit carefully, then fled back up the steps, tripping in her haste.

'Sovereign Generators. Clive Brown speaking.'

She could have kissed Clive Brown just for being there – no flu, no protective wife. '. . . So if you could send someone round immediately . . .'

'I'm very sorry, Mrs Pearson, but we only have a next-day service, and we don't work Christmas Day or bank holidays, so I can't get an engineer to you until the twenty-seventh.'

'But I've been told that in an emergency you're legally obliged to send someone.'

'The next day, yes, in normal circumstances, but I'm afraid we're closed as from tonight.'

'Look, this is ridiculous! The whole point of having a standby generator is to cover us in case of a power cut, yet the first time we need it the damned thing doesn't work. It cost enough, for Christ's sake!'

'I apologize, Mrs Pearson. I feel for you, believe me. It's most unusual for a new generator to go wrong. I can't imagine what the trouble is. It's unlikely to be flat batteries because there's a built-in battery-charger, and the only other – '

'Never mind what caused it. I want it put right. And I'm willing to pay – anything within reason.'

'It's not money, Mrs Pearson. I have to abide by company rules. As I've said, I sympathize with your position, but unfortunately my hands are tied.'

She swore under her breath. 'What do you suggest then? I just have to get the power back on. It's a matter of life and death.'

'You could give Power-Mate a bell. Or LBH. I probably have their numbers somewhere . . . Bear with me . . . '

Lorna cursed each second wasted. But, as it turned out, the two other firms were no more help than Sovereign.

'Sorry, we only service our own make of generator.'

'I'm afraid both our engineers are already out on call.'

At that moment Kathy appeared, with a cardboard folder tucked under her arm and holding a halogen torch. 'Any luck?'

'No. Eddie's wife won't let him come, and I've drawn a blank elsewhere, so far.'

Kathy passed her the folder. 'Here, try the Help file. Everybody's listed – Seeboard and what have you. Or another home or hotel might lend us their maintenance man. Work through until you find someone. OK?'

'OK. How's it going your end?'

'We're coping, just about. Miss O'Brien's a godsend. She's taken the children home and promised to come back with as many oil-heaters and torches as she can lay her hands on.'

Lorna checked her own torch, relieved to see the beam was still strong.

'And some of the relatives are helping too. We're bringing everyone down to the lounge with their blankets and coverlets. I prefer to have them all in one place where we can keep an eye on them. But of course a few are too ill to be moved. And those Bartletts are a right pain. The kids are running riot and Mr B's kicking up a stink. He seems to hold us personally responsible for the power cut. Anyway, must fly. Julie's in a bit of a state and I don't want her upsetting the other carers.'

'Good luck! I'll come and find you as soon as I've sorted something out.' With the aid of the torch, Lorna started leafing through the Help file.

Three numbers were given for Seeboard. The first had only a recorded message: *'I'm sorry, our offices are now closed. Our opening hours are between eight and six, Monday to Friday, and Saturday eight till two. Please try again later.'*

She shone the torch on her watch. It was half past five and a Tuesday, albeit Christmas Eve. Through gritted teeth she dialled the second number. *'If you have changed your energy supplier and are no longer supplied by Seeboard, please hang up and telephone our Change-of-Supplier Team on 0800 . . . '*

'I'd hardly be ringing if you weren't the bloody supplier,' she muttered at the disembodied voice.

Then a more fruity voice piped up: *'For news or advice on ways to make your business more energy-efficient, please say "One" after the tone.'*

She refrained from saying something less polite.

'For details of Seeboard's exciting new business products, please say "Two" after the tone. For all other enquiries, please stay on the line. Our dedicated business teams will be pleased to help you.'

Far from a dedicated business team, she got just a ringing tone, which shrilled on and on, then unaccountably stopped. Should she go through the whole rigmarole again? No. She'd try the third and last number.

'Welcome to Powercare, Seeboard's emergency service.'

This sounded more promising at least.

'Please listen carefully to the following two options. If you are calling to report a power failure or dangerous situation, please press One.'

She did so.

'You are through to Powercare, Seeboard's emergency service. We are busy dealing with emergency calls at the moment. Your call is held in a queue and will be answered as soon as an operator becomes available.'

'Shit!' she grunted, expecting to be regaled with a spell of schmaltzy music. Instead there was another ringing tone, which eventually gave way to yet another recorded message: *'You are through to Powercare*

Technical Help Desk. If you are calling about advice on earthing connections, voltage enquiries or electrical protection, please wait and you will be answered shortly.'

Somehow her call must have been misrouted. She rang off and redialled, only to be taken through an identical process. To hell with Seeboard! At this rate, it would be New Year before she managed to speak to a real person.

She went back to the Help file and worked through every appropriate number, starting with electricians and general emergency lines, then moving on to local homes and hotels.

After an hour she was practically weeping with frustration. Most firms were closed for Christmas and New Year and wouldn't be reopening for ten days. None of the hotels could help, and, although two homes had said she was welcome to ring their maintenance men, again she got only answering-machines. She had even tried Oakfield House, terrified that Oshoba might pick up the phone (as care assistants occasionally did at Oakfield, in the absence of a proper receptionist). As far as she knew, Olu hadn't carried out his threat to reveal everything to Ralph, but just thinking about it added to her fear.

And to make things worse the torch-beam was growing weaker. Once solid objects in the room – chairs, shelves, cabinets – seemed to be losing substance, unravelling. As *she* was. She felt faint, dizzy, frighteningly unreal. Her instinct was to run, but where? The whole area would be in darkness. Besides, she should be helping Kathy, who would have her hands full trying to rally staff and calm nervous residents. She despised herself for sitting paralysed, but panic had reduced her to pulp again.

With shaking fingers she dialled Seeboard's emergency number one last time. After the now familiar recorded instructions, she finally got through to a real person. 'Have you any idea how long this power cut might last?' she asked.

'It could be up to fourteen hours.'

'*Fourteen?*'

'I'm sorry, dozens of lines are down and it'll take that long to repair them.'

The tight band round her chest was squeezing tighter, tighter, and she was sweating despite the cold. In a hoarse, unnatural voice she explained the situation again. 'Isn't there anyone there who could help?'

'No, if it's a privately supplied generator there's nothing we can do.'

'What about other private firms? I've tried a lot already, but perhaps you know someone that really *does* work round the clock . . .'

'I'm sorry, we're not allowed to give out numbers.'

Lorna banged the phone down and sat hunched over her desk. There was one last possibility . . . It would probably be useless, self-defeating. But she had to do something other than tremble and dissolve.

'Please, God,' she whispered as she dialled. 'Let it work.'

This is how it must have been in the war, she thought: rows of frightened people huddled in blankets waiting for the blackout to end. There were in fact two guttering paraffin-lamps and a couple of evil-smelling oil-heaters; nevertheless the room was dim and shadowy, and had grown increasingly chilly during the last hour. She moved from person to person, trying to rally their spirits, offering them drinks and snacks. It was her job to hold the fort downstairs while Kathy stayed upstairs with the most serious of the flu cases.

'No, I'm sorry, Julie, you can't go home. I know you've done your shift. So have we all. But this is an emergency.' Apart from Julie, the staff were showing remarkable dedication. And the doughty Winifred was helping out, passing round her own tin of Christmas biscuits.

'Eric tells me you've found a man to mend the generator. Is that correct, my dear?'

Lorna lowered her voice. 'Well, he's *trying*, Winifred. He's down there now, but I don't want to publicize it in case he doesn't succeed.'

'I won't say a word.' Winifred proffered the biscuit-tin. 'Do have one of these – they're Belgian and rather nice.'

'Thanks, but no – I had a big lunch.' How could she eat? Her stomach was churning, her heart racing out of control. It was extraordinary that no one had noticed. Inwardly she was a wreck, yet they all seemed to regard her as a calm, efficient wonder-woman – Ms Courageous, in short.

'Yes, of course you can use the toilet, Mrs Alexander. Rowan will take you. Just be careful how you –'

The blaze of light took everyone by surprise. Lorna blinked, gazing up at the suddenly brilliant chandeliers. The Christmas-tree lights were glittering once more and the table-lamps casting their soft glow.

There was a spontaneous cheer from staff and residents alike and a burst of triumphant applause.

'Well, whoever's responsible for *that*', said Julie, 'deserves a bleeding medal! Bring the lucky bloke in here and I'll kiss him from head to toe.'

30

Lorna swerved to avoid a huge puddle. The overnight thaw had brought new driving hazards, and although the roads were no longer impassable her headlamps lit up swathes of snow still clinging to verges and hedges. She stopped to consult the map. Kendrick Grove was proving hard to find, and it was past seven when she finally drew up outside the house – a decrepit-looking property in a run-down part of Woking.

Suddenly apprehensive, she sat in the car wondering if it would be wiser to turn back. What was she going to say? How could she appear casual and not betray any emotion? He might well be annoyed that she'd turned to him only in a crisis, after avoiding him for months. She checked her reflection in the rear-view mirror and tried to rub off some of the lipstick. She didn't want to look as if she'd spent ages on her appearance – which she had.

A complete waste of time, no doubt. In fact she might as well leave the stuff in the car. No point lugging glass dishes through the slush if nobody was in.

She squinted at the list of names beside the bells. His was the only one neatly typed.

She rang, then negotiated the narrow steps to the basement, catching her breath as the door opened a crack.

'Lorna!'

She too was shocked – by his pallor and by the amount of weight he'd lost. Last night, in all the confusion and the darkness, she hadn't really noticed. And afterwards he'd fled, evidently unable to face her. Thinness apart, though, he still looked distinguished, dressed in dark cords and a navy sweater. 'I just wanted to thank you,' she said, 'for yesterday.'

'Come in.'

She followed him into the hall. It was dark and smelt of damp.

'May I take your coat?'

'Thank you.' They might be strangers: stilted language, stiff formalities. Should she reach out and take his hand?

But he was already standing aside, ushering her into a poky room with sludge-green walls and bars at the window. 'Do sit down. I'm afraid it's a bit of a mess.'

In fact it was meticulously tidy, just impoverished and bare. She sat on the edge of a chair, recognizing a couple of pieces from Queen's Hill Drive: a small mahogany writing-desk and an antique carriage-clock that had stopped working years ago. Throughout their marriage it had said ten past ten. Both items looked incongruous here, and seemed to recoil from the hideous sofa and scrappy rug. When the house-sale was going through he had offered her the pick of the furniture, but she had refused to take anything, determined to break all ties. Impossible. The ties were extraordinarily strong.

He picked up his pipe – another familiar object: the Peterson with the straight-grained briar and the silver band at the base of the stem. A number of other pipes sat on the writing-desk – a source of comfort, perhaps, in this prison. The room was disconcertingly quiet: no sound from the other flats or even from the street. She felt a sudden sense of shame that all this time she'd had no idea where or how he was living – her husband of eleven years. Kathy had advised her not to meet him, to cut contact to a minimum, just brief phone-calls about the finances. Kathy wasn't always right, she realized now.

She cleared her throat. 'I, er, hope you know how grateful everyone is. You were the hero of the hour!'

He shrugged. 'It wasn't difficult. I told you – there was an airlock in the system and I just had to bleed it through.'

'All the same, it saved our bacon. Or turkey, I should say!' She flushed at the trite joke. Nervousness was making her gabble. 'And the whole thing was such a drama I think the residents rather enjoyed it – once it was over, anyway. They were reminiscing about the Blitz and the General Strike and what have you, and it created quite a festive mood.'

He refilled his pipe and tamped it down with his thumb. 'It's a lovely house.'

'Mm.' Was he bitter about their very different circumstances? The coach-house was a palace compared to this slum. But he didn't *have* to live in such surroundings – what had happened to the money she had given him? 'What are you doing at the moment, Ralph?' she asked. 'Did you manage to find a job?'

316

'Of sorts. I'm using the van to do light haulage work. It's a bit sporadic, but it pays the bills. And before that I worked as a minicab-driver.' He gave the ghost of a smile. 'But the pipe didn't go down very well with customers. I've sold the car now, in fact.'

'Oh, *Ralph* . . . ' He had loved his car almost as much as the house.

Forestalling protestations of pity, he stood up and moved to the door. 'Would you like a cup of coffee?'

'Well, if it's no bother.'

She too got up, and en route to the kitchen had a quick look round the flat. There was only a tiny bathroom and one other room, his bedroom. Warily she put her head round the door. Would there be evidence of another woman: a photograph? belongings?

She froze. The woman in the photographs was *her*. There were four in all. The one beside his bed showed her sitting on the lawn in a halter top and shorts. The second, on the chest of drawers, had been taken at the company dinner-dance soon after they'd met. The third was just a snapshot, propped against the clock, and on the window-sill stood their wedding-photo, resplendent in its silver frame. She turned away from her smiling faces. The room was practically a shrine to her, whereas she had assumed he would throw her photos out, if not destroy them. This was surely proof that Olu hadn't approached him.

'Lorna?'

'Coming.'

'D'you mind tea instead? I don't seem to have any coffee.'

'Tea'll be fine.'

The kitchen was little bigger than a cupboard and again depressingly bare. When he opened the fridge to get out the milk, she saw there was nothing else in it except a carton of orange-juice. While she'd been tucking in to a splendid Christmas dinner at The Cedars, he had probably made do with a liquid lunch.

His hands weren't quite steady as he made the tea. She had no idea what he was feeling – pleasure at seeing her again, resentment, even anger? 'I . . . I've got a few things for you, Ralph. They're in the car. I'll fetch them.'

He didn't offer to help. Perhaps he just wished she'd leave. Certainly she hadn't been prepared for the effect the visit would have on her: desire and distress in equal proportions. She wanted to hold him, kiss him, yell at him, comfort him – all dangerous reactions. She *would* leave – it was safer. But at least he must have the trifle. She had taken great pains with it: begging the ingredients from Marco, borrowing a cut-glass bowl from the kitchen, decorating the top with holly made from glacé cherries and angelica strips, and spelling out 'Happy Christmas' in silver balls.

She carried it carefully in from the car and placed it on the work-top. 'I put in lots of almonds and ratafias. And masses of sherry of course!'

'This is for *me*?' He was gazing at it with an expression of disbelief.

'I always make you a trifle at Christmas.' Used to make, she should have said. 'And Kathy sent you a token of thanks.' She drew the bottle of single malt from her shoulder-bag and held it out to him.

'I don't drink.'

'*What?*'

'I don't drink any more. Not since you left.'

'You mean . . . you've kept off it all that time?'

'You seem surprised.' Now he did sound bitter. 'A lot of things have changed, Lorna.'

'So I see.' She was more than surprised, she was stunned – that he had found the strength to give up drinking during such a stressful period. When he had quit before it had lasted two days; this had been nine months. What will-power it must have taken. She couldn't walk out – not now.

She took the tea-tray into the sitting-room. A surreptitious glance confirmed the absence of glasses and bottles – there wasn't so much as a coaster.

He gave an awkward laugh. 'Actually, I did it for you.'

For her? She was dumbstruck. They weren't even in contact; he might never have seen her again. She sank down on the sofa, suddenly angry with its broken springs, angry with the sagging curtains and grimy ceiling-tiles. 'Ralph, this place is a *dump*. The whole point of Agnes's money was to help you get a decent flat.'

Without speaking, he poured the tea. The cups were thick white china; the teapot lid was cracked.

'Ralph, did you hear?'

'If you honestly imagine I'd take your money . . .'

'Look, we've been through all that already. You know I wanted you to have it.'

'It's not what you want, it's what's right. Agnes left it to *you*.'

'Yes, to do what I like with.'

'Well, the same applies to me. If it's mine I can do what *I* like. I've put it in an investment fund, in your name. With your share of the proceeds from the house. Then, if anything should happen, you'll have some security. For instance, if you decide to leave The Cedars – '

'I shan't,' she retorted.

He stirred his tea with enormous concentration.

How brusque she must have sounded, and ungrateful. Ralph had always been generous. He had never asked her for a penny; never would. And his concern about her future when that future didn't include him was genuinely unselfish. But he mustn't harbour the illusion that she might leave The Cedars. 'I love it there, you see, Ralph. It's the perfect job for me, living in a community. And I especially like the coach-house and sharing it with Kathy. We often have friends over and . . . '

Enough said, or she would seem smug. 'Ralph, thank you – honestly. It was a lovely thought, and I'm touched. I just wish you'd spent the money on yourself. And as for your giving up drinking, I'm incredibly impressed.'

Embarrassed, he started fiddling with his pipe again. After a long silence he leaned forward, frowning. 'There's something I ought to tell you, Lorna.'

She tensed. He'd been offered a job. Up north. Abroad. He was about to say goodbye.

'Since last night I've been debating whether to mention it or not. I don't want to land your maintenance man in trouble. On the other hand . . . '

She put her cup down. 'Ralph, what are you talking about?'

'Well, when I was mending the generator I could see that the diesel line had been tampered with. And of course that would account for the airlock. I have a strong suspicion that someone's been stealing fuel.'

'Good God! You mean . . . Eddie?'

'Yes, it looks like that. It's highly unlikely that a new generator would break down otherwise.'

319

'I can't *believe* it!'

'Well, the signs were pretty clear. And it would be easy enough to do. No one could see what he was up to in the cellar. He may be using the diesel in his car.'

'What a shit! And to think his wife had the nerve to say he was overworked.'

Ralph banged his pipe out on the ashtray. 'And, while we're on the subject, I noticed a few other problems. The fuse-box is far too small for a house that size. In fact the wiring looks a bit dodgy altogether.'

She grimaced. This was worse and worse. 'But the entire place was rewired before we opened.'

'Well, they seem to have made rather a mess of it.'

'Bloody hell! Chris will go berserk. She spent a fortune on the conversion. And I don't know what she'll say about Eddie – she interviewed loads of people before she took him on.'

'Staff do tend to take advantage, though. It happens all the time.'

Not at The Cedars, she thought. After their insistence on high standards, she felt deflated and betrayed. 'Ralph, would you mind terribly if . . . ?' She bit her lip, unwilling to ask more favours.

'If what?'

'Oh . . . nothing.'

'What were you going to say?'

'It doesn't matter.'

'For heaven's sake, don't start and then clam up.'

'Well, I was wondering if you could possibly come round again some time and show me this diesel line or whatever it is. Then I can explain the situation to Chris when she's back. And you could let us know exactly what needs doing in the house.'

'Yes, if it helps, why not? I could make it tomorrow if you like. Just tell me who I'm meant to be.'

'What do you mean?'

'Well, am I your husband or an odd-job man? Have you said?'

'Not really. Well, Kathy knows, of course, but no one else. They're not aware I'm married.'

'But isn't that a wedding-ring you're wearing? – on the wrong hand. Whose is it?'

'My . . . mother's. Agnes gave it to me.'

320

'And where's the one *I* gave you?'

She flushed. She had taken it off when she went to work at The Cedars, then somehow managed to lose it – on purpose, Kathy said. In fact Kathy kept urging her to press for a divorce, since it was obvious she wanted to be free of Ralph. 'I . . . don't wear it now.'

'But you wear the bracelet.' He leaned across and touched it.

'Yes.' Kathy was mistaken: she *didn't* want a divorce. She could never go back to him, she knew that. And yet . . .

'Remember what I said to you in the hospital? – diamonds are for ever.'

'For ever' – engraved on the ring she'd lost. A double loss, she saw now. The men she'd been out with recently were pleasant enough, but of no lasting significance. Like most of the men in her past. Tom, who had stayed the longest, was basically a good-time guy who distrusted the word commitment. Only Ralph had felt able to promise 'for better, for worse'. She stood up. 'Look, I . . . I think I ought to be going . . . '

'What for? You're not still on duty, are you? At least let's have the trifle. I don't want to eat it on my own. I'll go and get it.'

'No, let me,' she said, escaping to the kitchen. Her mind was in a turmoil: fury with Eddie and worry about The Cedars mixed up with her emotions over Ralph.

She stood leaning against the oven, a monstrosity with rusting claw-legs. On the opposite wall hung the Castles of Britain calendar they'd had in the kitchen at Queen's Hill Drive, open not at December but at May – the month she had left.

'Need any help?' he called.

'No, it's OK. Won't be a sec.'

She hunted through the cupboards for some bowls. There seemed to be a minimal supply of crockery and glassware, but what she did find was the old handwritten recipe-book started in the first year of their marriage. She had laboriously copied out recipes for banana-bread, steak-and-oyster pudding, apple fritters – and of course trifle. But why had he kept it? Clearly he did no cooking and seemed to be existing on thin air . . .

Because he loves you, you fool, and misses you. Why else has he got those photos in his bedroom? And you love *him* – admit it. You didn't have to come here. You could have written him a note.

'If you can't find bowls, use cups.'

'Right. Coming!' Hastily she closed the tattered recipe-book, spooned trifle into two mugs and carried them in. 'It looks as if you could do with a little more china,' she said, handing him a mug and a teaspoon.

'I could do with a lot of things.'

He ate slowly, yet with unaccustomed enthusiasm, taking his time to savour every raspberry and nut, to relish the flavours in each spoon-ful of sherry-rich sponge. As she watched, an idea began to take shape. The Cedars needed a new maintenance man – someone honest and reliable. And Ralph needed a new job – something stable, with paid holidays, a pension scheme, a decent midday meal. It wasn't high-grade work, admittedly, but no worse than driving a van. And it would mean they'd be together again – together on *her* terms; together yet apart. She would remain at the coach-house while he lived here, or somewhere more salubrious. They'd stay married, which was impor-tant. More important than she'd realized. When she'd sat with James Tate, sipping vintage claret, she had felt nothing for the poor man. And nothing for Ian or David or Andrew, although she was flattered that they'd asked her out. She'd assumed she was becoming more like Kathy, developing a taste for being single, permanently perhaps.

But Kathy would have no conception of what she was feeling now, faced with the man she'd married: the value of continuity, the pull of memories. Nor would Kathy understand that you could love someone for what they might have been if life had treated them better; someone with whom you shared a bond because you'd both missed out on child-hood; someone who'd stuck by you through panics and miscarriages. There would be no more miscarriages, and she had learned to handle panic on her own – last night was proof of that. She didn't need a pro-tector. She needed someone special. And Ralph was special. Still.

But would he want the job at The Cedars? The long hours didn't matter – he was used to working round the clock, although being surrounded by old people wouldn't have great appeal. However, a well-dressed, well-spoken maintenance man would appeal to *them*, considerably, and since he was bound to be superior to most potential candidates Chris might agree to a higher rate of pay, maybe even create a new post for him as an on-site engineer.

'Get real, woman! Kathy wouldn't want him within a mile of her. Anyway, what's in it for him? He'd just be your poodle and everyone else's too.'

'Heel!' she snapped, but the Monster paid no heed this time.

'It's all too pat – pure fantasy. You think you can have your cake and eat it. But life doesn't work like that.'

It *could*, she thought, refusing to be cowed. Ralph had changed so much that anything was possible. Even now he was gazing at her intently, whereas he used to find it difficult to look into her eyes. And going on the wagon after years of serious drinking; savouring his food, which before had been mere fuel . . .

'Don't be an idiot! If you're not careful you'll end up at his beck and call again, even if he *has* changed.'

The Monster had touched a nerve. The last thing she wanted was to return to her old dependency. Besides, perhaps she *was* deluding herself that she could have the best of all worlds.

'Any chance of some more?' Ralph asked almost bashfully.

'Of course. You can eat the lot if you like!' The Ralph she knew had rarely finished what was on his plate, let alone asked for second helpings. How might he react if she put her arms around him? Would he savour her, like the trifle?

She took his mug out to the kitchen and stood looking at the cream-swirled custard. Although 'Christmas' had been eaten or dislodged, 'Happy' remained intact, spelled out in silver balls. She lifted them off with a spoon and crunched the word down. Happiness was new, and far too precious to risk losing. She would say nothing to Ralph until she was absolutely certain that she was acting from strength, not weakness. Yet already new ideas were springing to mind. She and Ralph could pool their resources and use Agnes's money to buy a share in The Cedars. That would enhance their status and security.

'Now you're talking crap! You and Ralph are on the breadline. You can't compete with the likes of Chris.'

She did some quick sums in her head. A modest share might be possible. Agnes's cottage had sold for more than expected.

'Aunt Agnes,' she whispered, peering up at the starlit sky through the uncurtained square of window, 'was this *your* plan?'

Agnes had been delighted about the wedding and had invested in a new hat – pale straw, with a bunch of cherries on the brim: the only frivolous item of clothing she had ever bought. She would certainly approve of the marriage continuing, even if she were dubious about its unconventional style.

'But you know what Ralph's like, Aunt. An unorthodox relationship might suit him rather well.'

And suddenly Agnes was *there*, her face transfigured as on her deathbed, and fixing her with the same intense and piercing gaze.

Shaken, Lorna stared into her eyes. Again, as at the moment of death, she seemed to be trying to communicate. But what was she saying? That love was imperfect but none the less precious? That, although Ralph had never been demonstrative, he had proved his love? – like Agnes herself.

She couldn't tell. The fleeting vision vanished and she was alone in the shabby kitchen again, with a trifle-spoon in her hand. She felt unnerved, yet also elated, with a sense of possibilities . . . Things might work out.

Maybe.

And if they didn't, well, she'd be fine. 'Fine,' she said aloud, startled to realize that 'fine' was no longer bravado, but true at last.

And there wasn't a peep from the Monster.